D0240040

Withdrawn

995194182 6

Lily

A Tale of Revenge

ROSE TREMAIN

Chatto & Windus
LONDON

1 3 5 7 9 10 8 6 4 2

Chatto & Windus, an imprint of Vintage, is part of the
Penguin Random House group of companies whose addresses
can be found at global.penguinrandomhouse.com

Penguin
Random House
UK

Copyright © Rose Tremain 2021

Rose Tremain has asserted her right to be identified as the author of this
Work in accordance with the Copyright, Designs and Patents Act 1988

First published by Chatto & Windus in 2021

penguin.co.uk/vintage

A CIP catalogue record for this book is available from the British Library

HB ISBN 9781784744564
TPB ISBN 9781784744571

Typeset in 13.5/15.75 pt Bembo
by Integra Software Services Pvt. Ltd, Pondicherry

Printed and bound in Great Britain by Clays Ltd, Elcograf S.p.A.

The authorised representative in the EEA is Penguin Random House Ireland,
Morrison Chambers, 32 Nassau Street, Dublin D02 YH68

Penguin Random House is committed to a sustainable future for
our business, our readers and our planet. This book is made from
Forest Stewardship Council® certified paper.

MIX
Paper from
responsible sources
FSC
www.fsc.org   FSC® C018179

To Caroline Michel,
with love and laughter

She-wolf

She dreams of her death.

It comes as a cold October dawn is breaking in the London sky.

A sack is put over her head. Through the weave of the burlap, she can take her last look at the world, which is reduced to a cluster of tiny squares of grey light, and she thinks, Whyever did I struggle so long and so hard to make my way in a place which was bent on my destruction ever since I came into it? Why did I not surrender to death when I was a child, for children's pictures of death are fantastical and full of a strange beauty?

She feels the noose, made of thick hemp rope, go round her neck and knows that the noose's cunning is to be in perpetual coitus with a huge and bulbous knot behind her head. The knot nudges the base of her skull. Soon, a trap beneath her feet will open and she will drop into the void, her legs dangling like the legs of a doll made of cloth. Her neck will snap and her heart will stop.

Nobody but she knows that her dream of death is a rehearsal for what will surely happen to her one day. Nobody knows yet that she is a murderer. She is seen as an innocent girl. In one month's time she will be seventeen. Her cheeks are dimpled and her hair is brown and soft. Her voice is quiet. Her hands are skilled. She works at Belle Prettywood's Wig Emporium, which is famous

1

all over London. She goes to church on Sundays, wearing a blue serge dress. And she was named for a flower: Lily.

In the church, there is a man who watches her. He is older than she is. She estimates that he might be forty. But she likes the yearning she sees in his eyes. Perhaps it's because, when she becomes aware of this – this little flame of desire which is as constant as the many-coloured light falling from a window of stained glass – she forgets for a few seconds what she has done and how, in the end, she will be punished for her foul deed. Instead, what she starts to dream about is some kind of innocent continuation of her life.

She creates an imaginary moment, like a scene from a play. She sits in the churchyard with this unknown man. It is springtime, but the air is cool. She and the man are side by side on a stone bench and she can feel the cold of the stone coming through her dress. She begins to shiver a little, so that the man will reach out and take her hand, and his hand is warm and strong. He holds her gently – not violently or forever, as the knot holds the noose in its grip, but with a fleeting human tenderness. And this creates in her a terrible longing to confess her crime, the enormity of which surges up in her heart from time to time, as though she had swallowed a stone. She turns her face to the stranger's face, which is serious and kind, and she says, 'You know I am a murderer?' And he replies, 'Yes, I know this, but I think I am going to choose to put it aside, for you had good cause.'

Good cause.

But this is only a dream, a fantasy, a story . . .

When she was a few hours old, in the year 1850, she was abandoned by her mother and left at the gates of a park near Bethnal Green in the East End of London. The gates were made of iron. Lily was swaddled in sacking. Before she was found, wolves who lived in the Essex marshes came traipsing through the November night, drawn by the complicated stink of the city, and they came into the park and heard the wailing of a baby, which they mistook for the wailing of a wolf cub, and their snouts burrowed through the spaces in the iron gates and a she-wolf put her jaw round the sacking bundle and attempted to drag it to her. Perhaps she tried to be gentle with the baby, but her sharp teeth bit into the infant's foot and blood flowed into the sack, and at the scent of blood, the pack sent up a yearning cry.

The crying of the wolves brought to the gates a police constable of the night watch. He held aloft his lantern and saw the child, wrapped in the sacking, shrieking into the night and bleeding from the foot. He picked her up. He was a very young man with no children of his own, yet he cradled the baby against his body, as a parent would cradle his own infant, to try to warm her, and his uniform was stained with her blood. He was filled with both wonder and terror.

He walked through the night to Coram's Fields. A great storm came on and by the time the constable reached the London Foundling Hospital, he was suffering a fever from the cold and wet. The guardians led him in and took the child from where it was clamped against his shivering chest. They asked him if the baby was his, but he told them no, he'd found it at the gates to Victoria Park and saved it from the wolves. He was informed there were none of these creatures in London any more, that in his fever he was imagining them, but he said he had surely seen them by the light of his police lantern, their eyes shining like silver in the near darkness, and he showed them the blood on the sack where the foot had been bitten.

The dawn was breaking and fires were lit in the Hospital and the policeman sat in his underwear by a fire, with a coverlet tucked round him, drinking hot tea, and the baby was laid on a table and the sacking was unwound from her body, which was still bloody from her birth and wrapped in linen rags. A nurse was called and the wound on the child's foot was washed and bandaged and she was wrapped in a little blanket of rabbit skin, to try to warm her. She was near to death from all that she had endured during her first night on earth. She sucked on the nurse's finger, which she had dipped in a pap made from flour and water.

The custom at the London Foundling Hospital, when a baby was taken there, was for the mother to leave a token behind with the abandoned child, to show remorse. These tokens might be a button or a broken coin or a square of material – some small and useless thing which had been precious to the woman who was about to part with a living being she should have nurtured and loved. Sometimes, there was a scrap of writing left with these objects, a note to say that the mother would one day return to claim the child and try to show it some kindness. Sometimes, the women had written down a name for the infant, perhaps not knowing that when the babies had been named by their mothers, then this name was immediately taken from them and replaced with another. For it was the Hospital Governors' opinion that mothers who couldn't care for their infants were shameful sinners. They belonged to the category of human souls whom society named 'the undeserving' and it was decreed that they had no right to bind a child falsely to them by any kind of christening. Those in charge at the Hospital preferred to let the babies be christened afresh by them, its benefactors.

Lily was later told that the sack was searched in case there was some token or label or note, hidden there with her body, on which a name had been written, but there was no token or label or note. What there was, at the base of the sack, was a strange quantity of white human hair, now tamped with her blood, and nobody knew what it was doing there. The guardians tried to read some coded message from the hair, but they couldn't work it out. Yet they kept the sack with the hair inside it, for what it might one day reveal.

After they named the child Lily, the Governors allotted her a surname, kindly donated by one of the lady bene-factresses, high-born people who had an oiling of compassion in their dry hearts and liked to think their money was helping children to steer a path that would not lead them to ruin. So she was given the surname Mortimer, after a certain Lady Elizabeth Mortimer, daughter of a duke and owner of a lakeshore castle in Scotland, but born with a hump in her spine, so that no husband would take her and all her unspent passion flowed towards charity. Lily was given a miniature portrait of Lady Elizabeth, but it showed only her face, which was unblemished and pretty, and not her poor back, which was the ruination of her life and hopes.

Sucking from the nurse's finger, wrapped in rabbit skin, kept warm by the fire, Lily survived the breaking day. She was later told that, at her side, the young police constable fell into a fevered sleep and was carried to a bed, lest he die an unplanned death in the Coram Hospital. But he did not die and she learned that he returned a fortnight later to ask whether the foundling he had rescued had survived. He gave his name as Constable Sam Trench. He told the guardians that in his walk from Bethnal Green through the rain and wind, pressing the baby close against his chest, he had felt great compassion for it, and now wished to hold Lily in his arms once more. But by the time he returned, she had been sent away.

'Sent away?' he said. 'Because of the wound in her foot?'

'No,' the guardians replied, 'sent away to a foster home in the countryside. This is our custom. We send babies away for a few years, to be nurtured by an honest family. And then we bring them back.'

Rookery Farm

When Lily's eyes were open and pictures of the world began to nourish her baby brain, what she saw at first was thistledown floating against a light-filled sky.

Later, she understood that thistles choked the land and kept the grass from growing and that although a struggle was being waged against them, they flew free of it and all summer long their seeds streamed up and off into the east wind. Above them, swallows and swifts flew so high that sometimes you could hardly see them, only as motes of dust being moved by the changing motions of the afternoon breeze.

So these were Lily's first memories: a bright immensity of sky, skeins of thistledown borne aloft, birds in the trembling heavens. And these images have stayed with her across almost seventeen years of life and bring her consolation, as though she imagined she could one day become part of that aerial world, to escape the earthly one, which was so kind to her in her first six years and then led her towards darkness.

The place where the thistledown grew was called Rookery Farm. It was buried so deep in the Suffolk countryside that it was difficult to find a way out of it to anywhere else. Deep woods pressed round it, like a rising sea, and the tracks which urged you westwards towards the long, rutted lane that led to the Swaithey Road were susceptible to every thought that Nature had about covering every inch of everything with thistles and burdock and briars.

All this meant that once you had arrived at Rookery Farm, you felt no inclination to leave it. It hid from your mind the immensity of the world outside it. You had no thought that seventy miles away there could be a city like London, where small children could be put to sweeping chimneys or breaking their backs over a weaving loom and living on bones and lying down to sleep four or five to a bed.

The outbuildings of Rookery Farm were crammed with broken carts and bits and shapes of rusting iron and a multiplicity of household things hoarded over time, then thrown away and now half buried by the grass of years. Rats were at home here and didn't care if you saw them or tried to chase them away, and Perkin Buck, who owned the farm, let them be, as though he believed the rats' intention was to gobble up what the humans had discarded, piece by terrible piece, and one day leave the barns empty and clean. But all they did was add to the accumulation of life on the farm by rearing their young in the dark spaces between things and then you saw these baby rats, naked and small, making their first forays into the dusty, thistledown universe of Rookery Farm, and noted how they slipped and rolled and fell and struggled to right themselves.

Near the barns was a pond, choked with blanket weed in summer and leant upon by ancient willows. In winter, the water became clear and bright and the mallard reared by Perkin Buck preened themselves at its edge, like actors preparing for their roles before a big shimmering mirror, and bad-tempered geese arrived to shoulder the vain ducks away and glide into the water. At Christmas-time,

Perkin Buck fattened up the geese and chose the biggest one to kill and pluck and bind and salt, all ready for the oven. Over the Christmas table presided Nellie Buck, Perkin's wife and mother of his three children.

Nellie Buck looked out at the world over the big shelf of her bosom with a regard so tender, so full of consolation that everyone who knew her felt in her presence that elusive quietude of mind which is not far from a state of happiness. And it was this regard which fell on Lily when she was sent into Suffolk from the London Foundling Hospital as a baby with a wounded foot, to be cared for by Nellie.

Nellie was paid ten shillings a month as a foster-mother to abandoned children and over eleven years, as well as caring for her own three sons, she had mothered four foundlings – all of them also boys. Lily was the fifth child, the first girl Nellie had taken in, and here was the only bit of true good fortune ever to fall upon her. To be a child at Rookery Farm and to be tucked into her cot by Nellie Buck each night and to cling to her skirts as she went about her housework and her farm work was very heaven. Nobody told the foundling that when she was six years old she would be sent back to London, to Thomas Coram's mighty Hospital. Nobody warned her how she would be beaten there for grieving for Nellie Buck and for one day attempting to escape from the home, to try to make her way back to Rookery Farm.

Nellie Buck, in her stillness, in her sweetness of disposition, had the power to bring those around her to a contemplation of their own best selves, and when Lily was in her care, she was a good and obedient child. If you had told Nellie that her little foster-girl would one day commit murder, she would have pushed you away, just as, when she went out with winter feed for the bullocks and they crowded round her too closely, she would make a gesture with her hands, as if she were dusting down her bosom, and tell them to move away. 'Get you gone!' she would have said. 'For I know my Lily and she is not capable of hurting a soul. She will sit down and laugh when my boys tease her. She strokes the lobes of my ears, when I sing to her at night-time. She will hold a baby rat in her hand.'

Nellie's three boys had been named for their three uncles on Perkin Buck's side of the family: Jesse, James and Joseph. These three Uncle Js had, each in his turn, travelled away and away and away to India and to Africa to seek his fortune and each, in his turn, lost his life to disease, violence or the falling of a locomotive from a wooden bridge into a ravine. So, Perkin Buck (who had been baptised John Perkin but let go of the 'J' bit of his name) was left all alone to inherit Rookery Farm and to try to keep alive the memory of his dead brothers in the children he fathered with Nellie.

The fostering of babies at ten shillings a month added to what Perkin Buck could earn from the rearing of bullocks and fowl and the growing of wheat for Swaithey Mill, and for him, these little strangers inhabiting his house were also seen as ballast against the deaths of his own children. For it was the fate of so many to die. Fever could take them between the budding of a primrose and the spreading of its petals into a flower. A winter chill could turn their green bones to dust before a week of snowfall was out. Or they perished simply from their ignorance that they were alive, for being alive asks something colossal of the body and the soul: a *striving*, which they had no means to understand or to undertake. One boy in Nellie's care had died and when Lily asked why, Nellie said to her, 'He passed on to another world, pet, because he did not yearn to tarry. His name was Tom and I kept saying to him, "Hold fast, Tom. Live one day and then another and then another." I gave him all I could, but he had this little sly way of looking at me, as if to say, foolish woman, to keep hoping. As if to say, can't you see that I'm impatient to be gone?'

The Buck children remembered this 'impatience to be gone' and looked for it in the new foundling, but didn't find it. Lily was their contented plaything. When she was two years old and running around the yard, chasing the hens, Joseph was five, James was six and Jesse was eight. It was the chief delight of James, who went about the world counting what he saw ('eight dandelion clocks, two pheasants, seven swallows in the sky'), to sit her down in the grass and count her toes. For she had only nine of these. When the she-wolf had arrived at the gates of Victoria Park, she had bitten off the little toe of Lily's left foot and this tiny nub of flesh and tender bone had fallen into the burlap sack, to be wrapped all about by the unexplained locks of human hair.

Lily sometimes thinks now that if she goes barefoot to the gallows, the world will gawp at this deformed foot hanging in the air and see it as a sign of the Devil, marking her out from birth as a bringer of death. But for James Buck, her nine toes were just part of his daily lesson in arithmetic and Joseph and Jesse sometimes fashioned a tenth toe out of mud and tried to stick it onto her foot and she would take it off and squash it in her hand, or throw it across the meadow for the dog, Shadow, to chase and find.

Shadow was a thin, nervous collie with eyes which looked yellow in bright light. She would sometimes be sent to round up animals who had strayed into the wheat or had nosed their bulky way into the old, rumpled hedgerows to gorge on the rosehips Nellie liked to cull for syrup, but mostly she did not really work at all, only ran in swift circles about the place, with her yellow eyes all wild and aflame with the joy of speed for its own pointless sake.

After Nellie, the living creature Lily and the boys loved most was Shadow. They called her to them all the time. They put their arms round her thin, silky neck and took the burrs out of her ears. They made a ball for her out of cloth and flour paste and hurled it down the lane or across the meadows and watched her fly after it, quicker than a bird, with her black-and-white tail streaming after her in the wind. At night, one of them would often creep down to the kitchen, where she slept on the hard Suffolk pamments in front of the range, and try to lift her up and take her upstairs to lie on their little beds, so that they could reach out in a cold dawn and feel her warm head near to hand. And this is something Lily still does in her dreams: she reaches out for the comfort of Shadow's sleeping form. She even hears her breathing. And then she wakes up and thinks, Shadow is dead now; she is gone. Neither she nor I will ever return to Rookery Farm.

Once a week, on Saturday – market day – Lily and the Buck family all rode in a wooden cart to Swaithey Village. Jesse sat up front with Perkin Buck, driving the stubborn old shire horse, Peggy, along the narrow road, and Lily and the other boys sat with Nellie in the back, watching the woods go by. Lily liked to be on Nellie's lap, but so did Joseph, so poor Nellie tried to hold both children steady on her broad knees while the wheels of the cart bounced in and out of the ruts in the worn track and sometimes Joseph would pinch Lily's leg and she would slip down and land in the chaff and dust on the floor of the cart and everybody would laugh.

In winter, these rides were very cold and it could happen that a heavy coverlet of snow was shaken by the wind from the trees and landed on the family in the cart and on the horse. The children tasted the peppery flavour of the snow and the horse stopped dead and everything seemed to cease right there, halfway between Rookery Farm and Swaithey Village. That was when Nellie would decide to sing a song, to keep the children from fretting, or as though the sound of her voice might be the thing which would make Peggy decide to walk on. Lily would curl up in the crook of her arm and feel the great shelf of her breast moving up and down as she sang.

Perkin would bounce the reins and shout at the horse. Sometimes, she would shake the snow from her neck and get going again, but usually Jesse had to get down and take hold of her bridle and rub her nose, then blow into it, to coax her on. Peggy was a horse who liked human affection. Sometimes, when she was grazing near the house, she would decide to come up to the kitchen window and stick her huge head into the room and bare her stained old teeth in the approximation of a smile, and Lily remembers that the smell of her breath was like carrots steaming on the range.

When the cart reached Swaithey, Perkin Buck would go to the slaughterhouse to discuss payments for his bullocks, or to deliver pheasants to the butcher, or to take the horse to the smithy, then drink a jar of ale with him in the smithy's barn, where a great charcoal fire burned day and night, winter and summer.

Lily and the boys would trail along with Nellie through the market stalls and the little crowded place would be filled with people who knew and loved Nellie Buck and wanted to tell her all the things which had happened between one market day and the next, which was not much because Swaithey was a place where life moved more slowly than time and where people could forget how many days had passed between Wednesday and Monday. So they told her about small things: the colds and head-aches from which they were suffering, the way a goffering iron had overheated and burned a Sunday blouse, the rude remarks made by the coalman on his unprofitable rounds, the surliness of the bloater-seller, the failure of a kidney pie to puff up above the meat, the way the rooks were building their nests so high in the beeches ...

When they looked down at Lily, clinging on to Nellie's skirts, they would smile. 'Nice for you, Nellie, to have a *girl*,' they'd say and Nellie would put her wide, warm hand under Lily's chin and say, 'She's a good little soul. No trouble at all,' and they would wander on, stopping again at this stall or that, to buy knitting yarn or thread, or a pound of cheese or a pint of winkles, and once in a while, a pair of second-hand boots. To keep the children from running off and gawping at the stall selling pancakes that Nellie couldn't afford, she would buy them a packet of sherbet and they would sit on the steps of the market cross to eat it, passing it round and round from one to another and discussing how it tasted a bit like the snow that had fallen onto the cart from the laden trees.

★

From a young age, all the children had to work on the farm. Some tasks they liked and some they simply had to endure, because Perkin Buck reminded them that farm work was endurance and nothing less. The task which asked the most of them was stone-picking.

Once the fields had been ploughed, Perkin Buck would wait for a dry spell of weather to take the heaviness out of the earth, and as the earth sank down, so the stones which choked the Suffolk soil would rise up, quite as if they were living and growing things, and the children would gather them like a crop. They would work in a line, with sacks strapped across their bodies, into which they put the stones. Perkin Buck led the way. The winter sun would slant down on the little group creeping forwards across the plough. The sacks would get heavy and pull at the sinews of their shoulders. Their hands were chafed and cut, but they had no choice but to stumble on over the ridges of earth, bending down to their unending work, getting thirsty and morose.

At the edge of each field were hoppers into which they tipped the stones when the sacks were full, and Lily can remember that when she began to join in the stone-picking she was too small to reach the hoppers, so Jesse would gently lift her up and sit her on his shoulders so that she could empty her sack, and he would say, 'Well done, Lily, you're a farmer now.' And for all that she was parched and her back ached, she felt glad to be a farmer and knew that she wanted to stay at Rookery Farm forever, not realising then how soon she would have to leave it.

When the stones had all been gathered, builders' merchants would arrive with their carts and take the stones away, the good Suffolk flints to be used for walling or church repairs and the rest to be ground to dust for mortar. Perkin Buck made money from the stones and he liked to reward the children for all their work in the only way which appealed to him: on the season's last, long afternoon of the stone-picking, never minding if the weather was cold, they would lie down in the scant shade of an oak tree losing its leaves and Nellie would bring out a jar of cider and they would pass it around and around and drink and drink and, after a while, see the hedgerows begin to dance in the sky and then fall fast asleep with their snouts pointing into the grass. And Lily can remember this beautiful, crazed sleep, wild with dreaming, and how Nellie would later pick her up and carry her to her cot, and how these November nights were the deepest black, as though death had visited, and the morning, when it came, was a sweet surprise.

To the east of the farmhouse, just in front of a spinney which sighed in the wind, there was a stone well. It had been sunk a hundred feet into the earth, a hundred years ago, and a legend survived about a boy, near to Jesse's age, who had fallen into it on the day it was completed. It was said that he lived down there under the water, breathing like a fish and living on mud. Jesse, James, Joseph and Lily would sometimes take turns to climb up onto a milking stool and peer down the edge of the well into the darkness, to see if they could hear the boy or see his white limbs rippling the water. Once, they believed they had caught some whisper of sound coming from his drowned voice and they lowered the bucket down towards him and called to him to take hold of the chain and climb up. But they didn't know his name and Jesse said this was why they couldn't see his head and his arms suddenly rising up out of the dark: he would not realise he was being summoned. He said names were precious and if people didn't know your name, you were like shadows in the trees or like the thistledown flying above the fields – things of no substance.

When Lily remembers the well at Rookery Farm, it is not always the drowned boy that she thinks of; it's the sweetness of the water. When she left Suffolk and was brought back to the Foundling Hospital to be trained for a working life, she was ill for a long time. She couldn't keep her food down and she grew very thin and weak. The doctors, who couldn't tell why this should be so, punished her for being 'stubborn' and making herself sick. They put her on a milk diet and she was well again in a short time, but she got very thirsty and what she longed for was a jar of the cold, sweet water from the Rookery Farm well. She described the well to Bridget, the orphan girl with whom she had to share a bed, and Bridget said, 'What we drink in London is half water and half sewage, for everything comes from the river and the river is full of poison.'

The children of farming families had very little schooling in Suffolk. They learned what the government called 'the rudiments', for it was supposed that this was all they would ever need across their lives, lived within the confines of a few wild acres.

There was a small brick building between Rookery Farm and Swaithey Village, standing square on its own, which called itself a school, but always reminded Lily of a tea kettle. Two people came and went from this place, giving quiet lessons in divinity, spelling and mathematics on certain mornings and certain afternoons, and these seemed to change all the time, so that Lily and the boys would sometimes trudge along the lane and down the road to get there only to find that they had come on the wrong day.

One of the teachers lived in the attic of the school, which Lily thought of as the lid of the tea kettle. She was called Miss Oldroyd and she always carried a cloth-bound Bible under her thin arm and walked with a slow, careful step, as though the draughts coming through the small windows might be enough to blow her down, or even blow her right away, for she was elderly and her hold on the world seemed hesitant and provisional. She taught the divinity lessons and believed so fervently in the Resurrection of Souls that Joseph came home and told Lily that even Uncle Jesse, who had fallen with the train into the Indian ravine, would one day rise up from the parched riverbed and come walking into Rookery Farm. And Lily often imagined this man, or had strange dreams of him, shaking the dust of death from his clothes, smartening up his moustache, trudging up the rocky valley with astonishment in his heart and a glimmer of hope in his eyes.

Miss Oldroyd's assistant was the son of the vicar, an anxious twenty-year-old, known as Thin Martin, who should have been at Cambridge forging some intellectual destiny for himself, but instead found himself confined to Swaithey, teaching farm children their times tables and the reading and spelling of simple words. If you were a girl, you didn't have to pay much attention to the math-ematics lessons. It was thought that girls' brains were made of chaff and that all the numbers would tangle in the chaff for a moment and then fly out again. So, if they wished, the girls could sit on a bench and do their needlework or their knitting and the numbers being recited by the boys in the room would form a strange kind of music in their brains, which had a tendency to linger, so that even though they never uttered a word, their minds had absorbed the fact that nine times three was twenty-seven and that six and four could only ever add up to ten and nothing else. And for all that Lily only spent two years in the Swaithey school, her knowledge of numbers was formed by a kind of osmosis there and would later help in the life she had before she became a killer.

Nellie knew – from the moment Lily arrived at Rookery Farm, with her nine toes – that she would pass her first few years there and then a day would come when she would travel to London and return her to the Foundling Hospital, there to be trained in some apprenticeship to a lowly craft, such as spinning or weaving or haberdashery or the making of hemp rope. She knew that on that day she would have to say goodbye to the boys, goodbye to Perkin, goodbye to Shadow, goodbye to the preening ducks, goodbye to Peggy with her carrot-breath, goodbye to the windblown seeds streaming off from the acres of thistles. Goodbye to Miss Oldroyd in her tea kettle. Goodbye to the taste of sherbet and the taste of fresh snow.

Lily has always believed – and still believes – that Nellie Buck grew fond of her and that it pained her to enter the great gates of the Foundling Hospital and walk into its cold halls and leave her latest foster-child there, to her sad fate among strangers. But Nellie had to follow the law and the law decreed that children could not stay with their adopted families, 'idling in fallow fields', beyond the age of six; they had to repay their debt to the Hospital for taking them in as babies and be trained in some occupation that would be useful to society.

It was for this reason, in the hope that Lily's small hands might acquire some mundane skill, that Nellie took so much trouble to teach her how to sew. She would bring out her big work basket, with its skeins of silk thread, its collection of thimbles, its cards of lace and its little cloth book, filled with needles and pins. On torn pieces of cotton and linen, Lily first learned to do cross-stitch and to make patterns and short words with these tiny and ragged crosses, trying to emulate the work done on a sampler which Nellie kept hanging, framed in wood, in her bedroom: *Mary Wickham. Her Work. In the year 1846.* She kept telling Lily that if she put her mind to her cross-stitch, she could be as gifted as Mary Wickham. Lily didn't know who Mary Wickham was, or where she had gone, but for some reason felt great sorrow for her, as if she'd died without knowing that her sampler would become a precious thing for Nellie Buck.

Nellie's hands were large and coarsened by housework and farm work and her nails were ridged and torn, yet the moment her fingers took up a needle, they began a delicate little performance with it, as though conducting a tiny snatch of music. Her stitching was so precise and clever, its tension always so perfect and exact, that Lily came to marvel at what Nellie's coarse hands could do. She would examine her own fingers, scarred and grazed from the stone-picking, and wonder if she would ever be able to sew with such exquisite care.

The next thing she learned after cross-stitch was blanket stitch. She thought of the downward threads as soldiers standing in a perfect line and the taut loops joining them along the edge of the fabric as their arms reaching out and reaching out to one another, to give themselves courage, until the line was ended. She liked to use scarlet silk thread so that the soldiers would look smart in the red uniforms which James informed her British infantrymen always wore.

One day, Nellie told Lily to begin work on a small sampler. She'd painted the design for it onto a square of canvas. Lily knew her letters by then and what Nellie had painted onto the canvas was the letter 'E', garlanded round with simple flowers. When Lily asked her what the 'E' stood for, she said, 'Your benefactress, Lady Elizabeth Mortimer, who named you while you were still in the care of the London Foundling Hospital, is doing us the honour of a visit and you will give her the sampler as a token of your gratitude.'

Lily worked on the letter 'E' by daylight and by candle-light. The silk thread she was given to use was green and she sewed in rice stitch, which was the hardest stitch to make neat and even. She told Nellie she would do the flowers all in different colours, but Nellie said, 'No, Lily. Lady Elizabeth is a person of good taste. Too many colours might trouble her.' Yet when Lily came to work on the flowers, she couldn't but see them as being purple and yellow and red and orange and she thought how Nellie might be wrong and that Lady Elizabeth would be cheered by all these bright assorted things. For she had been told that Lady Elizabeth was a sad woman with a lump on her spine and how she had to walk about the world bent over like a question mark.

She arrived in a grand carriage, which shook and trem-bled on the rutted lane. Shadow ran out and began barking at the horses, her yellow eyes all aflame with outrage. But the coach came on and stopped a little way from the house. Lily clung to Nellie's skirts and held her sampler ready to be presented to Lady Elizabeth. The family waited in silence. Perkin Buck stood like a penitent, holding his farm cap in his blackened hands. The boys had put on their best Sunday clothes and were standing to attention, like infantrymen, but when, at last, Lady Elizabeth stepped down from the carriage Lily could tell that they had to stop themselves laughing, on account of how small she was. It was as though the great weight on her back had prevented her legs from growing, so that she looked almost like a child, except that her hair was dressed and curled and her cape was trimmed with fur.

A maid had travelled with her and now the two women walked towards the Buck family over the grass and the maid kept her hand under Lady Elizabeth's elbow, as though to hold her up.

Nellie had told Lily to curtsey to her benefactress, but the sight of this person was so peculiar she didn't want to let go of Nellie's skirt. She felt Nellie's hand on her shoulder, trying to make her fall into a little curtsey, but she only clung to her more tightly, because she feared, suddenly, that Lady Elizabeth had come to take her away from Rookery Farm, and she cried out, 'I don't want to get into the carriage! I shall not!'

When she heard this, Lady Elizabeth smiled and Lily looked carefully at her face, all furled about with dark ringlets. She saw that it was a beautiful face and she thought, She is like a person in a Cautionary Tale, such as those Miss Oldroyd sometimes reads to us in school, a person made up from bits and pieces of princesses and monsters, and perhaps she is an enchantress and can turn me into a dragonfly or a white owl ...

She came and held out her gloved hand to Nellie and said that the Foundling Hospital was grateful for all that Nellie had done. Then she looked down at Lily and said, 'Lily Mortimer. And tell me, how are your nine toes?'

She knew all about the child she was trying to help. When they went into the kitchen, where Nellie had set out a grand tea of fruit scones and gooseberry jelly, Lady Elizabeth began talking about the police constable who had saved Lily from the wolves in Victoria Park. She said he was a good man and that he kept up a conversation with the Hospital, just to know that she was alive. But Lily didn't speak. She kept staring at Lady Elizabeth. The sun fell on her ringlets and made them shine like treacle. The sampler was still in Lily's hand and she realised the piece of linen was all crushed and bent by now, so she got down from her chair and climbed onto Nellie's knee and gave the sampler to her, thinking she would hide it away somewhere, but instead she put it on the table and smoothed it out and said, 'We forgot to tell you, Lady Elizabeth, Lily made this as a gift for you, with your initial, very carefully worked in rice stitch, and she hopes you will like it.'

Lily hid her face in Nellie's breast. She heard Lady Elizabeth exclaim, 'Oh, but how very pretty! And what I can straight away see are all the hours of work that have gone into the making of this. And to see evidence of perseverance always makes me so glad, for it is a sign that a child will find its place in the world and commit to that place and have an honourable life.'

'You see,' said Nellie, 'Lady Elizabeth is pleased with your work. You must thank her for her kind words.'

Lily turned around and looked at her once again. She was sitting opposite her and all she could see of her was her beautiful face and her green dress and her white hands and not the lump on her back or her deformed legs, but still she couldn't summon the will to speak to her. And when at last Lady Elizabeth departed in her shaking and trembling carriage, Nellie said she was disappointed with Lily, for she wasn't usually so silent and shy and it was a shame to have been like this with her benefactress, who was going to help her in her life. Lily asked Nellie how she was going to help her, for she already knew that there were all kinds and conditions of help one person may give to another, like Jesse helping her with her bag of stones when it began to drag her body down towards the plough, and Perkin Buck helping the blacksmith to bellow up his fires, and Shadow helping the world to turn by flying in circles over the fields, but she couldn't think what her peculiar benefactress would be able to do for anyone.

'We don't know yet,' said Nellie, 'but she will find a way.'

And Jesse said, 'She might take you to India and you would sit in a railway train which did not fall and you would get a glimpse of a banyan tree.'

On the day Lily left Rookery Farm forever, an October rain was falling. She stood at the open door and looked out at the fields choked with thistles and at the hawthorn berries, dull red, drenched with the showers.

Jesse, Joseph and James set off on their journey to school. They didn't say goodbye to Lily. They went past her and just walked away down the lane, and when she tried to follow them, Jesse had to turn round and say,

'Go back, Lily. Go back. You're going to a different place now, the place where the other children went, and you must not cry about it.'

And she remembers that they began to run and she didn't know why unless they thought they could outrun the rain, but now she understands that they were choked by feelings which they couldn't name as sadness or guilt but which they were enduring just the same, and they were trying to run from these. They didn't turn to wave, but ran on until they were out of sight.

She thought she was alone in the house. She imagined Perkin Buck was clearing ditches with a scythe and a shovel, wearing his old tam-o'-shanter, and Nellie was collecting eggs. And this feeling of being perfectly and absolutely alone and standing in the doorway, watching the grey sky and the hawthorn berries and the boys running away from her, was something which she will never forget. She looked down at her boots, which were new and pinched the foot which had the five toes, and said to herself, 'I am Lily Mortimer and I will not cry.'

She stared beyond her own feet at the path, which was going to lead her away from Rookery Farm, its flags oily with rain, and she saw that there was a clump of ground elder pushing up at its edge. Perkin Buck had told the children to try to root out ground elder wherever they saw it because it was a weed which killed everything around it, and sometimes they would get rewards (a penny piece or a stick of liquorice) for pulling out the long tubers. So now Lily went to the patch of elder and squatted down and looked at it, but instead of trying to tear it out with her hands, just broke off a few green stems and clasped them into a little bunch, and she thought that if there was nothing green growing in

London – as Jesse had informed her – she would take the bitter elder leaves with her, to remind her of everything she had lost.

Then she heard Nellie's footstep at her back. She wasn't out collecting eggs but here in the house. She came to Lily and put her old brown coat round her, helping her to put her arms in the sleeves and knotting a woollen scarf at her neck. She didn't seem to notice the stems of elder in her hand. Lily could feel Nellie's body trembling as she said, 'We are leaving now, Lily, once Perkin has made ready the cart, and this is going to be a wonderful adventure.'

Sometimes, Lily asks herself why she didn't scream and fight and try to run away – to hide, perhaps, in the lid of Miss Oldroyd's tea-kettle schoolhouse – but perhaps she knew, even at the age of six, that this wouldn't save her from her fate, because her fate had long been there, like a shadow in her mind, like a dream that comes and goes, and now it was no longer a dream or a shadow, but a real moment in time.

She put the stems of elder into her coat pocket. Perkin brought the cart to the door. The rain kept falling. Peggy shook her heavy mane and a shower of raindrops made a dancing halo round her head, and while Lily was distracted by this sight, Perkin said to Nellie, 'Get her in the cart, Nellie. Soonest done, soonest mended.'

Nellie lifted Lily up and then climbed in beside her. Perkin had rigged up a kind of canvas awning to protect them from the miserable skies and they crouched under it as the cart lumbered off and then Lily saw the things Nellie had brought with her: there was a little Moses basket, made from reeds and rushes, like the ones in the Bible pictures, and folded into this was the coverlet made of crocheted wool, which had been on her cot at Rookery Farm for all the time that she'd lived there. And she said to Nellie, 'Why are we taking my coverlet?'

And Nellie took her hand and held it to her heart and said, 'This bit of me is hurting. It is hurting very much. But we are people of the world, Lily, and we have to do things according to the law. Or else there is chaos and confusion everywhere.'

Emporium

In London, she inhabits a basement room in Le Bone Street, near a muddy stretch of the Thames. It is winter and cold there and dark and the river's eternal conversation with itself is often made loud by the wind. There are mornings when Lily wakes, not with any joyous start of freedom, or pride at what she (alone among so many) has dared to do, but with a feeling she didn't anticipate and this is a stubborn reluctance to move any part of her body, as though she finds herself in a place where all movement is considered to be a futile and ridiculous human endeavour and where lying straight and still in a bed is all that is asked of her.

Her appetite is poor. The bread and treacle left out by her landlady for her breakfast she gives to the pigeons and starlings who strut up and down the greasy stone steps outside the window. She drinks a little tea, to warm her. She makes herself put on her clothes, but she begins to discover, as the days pass, that she has grown so thin that they no longer fit; it's as if they are the clothes of some other girl, a person who has done no wrong. But they are the only clothes she has. She didn't kill for money or possessions. She has neither. All she has is her work at the Wig Emporium and the joy of Sundays when she can go to the church – not because she believes any more in God or Jesus Christ and his Resurrection, but because the light coming through the stained-glass windows is beautiful, and because she can look round and see the man who watches her and feel distracted from her own terrors by his steady gaze.

She spends some time staring at herself in a scrap of broken mirror-glass nailed to the bedroom wall. What she sees is a face so pale, it's as if her heart, recently, had not been able to push any blood towards it. In the winter dawn light, it looks almost blue. But Lily knows, despite her reluctance to get out of bed, despite the pallor which has stolen into her cheeks, she must try to keep on working. Belle Prettywood has a grand commission from Her Majesty's Opera House to make the wigs for their production of Signor Giuseppe Verdi's *La Traviata*. Belle has told her girls that time is short, extra hours must be put in, the cast of the opera is large, with scenes from balls and salons, and then there are the several wigs to be made for the singer in the role of Violetta, for the director has explained to Belle that the hair of a consumptive woman would surely thin as her disease progressed and that he wishes to strive for realism in his production.

Lily has been given the task of making 'Violetta's final wig'. The hair she is using is black and long and she is working with single strands for the knotting, as instructed by Belle. As she works, Lily imagines Violetta, thin and pale like herself, with blood staining her nightgown and her eyes grown huge and wild, waiting for her lover, who does not come to save her (for no one can save her) but only to hold her in his arms as she dies.

The Emporium is housed in a narrow building on Long Acre. On the ground floor is the wig shop and Belle Prettywood can only wish that the fashion for elaborate wigs had not faded at the end of the last century. In these times, the 1860s, women are supposed to make the most of what Nature has given them, so that many of Belle's clients slip furtively into the shop, wondering if they dare to succumb to the idea of fabrication. Some are easily tempted by the sight of lush curls and ringlets framing their faces; others opt for a 'modestly priced hairpiece' to match their own locks and discreetly bulk them out; others again walk away with nothing, overcome by guilt at their vanity, resigned to remaining ordinary. So the fortune that Belle Prettywood is steadily amassing comes mainly from the London theatres and from the gentry's fondness for elaborate costume balls. It comes from other sources as well, but Belle doesn't talk about these to her workers at the Emporium.

Above the shop is the wig factory itself, a long room which smells of cedarwood and glue, lightly touched with the scent of bitter almonds. At one end, the head moulds are made by master craftsmen, chiselling and sanding. Down all the middle of the room, the wig-makers sit at their tables with their tools spread out in front of them, their hooks and hackles, their blocking pins and hammers, their bolts of muslin and bobbins of twine. And the hair. Some of this – the best, most expensive hair – is imported from India, but mainly it's bought from the London poor and may sometimes be crawling with lice. It is fumigated with Scheele's Prussic Acid, the poison which lends the room its almond perfume, and washed and tied into bundles by a group of unskilled women known collectively as 'The Shift'.

The bundles are then hung by The Shift around the walls, sorted by colour and thickness, ready for use by the likes of Lily, who has received an apprentice's training from Belle and whose deft and quick use of the hook, which pulls and knots the hair onto the lace 'cap', is a source of admiration in her fellow workers. She tells them that her fingers are nimble because her foster-mother Nellie taught her to sew, and whenever she says Nellie's name, she feels a weight pressing on her heart.

But she likes her work: cutting the lace and pressing it carefully onto the head mould, fashioning the darts and fixing them with blocking pins till all are shaped and blocked and they can be whipped with cotton thread to complete the cap. Then beginning to hook in the hair, strand by soft strand. Always, at this moment, her mind strays in wonder at the great subterfuge she is going to create.

Belle Prettywood has a small office within the room, but glassed off from it, so that she can look up from her mountain of invoices, hair samples, ledgers, cheques and banknotes to survey her 'girls' and make sure that none are daydreaming or have fallen asleep at their benches. Belle is a woman of forty-one, who manages to look younger by dousing her face in rose water, who dresses in silks and satins every day and who has gentlemen 'admirers' all over London. She smells of the rose water and of something else, something heavy, which Lily can't quite identify, but which she thinks may be the stench of an unsatisfied soul, for however much money Belle makes, she always hungers for more; however many men she seduces, there are always others in her sights.

Sometimes, Lily thinks that were she to confess her crime to Belle Prettywood, Belle would be transfixed with excitement. She would gasp and swoon. She would make her repeat the details more than once. She would look upon Lily with a new admiration. And then she would hold the secret inside her, safe as a child in the womb.

Days pass and the winter creeps over the surfaces of everything and Lily doesn't know what to live for except for the promise of Sundays and the multicoloured light coming through the high church windows and the gaze of the stranger, as constant as that light.

He never speaks to her. It always seems as though he is about to speak to her, and then he hesitates and looks away. She walks out of the church and his eyes follow her again as she steps carefully through the graveyard, but after that she is gone into the throng on the street and he does not follow.

Then, one Sunday in December, he is not there. Lily knows, without really looking, that there is an absence, an alteration in the way things are. When the service ends, she walks straight out, barely glancing to left or right. 'There is no purpose,' Nellie Buck once said to her, 'in searching for something that we are never going to find.'

So she goes on towards her lodgings, but is revolted by the idea of them, by the way they squat under the pavement, blanked off by their eight greasy stone steps, unblessed with light. They imprison her, or rather, when she is there alone, she is imprisoned by the fear of what lies in wait for her. And she sees now that she has put her faith in the longing of the stranger, as if, somehow, he might redeem her, as if, through him, she might finally be granted the feeling of freedom she'd hoped would come in the wake of her crime, and which did indeed arrive to comfort her heart for a while, and then somehow faded away, as if the whole thing had never happened and so needed to be done again.

She walks to the river and stands watching ragged children combing the mudbanks for treasure, for green glass bottles, for matchboxes, for old shoes, for sticks of wood to burn against the December cold. Red worms rise up in the mud, like arteries of blood, but the children are barefoot, seeming not to mind them, just stumbling this way and that, investigating the slime with their hands, as intent on their task as stone-pickers in a country field.

Miss Disobedience

When Nellie and Lily drove through the gates of the London Foundling Hospital and saw the great building rise up before them, like the hand of God planted on the earth, Nellie looked at the basket she had brought, in which to collect her new foster-baby, and then looked down at six-year-old Lily, holding some broken stems of elder in her hand, and what she felt was not so much sadness as a colossal weariness come over her. She thought, Life is repetition, endless and without pause, and then we die and that is all ...

Of all the children that had been placed in her care, she had loved Lily the most. Or else she had not loved the others at all – even little Tom who'd died – but only tolerated them, with a meagre show of affection, for the price of ten shillings a month. But Lily had been different, Lily had been 'her girl', Lily had worked at her stitching by daylight and candlelight, Lily had compared sherbet to fallen snow and laughed when she fell over in the cart, Lily had hugged and kissed her at bedtime and caressed the lobes of her ears with her tiny hands. That she should now be cast out made Nellie Buck want to lie down in some dark place and weep away the rest of her life.

She put a gentle palm on Lily's brown curls. She knew that the first thing that would happen to the child would be the shaving of her hair. The nurses at the Hospital believed that parasites from farm animals – ticks, fleas and nits – could be brought in on the heads of those who had 'lived and worked in cowsheds and pigsties and slept among mice and washed themselves in stagnant ponds'. If Nellie were to protest that her children had been kept clean and free from vermin at Rookery Farm, washed three times a week in the sweet water from the well, she would not be believed. Or if she was believed, it would not count. The routine was the same for every child returned to the Hospital: the head was shaved, then scrubbed in carbolic with a hard brush and doused with vinegar.

Lily knew nothing of this. All she knew, now, was that she was walking with Nellie up the steps of the Hospital and a harsh wind was blowing and the ground-elder leaves in her hand were dead.

They entered a vast, cold room. Lily gaped for a moment at the ornate ceiling high above them and when she lowered her head again, Nellie was gone. Nellie had vanished into a crowd of women, who seemed to be talking all at once in loud, unhappy voices, and Lily was being tugged by the arm through the room by a thin uniformed nurse. She tried to turn, to call out to Nellie, but a hand was clamped over her mouth and the nurse said with a sneer, 'None of that! We do not tolerate senti-ment. You are the child of an undeserving mother and you should fall on your knees and thank the Lord Jesus that you were saved by us. That is all that must fill your mind now: that you have been saved.'

Lily tried once again to turn around, to pull free of the nurse, to run to wherever it was Nellie had gone with her burden of the rush basket and the woollen crocheted coverlet, but she couldn't see her. 'Stop that!' said the nurse. 'She is gone and you will not find her.

There are no sentimental goodbyes here. We forbid them. Your foster-mother did her duty and that is all. Now, she takes in another baby and you will be forgotten.'

But surely it wasn't so? *Forgotten*? How could Nellie forget the hours and hours of sewing together, the pegging of washing together in the wind, the gathering of rosehips together in the autumn sunlight, the songs sung together when the night came ... ? How could this nurse, with her pursed lips and her thin face, suggest such a terrible thing?

Knowing that this person must be lying made Lily angry. She was wearing the new boots, bought by Perkin Buck in Swaithey Market, and with her left foot, she kicked out at the nurse's ankle, just visible under her white uniform. The nurse cried out in pain and was distracted by the kick long enough to let go her grip on Lily's arm, so that in an instant, Lily turned and began to run towards the crowd of women at the other end of the colossal room. She ran as fast as she could, as fast as she used to run with Shadow, chasing sheep in the thistle-down fields. When she reached the place where the people congregated, she didn't stop, but pretended she was an angry bullock shouldering its way through the herd and with the loudest voice she could manage, she cried out, 'Nellie! Nellie! Where are you?'

Hands tried to grab her – this ill-mannered little foundling barging among them like a farm animal and shouting like a costermonger – but she pressed on, pushing everybody away, until at last she saw Nellie, who was standing frozen to a spot near the door. Lily charged towards her and when she reached her, threw up her arms and began to beat her with her fists. She kept hitting and hitting and hitting. The dead elder leaves fell out of her hands and as these fell, so Nellie was forced to drop the Moses basket, as she tried to push Lily away. But Lily used her head now to butt into Nellie's broad stomach. She was no longer calling out Nellie's name. She had no words any more, only a feeling of sorrow and despair unlike anything she had ever known.

When her neck and her arms began to tire, she let Nellie kneel down and hold her and they clung together, crying and rocking to the rhythm of their broken hearts until at last they were still and the nurse returned to snatch at Lily's curls and pull her away by her hair.

Lily prefers not to remember her first days and nights at the Foundling Hospital. She has always tried to consign them to oblivion, but they have always resisted. They are like a wound that will not heal, like a snatch of melancholy music that will not fade, like a mathematical sum which never alters but is never solved.

After her head had been shaved, she was stripped of her clothes and told that these would be burned – all except the boots. These were 'serviceable' and they were to be given to one of the foundling boys, who had 'greater need of them', and replaced with shoes made of cloth, 'suitable for girls'. Lily began to protest. She had been proud of her boots, even though they pinched. Perkin Buck had bought them as a parting gift to her and they had cost a precious florin … But once again the nurse's hand was clamped across her mouth and she was commanded to be silent. As the nurse began scrubbing Lily's little body with carbolic soap – scrubbing so fiercely with a loofah that welts were raised on her arms and on her back – she informed her that she would be 'remade' here at Thomas Coram's great Hospital and that 'whatever kind of stubborn, undisciplined child' she had been, she would no longer be that person, but a different being, who existed only to obey God's Holy Law. 'And', said the nurse, who was to be addressed as 'Nurse Maud', 'whatever affection you may have formed for your foster-mother, you will let this go from your heart. God despises children who are not committed to their new life, but yearn in a sentimental way for an ignorant, pagan baby-hood. You love your benefactors at the Hospital and you love God now. And that is all.'

Lily remembers that Nellie had once told her that God was everywhere. God was in the wind which bent the willows down towards the pond; God was in the new-fallen snow, tasting of sherbet; God was in the sunlight shining on the plough. He was not a 'separate body', but present in all things, even in the dark night, even in times of sadness, and Lily began to tell Nurse Maud that this was how she had been taught to think of Him. But Nurse Maud snatched up a grey towel and threw it over Lily's head so that it smothered her face, and shouted, 'Dry yourself, Miss Disobedience! And learn never to talk back to your betters!'

Lily was dressed in a red and beige uniform and beige drawers and stockings, with a white kerchief tied around her neck and a white and red cap pressed onto her bald head. Her old clothes were put into a sack. She was dragged in front of a long mirror, silvered with wear and time, but didn't recognise the angry person she saw there, with a face distorted by weeping. She began to tug off the cap, which made her scalp itch, but Nurse Maud pulled her arm away and the cap fell onto the damp stone floor. 'Now look!' said the nurse. 'You have not been here two hours and already I can tell what trouble you are going to cause. And do you know what happens to troublemakers here? They are beaten. What is your name, so that I can warn the governors that you will be difficult and must be put on watch?'

Lily stared at Nurse Maud. She remembered Jesse explaining how the boy at the bottom of the well would not answer because they hadn't called him by name, and that if a person had no name, then he or she was like the shadows in the trees or like the thistledown vanishing into the sky – things of fragile substance. Lily told herself that – with her hair shorn and her boots confiscated – perhaps her name was the only thing left to her and she decided that she would not say it aloud to anyone.

Nurse Maud took her by the shoulders and shook her. 'Tell me your name, child!' she shrieked. 'It is the law!'

The little cap was still on the floor and Lily kicked it away with her cloth shoes, through which she could feel the hard ground, and she thought, This is how it will be now, wherever I walk on the earth, I will feel the stones of the earth hurting my bones. She whispered aloud, 'Perkin Buck would not have wanted this.'

'What? What did you say?' said the nurse.

'My foster-father—' Lily began.

'Never mind him. I've told you, your foster-parents have already forgotten you and you must put them out of your mind. Now pick up your cap and tell me your name.'

'He spent two shillings on my boots—' said Lily.

'Stop it! Stop it! Really, you are an unendurable child. Say your name, or you will be punished.'

But Lily wouldn't. She pressed her lips together, made them as thin as the mouth in Nurse Maud's mean face, so that no words could come out. She knew that she should have been afraid of Nurse Maud, but she felt hatred, not fear. She let the cap lie. She saw the nurse raise her arm and thought, Now it will come, the physical pain this Maud longs to inflict, but Lily was too quick for her. She ducked down and turned and began to run from the washroom. She ran past other children with shaved heads and naked bodies, crying as the soap stung their eyes and the loofahs scraped their skin, crying for the things they had lost. She ran along a stone passageway and came to a flight of stairs which she couldn't remember having climbed, but she decided that perhaps they led back to the high-ceilinged room where she had been torn away from Nellie, and so in turn to the entrance to the Hospital and an open door and the great courtyard beyond, bounded by high walls, but with a gateway that led to the world outside …

She was halfway down the stairs, still running, when a door opened on a landing and a white-haired man came out, wearing a priest's cassock. As Lily charged towards him, he flung out his arms to bar her way and said, 'Now, now, what's this? You know the rules. Children do not run.'

She collided with his body, almost knocking him over, and was assailed by the dry reek of him, the scent of incense and unwashed skin. He reached out and held her arms in a tight grip and looked at her – at the head newly shaved, the small face red and puffy from weeping – and saw, perhaps, what he had seen a hundred times before: sorrow and confusion in the body of a child, but also defiance, the sudden assertion of a will that found it would not bend to the alteration being forced upon it. And he knew what Nurse Maud did not know – or had not chosen to remember – that there was only one way to bring about some calm and acceptance and this was by showing kindness.

He knelt down, so that his white head was level with Lily's, and he smiled at her and said, 'I know this is all very sudden for you, and difficult to comprehend, but just let me tell you that God knows you are troubled. He understands that you feel alone. But you are not alone. God is with you. And we, the chaplains and teachers and nurses here at Coram, are with you too and only wish to lead you to a happy and useful life. Can you trust me on this score?'

No. She couldn't trust anybody or anything, not even this chaplain with his stale, holy smell. All she could trust was the knowledge that some mistake had been made. The day was turning towards darkness and she should not be here. She should be riding in the cart up the lane towards Rookery Farm, seeing the first star appear above the pond, knowing that in a short time she would be safe in her bed, with the crocheted blanket pulled up to her chin and Nellie's soft lips whispering across her cheek in a goodnight kiss . . .

She shook her head. She expected the chaplain to become angry. She remembered the vicar of Swaithey sometimes banging his fist on the edge of the pulpit and telling the farmers and the shopkeepers and the shoe-makers and the brewers of ale and the milkmaids and the growers of cabbages that they were 'addicted to sin'. But this white-haired man stayed calm. He just stood up and took her hand and said, 'Never mind. I'll take you to your dormitory. I wonder if you would like to tell me your name, so that we find the correct room. Would you do that?'

They were climbing the stairs now and Lily could feel the coldness of the stone through her cloth shoes. She said quietly, 'My name is Mary Wickham.'

So she was Mary Wickham for a while. Needlework preoccupied her mind.

She was 'Mary' on her first night in the dormitory, sharing a bed with a girl named Bridget O'Donnell, who reminded Lily of a thrush. Bridget's skin was speckled with brown spots, her eyes were nervous and bright and the touch of her hand on Lily's arm was as soft as a bird's wing.

In the damp darkness of the dormitory, Bridget clung to 'Mary' and described to her the foster home she had come from, in the village of Baldock in Hertfordshire, which was half a house and half a dry-goods store. She said that her foster-mother, Mrs Inchbald, kept the house and her foster-father, Mr Inchbald, kept the store and the children went between the two, sneaking from their lessons in the back parlour to watch Mr Inchbald weighing flour and making neat paper packages for tea leaves, and longing to run their fingers through the coffee beans which had come from Africa and which sat around the store in bulging sacks, smelling of a strange land.

Bridget said everybody in the village loved the store and loved the Inchbald family and that strangers would buy treats and trinkets there for the children. She said nobody told her that she wasn't a real part of the family, until one day Mr Inchbald sat her down on the counter of the shop and put up his 'Closed' sign and came and told her that she was only 'on loan' to them from the Foundling Hospital, just like the house and the shop were 'on loan' to them from the bank, and that one day soon the Hospital would take her back.

Bridget began to cry at this point in her story. She said, 'I didn't know a girl could be "on loan" to the people she thought were her parents.' She said she was crying for the gorgeous smell of coffee and for the little attic she slept in, where the moon travelled up and up the tiny window and talked to her as it passed, in a friendly conversational voice. She was crying for the pork roasts on Sundays and for Mrs Inchbald's ironing table, beneath which she liked to sit and listen to the iron hissing across the skirts and petticoats and to Mrs Inchbald trying to remember snatches of song from a distant past.

Lily tried to dry Bridget's tears with her nightgown sleeve. All around them in the dormitory, they could hear other girls crying and gulping with misery, and Lily said, 'I suppose all of us were "on loan" and there was nothing we could do about it. And now we're prisoners.'

'We could run away,' said Bridget.

'I tried to run away today,' said Lily. 'I was stopped by a chaplain. But we could try tomorrow.'

'Do you know the way to Baldock?' said Bridget.

'No,' said Lily. 'I don't know what Baldock is.'

'There might be an omnibus which knows the way.'

'You have to pay money to ride on an omnibus and we don't have any.'

'I do,' said Bridget. 'I'll tell you a secret. I've got a sixpenny piece hidden up my arse. Mr Inchbald gave it to me and told me to put it in a safe place. That was the safest place I could think of. But I could take it out and wash it. Unless it's fallen out by now.'

Lily was silent, wondering what it might feel like to hide a sixpenny piece in your BTM. Then, she said, 'I've got a secret, too. My name isn't Mary; it's Lily.'

For breakfast, they were given porridge and for lunch, hard bread and cheese and for supper a thin soup, in which a few things might be floating: cabbage leaves, grains of rice and little slivers of carrot or turnip. On her first evening, Lily found human hair in her bowl of soup, but did not see it until too late and it collected in her throat and began to choke her. She reached into her mouth with her hands to try to pull the hair out, but it seemed to fasten itself to her windpipe, so that her breathing suddenly ended and she felt blood surge into her face and she thought, This will be the last thing I know on this earth – what it is like to die, choking on hair. Then somebody slapped a heavy palm on her back, once, twice and then again, harder and harder, and Lily vomited it out, as a cat will vomit out a ball of fur gathered in its stomach, and she saw it in her soup bowl, wet strands clinging together, flecked with carrot stain.

They gave her water and she drank and drank, not knowing that the water at the Hospital was tainted and would make her sick. But the following day she couldn't eat her breakfast porridge and as the hours went on and she was seated on a hard stool and given a bundle of wool to card and comb, she began to sweat. Her arms and hands felt weak and she let the wool fall. Then she knew that everything in her stomach was rising up and was going to come out of her. She tried to put up her hand, to warn the teacher, but her body convulsed and a great stream of bile and half-digested food splashed onto her cloth shoes and onto the hard brick floor. Then she felt herself falling, as if off a vast mountainside, going down and down through the air, past rocks and stones, past fragile vegetation clinging to the scree, to land somewhere miles below, where no light ever came.

Lily woke up in the arms of a nurse. Her beige and red uniform had been taken away. The nurse, who was not Nurse Maud, but someone with gentler hands, laid her on a bed and put a coverlet over her. Lily reached out to see whether Bridget O'Donnell was in the bed beside her, but she was not, and this bed felt soft, as if the mattress might have been filled with chicken feathers.

She felt herself being lifted up and a beaker was pressed to her lips and she drank a few sips of water, but then pushed it away. It wasn't the sweet water from the well at Rookery Farm, but some other liquid, which might have come from a pond.

'You must drink,' said the nurse.

But Lily paid no attention to this. She laid her head down and closed her eyes and knew she was travelling towards a sleep too absolute for dreams.

But in another hour she was awake again, cold with sweat. She hung her head over the side of the bed and vomited onto the floor. When the nurse came and chastised her for not calling for bucket or a bowl, she couldn't stop herself from crying and when the nurse tried again to make her drink the foul river water, she hit the beaker away and water spilled over the place where the pool of sick had been cleaned away.

She lay still when the nurse had gone. She turned her head and saw that her bed was one in a long line of iron beds, but all except hers appeared to be empty. She remembered that Nellie Buck sometimes used to say to her friends in Swaithey that she had confidence that Lily would 'make something of her life', that she would 'find her place in the world'. And she thought that now she was in 'the world' – the dark world beyond Rookery Farm – and this was how she would always be, sick and alone in an empty room, with Hospital furniture arranged in rows all around her and sweat beading on her shaved head and a bell tolling somewhere, and then another bell and another, and all of them tolling for places and people she would never see again.

Like a Bride . . .

The winter is so hard in London that frost caresses the black railings, like a sugar-coating, and even the slops in the gutter freeze over in a caramel-coloured glaze.

Belle Prettywood can't endure the cold. She's installed a pot-bellied stove inside her glass booth and it is the job of the head-mould makers to keep it jammed up with fresh cuts of wood, arriving there early in the morning to make sure the stove is burning brightly before Miss Prettywood sweeps in for the day.

Some warmth seeps out into the room from Belle's booth, but the wig-makers struggle to manipulate their tools with frozen fingers, so Lily is deputed to ask Belle if the door to her heated sanctuary can remain open, so that the temperature can rise just a little in the room.

Belle looks at Lily, takes in the alteration to her body, the pallor in her cheeks, and says, 'Is it the cold doing this to you – making you so thin?'

'No,' Lily wants to say, 'it's the memory of a killing I recently performed. I thought the crime – which rid the world of a wicked person who did not deserve to live – would release me from the things that have haunted my life. Instead, I find that I feel so afraid of what lies in wait for me, that I have lost my appetite.'

But she doesn't say this. She smiles at Belle and replies, 'Yes, I suppose it might be this – my body consuming itself to try to get warm. But if you would open your door a little, Belle, that we might share in the heat from your stove …'

Belle adjusts the floral shawl she wears round her shoulders. 'I am far more susceptible to the cold than any of you,' she says. 'It's in my blood. All the Prettywoods suffered from what I have heard termed "winter petrifi-cation". And it was in my mother's family, too. If I open my door, I will have to come to work swathed in fur, with fur-lined galoshes, and then I will no doubt become a figure of mockery in the atelier.'

'We wouldn't mock you for wearing fur, Belle. And we are finding it very difficult to work in these condi-tions. We are only thinking about the time constraints on the *Traviata* wigs …'

At the mention of *Traviata*, Belle appears immediately flustered, as if her mind had let go all the work still to be done for the opera and only just remembered it, together with all the new instructions that keep pouring in from the director, Maestro Arditti, who has taken to arriving unannounced at the Wig Emporium, carrying a fly swat made of horsehair, which he taps on the shoulders of the workers, on the half-completed wigs and on the bolts of hair hanging round the walls, as if to identify everything as belonging uniquely to him.

'Oh, the *Traviata* undertaking …' sighs Belle. 'It is both quite marvellous and impossibly demanding! See here, Lily, a bottle of gin at my elbow and I never used to touch a drop of this. I expect it is already eating away at my personality and I shall soon become an intolerably dull and stagnant person. Do you already notice my becoming boring and stupid?'

'Not at all, Belle. We love you like a mother, or like a revered teacher. Every few moments, we look up from our work, to make sure you are still there, watching over us.'

'Oh, what naughty mockery! But this is good. I don't mind it at all. It shows me the spark in you. Some people have no spark at all – none. Shut the door, Lily, and I will tell you something.'

Lily looks round to see the patient Shift women unpacking a new consignment of dirty hair from East London and her fellow workers pausing in their tasks to watch her, hoping, no doubt, that Belle will agree to leave her door ajar, but she closes it as instructed and Belle beckons her nearer the mighty desk, piled with orders and invoices.

'Now,' Belle says, 'I don't know where you learned your skill. You are still very young. But you are quite and by miles the best of my women. The speed at which you work, the dexterity of your hands . . . I have been thinking how to reward you. I cannot pay you more than the others, or else I will face a mutiny, but perhaps I can take you out of that hovel you inhabit in Le Bone Street. There is an attic in my house, not much used. I could furnish it a little. I would charge you a fair rent.'

Lily gazes at Belle. She has never been to Belle Prettywood's house at Seven Dials, but she has heard rumours about it – that there is a luxurious boudoir in it to rival any in London, with a ceiling painted blood-red, a bed hung with turquoise tassels and mirrors placed all around it . . .

In the sudden warmth of Belle's booth, Lily feels slightly faint. She would like to sit down on the hard chair, from which men in dark coats – bankers, lawyers and merchants – frequently come and go, to pore over balance sheets and bills of lading, but she stays standing.

And she thinks how her life might change if she went to live at Seven Dials with Belle, or rather, she does not really wish to think about it because she knows she would not be able to live as she would be expected to live in a place like that. Her room under the road asks nothing of her, only that she *exist* there, in semi-darkness, to brood on her crime, to relive it, to wait for the day when she and the murder break forth into a storm of light. And she thinks, suddenly, that perhaps only then – when everything is known and can be judged – will she be free.

'Well?' asks Belle. 'Would you not prefer my attic to your basement?'

'You are very kind,' says Lily. 'But I believe I am a little ill at the moment. I feel it is best for me to stay where I am until I recover.'

'Very well,' says Belle. 'If that is how you want to see it. But try to eat something. I can't afford for you to fade away. Arditti will whip me with his fly swat if the wigs are not ready for the dress rehearsal.'

The Sunday church congregation gets very small, because now there is a great weight of snow on the city. Although the verger himself has dug a pathway through the graveyard to the church door, there are many pathways leading to that pathway which lie buried in the deep whiteness, where nothing and no one can move freely, only birds looking in vain for patches of dark earth.

Lily remembers the snow falling in crusts like cake icing from the firs on the road to Swaithey and it holds no fear for her. She just wraps her head in a woollen shawl and makes her way to the church once more. The hem of her coat is saturated and becomes heavy, but she finds the whitened churchyard beautiful: everything softened and leavened by the snow. She bends down and scoops a tiny handful into her mouth and remembers the taste of sherbet and Nellie singing in the cold air.

She goes into the church, bows her head, then looks up at her favourite stained-glass window, depicting a sower with his basket of corn seed. She likes the strong muscularity of his calves beneath his workman's tunic and the tenderness in his outstretched hand. Birds hover above him, golden in the morning light.

Then she walks down the nave to the pew where she always sits, five from the front. She kneels and says a prayer, asking for the stranger to return, despite the weather, and when she gets up again, she turns round, knowing that he has come in. Of course he is looking at her and now, for the first time, she holds his gaze. She sees that he is quite ordinary, his dark hair thinning a little at his temples, his necktie clumsily knotted, but his face clean-shaven and open and his eyes large and intense.

Lily's heart begins to beat wildly. Now that he is there, she wants more. She wants to touch his arm. She wants to say to him that she has nowhere to go in her life except towards him. But she forces herself to turn away, to open her prayer book as the organ begins to play and the service unfolds as it always does, with the vicar liking to stand very still once he has ascended the pulpit, looking down with severity, but sometimes closing one eye, to seem to focus upon one person or one part of the congregation, like an archer taking aim.

The vicar's voice is loud. *For thine is the kingdom, the power, and the glory!* The assertion is made as though it were a royal proclamation and Lily imagines the great prayer travelling out of the church and across all the whitened graves and disturbing the air as far as the river, where, moment by moment, the surface of the water is forming tiny ice crystals which begin to mass together to make floating islands that press up against the hulls of the boats and barges. And this, she thinks, is where she would really like to be, standing by the river with the stranger, letting him take her hand and ask her name, both of them remembering that, in time, by slow-moving tides and eddies, the Thames led inevitably to the sea ...

Her anxiety, now, is that the man will slip away before the service ends, and it becomes a deep fear. Something tells her that if she doesn't speak to him today, then she will never see him again and this is unendurable, because she has come to believe that he is all that she has, the only person in the world who can steer her away from her death – from the knotted rope and the trapdoor and the void. And it is as if he knows this, as if he understands that this is his appointed task, to alter her future. For why else would he have returned to the church so many times, never speaking, but only watching and waiting for the moment when she would come towards him?

The service is over now. The four fat little choirboys grin above their ruffs as they hurry out. The vicar walks at a stately pace behind them as the organist plays tuneless music, like someone only practising fingering to pass the time.

Now, Lily allows herself to turn. And he is still there. He is still watching her.

She lets the rest of the congregation go out into the winter morning. The man waits. Lily waits. They must wait until there is no one else left in the church, and then ... She moves very slowly to him, holding herself tall and contained, like a bride moving down the aisle to a waiting groom.

As she nears him, he reaches out and gently puts a hand on her arm. So they stand, face to face, the organ music still going on, the cold air from the open door now reaching them and making Lily shiver.

'Forgive me if I am quite mistaken,' he says at last. 'I wanted to speak out before, but I refrained, in case you felt this to be too forward or in case I was wrong, but I believe you are Miss Lily Mortimer. Am I right?'

'You are right,' says Lily.

He smiles then. The smile is so wide, it looks as if it might break into laughter.

'Lily!' he says, seeming to marvel at the name. 'I've been searching for you for so long. When I last saw you, you were at the Foundling Hospital. I first glimpsed you only across the width of a classroom. They wouldn't let me disturb you or talk to you, because I was not part of your family.'

Lily doesn't know what to say. She asks herself why a stranger would 'search' for her, but has no answer.

'I came back another time and I was told that you had once tried to run away from the Hospital and were punished, but since that punishment, you had worked hard at all your tasks.'

What could she say to this? She hears Perkin Buck mumble that 'Certain things are beyond mortal knowing, such as why Uncle Jesse's Indian train went down into a ravine and all were slain.'

'Why were you searching for me?' she asks at last.

'Well . . .' he says, looking away from her, as though he were embarrassed or as though he might be about to weep. 'You may think this strange, but I felt it my duty, somehow, to watch over you and hope that as a child of Coram you would come towards a good life.'

Ah. A 'good' life. How can you live a good life if you have been precious to nobody and made to feel burdened by shame? How can your heart not be vengeful?

'Watch over me?' Lily says.

'I tried. I saw you from a doorway, helping the little ones with their needlework. I saw how still and patient you were. But again, they would not let me speak to you. They mistrusted me.'

'Were they right to mistrust you?'

'It was only ... they did not know who I was.'

'And I don't know who you are. But you had better tell me, or I will have to walk away from you.'

The man is holding a tall, stiff hat in his hands. He looks down at the hat, then puts it on his head, pressing it tenderly around his temples, as though without it he did not feel brave or complete enough for the moment he's living through.

'Well,' he says, 'you have the right not to believe me, but I think I was the person who saved your life.'

She ponders this. She wants to say, 'My life needs saving again. I'm becoming distant from all humanity because I have committed a crime,' but she stays silent and waits.

'You may have heard, indeed I know that you have heard how your poor mother abandoned you on a winter's night?'

'Yes. She left me at the gates to Victoria Park.'

'And the rain was falling and it was bitter cold, but a young police constable was doing his rounds near the park, when he heard the howling of wolves ...'

'Oh,' she says. 'Oh.'

So she knows that it was him. She remembers his name now: Sam Trench. He walked through the sleet, carrying her in her sack. At the Foundling Hospital, they cared for him, ill as he was from his great trek, and then he went back to his home and soon afterwards she found herself at Rookery Farm.

It moves her that not only did he save her from the cold and from the wolves, he gave himself the task of watching over her, quite as though she had been his own child.

'Police Constable Sam Trench,' she says. 'I was told the name long ago, by my foster-mother, and I have never forgotten it.'

He smiles. He allows himself to put his hand on hers.

'You are making something of your life, working for Belle Prettywood.'

'"Making something"? Yes, I suppose I am. Belle likes my work. And you? What have you made of your time on this earth, Sam Trench?'

'Quite a lot, I modestly say. A dedicated catcher of felons for the Metropolitan Police. I'm a superintendent now. Detective Department.'

Detective Department.

Now, Lily feels a sudden chill. In the churchyard, she sees that the snow is still falling on the graves. She draws her shawl around her.

'Those little Barbarians'

The first lesson the children learned at the London Foundling Hospital was the lesson of their own abandonment. They were reminded – sometimes daily – that they had nobody in the world to care for them and nobody in the world to love them, except a benevolent God.

'God sees you,' they were told. 'He sees your loneliness. But He cannot teach you to spin or weave. He cannot keep reminding you that you must carve out your lives by your own strivings, but you will come to understand that if you do not obey your teachers, why then you will be cast out a second time. Perhaps, then, you will think that you are free, but what kind of freedom will you gain? The freedom to starve. The freedom to grub for a life in the flotsam cast up by the river tides ...'

Their day began at five in the morning. Lily had been used to rising early at Rookery Farm, when the cockerels began their crowing at first light. But here, at Coram, the children were woken in darkness. A single rushlight would be placed in each dormitory and by this fragile gleam, they would try to dress themselves, as the nurses inspected the beds for 'accidents in the night'. And there were many of these. The smell of urine lingered permanently in the air. Sniffing and complaining, the nurses would bundle away the soaking sheets and cuff the heads of 'those little Barbarians who cannot contain themselves'. The bed which Lily shared with Bridget was often wet in the early morning and both heads were cuffed, but after a while, Lily grew used to the warm, heavy damp in which they slept and dreamed and began to feel that it was a bond between her and Bridget, one they had never asked for, but which was almost comforting.

Their first task of the day was to draw water from a pump in the courtyard and scrub the floors of the dormitories, but also the parquet of the great public rooms where the Governors and visitors to the Hospital assembled and where sacred music was often performed by musicians, donating their time and their talent to the Coram Foundation, free of charge. On certain evenings, when the children were in bed, nursing their raw hands after a long day's work, they could sometimes be lulled to sleep by a sweet, melancholy sound they couldn't place in their memories, but which quietened them and sometimes entered their dreams.

Once the cleaning was done, the foundlings sat down to breakfast. The milk poured onto their porridge was fresh, for two dairymen came every morning, bringing cool churns. After her illness, Lily was afraid to drink the water, and the nurses, who didn't want the trouble of her sickness to be repeated, allowed her to drink milk with her meals for a while, 'until your constitution accustoms itself to London water'.

She worked hard. Perhaps the milk sustained her? Bible lessons were usually followed by sewing classes, then by an hour of reading and writing. It had been Thomas Coram's intention that the orphans should 'by every means available' be educated towards an independent life. The thought that they could spend years at

the Hospital, 'at the country's expense', and then emerge
from it in the kind of helpless state that would lead them
to knavery or prostitution dismayed him. He saw himself
as a saviour, but was a man wise enough to know that
not everybody in the world wishes for their own salvation and that some can only hear, in the space between
their ears, the siren cry of wickedness and rage.

Coram also knew that many of those he took in at six
years old had formed attachments to their foster-parents
and that these partings caused them a virus of sorrow
from which they might never quite recover. All he could
do was suggest to those who had the day-to-day care of
the children that severity be demonstrated towards this
'illness'. They would be encouraged to 'forget absolutely'
the years spent with people who were paid ten shillings
a month to care for them, 'but to whom they meant
nothing'. They were to be reminded that in other lands,
in times not so long gone, men kept slaves to pick cotton
and cut cane and although they may have seen their
plantations thrive from the monetary value of these
people, they cared nothing for them – no more than for
the rats in a haystack. 'You are like them,' the foundlings
were told. 'You are like those slaves. For did you not
work for the people *paid* to care for you? Did you not toil
in fields, picking stones? Did you not go out into frozen
winter mornings to feed livestock? Did you not endure
captivity and loneliness? And at the end of it all, what did
you take from the place you had called home? A keep-
sake, perhaps. The clothes on your back. The memory of
a helping of plum pudding at Christmas-time ...'

Lily didn't argue, but she knew that she had never
been a slave to Nellie and Perkin Buck. She told Bridget
that Nellie had sung her to sleep, that Perkin often offered

her the choicest ripe tomatoes from his wind-wrecked greenhouse. Bridget said she didn't know what slaves had had to do exactly, other than pick cotton (which endeavour she somehow imagined, not as gathering a white, foaming crop, but as tearing multicoloured rags from thorn bushes and thistle heads), or how – or by whom – it had been decided that 'slaves' was what they were. But she didn't think they slept in a calm little attic room while the moon rode up and down the sky, and nor, in all probability, were they given toffee apples fresh from Mrs Inchbald's kitchen or allowed to put their faces near the coffee sacks to inhale the troubling perfume of faraway places.

In her workbook one morning, underneath lines and lines of half-perfected alphabet symbols written in heavy lead pencil, Lily began a letter to Nellie. She had often seen the post-boys arriving and departing from the Hospital with bundles of letters and she was confident that if she folded it and put *Rookery Farm, Swaithey, Suffolk* below the fold, it would reach Nellie somehow.

Dear Nellie, she put.

I did not like it when you went awy. I have weted my bed very ofton. Pleese send Perkin with Pegy and the cart to take me home . . .

She was about to describe how she was trying to do neat hemming and backstitch in the sewing lessons when she became aware of the teacher, who was a new addition to the Coram staff, standing and looking over her shoulder. The teacher slammed his white hand down onto the page.

'Now,' he said. 'Tear it up!'

He was a young man with the loud voice of a person who wishes to make a 'mark' in the world and who believes that the world is always listening to him and urging him on. He was called Mr Cherry and he had become flustered and cross when the children had laughed at the announcement of his name. He no doubt believed that his time teaching backward orphans at Coram would be but a staging post in a significant career of some kind, even if he didn't yet recognise what that career might be. Perhaps he would go into the Law? Being cruel to the children, especially the benighted girls in their silly red and white caps, with their piteous expressions and their ridiculous cloth shoes, sometimes touched his flesh with a shiver of excitement.

Mr Cherry made Lily stand up and tear her letter to Nellie from the workbook. He reminded her that all the children at Coram were required to cast out from their memories the years of their 'pagan childhood', and to remember only their state of abandonment. 'This woman, Nellie, whoever she may be,' said Cherry, 'has long ago forgotten you. And I want to make sure you understand this. So please stand up and repeat after me: "Nellie has forgotten me. I am quite forgotten."'

He hauled her up by her collar and the other children all turned to look at her. The room was suddenly so quiet that Lily could hear the teacher's breathing and hear the sudden palpitations of her own heart.

'Come on!' shouted the teacher. 'Say it: "Nellie has forgotten me! I am quite forgotten!"'

'It's not true,' said Lily.

'What? I didn't hear what you said. What did you say?'

'I said it's not true. I know it's not. Nellie has not forgotten me.'

'Are you contradicting me? Is this what you're doing – contradicting me?'

'I don't know what "contradicting" means, sir.'

'No, I don't suppose you do. Because you are an ignorant girl with nothing in that shaven skull of yours, nothing at all except self-pity. You can barely read. You cannot spell. Why would this "Nellie" remember someone as futile as you? I expect she chose a baby boy to take home when she left you here. Didn't she? She chose a boy, because boys are cleverer and can make something of themselves. Whereas you—'

'I was her "precious girl",' said Lily quietly.

'What? What did you say?'

'I was precious to Nellie.'

'You talk sentimental nonsense. Now say what you have been commanded to say, or I shall beat you.'

The silence came again in the echoey room. At the high windows, Lily could see a little flock of sparrows passing and she thought how, at Rookery Farm, sparrows were a lively brown colour and how here in London, their feathers were drab with dust and soot. She thought that it made sense to think about the sparrows and not about the thing she was being asked to say, because she knew that, as long as she lived, she would never agree to say it.

Mr Cherry took her by the arm and pulled her to the front of the class. She could hear Bridget begin to cry. He made Lily bend over the back of a chair. He took a cane from beside his desk, lifted up the skirt of her dress and began hitting her buttocks through her drawers. Then, not content with this, he pulled down her drawers and let the blows of the cane land on her bare flesh. And Lily heard his breathing become laboured, as if he, like one of the Buck Uncle J's, was hauling himself up a steep mountainside in Africa.

She refused to cry or even scream. But that night, she whispered to Bridget, 'I want to run away now. I want to go before the daylight comes.'

Bridget said they couldn't leave at once; that there would have to be a plan. They would make use of the sixpenny piece, which she kept every day in a different place. She said they would have to go to Baldock because Swaithey was a village in the middle of nowhere and they would never find it. She said when they arrived in Baldock, Mr and Mrs Inchbald would take them in and cook them some bacon and then send word somehow to Nellie Buck in Suffolk. They remembered their journeys to the Hospital, the last stage made by omnibus. All they had to do was get out of the locked gates and walk to where the omnibuses stopped outside Gray's Inn.

When they were sent out into the great courtyard to help the boys in their tasks of cleaving and carrying wood, they wandered down to the gates, to see if they might climb over them, but they saw that the gates were heavily guarded and supposed that this might be true even during the night, that sentries would keep some kind of upright vigil there, fighting off sleep, their bones weighed down by the heaviness of their muskets.

They knew, however, that carts and wagons containing food had to drive in and out at dawn most days. Bridget informed Lily of all the commodities needed for life sold in the Inchbald store: tea, flour, oats, sugar, coffee, molasses, baking soda, dried beans, arrowroot, salt, pepper, rice, cheese, eggs, onions, carrots, cabbages, potatoes, lard, butter, bacon, semolina, canned fish, currants, angelica and almonds . . . She said everyone at the London Foundling Hospital would die unless these things were brought in, so they had to be delivered very often. All she and Lily had to do was to wake earlier than five o'clock and creep down to the yard, wait for the goods to arrive and while the drivers were taking them to the kitchen, conceal themselves in a wagon and keep silent and still while they were driven out safely through the gates.

Lily lay in the shared bed and even in the darkness knew that Bridget had gone to sleep. She reached out and gently touched her spiky short hair, without waking her, as she used to reach out and touch Shadow in the deep silence of the Suffolk night. She longed for the feel of the softness of Shadow's head and she longed for that Rookery Farm silence. At Coram, there was always and ever some distant sound of lamentation. Sometimes you couldn't tell if this was the cry of a child or only the wind tormenting the high walls or the great sighing of the city itself as it tried and failed to sleep.

But this melancholy resonance had, for reasons she couldn't name, made Lily think about the night of her own birth and the crying of the wolves who might have carried her away to her death if the policeman hadn't saved her, and of the mother who had wrapped her in sacking and left her at the gates of a park. Though she had been told this story by Nellie, it had felt to her, while she was at Rookery Farm, that it couldn't possibly be real. Nellie was her 'true mother'. That other mother, the one who had put her out to die on a November night, had belonged in a storybook, with evil witches and ghosts who danced in graveyards. She had no substance, no flesh. Her hair was thistledown, her feet were fallen leaves. But now, she took on form and shape in Lily's mind. She conjured a cruel person, thin and cruel, like Nurse Maud, with teeth that sloped inwards behind lips so pursed together they were almost no lips at all, but just a thin line of puckered skin, like a scar ...

And here she came now, walking out into the winter dark, headed for the gates to the park, carrying a bundle, carrying it carelessly so that it might have been dropped at any minute, dropped as she, who moved in an awkward way, stumbled over a paving stone or a loose cobble in the road, like Perkin Buck used to stumble when he drank cider. Rain began to fall on her, but she gave no thought to how her newborn baby might suffer and die in the cold and damp.

When she reached the gates, she bent down and placed her bundle against the iron railings. Perhaps she stood still for a moment, pulling her shawl over her head, and stared at the 'thing' she was leaving to its terrible fate, or perhaps she didn't even look at it, but hurried away, glad to be rid of it, never bothered for a moment by feelings of love or tenderness or sadness, but only telling herself that now she was free.

Lily wanted to fall asleep, but her vision of her mother moving away from her through the darkness, never looking back, never giving her another thought, was now so vivid in her mind and troubling to it that it kept her wide awake, staring into the shadows of the dormitory. Bridget turned in her sleep and her soft arm fell across Lily's face. She removed it gently.

Then came an early morning with the stars not yet gone from the sky and a fog beginning to creep down over London ...

Lily and Bridget, both seven years old, wearing coats and mufflers, but with their feet still shod in their worn cloth shoes, climbed into a tea merchant's dray under a tarpaulin and lay down among the sacks, trying to make themselves as small as mice. In Bridget's coat pocket was the silver sixpence.

The wagon creaked as the driver hoisted himself onto his seat and jolted as the dray horse began pulling and hesitating, pulling and hesitating, but at last let itself be turned and begin a slow walk. At the gate, the wagon stopped and Lily imagined that one of the guards might point his musket into the tea-scented darkness. She whispered to Bridget to close her eyes. She was afraid that her eyes and Bridget's might gleam with some kind of borrowed light, like the eyes of rats in Perkin Buck's barn, and that then the musket would be fired and their heads would fly off their bodies and bounce into the sacks of tea.

But no musket appeared and the dray went on and Lily knew that they were outside the walls of the Hospital now and a strange excitement mixed with terror began to take hold of her, thinking how she was being carried through the great city, where all the chimneys were crammed with little boys holding brushes on long poles to scrape away the soot and where children lay down to sleep in the mud at the river's edge. She tried to imagine moving beyond the darkness that was London to Baldock, where Mrs Inchbald would be frying bacon in a skillet. Bridget had said that wherever the dray stopped, they should climb down and go out into the street and look for an omnibus to take them to Baldock for the price of sixpence, but Lily wondered what they would do if all the omnibuses were going somewhere else, or charged more than sixpence, or didn't know the way to Baldock, for then they would have to walk there on the frozen roads and their cloth shoes would be torn to rags.

The dray went swaying on. The smell of the tea leaves was scented and strong. The girls huddled against the sacks for warmth, as though they might have been animate things who would console them for their plight. They talked in whispers, wondering which way the dray was heading and whether they had yet passed the place where the omnibuses gathered. They heard a church bell chiming the hour of five and knew that the winter darkness was still massed all around them, mingling with the early-morning fog. Hearing the tolling of the God-fearing bell, they were reminded that what they were attempting was wicked and that if they were returned to the Coram Hospital, they would be beaten with stems of willow.

'Did Mr Inchbald ever beat you?' Lily whispered to Bridget.

'No. Sometimes he got angry, when customers didn't pay, and beat his fist on the shop counter, but he never hurt me.'

'Why did the customers not pay?'

'I don't know. They'd say, "Put it on the tab, Mr Inchbald. Put it on the tab."'

'What's a tab?'

'It's a piece of paper and you write down numbers and then you add all the numbers up and give it to the customer and ask for payment, but often he says, "All fine and good, Mr Inchbald, but I need more time for the necessary."'

'What's the necessary?'

'It's the thing he doesn't have, like a silver sixpence or a half-crown. And that's when my foster-father struck the counter with his fist. He said certain people made him want to howl.'

'But we do have your silver sixpence.'

'It will pay for the omnibus. But if we get hungry, we'll have to steal.'

'Or we could pinch a sugar bun and say, "Put it on the tab, Mr Inchbald!"'

This made Bridget laugh. Her laughter was a little shriek, loud in the darkness of the dray, and straight away they heard the drayman call to the horse and felt the wagon shaking and rumbling to a halt. Bridget and Lily pressed themselves more closely to the sacks of tea, but after a few moments, the tarpaulin was lifted up and a lantern shone its yellow light on them and they heard the drayman swear.

'Coram scum, are you?' he said. 'Not the first and not the last. Now I'll have to waste precious time taking you back.'

'We don't want to go back,' whispered Lily.

'Want? *Want?*' said the man, who was as bulky as a mattress and wore a cloth hat all askew on his head to try to keep the mattress from the cold. 'You can "want" all you like, but it never pays. Not in this forsaken city.'

The Brass Crucifix

The street was called Mauritania Road. People said that two centuries ago a potentate from Eastern Europe had built a palace there and it was burned down by the poor at its gates and never rebuilt. What stood there now was a line of sooty houses, joined each to each, some of them garlanded with the painted signs of small trade: *Honesty & Son, Pawnbrokers, Gallup & Co., Shoe-menders, Greengrass Associates: Purveyors of Pure Gin.*

And then at the end of the row, on the last building, leaning at an almost imperceptible angle towards the empty sky, there was a sign which read: Salvation House.

It was Belle who had inadvertently led Lily here.

Talking about the past, about the good workers and the bad, she'd said to Lily one day, 'I only had one as naturally skilled as you. Years ago now. I can't remember her name. But all I know is that trouble came to her. She was a pious girl and she couldn't bear her shame.'

'What shame?'

'She was unmarried but she was carrying a child. I let her stay and keep working for me. I told her that I – of all people – was no arbiter of morals. But she left when she was near to her term. And we heard a rumour that she gave the baby away.'

Lily stayed silent. She saw Belle take up the small mirror she kept on her desk and examine the dabs of rouge on her face and begin to spread them more evenly on her white skin. 'How can you look yourself in the eye,' said Belle, 'if you do a thing like that?'

Lily took this information back to Le Bone Street and lay on her narrow bed and shivered. The next day she went back to Belle and asked, 'Did you ever see that woman again, the one who was shamed?'

'Who? Oh, that poor soul. No, I never saw her again.'

'Or hear what became of her?'

'Only another rumour – got from one of my head-mould workers, who's long passed away. He told me that he thought he saw her, or someone very like her, in Bethnal Green. He followed her, while still not sure that it was her, and saw her go into a shop that had no real frontage, only a name above the door: Salvation House. And then, over the years, we forgot her.'

The day had been warm – a suffocating, dusty August afternoon. Lily felt a slime of sweat on her forehead and her hands were clammy. She stepped up to the heavy-looking door, on which the door-knocker was in the form of a brass crucifix. The sun burned down on her head in its old straw bonnet. She looked along Mauritania Road at the shopfronts and saw two elderly women outside the shoe-menders staring at her. This was a poor part of the city and the women clung together in their shabby clothes and pointed at her, as if they recognised a wicked soul, come here to beg for some instrument of atonement.

Lily took up the crucifix in fingers marked by the knotting hooks and blocking pins of her trade, and let it fall. It made a thin, rattling sound, which immediately faded into the hot air of the summer day. Lily waited. Nothing was heard inside Salvation House. She turned her head and saw that the women outside Gallup's were still watching her.

'You have to knock firmly on that door,' said one.

'She is very deaf,' said the other.

Deaf? Was she always deaf and couldn't hear the wolves baying and the child screaming and just went on her way in the silence of the night?

'Can you tell me her name?' asked Lily.

'That's Mrs Quale in there. With a first name Frances. She told us once she'd been named for St Francis of Assisi, but she took us for fools, eh? That old St Francis was a man. A man who liked birds.'

'Oh yes,' said Lily. 'A man who liked birds. Thank you.'

The brass of the crucifix burned in the sunlight – almost too hot to hold. But Lily took it up again and knocked three times with it. After a moment, she heard a shuffling sound, something like a straw broom being dragged lazily across a floor. Then a lock was turned in the door and it opened and straight away she was there, blinking into the sunlight, rather short of stature but bulky and holding her head very high, to see above the mass of her own flesh, wearing a lace cap on tired grey curls.

Lily had imagined her – if indeed she might be her mother – as a woman of about forty, but this person appeared nearer to fifty-five. She wore a black dress with a high neck. Her nose twitched in the warm air of the afternoon.

'Frances Quale?' asked Lily.

'*Mrs Quale* to my customers, if you don't mind. But come in, now that you're here.'

It was dark inside Salvation House. There was one window, facing onto Mauritania Road, but this was curtained with heavy velvet. The room was lit only with

70

two oil lamps, one in a sconce on the wall and another on a shop counter, where ledgers and bills sat amongst a quantity of merchandise. This merchandise consisted of twenty or thirty identical Virgin Marys, made of plaster and with their gowns painted blue, but their faces left blank and white. Frances Quale settled herself behind the counter, heaving her weight onto a high stool. She picked up one of the Marys and said, 'These are my most popular item. Light enough to carry with you on your person. Is this what you came for?'

'No. I don't know ...' said Lily.

'Beg pardon, dear? You'll have to speak up. I only hear one word in ten.'

'Ah. I'm sorry for your affliction. I came here ... just ... just to see what I would find ...'

'To make absolution for your sins? The young can be wicked. We know that. Roam the premises, dear, and see what fits. I have amphoras of Holy Water from the blessed River Jordan. I have slivers of bark and shards of cork from trees in the Garden of Gethsemane. I have Roman nails, such as were used to pierce the limbs of Our Saviour on the cross. I have stones brought all the way from the Redeemer's tomb. And if your sin is great, then for a price you can buy some strands of white hair from Blessed St Peter's head ...' Lily listened but didn't move. She stared at Frances Quale in the low, flickering light. She got the impression of a closed face and eyes that did not shine but only regarded her with a dead stare. She was, of course, looking to see her own face reflected in the other, but recognised that it was too dark in the room to identify anything clearly.

'What would you like me to show you?' asked Mrs Quale.

Show me if you were the one who carried me in your womb and then left me to die.

But Lily said nothing, only turned her gaze to the merchandise hanging from hooks on the wall: rosary beads, small crucifixes made of wood, palm crosses, tiny vials attached to ribbons, and beneath these, on a narrow table, a line of plaster saints, crudely painted.

'The hair,' said Lily.

'What?'

'I'd like to see the hair.'

'I can't understand you. Let me find my ear trumpet.'

Frances Quale bent down and began to search under the counter. Her jolting movements made the Marys tremble. Lily picked up one of these and looked at its blank face. Frances Quale re-emerged, holding a brass cylinder, and put its narrow end to her ear.

'Now,' she said, 'that's better. Age kills us piece by piece. But tell me what you'd like to see.'

The reek of incense was strong. Though the place was protected from the August heat by the thick curtains, Lily was sweating. She wished she were back in Le Bone Street, lying in a cool bed, but she made herself stay where she was.

'St Peter's hair,' she said. 'I'd like to see that.'

Still holding the ear trumpet to her head, Frances Quale moved into the darkest bit of the room, where a bookcase stood, full of missals bound in leather and gleaming ivory. Frances took down one of the missals and put it to her thin lips.

'I swear,' she whispered, 'on this beloved book that what I'm about to show you is the thing it purports to be.'

The lamplight fell on a line of small boxes set out on a table. They were wooden, with lids made of glass.

Displayed under the glass in each one was a limp curl of white hair.

'There you are,' said Mrs Quale. 'From the head of our blessed St Peter. Preserved over centuries and you know why? Because of the blood. St Peter was crucified upside down, so all the blood flowed to his head and nourished the hair and made it strong for all time.'

Lily bent down towards the boxes.

'How did you acquire it?' she asked.

'You wonder what everybody wonders. They accuse me of subterfuge. They don't believe that somebody like me would have the courage or the energy to travel to the Holy Land to seek out the most precious relics I could afford. But I was guided on my journey by Our Lady and she protected me from charlatans and liars. That's all you need to know.'

Lily picked up one of the boxes, each priced at five guineas. She wanted to take the hair to the light to examine the curl. At the Wig Emporium, they worked with Asian hair and the hair of poor Londoners but also with mohair and hair from a yak's belly. She could tell one from another with a swift glance, as Belle had taught her. This looked to Lily like English hair, but she couldn't be certain. All she knew was that a trick had certainly been played here and she wondered how this person – who might or might not be her mother – thought about that trick and what that thinking might reveal about her.

She replaced the box on its table. She told Frances Quale that she would buy one of the cheap Marys.

When she got back to Le Bone Street, she took the Mary to the basement window, where some light entered from the street, and examined it. With the Virgin's garments so carefully painted, it felt odd to behold the blank white face, but after staring at it for a while, Lily began to see some cunning in what Mrs Quale had decided to do. For what was the Mother of God but the intercessor for all Roman Catholics, and thus differently imagined by each fretful soul? And when those souls held her statue in their hands, it was their own unique iteration of Mary they longed to see. And so they themselves could give her colour and definition. With tiny pointed brushes, they could put in dark eyebrows, thick or thin, then lips a solid carmine, or in some cases a fragile pink. And her complexion? It could be left white as a marble tomb or made rosy with health or darkened by the Judaean sun. And then there she was, whatever choices they'd made about her face: the Mary of their individual hearts.

These thoughts, which Lily knew were no more than suppositions, led her on to believe that Frances Quale, although half deaf to the world now, might be a person who tried to see *beyond* any present moment to the consequences of that moment. For was this not precisely what she'd done when she abandoned her baby? She'd understood that she wouldn't be able to bear the daily proximity of such a helpless, needy bundle of flesh, a constant, unyielding reminder of her own surrender to sin. And so she didn't let herself imagine the sufferings of a newborn child left out in the cold. She just had to be rid of it, not caring if it lived or died ...

But all of this was her mind jumping about from one wild thought to another. She had no proof that Frances Quale was her mother. All she had was the story of a 'fallen' woman who had once worked for Belle Prettywood, and Lily began fervently to hope that nothing in the world connected her to the devious and unlovely proprietor of

Salvation House. In the darkness that felt ever-present in that place, Lily hadn't even been able to examine her features closely, to see if anything in them resembled her own face. What she needed to do now was to go back there and somehow coax Mrs Quale out into the light.

Kept tied to her daytime work for Belle, Lily made her next visit to Frances Quale one early evening, when the August heat was just beginning to falter. Mauritania Road was busier than it had been before, with people returning home from work and ragged children playing in and out of the sunlight and the shadows of the houses. The door was closed. Lily tapped gently with the crucifix knocker and waited, but no one came. She waited and tried again, but the door didn't move. She was just beginning to imagine Mrs Quale embarked on another pilgrimage to the Holy Land, to scour the bazaars and the dry hills for more Christian souvenirs to sell, when a window above the shop opened and the wild-eyed figure of Frances Quale leaned out and announced in a choked voice, 'Closed for the day.'

Lily looked up. The sun was still on the window, but at that moment went from it, leaving it suddenly dark, yet Mrs Quale's face appeared a peculiar ghostly white in that darkness and it was now making odd movements with its mouth, as though trying to speak or call out but not finding the right sounds. Lily waited and watched. It occurred to her after a moment that Mrs Quale was drunk and Lily felt that there was dread inherent in this fact, for who knew what the woman might do in such a state. Yet she would surely also reveal more of herself if she could be persuaded to come down and open the door.

'A friend has sent me on a mission to you,' Lily called out. 'She is in grave trouble and asked me to see whether she can afford the relic of St Peter's hair, to intercede for her.'

'I can't hear you,' Frances Quale managed to say, yet perhaps she had picked up the words 'St Peter', for she disappeared from the window. Then, from inside Salvation House, Lily could hear a bumping and banging, as though the furniture had taken on life and begun to tilt and topple slowly down the stairs. After long minutes, the door to Salvation House opened a crack and Mrs Quale's fleshy face peered round it.

'What?' she said. 'What?'

'A friend,' Lily said. 'A friend in trouble ...'

'Trouble? I don't want no trouble.'

'I've come to see if she ... if I ... could afford one of the boxes of St Peter's hair.'

'St Peter is precious,' she said. 'I don't sell that cheap.'

'Let me come in.'

'I was sleeping ...'

'Yes. But now you might make a beneficial sale.'

Mrs Quale's gaze seemed to hang on the word 'sale', as if it had curative properties for whatever she was suffering. Slowly, her eyes grew brighter and she held the door wide for Lily to walk in. She shuffled over towards the table where the Marys stood and picked up her ear trumpet. Lily followed her, but didn't close the door, so that a square of light illuminated the room. She watched Frances Quale closely. The soiled shift she wore trailed on the dusty floor. Her arms were bare and showed patches of bruising and Lily thought, She is surely nobody's mother, for no man has ever loved her. She's a drunkard who stumbles and falls and her mind is clouded.

A chair set out for customers as they inspected the Marys now came to Mrs Quale's rescue as she threatened to topple over. She bumped down into it with the long sigh of someone whose habit it was to sound a lamentation on her daily quota of existence. She blinked at the light from the door, then held the rag to her eyes.

'Close that,' she said.

'You don't like the daylight?'

'No. So you shut the door.'

Lily didn't move but stood looking at Frances. It had always seemed to her that with both men and women addicted to grog or gin, it was as if their faces concealed another face, a face you might sometimes glimpse because it wasn't completely lost, only masked by long and corrosive habit. Now, she tried to see Frances Quale's face as it might have been when she was young and slim and to compare this to her own features. What she noticed was that the eyes, bunched round by flesh now, were brown, like her own, but here all comparisons seemed to end.

'Close the light,' Frances said again.

Lily turned and pushed the door so that it was almost shut but not quite, because now she felt suddenly afraid to be locked in with a person who'd drunk her afternoon away and who held the heavy ear trumpet like a weapon in hands that appeared clammy and trembling. But she moved nearer to her and began to speak.

'My poor friend,' she said, 'has done a most terrible thing. She did it out of desperation and shame and it cannot be undone. But she believes that if she could hold in her hands the hair of the blessed St Peter, then he would intercede for her and God would forgive her, even if she cannot forgive herself.'

Frances Quale had not moved, except to put the trumpet to her ear. Her mouth hung open. She stared at Lily, but said nothing.

'My friend asked me to describe to you,' continued Lily, 'what she has done, so that you would take pity on her and sell her the hair at a price she can afford. So I will tell you now. She gave birth to a baby girl in the cold of winter. She had no means to support the child and no man would help her. So she wrapped the baby in some rags – I believe they were rags of sacking – and left it at the gates to a London park. She left it to suffer and die.'

Lily paused and looked again at Frances Quale. Her expression was vacant. The ear trumpet trembled in her hand.

'Knowing this,' Lily went on, 'knowing what a terrible sin was committed by my friend and how she is sad and sorry, day and night, for the child she abandoned … can you find it in your heart to let me purchase the holy hair for a low price?'

Frances Quale shook her head. 'No,' she said, 'I never sell St Peter for a low price. Now get you gone.'

Lily went out into the calm evening and as she walked away down Mauritania Road, her first thought was that she never wanted to come back. Yet she knew that, sooner or later, she would force herself to return.

Yellow Apples

Before he reached his next delivery stop, the driver of the tea cart had tied the tarpaulin down tightly over Lily and Bridget, cursing them as he did so, and then driven on.

Arriving at a grocer's premises in Barley Street, he had to untie it again, to take out the sack to be delivered there, and as he reached in and lifted this out, the girls crawled to the edge of the dray and jumped down and ran into the swirling fog of dawn.

In the dirty air, it was hard to see where they were going. They only knew that they had to keep running, away from the tea cart. They joined hands and held on tightly as they skidded along the frosted pavements. Their lungs soon began to hurt. When they saw a railway bridge rise up ahead, they went into the ghostly arch of it and stood still, pressed against its sooty wall, choking as they struggled to catch their breath, but seeing the fog move in eddies towards them, as if it and not the drayman had been the thing which had followed them.

Their breathing gradually calmed, but when it had calmed they knew that they were lost. Bridget said when the light came, they'd begin to search for an omnibus or else start walking towards Baldock. All they had to do was travel northwards, keeping the sun to the right of them and looking out for milestones as they went. But the knowledge that they were lost made them feel dizzy and when a train came grinding overhead, making the bridge tremble, they understood that they'd put them-selves into a world where things unknown could smite them down. But from the far side of the arch, now, the girls could see a silvery light trying to expand and grow through the fog and they knew that it was the winter day struggling to break.

The air they breathed had a taste to it of things burned and gone. And it was not still. It moved in strange patterns, like a wispy black scarf threatening to touch their faces, then suddenly disappearing to reveal the way ahead. The sun was up now and they could see that they were walking northwards along a wide thoroughfare, where a few carriages came past them, carrying men wearing top hats, on their way to their money-getting in London, and where costermongers, bare-headed yet strong, tried to hurry on, pulling heavy carts.

Lily and Bridget soon felt thirsty. On parts of the road, water flowed freely in wide gutters and they wondered if they could stoop to drink it, but Lily said no, the water was tainted with sewage and would make them ill, but when they reached the limits of the city, they would find a stream or a clean river.

They seemed to know now that no omnibus would come by, that they had a short day in which to walk to Baldock and then the night would come down and freeze them and all might be lost. They kept watching out for a costermonger going the other way, from whom to beg a lift in his barrow, but none came along. The traffic was all converging on London. They had no choice but to keep walking and when the fog disappeared, they saw the road ahead narrowing and making its way between hedgerows and trees and Bridget said that this was a good sign, it was countryside and this was how you found Baldock: you first found some fields and walked across them for a while and then you started looking out for a church spire and a cluster of roofs neatly tiled and when you saw these, you were almost there.

Their legs ached, so they sat down on the damp verge of the road and plucked handfuls of grass, to suck the moisture off it, and while they were licking the grass a sheep appeared a little way off and stared at them. It was a ragged animal, in need of shearing, with a smudged and foolish face. It didn't move when Lily got up and began walking towards it. She held out her hand and talked to it softly, as Perkin Buck talked to his ewes with newborn lambs, making a low whistling sound with his mouth. The sheep let her approach and when she reached it she held it – as she had seen Perkin do – by its two ears and led it over to Bridget.

Bridget said, 'Poor thing. Let it go. See the wool, all hanging off its backside ... ?'

'No,' said Lily, 'we should take it with us. Then if the night comes down before we get to Mr and Mrs Inchbald, we can find a barn and lie next to the sheep and be warm.'

Bridget laughed at first at the idea of the sheep travelling along with them, but seeing Lily now stroking the animal's head, she said, 'You mean it's going to be our pet?'

'Yes,' said Lily. 'Why not? Sheep are more obedient than dogs. You follow close behind them and they stay on a straight road. We could give it a name.'

'What name?'

'Names have to sound right. We could call it Bessie, short for Elizabeth.'

'That's a cow's name, isn't it? What about Bert?'

'I think it's a girl sheep, Bridget — a ewe. The rams have horns.'

'It doesn't matter. Bert is a friendly name.'

'All right,' said Lily. 'We'll call it Bert.'

They began trudging on once more, with Lily talking to Bert, to keep it close to them, and they soon felt that, strange as it was, the sheep had cheered them and they were glad to be out under the sky with it, far away now from the prison of the Hospital, headed north under a pale winter sun.

When the track crossed a wooden bridge, they stopped and saw a clear stream running in a narrow culvert and clambered down the steep bank, pushing Bert ahead of them, and stood at the stream's edge and scooped up the icy water and drank and drank and the sheep drank, too, shivering as it did so.

They walked on. Their cloth shoes were torn. Bert trotted beside them with a dainty step. After a while, they came upon a grey apple tree, bare of leaves but holding on to a cluster of yellow fruit, pinched by successive frosts yet still offering a bite of tart flesh. They shook the tree and the apples spilled at their feet. While they ate, they also filled their pockets. Bert's smudged nose rolled the fruit around and around before beginning to gobble it up, while letting fall from its ragged arse a comical cascade of blackish pellets, not much smaller or less round than the apples.

'I love Bert,' said Bridget.

'I love her, too,' said Lily.

The day seemed to be very short. The coming of the dusk reminded Lily of winter afternoons at Rookery

Farm when she was helping Perkin Buck clean and oil the wheels of his cart in the barn, and the rats scampering round in the piles of hoarded things would suddenly become invisible. She would look towards the barn door, to reassure herself that the sky was still there, and then, moments later, it, too, would disappear and Perkin would say it was time to go home for tea, but when they walked back to the house, their human forms cast no shadows, as if they were no longer standing upright in the world.

Bridget and Lily walked for a long while in the dark, seeing lonely stars above them. Their stomachs ached from eating the yellow apples and they longed to lie down and rest, but they kept going in their torn shoes. The air was very cold and still. Then, after another half-hour, what floated towards them was a sound they recognised, of women's voices gathered up in religious song. Lily held on to Bert and they stopped on the stony path and listened. They could see no church. It seemed as if the trees were singing. But then they saw a light up ahead and this single light gave form to the hunched outline of a large building.

Still keeping Bert close to them, they moved steadily towards it. The nearer they came to the building the more they both began to long for respite – for somebody to take pity on them and give them food and warmth.

The singing stopped. In front of them now stood a wooden door, studded with iron nail heads. Near this, in a heavy wall sconce, a torch burned and this was the light they'd seen. Bridget reached up and knocked as hard as she could on the door.

Near the top of the door was an iron grille. Neither of the girls was tall enough to reach the grille, but after some moments of waiting, they heard footsteps coming towards it. They stood back and waited. A nun's face appeared behind the grille, lit by a ghostly candle, and the face – cramped into its wimple, like an apple pinched by the frost, its eyes flickering this way and that – was trying to see what was out there, but blinded by the dark.

'Who calls?' the nun asked.

Lily felt Bert's body begin to shiver and the long cry she gave was one of lamentation, and hearing this unexpected sound of a sheep, the nun called out in bewilderment: 'Thomas? Is that you? Show yourself. I cannot open until I see you.'

Lily looked at Bridget, both of them wondering who should speak and what they should say. The face of the nun, with its frightened gaze framed by the grille, appeared to them as a thing of strange terror, so that they almost wanted to walk away, but the thought of food and shelter kept them standing there.

Lily reached for Bridget's hand, then she said: 'Sister, we're lost in the dark. We were trying to walk to Baldock, but we can't find it anywhere.'

'Baldock?' said the nun. 'What are you talking about? I can't see you properly. Are you children?'

'Yes. We are only seven,' said Lily. 'Please may you open the door?'

'Seven children, do you mean? And what is that animal cry? This is a sacred building, belonging to our Order ...'

'Not seven children,' said Lily. 'Just two of us and our pet. And we're dying of cold. Please ...'

'I still can't see you. Show yourselves.'

They stepped aside a little, so that they were nearer to the torchlight. At their backs, a wind was rising, setting the tops of the sycamore trees swaying before the starlight. Then the door opened a little and the nun in her long robes was revealed, holding her trembling candle. Afraid that she would shut the door on them, locking them out again, Lily and Bridget hurried past her, hauling Bert with them. When the nun saw the sheep she stepped backwards in terror, as though Bert might have been a lion.

'God save us!' she exclaimed. 'Whatever is this?'

Bert continued to bleat, and, escaping from Lily's grip on her ears, began to skitter round the place they were now in, which was a great hall made of stone.

Lily went racing after her while Bridget started to laugh, and these unfamiliar sounds quickly brought a cluster of five or six Sisters to the hall, where they stood and gazed in perplexity at the sudden alteration to a normality usually so obedient to their expectations.

In the great space was a dying fire, still offering a bit of warmth, and Bridget went to it and knelt down by it and held out her hands, stiff with cold and stinging from the juice of the yellow apples. But she was soon enough hauled to her feet by the nun who had opened the door to them and her red and white cap was snatched off her head.

'Coram!' said the nun, examining the cap with distaste. 'You're Coram children. What in the name of all that's holy are you doing out here?'

'We're cold,' said Bridget, 'and our shoes are torn.'

'I can see that! I suppose you're runaways. Is that it?'

'We were trying to find Baldock,' said Bridget.

'You said that at the gate. What nonsense are you speaking? You are miles from Baldock.'

At this moment, another tall nun came sweeping in. All the faces of the Sisters turned towards her as she took in the strange sight of Lily now wrestling with Bert, who didn't want to be caught.

'Sister Mary-Jane,' said the new arrival, 'please be good enough to tell me what is happening here.'

The nun now holding on to Bridget by the neck bowed her head in humility and said, 'Reverend Mother, I am at fault. I let them in ...'

'Two little sinners from the Foundling Hospital and a sheep! A fine arrival on a winter's evening, I must say. Sister Margaret, go and summon Thomas to take the sheep away and pen it in, and you children come here at once and kneel down before me and I will decide what is to be done with you.'

When Lily saw Bridget being forced to bow down at the Reverend Mother's feet, she felt a weariness come over her which was hard to bear. When she remembered the mossy bank where they had sucked water from the grass and where Bert had first appeared to them, she wished they had lain down there, clinging to their new pet's ragged wool, and slept without dreaming.

Now she, too, was kneeling.

'If I may venture, Reverend Mother,' she heard Sister Mary-Jane say, 'I think that we should ask Thomas to bring the cart straight away and drive the children back to London.'

'You may not "venture", Sister,' said the Reverend Mother. 'We will show compassion. For that is what we do. Are you hungry, children?'

'Yes,' said Bridget.

'And tired, I imagine?'

'We were going to find my room at Mr and Mrs Inchbald's house. The room where I talked to the moon ...'

'Oh, you talked to the moon. Pagan to boot, are you, but never mind that, at present. This is what is going to happen to you. You will be given some supper. We will find an empty cell where you can sleep. But in return, tomorrow, you are going to work for us.'

This statement brought about a quiet whispering among the Sisters, followed by a bout of coughing from one of them. When the coughing had died down, Bridget asked, 'What work are we going to do?'

'Laundry work. We have two young novices who have fallen sick and we are horribly behind with the washing. You're small, but you will be helped to sort the garments correctly and light the fires under the cauldrons. Sister Annunciata will give you some bread and milk now and tomorrow you will pay us back by working. I expect you are familiar with the procedures of the wash? Are you?'

Lily could have said that, at Rookery Farm, Perkin Buck had carpentered her own small washboard and that she and Nellie had stood side by side every Monday morning trying to scrub the farm dirt out of shirts and slips, handkerchiefs and drawers. She could even have told how the soap kept sliding out of her small hands and bouncing around the pamment floor and how she chased it as you might chase a living thing, and how Nellie and she would laugh and laugh. But she kept silent.

★

A young man came into the hall. He seemed a person of wide and cheery countenance, with a boy's grin but the big hands of a labouring man.

'Thomas,' said the Reverend Mother, 'we have visitors, as you see. We will set the girls to work tomorrow morning. But we do not wish to accommodate a sheep, so please take it away.'

Thomas looked over to where Bert stood staring at the burning logs with her backside embarrassingly half-clad with mere strips of dirty wool and was unable to stop himself from giggling.

'She's a sad sight!' he said, winking at Lily and Bridget.

Lily and Bridget tried to keep a hold on Bert, quite as if she had been an old dog who had pushed its way into their hearts, and Bridget said to Thomas, 'Don't take her, Master Thomas. She's our pet. Please don't take her.'

Thomas looked towards the Reverend Mother and she held up a slim white hand, a hand practised at commanding silence.

'We do not,' she said, 'entertain sheep within our walls. Do as I tell you, Thomas, and take the animal away.'

Thomas picked up Bert by her hind legs and dragged her, bleating, across the stone floor. When Bert and Thomas had gone, the nun calling herself Sister Annunciata led Lily and Bridget away from the fire, down a long corridor towards the refectory, where the nuns had recently eaten their supper. The girls' saturated shoes squelched rudely as they walked and left damp imprints on the stone floor and perhaps this would have made Bridget laugh if she hadn't been saddened by the loss of Bert and if Sister Annunciata had not fastened a pinching hand to her shoulder.

They were pushed down onto a hard bench and set before a table which stretched beyond the reach of the candlelight in the dining room, so that it was impossible to see if anyone else was seated there. A young girl, not very much older than Lily and Bridget, was still clearing away the dregs of a meal and it was to her that Sister Annunciata gave the command for 'hot milk and some bread crusts'. She disappeared and Lily and Bridget were alone with the great polished highway of the table and the nun who seemed to like to use her hands in a cruel way. She now sat herself down opposite them and examined their faces in the dim light. 'Runaways,' she sighed, shaking her head, as if in despair at some personal misfortune. 'You know that God does not like runaways and will punish you?'

'We're used to that,' said Bridget. 'We're punished all the time. Lily was beaten with a willow branch.'

'Ah,' said Sister Annunciata. 'But a beating is given always for a reason. What was the reason?'

Lily wouldn't look at Sister Annunciata. She let her gaze go towards the shadowy part of the refectory, where she wanted to be, so that no eyes would interrogate her, where she would not have to speak.

'I'm waiting,' said Sister Annunciata. 'What was the reason for your beating?'

'She can't say it,' said Bridget. 'It was a letter to her foster-mother, but she can't talk about her. It's too painful for her.'

'I merely want to know the reason why this girl was beaten.'

'I've told you: for writing a letter, but don't make her talk about it. You're meant to be sisters of mercy.'

This silenced Sister Annunciata. She stared at the girls in sudden fright, as though somebody had told her that her room was on fire.

The bed Lily and Bridget were given was narrow and hard, in a cell where a mouse came out of the wainscoting and began to rush about the wooden floor, followed by its own shadow, made large and liquid-seeming by the candlelight. A thin blanket covered them. They lay there, still wearing their Coram uniforms, and clung together for warmth and comfort and watched the mouse and tried to laugh at it. They wondered what had become of Bert.

A strong wind had risen with the winter moon and it seemed now to sing through the great stone building, quite as if a disappointed God had sent it to keep them awake to reflect on what they had done and begin to feel afraid.

They slept for a few hours, clinging to each other, but when they were woken by a bell at six o'clock, it felt as though sleep had never come at all, but that they had been kept alert and troubled through every one of the dark hours, while the mouse rushed without purpose in and out of its hideaway and the song of the wind engulfed the building.

Sister Annunciata, holding a tallow candle, pulled the blanket from them and told them to get up and kneel on the hard floor and say their prayers, and they tried to do this, side by side, but they felt too tired to remember many of the words. Then they were taken once again to the refectory, where the full complement of the Sisters now sat as still as fence posts around the great avenue of the table, while a grace was intoned by the Reverend

Mother. In front of each nun there was a bowl of porridge and a cup of water, and when the grace was over, they crossed themselves and picked up their spoons and began to eat and drink in silence, while Lily and Bridget, for whom there was no space on the bench seats, were led by Sister Annunciata to a cold corner of the room and told to sit on the floor.

They sat there, staring at their torn shoes, waiting to see if any food would be given to them. Bridget whispered, 'If we had got to Baldock, Mrs Inchbald would have fried us each a sausage,' and Lily felt that she could imagine this sausage, all golden brown and spicy in the pan and dripping with hot lard, but what came to them were small bowls of the grey porridge the nuns were eating, so they began spooning this into their mouths, while, in the high windows of the room, rectangles of flat grey sky suggested to Lily that in God's fashioning of the world, he had here run out of colour.

After a short while, they were led out of the refectory, along a curving corridor, then down a flight of steps, and Lily knew that the day's work was going to begin because from the cellar came the acrid scent of damp wool and soap and slaked lime. She could feel the cold treads through her broken shoes, but she was glad to realise that, if this was a washday, then the basement would be warmed by the fires lit under the coppers and by the hot steam.

It was dark there. Two oil lamps burned with slow flames and by the light of these Lily and Bridget could see two nuns moving about among great piles of linen. Sister Annunciata pushed the girls towards them and they stopped in their work and looked down upon them with surprise.

'Who are these?' said one of them. 'How old are they? Will they have the strength for scrubbing?'

'They are foundling girls,' said Sister Annunciata, 'seven years old and used to a hard routine. They will do the work you ask of them.'

Lily could have added that she knew how to manage the wash because she had helped Nellie with it a thousand times. First it was sorted, by size and texture, with all the dirty rags and kerchiefs separated from the shirts and petticoats and drawers. Then each pile in turn was soaked in a solution of slaked lime, boiled in a copper and left to settle. After rinsing and straining, the fire in the copper was made so unbearably hot it was difficult to go near it and all the garments were lifted back in and stirred and tamped with a 'dolly', which was an instrument like a three-legged stool on a long pole. And only after this did the clothes come out and were put on the washboard and the great labour of soaping began and this work brought a sweet agony to your arms and your hands grew chafed and sore and Nellie sometimes sighed with pain. When all the stains and dirt were gone, the wash was returned to the copper and soda was poured in to remove the soap and it was stirred round and round again with the dolly before it came out at last, heavy as a corpse, and you carried it to the mangle before hanging it up to dry above the kitchen range or, in spring and summer, out in the March winds and the sunlight of May, when all the thistles at Rookery Farm reared up again to spite the meadows.

Lily remembered another thing about washdays: there was no hot food made because there was no time and no room in the kitchen and the midday dinner would be a piece of bread and cheese or leftover pie with pickled onions and Lily whispered to Bridget that this was going to be a hungry day and she saw that Bridget's brave little thrush-like face was all crumpled with heartache and she thought, We were happy on the road with Bert because we thought we were going to Baldock and salvation, but these things never came our way.

Perhaps the nuns were surprised at how helpful the girls were with the wash because they seemed disposed to treat them kindly. They brought stools for them to stand on, so that they could reach down into the coppers with the dollies, and they saw that Lily and Bridget kept on with the stirring and tamping and that their arms didn't tire. Perhaps they felt sorrowful about their broken shoes, which revealed Lily's missing toe, or about the quantity of freckles on Bridget's small face. While they worked on starching the delicate white wimples, the nuns began to ask them questions about the Foundling Hospital and how their days passed there and when Bridget said, 'We have no love there,' they reached out with their steam-reddened hands and touched her head and said, 'But you must not care about this, for God is Love and that is all you need.'

Bridget began to tell the laundry nuns how, as punishment, the older foundling children were sometimes made to pick oakum, like convicts. But the nuns didn't know what 'picking oakum' was and it was Bridget who explained that it was an unravelling of thick rope with your hands and nails, so that the threads could be used by shipbuilders, for caulking the seams in the oak planking of the great seagoing hulls.

'Ah,' said the nuns, 'so it is very vital work for the Queen and Empire?'

Bridget said she didn't know if it was vital, but she knew that girls of nine or ten were sometimes put to this task, which tore your nails and burned your fingers, and this was why she and Lily had run away, 'because we saw what misfortunes could come to us in time'.

The Sisters looked at each other and both shook their heads in sorrow. Then one of them said, 'We would like to keep you here, to save you from that oakum-picking, but we're afraid that when the wash is done, you will be sent back.'

'We're not going back,' said Bridget. 'Mr and Mrs Inchbald are waiting for us at Baldock.'

'Oh,' said the nun called Sister Agnes, 'and who are Mr and Mrs Inchbald?'

Lily knew that Bridget would try to describe them and the little upstairs room which looked out upon the stars, and the fragrant sacks of coffee beans beside the counter of the shop, but even as her friend began talking, something told her that they would never get to Baldock, just as they would never get to Swaithey.

The long day ended and the darkness filled up the rectangles of the windows once again and the first batch of the wash was carried to the kitchen to be strung on pulleys to dry above the range.

When Lily and Bridget neared the kitchen, bent under the weight of a basket of damp rags and dusters, something beautiful surprised them: the scent of roasting meat. Their mouths filled with saliva as the realisation of how hungry they were made them tremble.

As they began pegging out the rags, they were greeted by Thomas, who was seated near the range, peeling potatoes. His expression was one of infectious cheerfulness.

He winked at the girls and said, 'I reckon you did us a nice favour, capturing that ole ewe. Well done, maidens! Not much to look at, was she, but there was plenty of flesh on her. She butchered nice and I nurtured a rosemary bush through the first frosts, so I flavoured her with some of that, and we'll all get a fine fragrant supper.'

The Colour of the Onions

Her saviour, Sam Trench. Superintendent in the Detective Department of the Metropolitan Police ...

She thought that what she'd seen in him was yearning. She has never known a man's desire, nor really wished to know it. But then, Sunday by Sunday, this gaze on her had never faltered and after a while she had begun to see him, this rather ordinary man, as the person who would bring her back — back from the loveless place where the murder had placed her, cast out from humanity by what she'd done. For she was dying in this lonely universe. At the moment when the deed had been done, it had felt rational to her, so rational and right that she was able to keep very calm. She'd killed coldly, without pity. She'd walked away from what she'd done, with a terrible euphoria inside her enabling her to hold her head high.

Yet the thing soon began following her night and day. In her Le Bone Street lodgings, although it took place far from there, the terrible *smell* of it seems to lie in every crevice of the building. Even at work, where the room is scented by Belle's perfume, waves of sickness overcome Lily. She has kept calling silently for somebody to rescue her and in Sam Trench she thought she had found that blessed soul.

But he's not a 'blessed soul' — not for her. He works in the Detective Department of the Metropolitan Police. She knows that to save herself she must walk away from him and go where he can't find her. She pulls her shawl tightly round her head. She hears herself mumble thanks 'for a good deed done so long ago' and turns to go out into the snow. But, as she half suspected, Sam Trench reaches out to stop her leaving.

'My wife …' he begins, then pauses as Lily stops and looks back at him. 'My wife requested me to invite you to our house … if you would care to join us for Sunday lunch.'

His wife.

Perhaps, after all, it wasn't desire she saw in his face; it was simply the steady and patient gaze of someone who can read on the features of criminals what lurks in their minds. She opens her mouth to refuse the invitation when he says, 'It's only tripe and onions. We live simply. But Mrs Trench told me to tell you that there would be marmalade pudding to follow.'

Lily hesitates. There is something so touching in this recitation of the lunch ingredients, something which seems so perfectly right for the unselfish man who once saved an abandoned child, that to refuse the invitation appears ungrateful and mean.

'Oh …' says Lily. 'Well …'

'Our house is very near, in Chestnut Street, and we keep a good fire.'

'I don't want to put you to the trouble. You have done so much for me. Why should you do more?'

'Because I want to do it. Why don't you take my arm, Lily, and together we will brave the snow.'

So she sets aside her fear and does as he asks. An east wind blows the snowflakes into their faces as they walk, and Lily surrenders to the icy moment, knowing that she can no longer see the way ahead.

★

Joyce Trench has laid the table in the parlour, setting out her best bone-handled knives. A coal fire burns in the small grate.

Joyce is one of those steady women who don't fret when middle age makes their bodies shapeless. She seems easy in her movements, easy in her plain brown dress. She smiles kindly as she ushers Lily to a comfortable chair and offers a glass of ginger wine. From the small kitchen comes the scent of frying onions.

'Sam,' says Joyce, 'is very particular about onions. There should be just the right amount of gold colour to them and no more – so I let him cook them once the tripe is browned and in the oven. I ask myself how many other police superintendents in London agree to help cook the Sunday dinner.'

'Ah yes,' says Lily. 'He's a superintendent now. He's given his life to protecting London from its own violence.'

'He has. And you know the reason he has risen up the ranks? My Sam has a strange talent for it. He sees what other men very often miss. Even in crime scenes which turn the strongest stomach, it's often Sam who notices clues hidden from the eyes or ears of his colleagues. It's his attention to detail, you see, Lily – such as his particularity over the precise colour of the onions. That's the kind of person he is.'

Attention to detail.

The phrase chimes in her head. First, there was Nellie pointing out the care put into the sampler made by Mary Wickham and her own working of the letter 'E' for her benefactress, Lady Elizabeth Mortimer. Then there were the thousand hours of meticulous sewing at the Coram Hospital. Then there was her deft work in the wig factory, and Belle Prettywood telling her she was the best wig-maker in the Emporium. Then, at the end of all this *attention to detail*, there was the scene of the murder and how, by understanding exactly what she could or could not do, she made the right choice and so the thing was done quickly, with almost no sound at all: a moment of choking and gasping, and then silence.

'Attention to detail may be very important,' she says.

Joyce Trench nods as she scoops more coal onto the fire. Then she continues with her praise of her husband.

'There is also his understanding that police work may often send a man on a detour he didn't expect,' she says.

'I suppose it must.'

'Take the night he rescued you, seventeen years ago. A lowly constable with little responsibility for anything. But he crossed half of London to save your life. And he's never forgotten what he did that night.'

'I didn't think I would ever meet him ...'

'Wolves,' said Joyce. 'He told me he was sure he saw the eyes of wolves near the gate – wolves in London! Me, I would have been afraid, wouldn't you? But Sam, he fought his terror and he fought the elements, making himself ill to bring you to safety. And do you know what he says about all this?'

'No.'

'He says it was the most important thing he ever did in his life. Sometimes he says it was the *only* good thing.'

'Why would he say that?'

'Well, there is some logic to it. He says so much of his work has been about looking at the dead when it was too late to save them. But you he saved.'

Lily's not certain what Joyce Trench expects her to reply. Mention of the dead has made her feel suddenly hot. She looks round the small parlour, wondering if she might open a window out onto the falling snow. The smell of onions is strong and Lily feels her habitual sickness begin to creep into her the way it always comes, like a slowly sliding, receding and encroaching tide. She'd like to say goodbye and leave, but Joyce is watching her so closely, it's as though she and not her husband had mastered the habits of a detective superintendent.

'And you know he did more than save you,' says Joyce. 'He made several visits to Coram's Hospital. He wanted to get to know you. Visitors pay to watch the children at work, as you will have seen for yourself. But they aren't allowed to talk to them. He told the Governors that he'd been the one to save you and tried to get a special dispensation to make himself known to you, but the Hospital wouldn't grant it. They didn't understand how precious you were to him.'

Sam Trench now calls out from the kitchen that the onions are ready and that he is going to serve up the meal. Lily takes her place at the table and sips the ginger wine, hoping that her sickness will fade. But when the steaming plate of tripe is put in front of her, she knows that her struggle is lost. She gets up silently and goes to the front door. She lets herself out and vomits into the snow.

She tells Joyce and Sam Trench that she will walk home. There's anxiety on both their faces. The plates of tripe and onions are returned to the kitchen.

Lily goes to fetch her coat, apologising for what has happened, telling herself that this was her punishment, this sickness, for her vain belief that she'd seen yearning in the gaze of Sam Trench. But Joyce won't let her leave.

'You're not well, dear,' she says. 'You're as pale as a ghost. Rest an hour upstairs and then Sam will see you home.'

Lily thinks only of being back in Le Bone Street, of a silent, lonely sleep, but her legs feel weak, too weak to walk out into the cold – and she lets herself be led up the narrow stairs by Joyce and into a small bedroom, painted green.

Joyce turns back an eiderdown on a narrow wooden bed and the sight of this little place of rest is so inviting that Lily at once begins to unlace her boots. And when she lies down and Joyce pulls the eiderdown over her, it feels to Lily that this is the most comfortable place her body has known since she left her cot in Rookery Farm all those years ago. She closes her eyes. She hears the curtains being drawn at the window. Then she feels Joyce's hand touch her forehead.

'I know,' whispers Joyce, 'that your life has been hard.'

Lily says nothing. She wants to ask, 'How can you – whom I've never met before – know anything about my life? Has Sam been following me for a long time? Did he see me on *that* afternoon, going out from Le Bone Street and coming back and creeping down to the basement, with the knowledge of what I'd done making me feel so excited and terrified and filled with glory and horror that I was as weak as an abandoned baby? Has he told you that he suspects me of vile wickedness?'

Joyce's soft hand strokes her hair, damp from her moments in the snow. In the woman's eyes Lily can detect nothing but compassion. There is something about her which recalls Nellie Buck's tenderness.

'Can you sleep a little?' asks Joyce Trench.

'This room is very calm,' says Lily. 'Was it once a child's room?'

Joyce withdraws her hand and places it in her lap. She looks away for a moment before saying, 'It was intended as a child's room, but Sam and I were not fortunate enough ... we could not ... it was not given to us ...'

'Oh,' says Lily.

'The only time that Sam held a baby was when he carried you across London. Now sleep a little, if you can. Perhaps, when you are rested, you could try a spoonful of marmalade pudding?'

Later, when Lily wakes, she finds that her sickness has quite gone. She feels that she has just experienced the most beautiful sleep she has had since *that* night. It seems to her that even her heart has known some rest.

It's late afternoon and dark outside and so silent that Lily thinks the snow must be falling again and she imagines it lying in great skeins and drifts on the branches of the trees, and sometimes sliding to the ground as it slid into the lane going out from Rookery Farm towards Swaithey Village. She doesn't move. She realises that every limb of her body is warm and comfortable and she wants to stay like this, in the quiet of this room, for as long as she can.

Joyce Trench comes in with a lighted candle and a small dish containing a helping of marmalade pudding. She puts these things down near the bed and bends over Lily and lays a gentle hand on her hair. Lily asks what the time is and whether it's snowing again and Joyce replies that it's near to six o'clock and that the snow is 'lying deep and showing no sign of wanting to stop'. Then she says, 'Sam and I have been talking. We think you should stay with us tonight and in the morning Sam will walk you to your place of work.'

'Thank you,' says Lily. 'Thank you.'

And all she can do after that is close her eyes and sail into another enchanted sleep, from which all her habitual nightmares are absent. And what is strange but wonderful is that, held in the arms of this deep unconsciousness, her mind is somehow *aware that it's sleeping* and doesn't want to relinquish this state, knowing that its need for rest is so great.

She sleeps until just before dawn, when a blackbird begins to sing from a snow-laden tree outside the window, and she remembers Perkin Buck explaining to her that birds start their 'noise' (which he never referred to as 'song'), not in celebration of the oncoming daylight – as is so commonly assumed – but 'as a *warning* of it, to ready themselves for the tireless vigil they must keep once the sky is light'. She lies still, listening to the black-bird, and thinks about her own daily vigil upon herself, trying not to betray her own guilt, and how, as the days pass, this struggle to present an innocent face to the world is making her sick and killing her, bit by bit.

She tries to set this aside, knowing that the beautiful sleep she's had has given her some new strength. She will do good work today for Belle. She will give all her concentration to Violetta's wig – this last wig, where the hair is thinning and falling out, the one she will wear only in the last scene, where she stands at the window watching the crowds in the street and sees ... or thinks she sees ... the lover she was forced to abandon walking towards her house ...

There is light at the little window of Lily's room now and then a soft tap on her door. It opens and, silhouetted against the flare of the gas mantle on the landing, is Sam Trench. He is dressed for work, in his superintendent's uniform. He doesn't enter the room but stays just outside it, holding on to the door.

'Lily,' he says, 'Joyce sent me up to ask if you would feel strong enough to come down to the kitchen for a cup of tea and a muffin.'

'Yes,' says Lily.

'We hope you had a good night's rest.'

'A beautiful rest. This room reminds me of the room I had when I was a child in Suffolk. Except the bed had no eiderdown; only a little crocheted coverlet.'

Sam Trench stands very still – as he always seemed to stand so still in the church – looking into the relative darkness of the bedroom, while behind him the white flame of the gas mantle sighs and flickers. He doesn't speak. And Lily wonders about this stillness and silence of his and whether this is something perfected by his profession; if he is the one who waits and says nothing, waits and only looks with that yearning stare of his, for the one who is guilty to break apart and confess her crime.

Lily brushes her hair and washes her face. She has slept in her woollen dress and the skirt is creased. She thinks she probably appears like a transient soul who has wandered into some temporary shelter from the snow-shrouded world, but there's nothing she can do about this. She looks around the small green-painted room before leaving it. She straightens the eiderdown and caresses it for a moment with her hand, almost as if she saw herself still lying underneath it and wanted to say to her sleeping form, here you can rest without dreaming, without rage and without fear.

She goes down to the parlour, where Joyce is pouring tea and offering a plate of home-made muffins and Lily finds that for the first time in a long while she is so hungry that she eats her muffin with desperate haste, like a starving child, spilling crumbs down the bodice of her dress. She looks up to see Joyce and Sam Trench watching her and smiling. As she brushes the crumbs away, Joyce pushes the remaining muffins towards her and says, 'Sam told me that he thinks no one is taking care of you. Is that right?'

Lily is about to reach for another muffin, but withdraws her hand. She begins to talk about Belle Prettywood eventually agreeing to leave the door of her little office open, so that the wig-makers can share some of the warmth of her stove, and how, for all her power over her small universe, Belle has a jewel of a heart and will cheer her girls with jokes and laughter . . .

Joyce looks at Sam and says, 'Belle Prettywood is known all over London, Lily. I have heard she is very beguiling, but you should not look to her to take care of you.'

'No,' says Lily, 'and I do not. I don't look to anyone to take care of me.'

Again, Sam and Joyce exchange glances. Then Sam clears his throat and says, 'Joyce and I talked last night. We've seen now how unwell you are, and how thin, and I said to Joyce, "I rescued Lily once, long ago, and now I feel that she needs rescuing again." And Joyce said she wonders whether something bad hasn't happened to you recently, and—'

'No,' says Lily quickly. 'Nothing bad has happened to me.'

'Well, that's good, but perhaps you have had some shock or sorrow that you don't want to speak of. It's the fate of girls your age. And we would never pry into your life, but—'

'There is no sorrow.'

'But there is something that brings on your sickness. Perhaps it is only that you neglect yourself, for this is very often the condition of the young ...'

'No. It is very kind of you both to worry about me, but I am quite well and now I think I should be leaving. Miss Prettywood doesn't like us to be late for work. We are very busy at the moment, making wigs for an opera, and the director is very stern and comes to Long Acre with a fly swat, to chivvy us on ...'

Lily stands up. Her appetite for a second muffin has gone. She looks around for where her coat might have been put the previous day, before the helpings of tripe and onions, before her sickness, but Joyce Trench puts a hand on her arm and says, 'Sit down a moment longer, Lily. We made a plan, a resolution, last night, and we would like to put it to you.'

Lily looks to the parlour window and sees that the sun is shining on the fallen snow, but she doesn't know what time it is or whether, by the time she's walked to Long Acre, she may already be late. As if reading her mind, Sam says, 'It's still early yet and I'll see you to your work, but sit down, Lily, and listen to what we propose, for we believe we can help you.'

They tell her that they crept into her room towards evening and watched her sleeping so soundly and took away the dish of marmalade pudding and the same idea crossed both their minds – the idea that Lily should come here, to live with them for a while. They thought they had seen something about her which was troubled and from which she might die if nobody rescued her. Sam said that if they let her die, then his rescue of a child would all have been in vain and his watching of her over the years would also have been in vain and he said, with complete honesty, to Joyce that this one act, of saving a life, had stayed in his mind to console him through seventeen years and had enabled him to go on and prosper in the violent profession he'd chosen, and he didn't want that life to be lost now. And Joyce had said, 'Of course that's right, Sam. Right and logical. And then there is the little room where she's sleeping. We have no other use for it.'

Lily listened and watched their faces. She found her heart to be beating very fast. She saw that she was being offered a beautiful gift, the gift of shelter and sleep, the gift of the silk eiderdown. When she thought about the quiet room upstairs and compared it to her poor base-ment lodgings in Le Bone Street, she knew in which of these she would rather be. But she also thought that she knew something else: if she came to live in the house of Sam Trench, he would in time release her from the cage of silence she was in and she would begin to tell him everything. She would spill out her terrible wickedness. She might even kneel at his feet – at the feet of Superintendent Sam Trench of the Detective Department of the Metropolitan Police – and there it would be, laid before him in all its horror, and he would listen and raise her up and escort her to the place where she really belonged, not to a quiet room which reminded her of the space where her little cot had been in Nellie's house, but to a prison cell.

When Sam and Joyce had finished speaking, Lily said, 'I never could have imagined an offer so kind. In all my years at Coram, though we all thanked the Governors and the teachers and everybody in that place for all they did for us, it never *felt to me* as though they did much at all. But you. You've offered me a place in your lives and I am full of gratitude. But I can't accept.'

Silence fell in the parlour. Lily could hear the blackbird outside the window still singing, still making his noises of warning. Then she noticed that Joyce's eyes had filled with tears.

'You must tell us *why* you can't accept,' she said. 'Perhaps, as you say, you don't have the habit of accepting kindness because you have found none? If that is the reason, then of course you are bound to hesitate, but we would urge you to consider the offer, wouldn't we, Sam?'

'Indeed,' said Sam. 'And I would add something else. Because Joyce and I had no children, we have often been lonely. If we had you with us every day, why then—'

'I understand!' said Lily, getting to her feet and once again looking round for her coat. 'But I *can't* come to live with you. Le Bone Street is near to my work and I must go on with my life in that place. I must go on alone.'

The Woollen Scarf

After three days of helping with the wash at the convent, Lily and Bridget were summoned by the Reverend Mother. They were told to kneel down before her and kiss her outstretched hand and she said a prayer for them, asking God to look benignly upon the wickedness that was 'innate' to them, a blood-wickedness which could lead them into deep thickets of sin and transgression. Then they were put into a cart, with their hands and feet tied with rags, so that they couldn't escape, and driven by Thomas back to London. As the journey went along, Thomas began whistling and Lily suggested that they all sang songs, as Nellie used to sing when Peggy refused to move in the snowdrifts on the way to Swaithey Village, but Bridget said that she had no breath for singing, her lungs were still full of smoke and steam from the laundry, and besides, what was there to sing about when what lay ahead of them were weeks and years of weary days?

They thought about what they had tried to do – to walk to Baldock – and about what the Reverend Mother had said about there being no escape from their own evil and Lily looked at Bridget, who, with her thin legs and arms bound together, and her face very pale under its sprinkling of freckles, looked more than ever like a poor captive bird, and she thought how the Reverend Mother must be mistaken: there was no wickedness in Bridget O'Donnell, only pain and sadness and a longing to run her fingers through the sacks of coffee beans on the floor of the Inchbalds' shop and to hold conversations with the moon from a silent upstairs room.

When there was a pause in Thomas's whistling, Lily said to him, 'In return for the mutton dinner we brought you, Thomas, can you drive us to Baldock?'

Thomas was silent for a moment, as the cart lurched on. Then he said: 'Sorry, maidens, but the pony only knows this one road. An' if I were to do that, I'd lose my employ with the Sisters, wouldn't I?'

'The Sisters wouldn't know.'

'You're wrong there. Those women have powers of divination. They seem to know exactly where I am and what I'm doing, like God has given them a special compass. You see? I can't scratch my arse without them knowing. If I got you to Baldock, they'd fathom it somehow with that compass of theirs and I'd be cast out. And then what's to become of me? But listen here, you know what I've got in my pocket?'

'No,' said Lily.

'A silver sixpence,' said Bridget.

'Wrong,' said Thomas. 'I saved you a little nub of cold mutton. It's all wrapped up safe in greased paper. You want to eat it now?'

When they arrived at the Hospital, they were taken in and beaten on their bare flesh by Nurse Maud and their damaged shoes were thrown away and no others given to them, so that although the season was still bitter, they were made to go about the place barefoot, in torn stockings, and the cold ground sent an ache up their legs and into their spines so that sometimes they heard themselves cry out. But they couldn't hear the other one's cries because they were separated and told never to talk to each other again, and at night they had to share a bed with different children, who sometimes mocked Lily for her missing toe, and she found this such a torture that she slept very little, but only called to Bridget in her mind.

The weary days they had foreseen unfolded without pause. The hard winter engulfed them. The great court-yard, where the traffic from the Hospital came and went, was flooded and the waters turned to ice and at playtime the children came out to slide about on it and invent running and toppling and bruising games and long for skates so that something beautiful could be imagined with their bodies, turning and gliding to soundless music.

Lily tried to join in with these games, but without shoes the ice burned her feet and in places it was thin, with sharp stones and frozen twigs poking out of it, and one morning she saw Bridget sitting down on the ice, nursing her foot and crying. Lily knew she wasn't meant to go to her, but she saw blood on the ground and so she ran to her and knelt down beside her. There was a splinter of glass in Bridget's heel and the blood flowed freely from the wound, mixed with all the dust and dirt of the floors she trod. Lily tried to lift Bridget's foot onto her lap, to see if she could pull the splinter out, and Bridget clung to her arm and said, 'Lily, help me!' But Nurse Maud arrived, well shod in sturdy black boots, and bent down and pulled Lily to her feet and told her she would be beaten for 'communing with a child as wicked as yourself' and pushed her away so hard that she fell over and bruised her knees. Bridget began screaming, 'Lily, Lily! Don't leave me!' But Nurse Maud's gloved hand clamped itself on Bridget's mouth and she was led indoors, limping and shaking with sobs, and the blood from her wound made little scarlet imprints on the ice, as though a wolf had come and gone, still steeped in the lifeblood of its prey.

But there was no beating. Lily waited for it to come. When she saw Nurse Maud in a corridor, she almost asked her to administer it, so that it would join the cavalcade of things which were in the past. But Nurse Maud pulled her aside and told her that Bridget O'Donnell was in the sanatorium 'with poisoned blood'. Then she said, 'It is most likely that she will die, so I have chosen the path of leniency towards you. I feel that a death is punishment enough.' Then she went on her way, leaving Lily standing there. And Lily thought, This is what happens in the world: somebody brushes by you and utters words that bring a feeling like a stone being lodged in your chest, and they go on their way and you are left alone and you put a hand to your heart, to try to get the stone away, but it doesn't move.

The winter came to its end. Trees around the perimeter wall appeared as if startled by the pink and white blossom which broke out from their grey branches. There was a consignment of new shoes and Lily was given a half-worn pair that had belonged to an older girl and the feel of shoes on her feet was strange, as though she had put on some kind of armour.

Lily didn't dare ask Nurse Maud about Bridget. She told herself that she would know somehow if Bridget had died. She began knitting her a scarf. The wool she was given was rough and unbleached, but it was thick and tough and she thought it would be warm and comforting, when it was finished. Its muddy colour reminded her of Bert and she thought that to have lived in a barn with

Bridget O'Donnell and Bert the sheep, drinking from a stream, eating yellow apples, would have been preferable to being where she was. There might even have been an owl there, with a stern white face, keeping watch.

Then one day, she saw Bridget in the courtyard, playing with knuckle bones in a place where the blossom had fallen and turned to pink dust. She looked very thin. Even her head seemed to have shrunk, so that her Coram cap came down almost over her eyes. She wanted to run and show Bridget the half-finished scarf, which she had in her hands on its thick knitting needles, but she saw Nurse Maud standing a little way off, so she stayed where she was. It was a fine spring day, with soft clouds above the Hospital grounds and sooty London birds flying high in the blue air.

Lily stared for a while at the sky, remembering swallows that used to wheel and float above Rookery Farm and the rooks themselves clattering about in the beech trees. When her gaze returned to Bridget, she saw that she had left her game with the knuckle bones and had begun to run. A big old rickety wagon had been driven into the yard, with a sign painted to the canvas saying *Inchbald & Company, Purveyors of Dry Goods*. Bridget was running towards it and calling 'Mr Inchbald! Mr Inchbald!' It was a limping run, as though her punctured heel still gave her pain, but she was going as fast as she could.

Lily drew near. The wagon pulled up and a man – Mr Inchbald? – climbed down from the driver's perch and was almost knocked off his feet by Bridget charging into him and throwing her arms around his waist.

Lily saw that Mr Inchbald was older than she had imagined him and a little stooped – perhaps from bending down to ladle coffee beans into paper bags – but his face, beneath a shapeless brown hat, looked tranquil and kind. He held on to Bridget, who was crying now, but he didn't look down at her or appear to speak to her; his gaze roamed all around the courtyard, as though begging for someone to come to his rescue. Lily saw that Nurse Maud hadn't moved, but only looked upon the scene with her lips pulled inwards onto her stained teeth, so Lily put her knitting under her arm and began to walk boldly towards Bridget and Mr Inchbald. Nurse Maud still didn't move, so Lily went on and when she got near to the wagon she heard Bridget say, 'Take me home, Mr Inchbald. I want to go home …'

Mr Inchbald was trying to release Bridget's arms from clinging so hard to him, but she held on to him and cried, 'Put me in the wagon. Please! I want to go home to Baldock and never come back!'

He released her arms at last and bent down, so that his battered hat cast a little shadow onto her face, and said, 'Listen to me, Bridget. Listen to me …'

Bridget stopped crying but was left with the shuddering that always comes in the wake of tears. Mr Inchbald put a tender hand on her cheek and said, 'You know the rules, Bridget. I would love to take you back with me. You were never ever any trouble to us. But I can't.'

'Please!' cried Bridget again. 'I tried to run away from here, to get to Baldock, but I couldn't find it and I was sent back and we were beaten …'

Another storm of weeping overtook Bridget. Mr Inchbald again looked around him for some help to come to him, so Lily went up to him and said, 'I'm Bridget's friend, Lily. She told me all about your shop and putting things on the tab and her room where she saw the moon, and I think you should take her back, because none of us are happy here.'

Mr Inchbald sighed and said, 'I can't do it, my dear. The law prevails. I explained this to Bridget before she left our household. After the six years were up, she had to be returned here.'

'You could just put her in your wagon,' said Lily, 'and drive away and no one would follow you because no one cares about us.'

'I'm quite sure they do. The Governors are good people. This is a charitable place.'

'And there are no sacks of coffee and no toffee apples ...'

'Bless me, but is that all?' said Mr Inchbald. 'Compared to some out there, sweeping crossings, cleaning chimneys, selling matches, you're in heaven! You and Bridget must learn to be more grateful.'

'And there are beatings. And after we tried to escape, they took away our shoes.'

'Yes!' said Bridget. 'They took away our shoes and a splinter of glass went into my foot and I nearly died of it ...'

'That's worrying news, Bridget. But you did not die and you must go on in your life. You cannot go backwards.'

'I want to go backwards!'

'I see that, but it cannot be. I'm here to collect a new infant. A boy this time. I have a little basket for him in the wagon.'

Bridget stopped talking then. She stared at Mr Inchbald and Lily stared at him, too, but they both knew that there was nothing more to be said. Nellie Buck had left the Hospital with a new baby boy swaddled in Lily's crocheted coverlet; now, Mr Inchbald had come here to collect their new foster-child. It was the law.

Seeing the shock and sorrow in their faces, Mr Inchbald took off his old, ruined hat and pressed it against his heart. 'I'm sorry ...' he stammered. 'You were a good girl, Bridget. You were the best girl. But what can I do?'

As if to answer that question definitively, Nurse Maud now descended upon Bridget, took hold of her shoulders and turned her round and began pushing her back towards the Hospital entrance. Lily followed and, defying the edict not to talk to her friend, held up the scarf she was knitting and said, 'See this, Bridget? I'm making it for you. So, when the winter comes back—'

Nurse Maud sniffed and said, 'You are breaking a rule, Lily Mortimer. Am I going to have to punish you?'

'No,' said Lily, 'I only said a few words. It wasn't really "talking". I just wanted to show Bridget the scarf.'

She held the scarf out and Bridget touched it tenderly. Tears slid slowly down her cheeks, over the brown freckles.

'Can you make it very long?' she said. 'For the comfort of it in the cold.'

'Yes.'

Nurse Maud tugged Bridget's hand away from the scarf. 'I don't know what this is, if it's not "talking",' she said. 'Go away, Miss Disobedience, or you know what will happen to you.'

Lily stood still and watched Bridget and Nurse Maud walk away from her. She looked back at Mr Inchbald's wagon and wondered for a fleeting second if she could stow away inside it and be driven to Baldock, rocking the new baby boy to quietness in her arms, and arrive at the shop to count the packets of semolina and rice and the number of boiled sweets in a jar, as James Buck had once counted everything in the world, including her nine toes. But she knew that the time for outlandish escapes from the Foundling Hospital was past, and besides, the shop was Bridget's paradise, not hers. To go there would be to steal from someone she loved.

She returned her gaze to the scarf. She hoped she would be able to ask for enough wool to make it longer than ordinary scarves so that Bridget would be warmed by it.

Lily kept the scarf with her all the time, afraid that someone would steal it. Whenever her hands were free of other tasks, she worked at it, until it could stretch from the end to the head of her iron cot. Then she continued on. She seemed to know that a bed's length wasn't long enough. She thought of the seasons going round and how slowly they turned, but how winter always came in the end. The scarf grew dusty and marked with mud stains, but this, she realised, was how everything became as time passed, so it didn't trouble her and she thought it wouldn't trouble Bridget; what mattered were the hours and hours she spent making it and how Bridget would know, in the way that it kept her warm, in the way that it still smelled a bit like Bert had smelled, that their friendship endured, even if they couldn't talk to each other, nor cling together, laughing, in a soaking bed.

It was high summer by the time the scarf was finished. Lily asked one of the boys who worked on the weaving looms to measure it for her and he told her it was 'a mad thing, seventeen foot and three inches!' She brushed it and brushed it to clean it, until she choked on the coarse fibres of the wool. She embellished the neatly cast-off ends with blanket stitch, worked in scarlet thread, like the 'soldiers' she'd made at Rookery Farm. Then she tied it into a bundle and asked permission to visit Bridget, who was once again in the sanatorium, not with blood poisoning this time, but with something the doctors referred to as 'brain fever', but which was really just a clouding of the soul, a falling into sadness for which, the doctors said adamantly, 'there could be no possible reason'.

Bridget wasn't lying in her sanatorium bed like an invalid, but sitting at a window, staring out at the yard and at the jagged roofs beyond. She said, 'Do you remember how the fog and mist seemed so black when we climbed out of the tea cart?'

Lily said, 'I have been thinking. I could try to write another letter to Nellie and I'd say that if I could go back to Rookery Farm then I'd have to bring you with me and you could help with the stone-picking.'

'It's too late,' said Bridget.

'What do you mean?'

'I will stay here now and then I will die.'

Lily held out the scarf. 'Look,' she said, 'I made it really long. You could wind yourself round and round with it.'

Bridget took the scarf and untied it from its bundle and the heroic length of it unrolled across the sanatorium floor. Bridget stared at it in wonder.

'How many stitches?' she said.

'I don't know,' said Lily. 'Thousands. As many as all the angry words that come out of Nurse Maud's mouth. Or even more than that.'

Bridget smiled a wan smile. 'I miss you, Lily,' she said.

Lily went to her and put her arms around her and kissed the top of her head, which had been shaved again and was bare of the Coram cap. Bridget clung to her and laid her head against her chest. She said, 'I could go to sleep like this. It wouldn't be hard.'

She was only allowed to stay with Bridget for the briefest time and then Nurse Maud came in and said, pointing at the scarf, 'That thing is nothing but a receptacle for grime. Now come away, Lily, or there will be punishments in store and they will be more serious this time.'

The following day, Lily was summoned to the chaplain's office. The man had a kindly voice and his movements were slow and gentle. He invited Lily to sit down in a wide armchair and she obeyed him and waited for him to speak, with her legs dangling in the air, her feet unable to reach the ground.

He told her that Bridget O'Donnell was dead. She had died on her eighth birthday. He said, 'Unfortunately, it is the kind of death which angers Our Lord very much, so we will not speak of it very often and we cannot bury her on hallowed ground. But, as her friend, I felt that you were entitled to know what happened.'

Lily said nothing. She didn't know how to bring any words into her mind. She just stared at the chaplain and saw how, above his white collar, his neck was grey and had a kind of egg-shaped thing inside the greyness, which moved up and down as he spoke.

'She died by hanging herself,' said the chaplain. 'She went to the weavers' atelier and climbed up on a chair and tied one end of a long scarf to the loom frame and the other around her neck. Then she kicked the chair away. We're afraid that the knitted thing wasn't strong enough to snap her neck, but that she choked to death in a very short while. We pray that she did not suffer too much.'

Lily couldn't look any longer at the chaplain. There was something about the pale dryness of him which repulsed her. She looked down at her hands and saw how limp and pink and idle they were without the knitting needles and the wool. She remembered how all the hours of work on the scarf had brought her a kind of dull peace, which had endured across a hundred days or more, and how, in the space of the last few minutes in the chaplain's office, that peace had vanished away.

Clothes: *none*

Proof. Lily had to have proof that Frances Quale was or was not her mother. The mother she'd imagined finding was nothing like this woman.

She spent long hours looking at the plaster Mary. Mary, Mother of Jesus, Our Lady, Mother of All. Frances had so many replicas of her in Salvation House, it was as if she might imagine that each one of these could atone for what she had done and then she would be forgiven.

Forgiven by whom?

Perhaps Lily had believed, all along the journey of her short life, that when or if she ever found her mother, she would forgive her. She would forgive her and the mother would repent and then some kind of affection between them could exist in the world. But now Lily knew that if that mother was Frances Quale, a drunken wreck of a being, pretending piety, making a mendacious living from lonely and superstitious people ... if this was the truth of it, she would be unable to forgive her; she would have to flee from her and never return.

She went to see the Governors of the Foundling Hospital.

Going up the steps and into the Hospital made Lily shiver. At her back, she could hear the voices of children at play in the yard and she thought how the sound of boys and girls running and playing chasing games in the open air was always a sweet thing, as though these little

121

people must be carefree and happy, with the truth of their sorrows for a time concealed from them, but she knew that it wasn't so. They knew that they were the children of the 'undeserving'. They knew that they clung to life only by the hand held out to them by their distant benefactors.

Lily had dressed herself as carefully as she could for her visit, wearing her best blue coat and bonnet and clean boots. When she was shown into one of the offices of the Governors, two bearded men regarded her coldly and when she told them who she was, one of them put a monocle to his eye and regarded her intently through the round lens and said, 'Lily Mortimer. Often in trouble, eh? Were you not? One of the ... uh ... unreconciled ...'

'Yes, sir.'

'But then, I seem to remember, you secured an apprenticeship to a wig-maker. Or have I muddled you with someone else?'

'I am apprenticed to Belle Prettywood, to her Wig Emporium, sir.'

'Good. And does this work suit you?'

'Yes, it does,' said Lily. 'Thank you. All the stitching instruction I received here has been useful for the skills I need for the wigs.'

'Ah. So we really gave you a great gift, didn't we?'

'I don't know, sir.'

'You don't know? Of course we did. And now you're able to earn money. You're happy in your labours, we presume?'

'Miss Prettywood is very kind to me.'

'And you knew kindness here, too, didn't you? Despite your attempt to run away.'

'I can't remember, sir.'

'Yes, you can. You've just admitted that the instruction you received here was very beneficial. We hope that in time you will look back and understand what was given to you. Or am I wrong?'

'I don't know.'

'Ah well. We've known many who lacked gratitude, like you. But we won't dwell on it further. Can we ask what you want of us?'

She knew it was allowed. Young people who had spent their childhood at Thomas Coram's Hospital sometimes came and asked to see details about themselves, which they had long forgotten, or else had never known. They didn't have to say why they wanted them. They just asked for them and because the record-keeping had never slackened at the Hospital, they were usually found. Lily asked to see the sack.

She was instructed to wait outside the room, while a clerk was sent down to look for the appropriate page of the billet book in which all the records were kept. She sat on a bench in a familiar corridor, listening to the sounds echoing through the building, smelling the beeswax with which the floors were polished, glad that when she had been shown the ledger she would be free to walk out of the gates.

A handbell was rung outside. Lily stood up and looked out into the great courtyard, where the boys and girls would be forming into separate lines at the end of their playtime, and she saw them come obediently to order, wearing their Coram caps ... so *many* children ... so *many* foundlings. And it was then that she caught sight of Nurse Maud. She had come out from the building and was walking towards the lines of children. With her was a girl of nine or ten and Nurse Maud was pressing her forward with a possessive hand on the back of her neck, so that the girl's head hung down. Lily stared. Just by looking at the way Nurse Maud was in command of the child, Lily believed she could tell that what had happened to her, to 'Miss Disobedience', was happening again. Lily had thought that when, at last, she had been set free from the Hospital to begin her apprenticeship with Belle Prettywood, it had ended, but now she saw clearly that it hadn't ended; there was only a different victim.

Nurse Maud shoved the girl into one of the lines and Lily saw that the child was weeping. She wanted to run to her and say, 'I know the shame you're feeling. I understand it all. And somehow – I swear on my life – I will make it cease.' But 'make it cease' how? Years had passed and there she still was, Vile Maud, with her heart full of cruelty. There she still was, no different from how she'd been, with her stubby hand pressing on a girl's neck, leading an innocent being towards suffering and degradation. And what could anybody dare to do about it?

When the clerk returned, Lily turned away from the window and was conducted back into the office of the two Beards, whose names she thought she should know, but couldn't remember. The heavy billet book was set on a polished table and the clerk's thin hand showed Lily where to begin reading:

FOUNDLING HOSPITAL, *November 8th 1850*
Newborn infant, female
Clothes: *none*
Marks on the body: *wound to left foot; smallest toe severed*
Christian name given: *Lily*
Observations: *baby's body wrapped in a sack*

Lily stared at the faded writing. Then the clerk stood back and unwrapped something heavy and limp from a rough paper package and laid it down beside the book. It was the sack. Time had darkened it but clearly visible on it were brown stains, where her foot had bled into it, and there was a rancid smell to it, locked away in the fibres of the burlap, locked away in darkness for almost sixteen years, but now released once again into the air.

The Beard who had pressed her to admit the kindness shown to her by the Hospital – whose name, Lily now remembered, was Mr Hudson – cleared his throat, as though this smell might be choking him, and said, 'A very terrible beginning, Lily. Poor infant. Perhaps this is why you were unreconciled? But the fact remains that you were rescued and brought to the Hospital. And for this we must all thank the good Lord. We saved you.'

'I think a police constable saved me,' said Lily. 'He risked his own life ...'

'Did he? Is that true? But we warmed you and fed you. Your life really began here.'

Lily touched the sack. She asked if she might pick it up. The thing felt stiff and greasy. It was difficult to open it because the edges stuck together, as though the intervening years had sealed it shut. But her hand reached in at last and her fingers found the thing she knew would be there: the handful of hair. She wanted to bring it out into the light, to examine it after all the intervening years, but she didn't want the Beards to see it. She'd noticed from the entry in the billet book that no mention had been made of the hair, as though nobody remembered that it had once been there, and so she thought that by rights, now, the hair belonged to her and she could do whatever she liked with it.

When Lily informed the Beards she wanted to borrow the sack 'for a short time', they looked at her in bafflement.

'It seems like a rather terrible, dirty object,' said Mr Hudson. 'Not at all like the things which are normally left with foundlings. I would suggest that we get rid of it for you. Let us burn it and you will try to forget all about it.'

'Yes,' said Lily. 'I would like to "forget all about it", but there is somebody I must show it to first. Then I will bring it back and you can burn it.'

'Well,' said Mr Hudson, 'I suppose it is really your property, strictly speaking, so we won't object to your taking it. Do you agree, Mr Rafferty?'

Rafferty – that was the other man's name. And Bridget had once said, 'It doesn't sound a proper name for a man like that: better for a clown.'

'Yes,' said Mr Rafferty. 'You can take it. But return it you must, Lily. Mr Hudson is slightly wrong in suggesting that it is your property. It was the "token" left with you, albeit an unusual one, and these tokens rightly belong to Coram unless they are reclaimed by the foundling's mother. Everything must be done here according to the law.'

Lily was silent. She wanted to say, 'Certain things were done here which transgressed the law – things which never could be told to you,' but instead she said, 'I was surprised to see Nurse Maud in the courtyard. I had thought she would no longer be here.'

'Why did you think that?' said Mr Hudson.

'Oh,' said Lily. 'I thought she would be in her retirement by now.'

'Well, yes, by rights she should be. She is of retiring age. But Nurse Maud is a pillar of the Foundling Hospital, so we have kept her on. We let her take Sundays off, so that she can rest in her room, and on Mondays she is quite as energetic as she always was.'

'I see,' said Lily.

'Why do you ask?' said Hudson. 'Were you very fond of Nurse Maud?'

'No,' said Lily.

Mr Rafferty looked hard at Lily, taken aback, perhaps, by the firmness of that one word, 'No'. Then he said, 'I'm surprised. I know she is strict, but we feel that Coram children come to value the rules of behaviour put upon them. Under the tutelage of people like Nurse Maud, they soon understand the difference between right and wrong. Do you not agree?'

Lily looked at Mr Rafferty. 'A clown', Bridget had said. 'And there is nothing much worth saying to clowns because, behind their paint, anything could lurk: lies, inventions, spite, or even wickedness.' So Lily turned away from him, looked down at the sack and pretended she hadn't heard the question.

When Mr Rafferty saw that she wasn't going to answer him, he stared hard at her and said, 'One thing we know is that children are often like wild animals when they come to us. You were one such animal – a runaway, weren't you? And look at you now: quite upright and well behaved and earning your living, but only because we tamed you and brought you to God. Now go on your way with your dirty sack and make sure you obey the law and return it.'

The stifling summer wound on and no rain fell. Belle Prettywood threw open all the windows of the workroom and loosened her stays. The filthy London gutters turned to dust.

Lily thought, I will go there tomorrow – to Salvation House. I will lay the sack down on the counter. I will watch Frances Quale as closely as the old grey owl used to watch the rats in Perkin Buck's barn. I will only have to watch and say nothing and then I will *know*.

But she didn't go. She let all the August evenings pass and only crept back to her lodgings, to lie alone in her airless basement, staring at the plaster Mary, at its blank, unmoving face, telling herself she would go the very next day, she would somehow gather the courage to find out if Frances Quale was her mother.

The Scarlet Gown

Maestro Arditti has chivvied and bullied. Belle Prettywood has kept the wig-makers working long hours and now Belle has her reward: Arditti has given her two tickets to the opening performance of *La Traviata*.

Lily is summoned to her office and the door is closed. Belle is holding Violetta's 'final' wig, the one with the thinning hair, made by Lily, and Belle is caressing it with her long white hands.

'Beautiful work,' she says. 'So careful, so real. Arditti is ecstatic. And now I will repay you.'

Lily looks back through the glass door into the work-room and sees all the faces of her fellow workers lifted up, watching her, and this makes her tremble. When she's being watched, she always feels that it's about to arrive, the moment when everything she has done is revealed and she is taken away.

'I will take you ...' says Belle.

Lily jolts, as if she has been asleep for a second and has suddenly woken.

'Take me?'

'You should not tell anybody.'

'What did you say, Belle?'

Belle leans forward and whispers now: 'I am going to reward you by taking you with me to *La Traviata*. But you should not tell the other girls. I have only the two tickets.'

'Oh,' says Lily.

'We will have a grand evening. Arditti wants to include us in his private reception after the performance. You will meet the opera stars.'

Lily looks down at the hessian apron she wears for work. She picks at a corner of it. She says, 'You are kind to have chosen me, Belle, but—'

'You were about to say you have no dress to wear, weren't you?'

'Well ...'

'I have thought about that. This evening you will come home with me to Seven Dials and you can choose one of my dresses. You will need to alter it because you are so thin, but I know you can do that.'

Lily stares at Belle. She has the thought that in her former state of innocence, in the time before *that*, she would have been entranced by the offer. Her cheeks would have flushed with excitement. She would have begun dreaming of some marvellous romantic outcome. But everything is tainted now. There is no point in imagining an altered future, because there is no future; there is only the prison cell and the hangman's rope.

'I'm not sure ...' she stammers.

'No. Of course you're not sure. You're afraid you won't understand the opera, or you're afraid you will feel lost among rich and cultured people, but I will show you how to be. You will stay at my side and we will be transported by the music. And then there will be champagne and perhaps blackbird pâté and I know not what else of an exaggerated nature, because Arditti is very grand and always strives to impress. And you and I will get a little *aerated* and laugh at all the wonder.'

Lily looks at Belle. She thinks, There is something magnificent about her, the way she strives for everything and never gives up. She is beginning to get old, but even to this she pays no heed, only to make sure her cheeks are correctly rouged and there is lace at her neck and her beautiful hands are white. And seeing this, as though for the first time, Lily is seized by a terrible desire to kneel at Belle's feet and confess her crime, to lay the whole repulsive thing before her, and then wait for judgment, for it feels to her that judgment – even of a murder – is not something fixed and foregone but that it can undergo surprising alteration, if only the judge is wisely chosen.

She's at the point of falling on her knees, to clutch at Belle's skirt, as an unhappy daughter might clutch at the skirt of her mother, when she remembers that what is said in Belle's office can sometimes be heard by the other wig-makers, even when their heads appear to be bent towards their work. She stops herself just in time, just barely in time, for she knows that her face is full of emotion, as if she's about to scream or cry out. She puts her hands up to her mouth, to suppress whatever sound she might be going to make, and Belle, seeing some kind of distress in her, gets up and moves to her and puts her arms around her.

'Lily,' she says. 'I know your life is hard. I know that it has always been hard. But I am here. Belle Prettywood is your friend. And do you not long to try the blackbird pâté? Even just a little morsel?'

Belle's rooms at Seven Dials are painted in bright, strange colours. Her parlour isn't scarlet as it had been reputed to be, but sea-green, with white, billowing curtains.

Her bedroom is coral and peach. These corals and peaches are reflected in an armoire panelled with mirror-glass, from which Belle now takes two dresses made of embroidered silk, their skirts ample and their bodices low-cut and edged with tiers of silvered lace. She lays them on the wide bed and says, 'I expect you will choose the grey, because you think that the scarlet dress is too bold for you, but try it on and see what it does to how you *feel*. Clothes are not just ornaments; they're also medicines.'

Lily looks at the silk gowns. Her first thought is that she will do them some harm by trying to wear them and that they, in turn, will protest by scratching her skin or cutting into her waist or tripping her up as she tries to walk in them. Belle sees her hesitate and picks up the red dress and holds it against Lily's shoulders and smooths down the wide skirt. She turns her towards the mirrored armoire.

'Look!' she says. 'Straight away it brings a bright tone to your face. See? It acts like a potion. You will be a glorious angel in this.'

Lily stares at herself – her white neck above the dress, her hair scraped back and knotted carelessly at the nape of her neck, her eyes startled by what she sees, her skin pallid and sickly. At Le Bone Street, there is no proper mirror, just the shard of glass she holds up to the light to see some part of herself, and now, seeing the whole, unpromising person, she wonders why Belle Prettywood is taking so much trouble with her.

Belle takes the dress off its hanger. 'Try it on!' she orders.

Lily undresses, knowing that her worn underwear will look like something embarrassingly dead in this garden of living colour, but she chooses not to mind this and when the scarlet gown is on, pinched in at the back by Belle, so that the bodice is tight on her and flatters her small breasts and her narrow waist, she is fascinated by the altered girl she sees in the mirror. It's as if she has been born this minute in a room in Seven Dials, created by Belle Prettywood to take a different place in the world from the one she's always occupied.

She drinks in the image. Standing behind her, Belle drinks, too. Then they laugh.

'I told you,' says Belle. 'An angel.'

Lily takes the dress, wrapped in a linen sheet, to Le Bone Street and hangs it up and lights candles and kindles a fire and basks in all the colours of flame.

She falls asleep, watching, and wakes in the deep of night with all the candles out and the fire burned away, and touches the gown, where it hangs from the wooden curtain pole, then gets into bed and covers her heart with her palm, because it beats so loudly and stubbornly.

The following evening, she unpicks the bodice of the dress from its skirt, then the side seams up to where they join the sleeves and lastly the seams of the sleeves them-selves and looks at the thing now in pieces and remembers Nellie Buck making dress patterns out of paper and pinning them to black cambric and cutting round them with heavy scissors which made a munching noise as Nellie guided them along. And when Lily begins to sew up the seams, to fit her narrow waist and small breasts, this is done with all the cleverness and care that Nellie taught her long ago. She ruches the sleeves by drawing two running threads from shoulder to wrist and the silk falls into soft, obedient folds which seem to attract little ribbons of light and make the dress more marvellous than it already was.

She works slowly, over several evenings, but when the alterations are finished, Lily props up her piece of mirror-glass on the chimney breast and clips to her hair two sets of ringlets that Belle has given her and these fall prettily to her shoulders. Then she puts on the dress, lacing it up as tightly as she is able, and turns and courts her reflection in the window that gives on to the dark well beside the basement stairs.

She is so preoccupied with this new (and almost beautiful) self that she hardly hears the sound of footsteps on the stone treads and is surprised when there's a knock on her door. She freezes. The hour is late. Few people venture along Le Bone Street at this time; only the night watchmen or a few drunkards in search of comfort, and sometimes ragged boys going from shadow to shadow with larceny on their minds.

Lily goes to the window, meeting her reflection eye to eye, and cranes to see out. She wonders if some stranger in the street looked down into her basement and saw her in her scarlet dress and took her for a whore. Instead of answering the door, Lily raises the window a fraction and calls out, 'What d'you want?'

'Lily,' says a familiar voice. 'It's Sam. Sam Trench.'

Sam Trench. Lily's first thought is, He shouldn't see me dressed like this: quite different from how I usually appear to him. She's about to tell him to wait, while she changes back into her blue woollen frock, but then she thinks, Why shouldn't anybody look at me in this new state, altered by Belle, a girl who is going to be taken to the opera? So she goes and opens the door to him and he takes off his hat and stares at her.

'The dress isn't mine,' she says quickly. 'I am only doing some alterations for my friend ...'

She sees him take it all in: the silver lace above her breasts, the tight waist and the ringlets in her hair. His face is in shadow, but she believes she can recognise in it the thing she first detected when he stared at her in church – a yearning he can't conceal.

He doesn't move. He says, 'I won't disturb your sewing. I only happened to be in the vicinity and I thought ... I thought I would reassure myself ...'

'Yes?'

'Reassure myself that you were well.'

'Oh yes, I am quite well, thank you.'

'Good. Well, I shall be on my way ...'

'Or,' says Lily, 'why not rest for a moment by my fire? I could make a mug of chocolate.'

'Oh no. I can't put you to the trouble.'

'It's no trouble. Come in. And you can tell me what crimes you have investigated this week!'

Lily fills a pan with water and sets it on the blackened range. She puts more coal onto the fire, taking great care with it, so that the dress is held far back from the flames.

Sam Trench, in his uniform, looks about the room, seeming to note each object with his superintendent's eye: Lily's sewing basket on the small table and the narrow cot where she sleeps, and her old clothes lying there. Then his gaze returns to her, and she remembers a while ago, before he invited her to meet his wife, how she had a waking dream of him sitting beside her on a stone seat in the churchyard and how she felt the warmth of his hand very lightly holding hers, and how, in that time, she wondered if this ordinary stranger would save her by some means.

Making the chocolate, she asks about Joyce and Sam tells her that there are times in the year when Joyce makes a 'retreat', a sudden withdrawal into the self, from which nothing seems able to rescue her, and that now is one such time. 'Even I,' he says, 'I seem to be incapable of bringing her out from where she's gone.'

'Oh,' says Lily, 'but I wonder why she goes there. If you knew the reason—'

'I know the reason. It is sorrow for the children she never had.'

'Oh.'

'It is difficult to be the one who is powerless to console.'

Lily thinks about this. She remembers the moment when the Inchbalds' dry-goods wagon drove into the courtyard at the Foundling Hospital and how Bridget O'Donnell ran towards it, believing Mr Inchbald had come to take her back with him to Baldock, and how, after that, when she knew that he would never do this, she had been inconsolable and had hanged herself with the scarf that Lily had knitted.

She decides to tell all this to Sam Trench, and the way sadness for her childhood friend sometimes overtakes her, and Sam says, 'This is how I see it, Lily: sorrow is always with us, like a London mist or fog, always there, even on fine days, waiting its time to come back. But do you know what I tell myself when this casts me down? I tell myself that I did one important unselfish thing in my life, which was to save you, and I have come to believe that this is what keeps me from despair.'

'Despair? Why would you despair, Sam Trench, when your profession is to bring the guilty to justice?'

'Very few are brought to justice, Lily. I see the bodies. I see the thousand ways flesh can be mutilated, but I don't always capture the people who are responsible for the suffering. Do you know how cunning a murderer can be?'

'Not really ...'

'With some, it's almost an art, so that you do not *see* the crime. And when I miss something that should be before my eyes, I curse myself. I cannot tolerate my own lack of purpose and resolve and my stupidity. It's then, at such times as these, that I begin to think about you.'

'About saving me from the wolves?'

'Yes. And then ...'

'What, Sam?'

'About what I feel for you now. I have tried to set this aside. I have told myself that my affection will not be acceptable to you, but the truth is that you have become precious to me ...'

Oh, Lily thinks, here is the scene: here is a virgin girl wearing a scarlet dress, with ringlets in her hair, and beside her, beside a fire on a winter's night, is the man who saved her, the man who walks in and out of her dreams, the man who seems to know what is in her soul, and he has made a confession, as the girl always seemed to know that he would ... but what is to be done about it?

She looks at him: Sam Trench, wearing his superintendent's black coat, warming his rough hands on a mug of chocolate. Lily sets her own mug aside and gets up. She says, 'I would like to feel it, what you feel. I would like you to hold me, just for a moment, just so that I can be comforted by the warmth of you, just as it is in my dreams, and then you must leave.'

'Lily,' he says, 'why did you say "in my dreams"? Are you telling me that you dream about me?'

'Yes,' says Lily. 'We sit together and you take my hand.'

'Are we here, in this room?'

'No. We're sitting on a stone bench and the stone feels cold, and the air is cold, but your hand is warm.'

She goes to him and he brings her gently towards him and kisses the top of her head. The smell of him is like the scent of snow, part bitter and part sweet. She clings to him and feels so comforted that she doesn't want to break away. She isn't certain how long they stay like that, while the fire burns and the light of it falls on her beautiful dress, but after a while she becomes aware that Sam is crying. Then, very slowly, he turns away from her. She sees how all his movements are slow and sorrowful and how his tears still fall. He retrieves his hat and lets himself out into the dark and she watches him climb the basement steps.

'Caverns measureless to man'

After Bridget died, Lily was ill with her old sickness and grew thin and weak and Nurse Maud said, 'What is wrong with you, Miss Disobedience, that you can't even obey the laws of sensible food digestion?'

She was put in the sanatorium. She had a bed to herself near a window and somebody had placed a china flower vase on the window sill, but there were no flowers in it.

The summer was ending. A cold wind blew from the north and the afternoons were beginning to darken. Lily thought about Bridget's body under the earth and how it had been placed beyond the graveyard of the church, in ground that was full of stones and rubble. She wanted to write a letter to the Inchbalds, telling them what had happened and asking them to dig up the cardboard coffin and rebury Bridget in Baldock, under the shade of some beautiful spreading tree. But she knew she might be punished if she did this and the thought of being beaten once again felt too cruel to be borne.

She had a dream that, down in the darkness of the earth, Bridget had grown wings and become the bird she had always resembled, the mistle thrush. When Lily woke up, she thought, When I next see a thrush, I'll pretend it's Bridget, but I won't try to catch it — as Jesse Buck once caught a baby owl and held it in his hands — but only let it fly to wherever it longs to go.

Of her own future she tried not to think, because what was in it, after eight years of life, except spinning yarn and picking oakum and making baskets and sewing and cleaning dormitories and sharing a damp bed with a girl who was not Bridget and never laughed and never made plans for escape and who had never owned a silver sixpence?

She lay without moving, looking at the empty vase and filling it, in her mind, not with roses or lavender, but with stems of ground elder, letting the remembered reek of them invade the air of the room, reminding her that life had become bitter and devoid of hope. When she thought about the little girl she had been at Rookery Farm, sleeping under her multicoloured blanket, eating sherbet from a market stall in Swaithey, gazing down into the sweet water of the well, it seemed to her that she was no longer that person, or worse, that none of what she could recall had actually happened, but was only a stubborn dream which wouldn't go away.

Broth and porridge and sometimes potato soup were brought to her in the sanatorium, but she left it all to grow cold. Her body became so light, it sometimes felt as if it might rise up from the bed and hover above it, like a plover above a field.

One day, the chaplain came to see her. He sat by her bed and she watched the egg in his grey neck going up and down as he talked. He told her that he had written to her benefactress, Lady Elizabeth Mortimer, to tell her that they feared for her life and that Lady Elizabeth was travelling down from Scotland to come and see her, bringing with her 'food to tempt you back to life'.

Lily had forgotten about Lady Elizabeth Mortimer. She had only met her that one time, when the embroidered letter 'E' she'd made stayed scrunched up in her hand and the sun had shone on Lady Elizabeth's hair, making it look like treacle. But now she felt glad that somebody beyond the walls of the Hospital had remembered where she was. She had difficulty imagining how far away Scotland was and how long it would take for Lady Elizabeth to travel from there to London, but she tried to picture the food she might bring: eagles' eggs, wild mushrooms, sweet chestnuts ...

And then, one afternoon, she came into the sanatorium, walking with her limp and her forward lean, with her maid holding her up. She sat down by Lily's bed and Lily once again saw the beauty in her face.

Lily's right hand lay limp and still on her coverlet and Lady Elizabeth picked it up and held it tenderly.

'They tell me,' she said, 'that you are finding it difficult to eat. But you probably know, Lily, that if you don't eat, then after a certain time, you're going to die.'

Lady Elizabeth had large blue eyes and her dark eyelashes were straight, not curled, straight and thick, like a perfect row of plain stitch. Lily stared at these eyes as she said, 'My friend died.'

'The chaplain told me,' said Lady Elizabeth, 'and I know when sorrow like that comes, it's often difficult to want to persevere with life. But listen to me. I've brought you a book of engravings of the Scottish landscape. This landscape is very wild and beautiful. Some of its crags and waterfalls are so mighty to behold that we are lost for words when we see them. They are "caverns measureless to man", as in Mr Coleridge's great poem. And I've brought the book, to show you what Scotland looks like, because I've begun to wonder whether it might be possible for you to leave the Hospital and come there, to live with me. I shall never have a child of my own and I'm sure, in time, you and I could get along well and be happy together.'

Lily lay very still. She didn't know if what she had just heard had actually been said, or whether her mind, which felt so strangely weightless, had merely dreamed it.

'Do you mean that I would leave the Hospital?' she said.

'Yes. I will have to get official permission from the Governors, of course, but I don't really see why they shouldn't give it. I would take full responsibility for you. All you have to do, Lily, is decide to live. And to live, you must start eating.'

Lady Elizabeth turned towards her maid, who put a little parcel into her hands. It was a bag of oranges. She took one out and held it near to Lily's cheek, so that she could inhale its sweet citrus perfume. Lily could recall that, long ago, Nellie Buck had been given an orange in return for some bantam eggs. She had taken a knife and peeled the skin from the orange in narrow sections, then splayed out the sections around the fruit, so that they looked like the petals of a water lily, and Joseph had clapped his hands and Perkin Buck had said, 'Well, bravo, our Nell.' Then Nellie had given everybody a segment of the orange and it tasted beautiful and seemed to quench a thirst which you didn't know you'd ever had.

And this was what Lily felt now: a terrible thirst. She wasn't sure whether it was a thirst for the orange or a thirst for something she couldn't name, but she tried to pull herself up higher in the bed, to ask Lady Elizabeth if she could eat the orange now, and Lady Elizabeth said, 'Yes. That's very good,' and sent her maid off to search for a plate and a knife. Then she picked up the book she'd brought, with all its engravings of the Scottish landscape, and put it into Lily's lap.

The book was heavy and pressed on Lily's body like an old church Bible. The pages were thick and crackled when Lily turned them. She stared at the images of mountains and crags and high trees and the sky above and all of it was dark, as though night was not far off. She found a picture of a wide river, and there was a grey light on that and little touches of white, where wavelets were forming in the wind, and on the banks of the river, women guarding a few nubbly sheep, who had come to drink there, and Lily thought about Bert and Bridget and the yellow apples and the quiet stream.

Then she found a picture of a castle, with high turrets, standing on a hill and keeping watch over a forest of oaks and elms, and beyond these a shining lake. Birds flew around in the cloud-streaked air above the castle, except that they didn't move, but only balanced there in a trembling kind of way, forever stilled by the picture. Lily thought this scene very beautiful, perhaps even more beautiful than anything she'd seen in Suffolk, and then Lady Elizabeth's hand alighted on the engraving and she said, 'That is a picture of the castle which belongs to me. And if you came to live here, you could have a room high up in one of the turrets and it would be a perfectly round room with three windows looking down on the forest and the lake.'

The maid returned with the peeled orange, sliced into circular pieces. Lady Elizabeth set down the plate at Lily's side and she began to eat the fruit. At first, it was difficult to swallow it, but soon the sweetness of it was so consoling that she forgot about this difficulty and began cramming her mouth with piece after piece of the orange. And she wondered whether, if she went to live in the castle, there would be oranges in a glass bowl or a wooden bowl, for her to eat whenever her thirst for them overcame her.

She returned her gaze to the engraving of the castle. She pointed with a finger, sticky with the juice of the orange, to a window in one of the round towers. 'Can that room be mine?' she asked.

'Yes,' said Lady Elizabeth. 'That can be your room. And you can have a brass bed in it, and feather pillows. And a chair where your dolls can sit.'

'I don't have any dolls,' said Lily.

'Don't you? But in the future, we will buy some for you, if you want them.'

'A rag doll,' she said.

'Or a beautiful baby doll with a china face?'

'No. I like soft things. And china can break.'

'True, it can. So we will go and look for a rag doll. But you will never get her, Lily, if you die, will you? So what are you going to do about that?'

Lily didn't know how to answer this. She looked down at the forest surrounding the castle and wondered what lived there. She remembered that in the woods between Rookery Farm and Swaithey, where she and Nellie gathered primroses in April, there was a world of shy animals and birds, scuffling and searching and jumping about in dry leaves: red squirrels, weasels with bright eyes, dormice, pheasants, woodcock and wandering wood pigeons. But the forest in the Scottish picture appeared so dense and dark that perhaps there was only room for the trees and a few boulders covered in moss by all the winters that had come and gone. Perhaps it was the kind of place where a girl could get lost and never be found? Yet Lily wanted to see it. She wanted to be driven away from the Hospital and put on a train to Scotland, to find herself surrounded by oaks and elms and sprinklings of sunlight and to hear the trees sigh in the wind and then make her way to the brimming lake. And she thought that if only this could be her future, she would decide to stay alive and wait for it to come.

After the visit of Lady Elizabeth, Lily tried not to think about Bridget any more, or about the scarf with which she had hanged herself, but only about the high room in the castle and the rag doll with a flat, endearing face who sat in an armchair, watching the clouds.

Lady Elizabeth had told her she would talk to the Governors and then she would write to her to tell her what was being arranged. While she waited for this letter to come, Lily forced herself to eat the soup and porridge that was brought to her and after two weeks, she was taken away from the sanatorium and put back into the day-to-day life of work and fugitive rest.

Because her sewing was so good, on her ninth birthday she was told she would be transferred out of her needle-work class and put to help the younger girls who were struggling not only with their stitching but with their homesickness and who cried for their lost foster-mothers just as Lily had cried for Nellie. Told that she could help them make handkerchiefs or Coram caps or calico drawers or embroider samplers like the one made long ago by Mary Wickham, Lily decided to ignore this and to use the calico to make rag dolls.

The dolls had no fingers or toes, no hair yet and no features. They were flat pieces of calico in the rough shape of gingerbread biscuits. But Lily made sure that every child had her own doll with its own name: Hattie,

Tattie, Daisy, Rosie, Penny, Molly, Marjorie and Meg. She showed the girls how to stitch the seams all around the head and body, leaving gaps here and there, where the stuffing would go in, then turn them inside out, so that the seams wouldn't show. Their faces would be painted on and they would be coiffed with wool. She said, 'Doing all of this work will take quite a long time, but you must be patient.' She said that when the dolls were complete, they would be taken outside into the yard for the birds in the air to see and the birds would capture souls for them and send them down into their heads, and after that, they would have to be cared for, as mothers are supposed to care for their children.

Lily noticed that the girls were very solemn and quiet as they worked on their dolls, and that those who had cried all the time when they were sewing Coram caps forgot to cry, and she thought, This is what will happen to me when I go to live with Lady Elizabeth in Scotland: I will forget to cry for Bridget. I will have my own doll and name her Bridget. Bridget and I will go into the woods to look for primroses and listen to living things making nests with twigs and leaves, and there will be a waterfall nearby and we will sit and wonder at the sound it makes.

One evening, as Lily prepared for bed, Nurse Maud came into the dormitory. She held a letter aloft in her hand, as though she were showing people the way to somewhere or other, then she brought her arm down and thrust the letter into Lily's face.

'It seems,' she said, 'that you have a benefactress. I cannot myself see why she has chosen you, Miss Disobedience, but there it is.'

Lily took the letter, on which the seal had already been broken, and there was the kind of smile on Nurse Maud's face which suggested that it was she who had broken it. Lily put the letter into the pocket of her nightshift without glancing at it, but she knew it must be from Scotland. She didn't want anyone else to see it and decided she would wait until everyone in the room was asleep, then she would get up and go out into the passage, where an oil lamp was left burning, and read it there, by that small consoling light.

She had a bed to herself now. At nine – two or three years away from leaving the Hospital to be apprenticed to a trade – she was too big to share with another girl. In the darkness, she unfolded the letter, to see if she could guess what was in it without following its actual words, but she couldn't. She tried to imagine what it would say but Lily knew that trying to imagine something that you can't properly see was like trying to get to Baldock with no map, but only a sheep for a companion and a silver sixpence hidden up your BTM. She fell asleep with the paper in her hands and didn't wake till morning, and when she woke, the letter was gone.

Never

It was late evening when Lily arrived at Salvation House. The road was quiet. Only one person came towards her, an eel-seller, dragging his cart, his body bent over with exhaustion, his eyes on the pavement.

'Eels?' he said sadly. 'Best live eels?'

'No thank you,' said Lily.

'Godspeed, maiden,' he said and went on his slow way. Lily watched him until he was out of sight and she thought, I am like him. I am no luckier than him. He drags his heavy cart through the streets all day till his sinews feel they are breaking, and what weighs my flesh down and sends an ache all through me is my dread of discovering that Frances Quale is my mother.

She turned away. She had seen that, to the left of the house, there was a narrow alley, unlit. She would slip like a shadow down this passage, then turn left and hope to come upon Frances Quale's back door, for she knew that there was something about a knocking on a back door which was difficult to ignore, something portentous, especially in the dusk of evening, when the occupant of the building had closed her shop and believed herself safe from customers and callers.

The alleyway was foul, strewn with household rubbish, including a torn mattress, smelling of piss, with its horse-hair stuffing exploding out of it.

And there was movement around Lily's feet, which she knew had to be mice or rats, even though she couldn't see them in the darkness. And it made her smile to think that all Frances Quale's clean and supposedly sacred religious objects, dusted with the patina of eternity, existed just one brick wall away from discarded things and vermin and human waste.

She stood in the alley for a few moments, pressed close to the wall, listening, to see how many more people passed by in the street itself, but she heard no footfall, no carts, no cry of a child. And she imagined the thousand strangers who occupied this corner of London at rest at home, or drinking in the Rose and Crown, tired from their day but with their minds in a state of tranquillity, and she envied them that it hadn't come upon them to find out that they had an ogre for a mother.

The back door of Salvation House was an old collapsing iron structure, which might almost have been the portal to a prison cell. Lily stood before it now, holding the sack. Her mouth was dry and she shivered in the evening air. But she knew that she wouldn't walk away. She was 'Miss Disobedience', wasn't she? Miss Disobedience had always stood her ground.

She thought that the iron door would reverberate with her knocking and attract the attention of the neighbours, so she picked up a stone from the dusty road and tapped lightly on it with this. She waited. After a while, she heard the familiar shuffle of footsteps. Then Frances's voice sounded near and whispery and tender as she asked, 'Who calls?' As though she might have been expecting somebody she longed to see.

'Lily Mortimer,' said Lily. 'I have a gift for you.'

'Who?'

'Lily Mortimer. I bought a Mary from you and now I have something important to show you.'

There was silence. Lily was going to knock again, but then the door opened slowly. Frances Quale stood there, holding aloft an oil lamp. She was wearing an old quilted gown, made of satin, once grand and shiny, but stained by time. Her hair was wild, gone into a kind of rebellious frizz that risked being set alight at any moment by the lamp.

'What gift?' she said.

Lily held out the sack, which was wrapped in clean linen.

'I'll show you,' she said, 'because this is something you will want to see. But you must let me in. I'm sorry for the late hour.'

As Lily stepped inside, Frances Quale stared at her with her mouth agape and Lily knew that she didn't recognise her from her previous visits; she was just another stranger who came and went from the shop and never, in all her life of subterfuge, was she yet thinking that there might be some fearful connection between them.

They walked through a dark hall and Frances Quale opened the door to a back parlour, furnished with green chairs and a sofa and a mahogany sideboard stacked with bottles of some amber liquor. Mrs Quale was yawning. Her breath was foul. Either she had been woken from sleep or else she had been sitting in one of the green chairs, drinking. Then Lily noticed that beside the sofa, on a low table, was a heap of silver half-crowns and a pile of creased banknotes, and she thought, Well, this is what she does in the evenings: she counts her money. And it was an important realisation, for she saw how easy it would be for someone to slip into this back parlour and commit a robbery. And she shivered because the idea of stealing from her, of getting money for some of the things she yearned for, suddenly excited her, and for some reason she thought of her dead friend Bridget and her silver sixpence, and said to herself, If I steal the money, I will feel no shame about it because it will be for Bridget, and then I will buy coffee and butter and lard and flour and somehow make a meal out of the goods that were sold in the Inchbalds' store and the thing I will remember is Friendship, which is one of the precious things of the world.

Lily and Frances Quale sat down and Lily's hands hovered over the sack, wrapped in its linen. She noticed that her hands were trembling as she said, 'I've brought you something which I think once belonged to you. Open it and see if you recognise it.'

She passed the bulky object to Mrs Quale. Frances Quale yawned again, then her arthritic fingers began to peck at the ribbon. A clock ticked somewhere in the room and the summer darkness outside grew more absolute, as though a storm was waiting to break from the Essex marshes and drench the city.

When the sack was unwrapped, Mrs Quale unfolded it and held it towards the oil lamp, the better to see what it was. Her expression remained blank. Then she opened the sack and reached into it, but she seemed to find nothing inside it and withdrew her hand.

'You've brought me an old, empty sack,' she said. 'What use is that to me?'

'Its use,' said Lily, 'is to jolt your memory. Have you not seen this sack before?'

151

Mrs Quale brought it near to her face, all the while feeling its weave. At any moment, Lily thought, she will remember, and then my future life will be damaged by its proximity to this woman. Now, she kept watching – for every tremor, for every little movement of anguish in this woman she had come to detest. She almost willed these outward signs of her guilt to show themselves quickly, so that then it would be over. But Frances Quale seemed to stay very calm. The look on her face was one of puzzlement, nothing else. And Lily felt vexed; she wanted to hurry it along now, the moment of revelation, the moment when everything would change.

'Look inside the sack again,' said Lily. 'Then you'll remember ...'

The arthritic fingers reached in and down and found the locks of hair and brought a handful out into the light. The hair was white.

'Hair?' she said. 'Whose hair?'

'I've never known who it belonged to,' said Lily, as calmly as she could, but finding it difficult to speak, her mouth was so dry. 'Perhaps you used some of it to make a wig, when you worked for Belle Prettywood.'

Frances Quale put up a hand to try to suppress another yawn.

'Who is Belle Prettywood?' she asked.

'You don't remember her?'

'No. I never heard that name.'

'Yes you have. You know perfectly well who Belle is. You worked for her at the Wig Emporium in Long Acre. When you were young.'

'Wig Emporium? No ...'

'You did. You worked for Belle, and then when the shame came upon you—'

'Shame? What shame?'

'The baby. And then ...'

Frances Quale was now staring at Lily. Her gaze, made a flickering and sliding kind of gaze by her drinking, suddenly hardened.

'I'm sorry, dear,' she said. 'But I haven't the faintest idea what you're talking about. Begin again, can you?'

Lily saw her return the hair to the sack and lay it aside, but she did this carefully and gently, not like one who was fearful of it or repelled by it, and suddenly hope rose in Lily's heart that after everything, she had imagined it all wrongly. She willed her voice to be calm as she said, 'I heard that you took a job at Belle Prettywood's Wig Emporium. She told me you were one of her best workers. And then—'

'No,' said Mrs Quale. 'Wherever did you fabricate that idea? I've never been near Long Acre in my life. Never. And I would have had no talent for wig-making. I don't know what brought that into your head.'

'I was informed, on good authority—'

'Whose authority?'

'Belle Prettywood's. And one of her workers followed you here to Salvation House.'

'Well, whoever she followed, it wasn't me. I've told you, I don't know Belle Prettywood. I worked in service when I was young. I cleaned and scrubbed for a bishop, a holy man, and he kept me on doing that work, because I did it well, and it was from him that I once stole an ivory-bound prayer book – my only transgression, bar those he forced upon me – to make up for the low wages he gave me. And I sold the book for ten shillings and that was how I got the idea for Salvation House. Bishop Thomas Maggs was his name. Happen he's dead now, but you ask in his household in Streatham if I didn't labour there for all the best years of my life and wear out any beauty I may have had, but don't mention the prayer book because Maggs never worked out it was I who had stolen it, just as he never worked out certain other things. He thought me too honest to commit a crime like that.'

Lily was silent. For the first time, she turned her head away from Mrs Quale, to look around the parlour, as if searching for proof there for what she had come to believe, but the parlour was all in shadow. She stood up and walked through into the salvation shop, where all the holy relics were displayed. She took down a Bible from a high shelf and returned with it to where Frances Quale sat, with her jaw all stretched out in another yawn.

Lily held out the Bible. She said, 'I know you're tired and I shall leave you in peace in a moment, but first you must put your hand on the book and swear to me, swear on the words of God, that you were not the one who put a baby in this sack and left it to die.'

'Put a baby in the sack? In heaven's name, dear, how could you dream up such a thing?'

'I *dreamed it up* because I was the baby. I was left to die at the gates of Victoria Park and rescued by a young man and taken to the London Foundling Hospital, where I lived a life of suffering.'

Frances Quale stared at Lily. For the first time, Lily saw something in her eyes that was kindly and tender and she thought, Perhaps this is how she was when she was young, before she started slaving for the bishop, before her drinking, before all her dreams of making money from humanity's longing for salvation.

'You lived a life of suffering in that place?'

'Yes. But it's in the past now.'

'Do you want to tell me about it?'

'No. I'll go back there one last time, to return the sack, and then I will never set foot in it again. I try not to remember what was done to me there.'

'Well, the world can be cruel to children and it can be capricious. I had a son years ago and I loved him, for all that he was the child of the bishop, damn his eyes!'

'You had a son?'

'I began raising him as best I could on my own, with the money I got from my relics. He came with me to the Holy Land when he was four years old and he caught one of the diseases they have in those dry places and died, and I buried him there and came back alone. I had baptised him Michael.'

'Michael?'

'Yes. A darling boy. Laid to rest in the dust of the Judaean Hills. But he was my only child. I'll swear on the Bible, if you want. There was only Michael, the son of Bishop Maggs; never any other child.'

Lily walked home to Le Bone Street, carrying the sack wrapped up in its linen, and it felt somehow lighter in her hands.

London was full of revellers at this hour and Lily's pathway was through clusters of men and women, young and old, swaying along to the music of their inebriated minds. But she paid them heed only so far as to think, If she is not dead, then she could be one of them, my poor mother; she could be any ancient soul still striving for life in the blighted city. She could be the grand-dam of an eel-seller, or one who paints the cruel faces on the Punch and Judy puppets, or a tired landlady, dreaming of the Essex sands and oysters and the fragrance of the sea.

She might be the owner of a dog-grooming parlour, or a skivvy at the Blue Anchor tavern, watching men set fighting terriers upon rats. She could be a cleaner at the Merchant Taylors' School, cuffing the fresh-faced boys for not pissing straight into the urinals, or fate might have used her so poorly that she languished in a work-house, with no hope left in her heart. She could be any of these. Any one of these and a thousand others. But she is not Frances Quale.

After some time, Lily grew warm from her walk and became aware that there was a foolish smile on her face. She wondered whether now, freed from the horrors of Salvation House, her search for her mother would cease. For she seemed to know at last that she would never find her and that, for the sake of her own sanity, she had to be reconciled to this – to an unknowing which had no end. She looked up at the sky above the roofs and chimneys and her eyes lighted upon a few beautiful stars – not many, just a shy few, momentarily glorious.

No Entry to Children

Lily had searched her bed. Then she'd searched underneath her bed. Then, as the girls in the dormitory began dressing for the new day, she'd asked them one by one if they'd taken a letter out of her hands while she was asleep? She knew, because letters so seldom came for anybody, that even a letter that wasn't yours had a kind of fascination about it, as if it might be an object of intrinsic value, or contain secret information about the world, or bring news of some wonderful day in which everybody was going to share. Lily explained that this was an important letter from her benefactress, Lady Elizabeth Mortimer, in Scotland, a letter that could change her life by promising that the time had come for her to inhabit a high room in a castle, and the children looked at her in awe, trying to imagine such a wonderful place, but they denied ever having seen a letter.

The day wound on and all Lily could think about was the engraving she'd been shown of the castle on the hill, with the forest all around and a lake shining at its feet. She had wanted to keep the book of engravings, but Lady Elizabeth had said it was too precious to be left at the Hospital, somebody would steal it. And now Lily decided that if a book could be stolen, then so could a letter, and one day the thief would come to her and ask her to pay a price for getting the letter back, and if she had owned a silver sixpence like Bridget, she would have given that, but she had nothing, only her Coram clothes.

At bedtime, the occupants of Lily's dormitory helped her search the large room. There was very little furniture in the room – just the iron beds and a few oak chests where new linen was stored and a cupboard full of chamber pots and rags – and for the children to look in these places was considered by Nurse Maud to be 'unnecessarily inquisitive', so that when Maud arrived to supervise the bedtime prayers and found the girls examining Hospital property with their 'dirty little fingers', she told them, not for the first time, that they were evil and that all through their lives this evil would be in them, inherited from the vile acts their mothers had performed to bring them into the world. She made them kneel by their beds and confess their wickedness to God with their hands over their eyes and as they silently prayed, she went from bed to bed, cuffing their bent heads, round and round, cuffing with her hard hand on their necks and on their ears until some of them began crying and the crying seemed to satisfy her and she stopped. But then it seemed that she wasn't satisfied. Lily raised her head and opened her eyes and saw Nurse Maud march to the place where a few chamber pots had been taken out of the cupboard. She lifted up one of them, made of white china, took it over to the chimney breast and let it drop there, where it broke into pieces.

She turned and saw Lily watching her. 'Right,' she said. 'Miss Disobedience, please tell me why you have wilfully destroyed this precious piece of Hospital property!'

Lily said nothing. She felt dizzy from Nurse Maud's cuffing. She seemed to know that she was being accused of breaking the chamber pot, but it felt to her as though

Nurse Maud had said this in another language which she couldn't understand.

'I'm waiting,' said Nurse Maud. 'I wish to hear from you why you have committed this act of vandalism.'

'I didn't do it,' said Lily quietly. 'You broke the pot.'

'What? What did you say?'

'You let the pot fall.'

'Children!' screamed Nurse Maud. 'Raise your heads! Our Lord does not hear your prayers anyway. He is deaf to such vain entreaties. And now there is one among you who is telling the filthiest lie and it poisons you all if you take her side and you will be punished in a way you would not like. So will somebody tell me please who broke the chamber pot?'

Nobody spoke. The crying which had broken out at the cuffing seemed to have taken the breath from many of the girls, so that they knelt there, gulping and twisting their fists into their eyes, perhaps hoping that if they couldn't see Nurse Maud then she couldn't see them.

The silence in the room seemed to act like a potent medicine on Nurse Maud. She hurled herself across the room with a kind of wild strength Lily had not seen in her before. She pulled Lily to her feet and twisted her arm behind her back and pushed her to the centre of the room.

'Girls!' she cried out. 'I have had enough of this child! It is not for nothing that Lily Mortimer is known as Miss Disobedience. Only those filled with pride are disobedient, and as you should know by now from your religious education, pride is a mortal sin. And I expect you know what awaits a mortal sinner, don't you? Perhaps you are unable to imagine it, so I will tell you. When the mortal sinner arrives in Hell she will suffer perpetual thirst. Her body will burn with inextinguishable fire, from which there is no escape. And all her senses will be assailed by visions of foul and stinking things and by noise beyond imagining, and none of this will falter; it will give no respite, it will be suffering to be endured forever.'

The crying in the room broke out again. Lily didn't cry. The pain in her twisted arm was fierce and she knew that Nurse Maud expected her to break down, but she refused to grant her this satisfaction. If she was 'Miss Disobedience', then she would never give in to this woman, no matter what punishments would be forced upon her.

'Stop crying!' Nurse Maud commanded. 'Everybody stop crying, and you, Verity, and you, Venetia, pick up the broken pieces of the pot and then find a brush and pan and sweep them away, and then all of you get into your beds and be silent until I come back.'

The chosen girls, Verity and Venetia, stood up, both faces red from weeping. Lily knew them to be kindly children, one of whom had been fostered to the family of a cabinetmaker and kept trying to make tiny pieces of furniture from sticks and cast-off ends of wood she found in the yard. Nurse Maud began pulling Lily towards the door and she saw Verity and Venetia stare at her in terror, wondering where the nurse was going to take her. Lily wanted to say to them, 'Don't be afraid for me. Whatever she chooses to do to me, I'll endure it and not break, because she is my enemy now, but I am a scarlet soldier and I will fight and not give in.'

She didn't know what lay in wait for her.

She was taken out of the dormitory and along a familiar passage, and then through a door she had never opened, a door which displayed a notice saying *Private. No Entry to Children*. Beyond it was a flight of narrow stairs. As they approached this, Nurse Maud released her grip on Lily's arm and pushed her onto the bottom stair and kept pushing until Lily fell over, bruising her shins on the treads.

'Up!' said Nurse Maud. 'Go up!'

It felt cold in this stairway and there seemed to be no light coming from anywhere and Lily thought, This must be the very centre of the building, the heart of it, with no windows, the place that children are never allowed to see.

She stumbled on, with Nurse Maud's hand now pressing the small of her back, and to stop herself from being afraid, she began thinking about poor Lady Elizabeth's deformity and how she, Lily, was lucky to have a spine that was straight and green as a wand of willow.

They reached a dark landing which smelled of lye and reminded Lily of the convent laundry where she and Bridget had worked for three days before being brought back to the Hospital in Thomas's cart and then she remembered Bert and how Bert had been eaten in the end, cooked with rosemary to flavour the flesh, and how these things appeared almost to have been part of some ancient happiness that was lost when Bridget died.

Nurse Maud opened a door and pushed Lily into a bedroom which had one high, tilted window staring up at the sky. There was a narrow bed in the room, with the sheet and blanket stretched tight over the mattress, and Lily also noticed a rag rug in front of a small, unlit fire and a rocking chair and a thin bookcase and a sewing basket, and she understood that this was Nurse Maud's own room, the place where she came when she wasn't supervising the children, and she couldn't help but imagine her enemy sitting in the chair and rocking back and forth, back and forth so determinedly that she lost all control of the chair and was pitched face first onto the rag rug and then a spark from the fire was catapulted into the air and landed in Nurse Maud's hair and set it alight and travelled down her neck and onto her arms and her back and burned her whole body with perpetual flame, like those to be found in Hell . . .

Nurse Maud now gestured to the bed. 'What is undergone in here,' she said, 'for those who have sinned, as you have done, too many times to be borne, is what we call the Chastity Test. It is the penance you must perform. But the way I administer it, as you will see, allows you to reach absolution. It is like a confession. You are not a Roman Catholic, but you know what confession is, don't you?'

Lily said nothing. She saw that to the left of the bed there was a screen and she supposed that behind it might be the place where Nurse Maud washed herself and looked in an old silvered mirror to brush her hair and put on her nurse's cap.

'Lily Mortimer,' she said, 'I asked you a question. Do you or do you not know what confession is?'

'Yes,' said Lily.

'Right. Well, we shall proceed with it now. Out of the goodness of my heart, I am performing this to save you. Take off your nightshift and lie on the bed.'

'No,' said Lily.

Nurse Maud now strode to the door and locked it and took away the key.

'There is no escaping this,' she said, 'but in the end you will thank me because this is a very potent punishment and when it is over – in the mystical way that I perform it – I will give you absolution and your soul will be calmed and you will go about your life here in a state of obedience.'

Before Lily could say that she hadn't understood this, Nurse Maud threw her onto the narrow bed. She lifted her nightshift and with one hand held her down and with the other parted her legs and then let her hand rest on the mound between them, the place Nellie Buck had said should never be touched except to be cleaned and dried, a private and sacred place, the purpose of which would only be revealed to her when she was grown up and wanted children of her own.

'Now,' said Nurse Maud, 'we are going to gauge how much of a sinner you are.'

It was late when Lily returned to the dormitory, but most of the girls were still awake. Lily got silently into her bed, but Verity and Venetia came to the bedside and asked, 'What did the Monstrosity do?'

The Monstrosity. This was what they called Nurse Maud now. It was discussed between all the children: Nurse Maud had the soul of a wild animal. She could fall into a swoon from her own cruelties.

Lily was fond of Verity and Venetia, but she wanted them to go back to their beds and leave her alone. She couldn't speak about what Nurse Maud had done. She knew that those moments in the high room with its window tilted upwards towards the sky would have to be consigned to a part of her mind she seldom visited, but already she was afraid that somehow they would seep out from there, like some invasive disease, and bring her low. She told Verity and Venetia only that Nurse Maud had pretended to be some kind of priest and had made her confess her sins and then given her absolution.

'What sins did you confess?' asked Verity.

'I didn't,' said Lily. 'She confessed them for me, how I once ran away from Coram and how my mother was a whore. But I want to be quiet now and go to sleep.'

'How did she know your mother was a whore?' asked Venetia. 'Because you told us nobody knows who your mother is.'

'Yes,' said Lily. 'Nobody knows. Nurse Maud is full of lies. But I can't say anything more about it.'

She lay in the dark and heard the bells chime out in the London night and tried to sleep, but every time sleep came near, she began to sweat and she felt it all go through her once again, the horror that had been performed on her, and she curled her body into a circle, holding on to her ankles. At Rookery Farm, she had seen hedgehogs do this, make themselves into a ball to ward off danger, as if they thought, like this, they could be mistaken for a prickly chestnut pod or a fallen bird's nest and protect themselves from suffering. But folding her body up didn't bring her any comfort. It was as though shame had taken on liquid form and tainted her blood and she didn't know how she would ever be free of it.

To try to ease her mind, Lily began to imagine again an escape to Scotland. She tried to hear the wind in the oak trees and the sounds the lake made as it was lifted into waves which broke softly onto the little shingle beach. She imagined golden eagles flying above the forest, their great spread wings passing close to the window of her high room, their cry like the call of a child lost and found. Then she saw Lady Elizabeth sitting in a vaulted room, beside a cheerful fire, and offering some delicacy on a silver dish: crystallised plums or hazelnuts dipped in chocolate. And she thought, That is where I would like to be, and all the horror of Coram would be in the past. But then she remembered the letter, with its broken seal. Now that it was lost, the only person who knew what it contained had to be Nurse Maud: the Monstrosity. But if Nurse Maud's was the only mind which knew what had been in the letter, then this knowledge would have to remain out of reach. For Lily decided that she would never say a word to Nurse Maud ever again and that whenever she saw her, she would jam her fists into her own eyes.

Traviata

Belle Prettywood arrives in a hired carriage at Le Bone Street. Being disinclined to step down into the muddy road, Belle sends the coachman to call Lily forth from her basement.

The man descends the area steps and knocks on Lily's door. The young person who answers the knock wears a striking scarlet dress, trimmed with silver lace, and her hair falls in glossy ringlets over her ears, and the coachman, who has seen many beauties in his time, is at once moved by her – by a certain fragility visible in her despite the proud way in which she holds herself and the tender regard she chooses to bestow on him. His thought is that here is somebody who needs a protector. He holds out his arm to steady her as they go up the steps towards the waiting carriage.

When Belle sees Lily, she explodes into exaggerated cockney speech.

'Lord love us!' she says. 'I never looked anything in that dress, but you are transformed, Lily! You are meta-morphosised – or whatever the bloomin' word is! Everybody at the Haymarket will want to lie down at your feet – kiss my arse if they won't. So climb in, Miss Mortimer, and off to the opera we go.'

Inside the carriage, Belle studies Lily's appearance more closely. She leans over and places a little peck of a kiss on Lily's cheek, leaving the smallest imprint of brilliant pink lip colouring just beyond the place where the brown ringlets fall, and says, 'I never really saw it in you until now, Lily. I expect it's because your head is always bent over your work, or else because I am more short-sighted than I care to admit, but you are indecently pretty, you really are. And all I can say about this revelation is that you must, from now on, be vigilant and careful.'

'Careful of what?' says Lily innocently.

'Of men, of course!' says Belle with a whoosh of laughter. 'For now you're coming to the time in your life when you will discover that all men are fiends. They are *wolves*. They howl for the scent of a woman, they *bay* for it, and then they treat her like meat – as poor Violetta is treated in the opera we're going to see. But I would not like to see you become meat. You are far too precious.'

Belle links her arm, adorned with several gold and silver bracelets, through Lily's and draws her close to her, just as an affectionate mother might draw a beloved daughter close, and it comes into Lily's mind to admit to Belle the thing which happened with Sam Trench, the moment that wasn't meant to happen, except in Lily's dreams, but which had suddenly occurred. She wants to say, 'There is a married man, much older than me, with a wife who is kind, a wife who does not deserve to be hurt, and he came near to me and I let myself be held by him and it was the most consoling feeling I have ever felt in my life. And I wanted to stay like that, with my head on his breast and his arms around me, forever.' But then she decides that to talk about that strange and powerful feeling, which should surely remain a secret thing, would be to betray it and betray Sam Trench, and so she keeps silent.

★

Maestro Arditti, his long neck charged with the significant task of keeping his chin aloft above his stiff white collar and white tie, is greeting the arriving audience in as flamboyant a way as his fearful heart will let him. He bows and pirouettes and laughs and adjusts his cuffs and manages to maintain on his handsome face a steady and encouraging smile, but he's as nervous as a bird. Is his production of *La Traviata* as good as – now and then – he believes it to be, or is there something predictable and flat about it? Does it fascinate and seduce, or has it somehow strayed into dullness, despite the beauty of the music?

It's for this reason, this anguish of not knowing, that Arditti is glad to see Belle Prettywood. If his production fails, then somehow Belle also fails with it. She and her work are part of what will either dazzle or disappoint. So he clings to her and whispers, 'Help me, Belle. I'm sick with fear. Tell me if I'm going to fall off the mountaintop.'

Lily stands by, watching Belle as she gently strokes Arditti's hair. She can't hear what Belle says to him, but it brings a laugh to his constricted throat and then he says, 'Oh, well, at least afterwards we'll have some champagne, plenty of champagne, won't we, my lovely? And if it's all collapsed into the gutter, we'll just join it there and decide not to mind, eh, Belle?'

'Of course,' says Belle. 'The gutter can be a surprisingly interesting place. Now, Maestro, you will not recognise Lily, who works with me, for she has suddenly become a beauty without giving anyone any warning, but do be chivalrous and kiss her hand.'

Arditti turns his anxious gaze on Lily. She has seen him before, when he's visited the Wig Emporium, but he always strides through the workshop into Belle's office, where the completed wigs are displayed for him, and it's almost as though the workers are invisible to him, except, now and again, to be touched fleetingly by his fly swat. As instructed by Belle, he takes up Lily's hand and kisses it, but he has no idea who she is and only murmurs politely, 'Charmed, mademoiselle. Now, in the box reserved for you, you will find a little ensemble of sweet-meats, for your delectation, to help keep you awake through all the Italian songs. Are you partial to sugared almonds?'

'I think, by the sound of them, I could be,' says Lily.

'Oh, "by the sound of them"! How adorable. You have never tasted a sugared almond! I love you instantly. And your red dress is very fine. You had such a dress once, didn't you, Belle?'

'Something of this colour, yes. It didn't suit me. I prefer pink for my complexion.'

'Quite right. Pink. Absolutely right. Now forgive me, there are a few counts and barons and baronesses I must flatter before I disappear to soothe my singers. Wish me luck, ladies.'

'We do,' says Belle. 'We do.'

Arditti hurries off. He has the upright walk of a dancer, measuring his strides as if in time to some internal music. Belle watches him go and suppresses a laugh as Lily asks her, 'What did you say to him when you were stroking his hair?'

'Oh,' says Belle, 'I told him he was a vain old cockerel who just longed for praise!'

The audaciousness of this makes Lily gasp, then she begins giggling and Belle joins in and Lily looks all around her at the opera-goers in their silks and satins and feathers and marvels at how tall they seem, as if they come from a different race from her, but she hears her own laughter carried in the air above them and how she has earned her place in this grand company, if only for a single night.

Belle had once told her workers the story of *La Traviata*. She had come into the workroom towards the day's end, carrying a mug of gin, and told everybody to stop work and listen. She had sat herself down at the long table, where a single, faceless head mould seemed to watch her and wait attentively for the story to begin. Belle set the gin beside the stand, took a grand gulp of it and said: '*La Traviata* is based on the story *La Dame aux Camélias* by the French author Alexandre Dumas, and it is tragic. But this appears right to me. When we do the great additions of fortune and misfortune, most human lives have tragedy in them.'

'Not all,' said Priscilla, one of the young wig-makers. 'Your life isn't tragic, Belle.'

'Well, but what do you know of it, my dear? I shall not comment. But listen now. Here we have Violetta, our heroine. She is a woman of the night, beautiful and young, but dying of consumption. Knowing her life will be short, she gives herself to superficial pleasure only. She declares that in what remains of her time on earth there is no place for love.'

'She's quite right,' commented Fleur, another of the assembled women. 'Love is a delusion.'

Belle ignored this, took another sip of gin and hurried on. 'Well,' she said, 'after resolving never to love, Violetta meets a man, Alfredo, whose unswerving affection makes her change her mind. He declares he will become "the watchful guardian of your dear life". And so, of course, Violetta can't resist him. How could she? For a brief moment, a few months, the couple know happiness together, but in deciding to live with her, a woman damned by her former "crimes", an erring soul, Alfredo knows he has brought dishonour on his family.

'His father, Giorgio, arrives at Violetta's house while Alfredo is away. He warns her that she can't escape her past except through sacrifice. She must renounce Alfredo, then she will "fly to regions of the blessed".'

'Humbug!' said Mrs Julia Buchanan, the oldest woman on the wig-making team. 'I sincerely hope she refuses.'

'She doesn't refuse. Giorgio reminds her that beauty is fleeting and that when hers is gone, Alfredo will leave her for somebody younger – for this is what men always do.'

'Oh Christmas! That old saw again!'

'Well, I know. It is wearyingly familiar. But what can Violetta do? She leaves her lover. She returns to her previous ways, under the protection of a certain rich baron. All that remains for her is to await her death.'

At this point in the story, Lily and every one of the other wig-makers stared at Belle in horror. Surely, they wanted to ask, the story cannot end like that? Belle gulped down most of the gin remaining in her mug before wiping her lips with a lace handkerchief and sighing with as much drama as the moment asked for and then saying, 'What other ending would you expect, girls?'

Everybody was silent. They were women for whom life was hard. Wig-making bought them a scant living and Belle Prettywood was a kindly employer, but perhaps some of them, the youngest ones, dreamed of love, or at least of 'watchful guardians' who might help them to an existence a little more easeful than the one they had. It was Lily who at last spoke up. 'Isn't it true that there can be no other ending, Belle?' she said.

'Why do you say that, Lily?' asked Belle.

'Because once you have committed sin, you might be free from its consequences for a time, but in the end, it will bring you down.'

'Well,' said Belle, 'that is to reckon without forgiveness – from the hearts of those we love and from God. Do you not believe in forgiveness, then, Lily?'

'No,' said Lily. 'I don't. I think if the crime is very bad, then forgiveness will never come, just as it doesn't come to Violetta.'

'Ah,' said Belle, 'but we haven't quite reached the end of the story. And who do you think needs forgiving here?'

She took the last dregs of the gin. Her bright cheeks were becoming even brighter in the late afternoon light. The wig-makers looked around at each other, as though they thought the answer lay with one of them – one who had the leisure to ponder questions of right and wrong, honour and betrayal – but nobody ventured a word.

Now, in Her Majesty's Opera House in the Haymarket, Maestro Arditti's performance of *La Traviata* is drawing towards its terrible conclusion.

Wearing the wig made by Lily for this last scene, Violetta is dying a painful death, alone except for her faithful maidservant. All seems lost. The audience in their finery are so held by the drama that they have mostly forgotten which tiaras or mantillas or hats or feathers they are wearing. The ladies are choked by strong feeling and long to cry. They search in tiny purses for even tinier handkerchiefs. Weeping at misfortune which is not theirs is such a deep pleasure! The gentlemen, too, are moved, yet wonder at themselves for being so. Wasn't Violetta, after all, simply a high-class whore, who lived only for physical pleasure? Why have they come to hope that Alfredo, the upright man who strayed from the upright path, will return to her? But hope they do.

And wait! Here he comes! Alfredo rushes in. He takes Violetta in his arms. He tells her that he will be hers for the rest of her life and all past sorrows will be forgotten. Sobbing is heard in the front three rows and in the box next door to the one where Belle and Lily sit. Love is going to save Violetta. Love can save everything, if it's strong enough. It will bind the lovers together forever and past sorrows and transgressions will fade to oblivion. The music swells and swells. Belle leans so far out of the box, her bosom is resting on the velvet sill. But then it comes, the tiny pause in the aria, and Violetta cries out: 'È strano ... Cessarono gli spasmi del dolore.' It's strange! ... But the pain has vanished! She begins to whirl about the room. Her thin hair whips around her face as she dances for joy. But of course joy is a delusion. There is only death. Alfredo has arrived too late. The curtain falls.

When it rises again, the marvellous opera ensemble stand in a line, smiling. It was only a story. They are alive and buxom and beaming and pushing Violetta and Alfredo forwards and the fragrant heat of their bodies is inhaled by the audience, who rise, applauding, to their feet and cry, 'Bravo! Bravo! Bravo!' They throw flowers onto the stage. Belle and Lily are standing too. Belle is crying so hard, her tears run down her neck and onto her white breast, but Lily can't cry. She feels choked by an internal fire that rises from her heart and gathers in her

throat and almost stops her breathing. She has the illu-
sion that what she's just seen – the wonder and the cruelty
of it both – was performed uniquely for her, but that
only in due time will its meaning be revealed to her.

Arditti is called up to the stage. He's soaked with sweat.
'Maestro!' the audience call. 'Maestro!' And he bows
low, as though he were a courtier in doublet and hose,
bowing to the sovereign, bowing in gratitude for the
cheers of the nation. The audience don't want to let him
go, don't want the high emotion to end. Their hearts are
so full, they feel they want to applaud forever, but slowly
there is a movement out towards the foyer and the night
beyond and the waiting carriages. The burning footlights
are extinguished. Arditti and his company disappear
behind the curtain. Belle blows her nose. 'Blackbird pâté,'
she says in a firm voice. 'Arditti promised.'

Towards midnight, finding herself once again in Le Bone
Street, unsteady from the champagne she has drunk, Lily
thinks about taking off her dress to put on her nightshirt,
but, looking down at the crimson skirt, she's unwilling
to be parted from it. She lies on her bed and spreads the
skirt out around her. She feels the touch of her false ringlets on her cheek and hopes they didn't fall awry in the
crush of people crammed into Maestro Arditti's rehearsal
rooms. In the midst of this crowd, Lily had thought: We
might as well be on an omnibus, except that the scent of
the bodies is heady with rose water and pomade and we
are all getting drunker and drunker.

Nobody talked to her. Belle had been led away by
Arditti to meet the singers and Lily had made her way to
a quiet corner of the large room and stood with her back
to a potted palm and watched the waiters trying to

circulate with champagne bottles and silver trays of tiny biscuits, which might or might not have been spread with blackbird pâté. She watched hands reaching out and glasses held up to be refilled. She wondered if all the weeping had gone from the soft and plump and bejewelled white bosoms of the women, or if it might suddenly return, with the ladies now crying, not for the drama itself, but because it was *over* and all that remained for the morrow was ordinary existence, full of hurry and disquiet and the faithlessness of young men.

Then, suddenly, the singer who had been Violetta was at her side, not wearing her deathbed wig any more, but with her own hair augmented by ringlets not unlike those Lily wore. She was large and smiling and Lily thought, Death, for her, is distant and she doesn't know that for me, the hangman's rope is coming near.

'My dear!' said Violetta. 'How young you are! You were pointed out to me as the one who made my wonderful Act III wig. I never saw such an artful piece of work.'

'Oh,' said Lily, 'oh, but the wig is nothing. Only the singing ... and that moment when Alfredo returns ...'

'Were you moved by it?'

'Yes! I shall never forget it. Never.'

'Do you mean it? Because that is exactly what we strive for – to present something that will endure in people's hearts. The world can be so ugly. Isn't that true? And so we try to take the audience away from it, just for a brief time. But let me drink to you – to your skill. Tell me your name.'

'Lily Mortimer.'

Violetta raised her glass. 'I drink to you, Miss Mortimer. And I drink to patience. For wig-making I know is arduous and needs infinite endurance.'

175

She drank and Lily drank. The taste of the champagne was glorious, making her mind dance, and she felt, just for the moment, that she had been singled out. But other guests had soon pressed upon Violetta and she was whirled away, to meet this or that person, because she was the heroine of the hour and Lily was nothing, just a girl who had studied needlecraft all her life and who looked almost pretty in a cast-off scarlet dress.

Lily closes her eyes. The silent room still spins, but the feeling isn't unpleasant, just unfamiliar, and the thought comes into Lily's mind that the night, in all its wonder, is somehow incomplete. And she knows what it is she wants. She longs for her own 'Alfredo', her own 'watchful guardian', to come in and take her in his arms. She wonders if, perhaps, he is on his night rounds and will pass by her window and see a light burning and come down the steps and see her lying there in her red silk gown and dare to approach her and say, 'Lily, I know I shouldn't feel what I feel, but I don't seem able to help it. I know I will be punished for my sin, but I want to be your lover.'

But of course he does not come. Sleep comes. And then the cold morning breaks and the cries of London begin once again to penetrate the sooty air.

Rag Doll

Lily had dreamed often about Scotland and Lady Elizabeth's castle above the forest and the lake. This dream always had a marvellous scent to it, the scent of applewood fires, for those were what she used to imagine she would find there: sweet branches felled from an orchard, grey with lichen, burning Vulcan red in wide grates under mantels of stone. Going from room to room, where pale sunlight fell in squares across polished floors, there the fires would be and sometimes she would stop and crouch down to warm herself and wait to see one limb of wood breaking and falling into the ashes with a soft, apologetic sound.

She'd never seen the castle, never set foot in Scotland. She assembled the beautiful place in her child's mind, just from the dark engraving she'd been shown. She kept hoping that a letter would come – a second letter to replace the one she'd lost – but time kept passing and there was no word from her benefactress.

The question of the lost letter had never been resolved. Though Lily believed that the only person who had seen its contents was Nurse Maud, she'd refused to give Maud the satisfaction of being asked for something that she wouldn't divulge. And she began to imagine that Maud had torn the letter into pieces and thrown the pieces into the fire and that the sealing wax had been baked to black shards.

Then one day, the Governors had sent for her and she was taken into a high, cold room and was told to sit down on a low embroidered stool, which tilted this way and that and reminded Lily of the cranky little milking stool she'd used to help Perkin Buck in the dairy at Rookery Farm.

Seated high above her on a tall chair was a very elderly man. His name was Judge Cantrell. Lily looked up at him and saw what she thought was kindness lingering there in the spaces between the lines and creases of his face. He was smoking a cigar which had burned to a little round nub and threatened, it seemed to Lily, to set alight the hair growing out of his nostrils, and she wanted to warn him about this, but straight away he began talking very fast, quite as if he were in a race to see how many words he could cram into a fugitive moment of time.

All the while watching the burning cigar and the judge's nose, and marvelling that this ancient man could smoke and gabble at the same time, Lily tried to take in what he was saying. She wondered whether she was really following what he'd been deputed to tell her: that Lady Elizabeth Mortimer had changed her mind about taking her to live in her wonderful Scottish palace. Lady Elizabeth was sorry, said the judge, she very much disliked going back on her word, but the plan would now have to be set aside. She'd sent a token: a rag doll, dressed in tartan. She hoped this would be some compensation.

The judge paused at last and looked down at Lily on her tilting stool.

'Do you understand?' he asked.

'No,' said Lily. 'She told me I could go to live there. I was going to sleep in a round-shaped room with three windows looking different ways.'

'I'm very sorry about it. Shall I try to explain it again?'

The judge extracted the nub of the cigar from his mouth and Lily saw that the end of it was all damp with spittle. 'Where is the rag doll dressed in tartan?' asked Lily.

'Oh,' said Judge Cantrell, 'the doll. Now what the devil did I do with that? Let me see ...'

He put the cigar end on a saucer on his desk and began looking in the desk drawers for the doll. Not finding it in any of them, he got up and went first to a mantelpiece and searched all along it, behind candlesticks and peculiar lumps of jade, but it wasn't there either. The judge turned in a little circle, as if beginning a game of blind man's bluff, then went to an upright piano and lifted up the lid, as if he might have absent-mindedly thrown it inside, but there was no tartan doll in the piano. Judge Cantrell returned to his chair. His ancient head was shaking side to side in perplexity.

'The devil of it is,' he said, 'I'm now not absolutely certain whether Lady Elizabeth said she *had* sent the toy, or whether she said she *was* sending it. And there is a consummate difference between the two. I will find out for you, Lily, and then, very soon, you will have your doll.'

Lily stared all around the room. She was partly thinking that there were still a lot of places where the judge hadn't looked for the doll, but she was also wondering why her benefactress had changed her mind about taking her in. Had she been told by Nurse Maud that Lily was 'Miss Disobedience', or even that she had been forced to commit acts of shame that would disgrace the owner of a Scottish castle? When she returned her gaze to the judge, she dared to ask, 'Why did Lady Elizabeth change her mind?'

Judge Cantrell picked up the cigar stub and though it had gone out, held it between his fingers, as if for comfort. He cleared his throat and said, 'The thing seems to be, I understand, that Lady Elizabeth has a suitor. Do you know what a suitor is, Lily?'

'No,' said Lily.

'Well, a suitor is a man who promises marriage. And for Lady Elizabeth, with her unfortunate affliction, which you've seen with your own eyes, this is a very great honour, a very great *wonder*, if you like. But – and I don't expect you will understand this – the suitor in question seems to be nervous about you, about *a child*, coming to live in the castle and taking up Lady Elizabeth's time. You see?'

'I wouldn't take up her time,' said Lily. 'I could go and play in the forest with the animals. I could make friends with a sheep. I could build a house in a tree. I could go and listen to the little waves on the lake.'

'Ah bless you, yes, I'm sure you could do all of those things, but of course Lady Elizabeth doesn't know this and her suitor doesn't know it either.'

'You could write and tell them.'

'Write and tell them! Well, yes, I suppose I could. But, to be honest with you about grown-up matters, Lily, I believe there may also be a money factor.'

'What is a money factor, sir?'

'I don't quite know how to put it. You see, Lady Elizabeth Mortimer, the only child of a Scottish laird, is very rich and I do believe her suitor might be worried that some of this ... this richness ... might, if you were adopted by the Mortimer family, pass to you instead of to him. I'm afraid that is just how the world is, Lily.'

Lily sat on her stool, trying to think what 'richness' would look like exactly. She remembered Bridget's silver sixpence, how she had sometimes shined it up on her sleeve and how, in the end, it was never used, to buy food or to buy a ticket on an omnibus to Baldock, and then, when they were taken back to the Foundling Hospital in Thomas's cart, it seemed to have disappeared and, like the stolen letter, was never found. She wondered how many silver sixpences could be hidden in a Scottish castle and how, if a suitor wanted to find them and take them all for himself, he would set about it.

'Do you like crystallised plums?' asked the judge suddenly.

'I think I would ...' said Lily.

Judge Cantrell looked again in his desk drawers and extracted a sticky earthenware pot and held it out to Lily and she leaned forward and saw that there was only one plum remaining in it.

'There's only one,' she said.

'Is there? Well, that's my fault. Mine entirely. I think I must eat them without noticing. But please take the last one. They are nice and sugary.'

Lily took the plum and it felt huge in her mouth but full of sweetness and consolation. The judge watched her eat it and smiled and then after a while he said, 'I must let you go now. I will put my mind to the question of the doll and hope to get it for you very soon. All right?'

She knew it wasn't 'all right'. She knew that, despite the letter which had been lost, she'd believed Elizabeth Mortimer would take her away from Coram one day and that she would see golden eagles flying past her window and a friendly moon, like the one which kept company with Bridget at the Inchbalds' house, sauntering up and down the velvet sky. But there was nothing to be done about it. In her life at the Hospital, there was never anything to be done.

She still has the doll.

Judge Cantrell found it, he told her later, in a most peculiar place, inside a long-case clock in his chambers, but he just couldn't remember ever having put it there. 'Perhaps,' he joked, 'it is a follower of Galileo and enjoys watching the swing of the pendulum?'

It was about a foot tall, with woollen hair and a flat face which Lily liked to hold against her cheek. The tartan dress was red and green with a full skirt and a white lace collar and when Lily examined this, she saw that it was very carefully made, with double seams, like something that could have been sewn by Nellie. It lay on her bed at the Foundling Hospital for three years and in the nights, Lily clutched it close to her heart. She named it Bridget.

Now, it sits on a high shelf in Lily's lodgings and looks down on the quiet, shadowy life of Lily-the-Murderer. The tartan dress is faded and worn thin. The flat face, once pink, is grey and stained by time, but Lily knows that she will probably never part with it. She could even ask permission to take it with her to the gallows and place some knotted string round its neck and let it go with her into the great void.

She still thinks about Lady Elizabeth Mortimer, whose name she bears, and sometimes wonders about her 'suitor' and likes to imagine him searching and searching – even inside long-case clocks – for the hoard of silver sixpences and not finding them. For a while, Lily composed letters to Scotland, begging to be taken in, even if she had to spend her days chasing squirrels and stoats in the forest, but she never sent them and now, when all that waits for her is death, it seems fruitless to imagine any other life but the one she has. She imagines Lady Elizabeth in one of her high rooms, bent over as she always was, but with her beautiful face lit by the pearly northern light, and in one of her hands the scrap of embroidery Lily made for her at Rookery Farm. But she is always alone.

Lily wonders whether the suitor became a husband and if so, for how long. In her mind, she sees a tall man, swaggering about the estate, carrying a gun. But she thinks that once this person had found the money, he would have disappeared, taking it all with him in leather suitcases, to set out for the place they call the New World. In this New World there would be vast ravines, like the one which had claimed the life of Uncle Jesse Buck, and in such a place he might now lie dead, unvisited except by birds of prey.

The Gate to Hell

Dreams, Lily decided, played a part in almost everything. They could turn the past into the future. They could send you forth on a path you had once thought of but never dared to take – until now. In the tangled mathematics of your brain, dreams can sometimes lay before you equations which are perfect and correct. And on a certain day, a Sunday afternoon, when she was almost sixteen and dozing by her fire, such a dream had seeped into Lily's mind.

She rose almost at once, without pondering what she was going to do, preferring not to think about it exactly, but only to *see* it, as though it had already happened.

She dressed herself with care, down to some soft-soled shoes, given to her by Belle, which made almost no noise as she walked, her best pair of gloves and a large bonnet that cast a shadow over her face. She took up the sack, wrapped in its linen, and went out. It was an autumn day and as Lily walked towards Coram Fields she saw that the soot-blackened plane trees, wearing their clusters of seeds like dangling jewellery, were shedding huge leaves of every colour of yellow, orange and brown and she thought how fine a thing it was that the world kept changing and that nothing lasted beyond some finite and allotted season.

With her mind preoccupied, she seemed to reach the gates to the Foundling Hospital more quickly than she'd expected. So then she stood before them and paused, looking up at the high walls, deciding that this would be the last time she would ever visit this place. She knocked at the main gate and was admitted and asked by the guards to state her business. She held out the linen-wrapped parcel and said that she'd come to return 'Hospital property' to the Governors. The guards looked at her sleepily. Lily remembered how, on a Sunday, they would often fall to drinking, losing track of the visitors who came and went, and sometimes breaking into ribald laughter at the sight of this or that thing – the Coram cats chasing birds, the boys who fought each other with broken sticks, a carriage horse gone horribly lame. So she knew they wouldn't pay her much attention or note the time of her arrival and she walked slowly away from them towards the entrance, with her mind still serene and her heart steady.

In the grand hall, as she expected, she found a press of people, mainly well-dressed patrons who had come to reassure themselves that the ornate ceilings of the reception rooms were kept painted and gilded and that the children had at least some flesh on their bones under their red-and-beige uniforms. But mingling with these were poor country folk in their fustian, returning fostered children to their unknown fate, women like Nellie, trying to quench the weeping and caterwauling which would break out without warning and echo around the room in gulps and shrieks.

Somewhere beyond the crowd, trying to remain tall and contained behind a desk, Lily saw Mr Hudson, but she didn't think that he'd noticed her. With her face shielded partly by her bonnet and partly by the sack, wrapped in its linen, Lily made her way through the public rooms and down a passage into the heart of the building. She was walking now in a kind of dream daze. It was as if a tiny hurting part of her brain had turned itself into a compass, its agitated pointer hovering perpetually upon North, and all she had to do was follow it. People passed her in the corridors, but paid her no heed and she saw no one she'd ever known. And just as her walk to Coram, with the grand autumn colours of the planes always at the edge of her vision, had seemed short, so now she found herself, in a matter of a few minutes, arriving at the place she sought and here she stopped and stared. In front of her still hung the notice: *Private. No Entry to Children.*

For years and years, Lily had called this 'the Gate to Hell' in her mind, but she'd never uttered these words, never told anyone what happened beyond it in Nurse Maud's room, and how, until she left the Hospital and was apprenticed to Belle Prettywood, the foul 'absolution' was administered again and again to 'Miss Disobedience' and how it grew worse as she got older because it seemed to drive Nurse Maud into a kind of shameless delirium. In this wild state, she would whisper to Lily that it was now the child's 'pious duty' to do the things she wanted and give her 'reciprocal absolution', as beautiful as any word from God. When she'd refused, Nurse Maud had spat in her face. She was told that it would only happen this one time and then she would never be brought back: it would be over. But it was not over. It was not 'one time', but many. Lily could be dragged out of bed in the dead of night by Maud, with the nurse's hand clamped over her mouth to prevent her from crying out. And she came to realise that it would never end. It was Nurse Maud's addiction and it fed upon itself. She was enslaved to it. She would utter foul animal noises. Sometimes she would weep.

Lily had often thought that if Bridget hadn't died, she would have told her what happened in that room, that Bridget and she would have gone together to the Governors and told them that it couldn't be borne, it was against all Christian decency and Nurse Maud should be sent away. But to do this alone ... To spell out the shame of it ... Lily knew that this was impossible. She had to exist in a shrieking forest of silence.

Everything now was done almost silently. This had been the way the dream had unfolded, as though the world had paused just for a brief while, just long enough for the thing to be completed, because it was going to be easy.

Lily opened the door where the notice hung: *No Entry to Children*. But she wasn't a child any more. She was an employee of Belle Prettywood's Wig Emporium, singled out for her neat work. Time had turned and brought her back, not as a helpless baby in a sack nor as a girl torn from her bed by the person some children called 'the Monstrosity', but as Miss Lily Mortimer, who was going to bring an end to the suffering of all those subjected to the warped inclinations of a wicked woman. She was going to lay the past to rest.

She walked quietly along the corridor until she came to the familiar door of Nurse Maud's room. She knew only too well that it could be locked and that the key always hung on a hook above the fireplace, too high for a child to reach, but in her dream it had not been locked.

She had just opened it and walked in, and there she had been, lying in her bed, as if patiently waiting …

Lily reached out to turn the door handle. She noticed that her hand was steady and that all she felt was a cold resolve, no pity, no compassion, no fear of what she was about to do. Her dream had told her the way and it seemed to her now that she had dreamed it not once but many times long ago, years ago, and was disposed to blame herself for not accomplishing the deed sooner.

The room had barely changed. There was no fire in the grate. The wallpaper, an innocent yellow patterned with tiny flowers, looked faded, but it was still there, the childlike backdrop to Nurse Maud's obscene tableau. The screen, behind which Maud had always retreated to wash herself when the 'absolution' was over, still stood to the left of the nightstand. And Nurse Maud? There she lay in the narrow bed, with the sheet stretched tightly over her, but the coverlet hanging down and touching the floor and one of her arms hanging there with it, limp and thin.

She was sleeping. Lily stood still and watched her. Her normally pinched mouth was wide open, showing her backward-sloping teeth, two of which were now missing. A constricted kind of snoring escaped from her throat. Her hair was white. When Lily walked into the room, she didn't stir.

Lily went to the fireplace and found the room key where it had always hung and took it down and walked back to the door and locked it and the sound of this key turning in the lock was so familiar that she could have heard it yesterday and indeed the way the room smelled of mothballs, but also of something else, something sickly, some terrible essence of Nurse Maud, brought back to her all that had happened there, as if no time had passed, as if there could not *be* any time between its passing and its ending, because it would always be with her, always until she died.

Anger, cold and bitter, now held Lily in its grip. She went to the bed and, still wearing her gloves, shook Nurse Maud awake. It would have been so easy to have acted while she still slept, but Lily wanted Maud to recognise her and then to be afraid. Put simply, she wanted her to suffer. The woman stared up at her, with her pale eyes blinking, trying to focus, and Lily felt the heat of her and remembered this, too, the terrible, crawling heat of Nurse Maud's body as it had sought its repulsive 'absolution' from Lily's hand.

'Maud,' said Lily, 'do you know who I am?'

The eyes were like marbles, round and small, moving just a little while the rest of her face, filmed with sweat, seemed to have suffered some kind of petrification and couldn't move. The mouth was still open and the breath coming from it was sour with a laudanum stink.

'Maud,' said Lily again. 'Tell me my name.'

Maud now brought her dangling arm up onto her chest and began kneading it and Lily saw that she was in pain. Then she tried to lift her head from the pillows and Lily acted swiftly. She snatched one of the pillows away and threw it on the floor and Maud's head fell back and Lily said, 'Do you wish to make a confession? If you do, make it swiftly, because darkness is coming. There will be no morning.'

'Miss …' said Maud.

'Yes, that's right. "Miss Disobedience". That's what you always called me, right from the day when I first came here. And you were right. You made me submit to you, but in my heart I never did. You put me in Hell and I endured, but I never surrendered to you. And now I am going to disobey the Sixth Commandment. Can you remember which that is? Yes, of course you can, but you are helpless now. The door's locked. And nobody will hear if you try to call out because I'm going to silence you.'

Lily now saw Nurse Maud's hand try to creep towards her nightstand, towards a little brass bell that stood beside the medicine bottles gathered there, among which was a laudanum jar. Lily whipped the bell away from her reach and carefully set it down further off. Then, leaving the bedside for a moment, she untied the sack from its linen parcel, reached inside it and took out a small handful of the ancient white hair. She moved silently back to Nurse Maud, leaned over her for a second, smelling her breath, feeling her heat, then she crammed the hair into Maud's mouth and closed it with her gloved hand, pressing her head down into the pillow.

The choking began straight away, except that the woman couldn't open her mouth to try to cough. Her throat constricted. Her chest heaved under the tight sheet. The face coloured itself a darkish red, like the colour in a Coram smock. The marble eyes bulged. One of Nurse Maud's hands tried to reach up to Lily, to plead, to beg for what couldn't be given. But Lily didn't even want to look at her any more. With her free hand, she snatched the pillow from the floor, then withdrew her palm from the mouth and with all her strength pressed the pillow down, right over Maud's face, and held it there until she felt the struggle to live begin to fail, and still held it, holding it down and down until her arms ached and Maud's body lay still.

Lily remained calm. She wondered at it, but felt proud and glad. She stared a while longer at Maud's dead face, before lifting up her heavy head and putting the pillow underneath it. Then she moved behind the screen, where the nurse had always kept her few personal belongings in neat array. She took up a pair of scissors. She returned to Nurse Maud's bedside, bent over her, not afraid to look into her marble eyes. Then she cut off a hank of her white hair, opened the dead mouth, filled with phlegm, and pressed in the hair scissored from the dead woman's head and closed her teeth around it, holding the jaw up until it remained closed.

It was at this moment that Lily heard footsteps in the corridor outside the room. She held herself very still. Somebody tried the door handle of the room and called softly: 'Teatime, Maud.' Then, whoever stood there knocked on the door and said, 'Teatime, if you want it, Maud.'

Lily waited. In that difficult moment, she recalled Nellie Buck telling her that stillness in the world was a wonderful thing because people moved about too much and hadn't learned how to patiently attend and not strive with their hearts and their limbs after all that they desired. So she was able to remain quite still, trembling a little, like the dog, Shadow, before she was given the command to round up Perkin's cluster of disobedient sheep. And soon enough, the footsteps resumed and then faded.

Lily cut more white hair and showered it over Maud's neck and over the sheet, which was still pulled tight over the body, like an unforgiving shroud. Then she lifted up Maud's right hand, gone cold, it seemed, in a matter of minutes, and inserted her thin fingers into the handle of the scissors and laid these – hand and scissors – across the nurse's chest. Lastly, she took up the laudanum jar from the night table, unstoppered it and pressed some of Maud's hair down into the liquid. She poured some laudanum over Maud's mouth and laid the bottle next to the hand, letting it spill onto the sheet.

She brushed a few hairs from her gloves and from her skirt. Then she stood back. She looked at the scene as though it were a little theatre tableau, perfectly realised in all its detail. She wanted, now, to go to the girl or girls who had been terrorised by Nurse Maud and tell them that it was over, that their shame was at an end, but she knew she had to try to glide away from the building without stopping for anyone.

Lily folded the sack and put it back in its linen wrapping. She unlocked the door and listened for footsteps in the corridor, but heard none. The public rooms were crowded on a Sunday, but this lightless part of the Hospital was deserted. She stepped out into the passage and closed the door. She turned left and made her way to some backstairs, out of bounds to children. She adjusted her bonnet.

Arriving home as the light faded, Lily felt so tired, it was as if she had spent days and days picking stones out of the earth. She longed for a cool jar of cider and a vision of the tops of the Suffolk hedgerows dancing in the bright air and then to lay herself down on the grass, next to Nellie, and hear Nellie say to her, 'I know what you've done, pet, and it's a fearful thing, but here is my token of forgiveness.' And Nellie would plant a little kiss on her head and then they would both fall asleep with their noses sticking into the meadow grass and only wake when the night came and the owls began calling.

She made herself stay awake long enough to build a fire and stoke it to a good blaze. She burned her gloves and then she burned the sack and when the fire caught at the remaining hair inside it, it flared suddenly with a peculiar yellow flame.

Wedding Picture

The mood at Belle's Emporium is sombre and quiet. After the triumph of *Traviata*, the wig-makers have too little to occupy them. Belle announces that she is in discussion with the Royal Victoria Theatre to provide wigs 'in the late-Georgian style' for a forthcoming production of the popular melodrama *The Murder of Lord Brigham-Twist*, but until this work is agreed, they have to make do with commissions for discreet hairpieces and orders from society hostesses wishing to dress themselves up as courtesans for their late-winter soirées.

London is tormented by freezing fogs, turning daylight to ghostly shadow. Lily walks to work with a shawl pulled over her nose and mouth and when she arrives at Long Acre she finds the shawl stained and damp. She begins to long for springtime, but knows that longing for a future she might not live to see is fruitless.

She hasn't been to church for several weeks, denying herself the consoling light of the windows, afraid of what she feels for Sam Trench, but on a Sunday of particular darkness, she decides that she *has* to see him.

He isn't there.

She keeps turning round as the service progresses. She can't see every face in the congregation, but she knows that, at the back, where he always sits, there is an absence. The absence is so palpable and absolute, it's almost like a presence. She hardly hears the sermon or the prayers.

Her longing, she knows, isn't rational. Sam Trench has a wife he cares for. He fries her golden onions on Sundays. They sleep in the same bed. But then she can't helping thinking about the moment in Le Bone Street when Sam found her wearing the scarlet dress and how he held her and kissed her hair, and how, after that, when he left her, he was overcome with weeping.

The service ends and Lily pulls her shawl around her face, ready to walk out into the fog. She feels sad and hungry, craving consolation, craving sweetness. She's remembering the treacle puddings Nellie sometimes made on Sundays, served up on little tin plates with a blob of yellow cream on top, and thinks, I could have eaten that forever and grown fat like Nellie and not been this thin and sorrowful girl. And I would not be here, longing to be held by a man who can never be mine.

As she leaves, a woman's voice says her name and she looks up and sees Joyce Trench. Joyce wears a fashionable bonnet and her round face underneath it is smiling.

'I was hoping to see you, Lily,' she says. 'I wanted to apologise to you.'

'Apologise?'

'Yes. I'm afraid we were much too forward and interfering in inviting you to stay with us in Chestnut Street. We can see, now, that this was not agreeable to you and I'd like to say that I'm sorry. It was my idea, but we had no right to decide anything for you.'

'Oh …' says Lily. 'No. You had a perfect right. I wouldn't be alive had your husband not saved me. And I'm sorry about the sickness. I'm quite well now.'

'I'm more than pleased about that, because I was hoping … if I saw you … I was hoping you might keep me company today.'

'Keep you company?'

'Yes. Sam is working a Sunday shift. Murders in the capital don't pause for the Sabbath! Especially in this dark weather. I have some lamb chops I was going to fry for my dinner with some cabbage, and we might take a glass of port wine with the meal. What d'you say? You could tell me about Miss Prettywood's triumph with her work for the opera company. I get out so little, I would love to hear about that.'

If it had not been for her hunger, Lily might have said no to Joyce Trench. But the image of the chops and the cabbage and the port is tempting and there's another thought behind this, that to be in Sam's house, where the smell of him – of his cigars or his winter uniform – might certainly linger, would be to feel a little comforted. So she walks through the freezing air, arm in arm with Joyce, and when they reach number 12 Chestnut Street, Joyce banks up a fire in the parlour and they sit beside it, drinking port, while the chops are frying in the kitchen.

Lily tells Joyce about *La Traviata* and the wig she'd made for Violetta's last scene and how Belle Prettywood's tears had spilled over her bosom and down onto the velvet rim of the box. Joyce says, 'Oh mercy, to be so carried away! How I long for that. My life has been very ordinary.'

Lily wants to say that she doesn't think it would be 'ordinary' to lie in Sam Trench's arms, to feel his heart-beat close to her own, to share his sadness, his bravery and his delight. But instead she keeps talking about the opera and how Violetta briefly believes that love can save her, that if only Alfredo would return to stay by her side, then she wouldn't die.

'I suppose that's the kind of thing they have to believe in a music show,' says Joyce, 'isn't it?'

'Yes,' says Lily. 'But perhaps it does turn out like that, sometimes, in a life, that if people show us love, we can come back from dying.'

'"Come back from dying"? I don't think so, pet. Love isn't a medicine, is it?'

'No. But love can give us hope.'

'Hope for what? Look what happens to your Violetta person: she hopes her lover will make her well and in the next ten minutes she's dead in his arms. Now, forgive me a minute, but I must go and see that the chops aren't burning. Drink up your port, Lily. It will bring a little colour to your face.'

While Joyce is gone, Lily looks around the small parlour, neat in its every particular, with antimacassars placed over the backs of the armchairs and a collection of china teapots on display in a glass cabinet. Then Lily notices that there is a daguerreotype hanging on the wall. She gets up and goes to look at it. It's gone brown with time and even the brown is fading from the bottom, as if encroached upon by rising sea foam, but above this, two faces – Joyce's and Sam's – defiantly stare out, and along the bottom of the picture somebody has written *Wedding Day, August 2nd, 1855.* So there they sit, side by side, holding still for the photograph, with, on their features, expressions of extreme solemnity, as if this might have been a funeral day. Sam wears a top hat and his high collar and knotted bow are neat. Joyce wears a lace cap, adorned a little with trailing ribbons, over obedient dark curls. Her face is smooth but plump. Sam's brown eyes look very dark and Joyce's rather pale, as though the light which reached them wasn't the same light, or else, just at the moment when the picture was being taken, something ghostly passed across Joyce's gaze.

Joyce returns and sees Lily examining the wedding picture and says, 'Oh, think now, twelve years ago, that was! Look how young we were.'

'You look beautiful, Joyce,' says Lily.

'You're very kind, but not really, pet. I never was anything but ordinary. And where were you in 1855?'

'Oh,' says Lily. 'I was still at Nellie Buck's farm in Suffolk. Nobody told me until the last minute that I had to go to the Foundling Hospital. I thought I'd be with Nellie forever.'

Joyce sighs. She puts more coals on the fire as she says, 'I've always thought it was a bad business, sending babies away and then bringing them back into that place. Because from what I've heard tell from Sam, when he tried to visit you to see how you were getting on ... from what I've heard, there's a lot of cruelty going on there. Aren't I right?'

'That's because the children mean nothing to anyone,' says Lily. 'We are just the carriers of the sins of our mothers. And so nobody gives us any love.'

'It's all wrong, I think. I always have. Probably, the Governors do their best, but you know bad things happen there.'

'I know.'

'About a year ago, there was a strange death. I don't know if you heard about it. One of the nurses strangled or poisoned or something, I can't remember. Sam was sent for. At first sight, it looked to him like a peculiar accident, the poor creature had choked on laudanum and her heart had stopped. But he told me, plain as daylight, he thought there was something contrived about it and that there might have been a crime.'

'Oh,' says Lily. 'What was contrived?'

'I can't remember. The local police had been called and concluded it was an accident, but they passed it to the Detective Department, just to be sure, and they asked for Sam because they knew that he knew the place. Sam interrogated some of the Hospital staff, but he learned nothing from them and he told me he thought they were keeping quiet, hushing things up, if you get my meaning.'

'I wonder why they would do that.'

'Well, Sam told me he'd heard rumours that this person – the one who died – was warped. That was the word he used, "warped". And whoever killed her – if indeed she was killed – then this was the reason: unmentionable things had happened.'

Lily returns quickly to her chair and drains the last sip of the port. She knows she's trembling and tries to conceal this by placing her hands firmly on her knees. Joyce moves away from the wedding picture and sits opposite Lily.

'Are you all right, pet?' she asks. 'You look pale.'

'Yes,' says Lily. 'It's only that when I remember the Hospital ...'

'It upsets you. I can understand that. We won't talk about it any more.'

Lily is silent for a moment, then she asks, 'Is Sam looking for a killer?'

'No. I don't think so. He says there are no leads of any substance. But if it really was a murder, he thinks there will be a confession.'

'A confession?'

'That's what Sam believes. He says he's certain of it. The children at Coram are taught to fear God so absolutely that if it was one of them who committed the crime, the burden of it ... the guilt ... these would become intolerable in due time and so a confession will come. And then he will understand the motive. In his work, so he tells me, you would be surprised at how often a murderer confesses. It's one of the things we find hardest, isn't it, living with our own wickedness?'

Lily looks down at her hands, trying once again to hold them still. She wants to say, 'I killed Nurse Maud, I stuffed her throat with hair. I was thrown to the wolves in a sack full of hair and I thought this was a fitting death for vile Maud, who almost left me to die a second time – die of shame. But I murdered her not just to avenge what happened to me but to protect the girls who came after me,' yet she knows that if a confession is going to come forth, then it will not be to Joyce Trench.

Joyce picks up a piece of embroidery on a frame and begins idly stitching.

'The chops won't be long,' she says. 'And I have a few stewed plums for afterwards, if you like those. Sam is hoping to be back in time for the plums.'

'Oh,' says Lily, 'oh ...'

The afternoon begins to slip by. The plums are sweet.

Then Sam is there. His face looks burnt from the cold. His hair is wet.

He hangs up his heavy police overcoat and sits down at the table. He addresses Lily as 'Miss Mortimer' and tells her he is glad to see her. She finds herself blushing and can't think of anything to say to him. She looks down at what remains of the dish of plums and passes it

to him, but he waves it away. He rubs his eyes. His tired-
ness makes him appear wounded. He says to Joyce that
he will take a glass of port and when she goes out to fetch
the bottle from the parlour, Sam raises his head and stares
at Lily and she knows what this burning look means; it's
the look of a stricken Alfredo watching Violetta, lost to
him for always.

The silence between them is difficult to endure.
Looking defiantly into Sam's troubled eyes, Lily ventures,
'Joyce told me that last year you went to investigate a
death at the Foundling Hospital.'

'Yes,' says Sam. 'The local police called me in. One of
the nurses choked to death on her own hair – or the
scene was dressed to suggest that this was how she died.
A most horrible way to die, and unusual, do you not
think?'

'Unusual?'

'I've never, in all my years with the Department,
witnessed anybody die this way. She had been drinking
laudanum, of course, and cutting her hair at the same
time and so might have accidentally got a tangle of hair
in her mouth. But I feel that it is unlikely.'

'Oh,' says Lily. 'I see. So the case is still open?'

'Yes. But we've not made much progress with it.
Nobody at the Hospital wants to talk about it. What is
your instinctive feeling about it?'

Lily manages to hold herself very still, very calm, as
she replies, 'Some of the nurses at the Hospital were
kind, but some were not. When children are treated
unkindly, their natures can turn towards darkness.'

'So you think it could have been one of the inmates?
I have heard rumours that this nurse was warped in her
mind and abused the bodies of her charges for her own

gratification, but I have no proof of it. Do you recall any such accusation?'

'No.'

'Rumours of that kind might easily circulate in an institution and the nurse may be quite innocent.'

Joyce returns with the bottle of port and pours a glass for Sam. He drinks gratefully. Joyce smiles at him – her caring husband, her hard-working man – and he smiles back at her and says, 'It's nice to be home and to find Lily here. I hope you have both eaten a good dinner.'

'Oh yes,' says Joyce as she sits down. She looks from Sam's face to Lily's and back to Sam's. A question seems about to form on her lips, but she thinks better of it and turns her head away, to stare for a moment at the darkening afternoon.

'The world is to blame'

The commission from the Royal Victoria Theatre comes through. Belle Prettywood gets out her sheafs of designs for Georgian wigs and places orders for a great quantity of yak belly hair and mohair 'to give bulk to these wonderful exaggerations'. Actresses of all ages and types come to Long Acre to have their heads measured and behave like exotic parakeets, fluttering round the work-room, squawking and exclaiming, and the room is scented with their perfume and with the dried sweat of their silken underarms.

Lily asks which one of them will kill Lord Brigham-Twist, but they refuse to tell her. 'Mustn't spoil a good murder, ducky,' they say, 'must we? You come and see the show and you'll find out! Do us some lovely pompadour hair and we'll stand you a fourpenny gallery seat.'

Winter is departing at last. On the limbs of the plane trees fresh little wounds of green appear. The air is clearer, the sun no longer a burnished coin, but a wide cloak of light. When Lily walks to work, she wonders whether the innocence of the weather might be telling her that death has moved further off.

The wig-makers begin work. Belle's sketches for the Georgian wigs are passed from hand to hand, all remarking on her fine draughtsmanship, and Belle yodels with laughter and says, 'Well, don't waste time comparing me to Michelangelo, make sensible use of the yak.' And

Lily notices that Belle is becoming more and more excited and restless. She begins new sketches, wearing out charcoal and pencil lead with heavy shading, smudging this with her thumb, then tearing up the drawings and throwing them into her little furnace. She seems to take refuge in her abacus, slamming the beads back and forth with passionate intensity, impatient with every sum. Sometimes, she rushes into the workroom and rummages in the new bales of mohair brought in by the Shift, holding strands of it to the light, then hurling them away. Sometimes, she whirls from work station to work station, moving blocking points on the muslin foundation caps or, where the stitching has begun, seizing a knotting hook and a strand of yak hair and performing a deft double knot so swiftly that the manoeuvre appears like a magic trick. Now and then, she utters what sound like little cries of terror and Julia Buchanan, always frank and direct in her utterances, turns to Lily and whispers, 'I really see no need for her to go around shrieking like that. We're not a tribe of monkeys.'

Then, one day, Belle isn't there.

The wig-makers go patiently on with their work. The colossal Georgian perruques are slowly beginning to acquire bulk and form. Only Mrs Buchanan remarks on Belle's absence and says the shrieking may have been a sign of something worrying that no one could foresee. Lily keeps glancing at the door, listening for the sound of her click-clacking footfall on the stairs and feeling troubled when she doesn't hear it.

The day draws to its end and the following morning arrives and Belle's booth remains empty. Lily goes in there and notices that her stove is choked with ash. Her desk is smothered with letters, bills, sketches, lists, press clippings, accounts ledgers, calling cards, broken pencils, sticks of charcoal, samples of muslin and an unexpected drift of five-pound notes, like translucent white leaves. Lily collects up the money and places it in the tin box where Belle keeps small change and assorted bits of jewellery and locks this away. But when she looks closely at the disorder on the desk, she sees that it's accumulated there very fast, in the brief time of Belle's hectic beating of the abacus, her intermittent cries and her whirlwind forays into the workroom, and wonders if all this didn't signal something strange going on in her head.

As soon as the workday is over, Lily sets out for Seven Dials. Arriving hot and tired at Belle's house, she is ushered in by Belle's maid, Hetty, whose expression of terror tells her everything she believes she already knew. 'Miss Belle is gone peculiar,' says Hetty. 'She won't move from her bed and whatever I give her to eat, she spits it away.'

'Did you call a doctor?' asks Lily.

'She won't have it,' says Hetty. 'She won't have anyone near her. She says she's being poisoned. And her waist is all on fire.'

'What d'you mean?'

'I don't know. A rash, I think. Or a sore. She won't let me see it. So what am I to do? I'm all alone. Gentlemen have called, as usual, but she won't see them neither. She says she hopes they'll burn in hell.'

'Can I see her?' asks Lily.

'I don't know, miss. You can try. But she cries out, you know. She cries out that she is dying, and the world is to blame. Happen she'll consider you a part of that world.'

Lily sits down on a settle in Belle's hallway and asks for a cup of water. As Hetty goes to fetch it, Lily looks around at the expensive panelling and at a portrait of Belle, ravishing and young in a scarlet dress. Hetty returns with the water and when Lily looks at this – London water, which is always and ever tainted – she finds herself thinking once again about the well at Rookery Farm and the nameless boy who lived under the mud a hundred feet down into the earth. And Lily is suddenly aware that even though eleven years have passed since she left Suffolk, her mind refuses to forget it, as if it were a magic-lantern show going on and on in slow rotation behind her eyes. On and on and never ceasing.

Lily is shown up to Belle's room. Belle lies in her big brocaded bed with her hair in a kind of tangled halo, almost covering the pillow. When she sees Lily, she reaches out for her, and Lily bends down and holds her and Belle begins to cry. There is sweat on Belle's neck and her body is clearly in the grip of a fever. As she weeps, she's trying to speak, but Lily can't make out what it is that she wants to say.

Hetty stands at the door with her fingers in her mouth, the sad picture of a person who feels that something is being asked of her, but who doesn't know what that something is.

'Go downstairs, Hetty,' says Lily gently, 'and bring a bowl of cool water and some rags.'

Hetty goes. Belle's weeping diminishes into a breathless gulping. Lily lays her back on her pillow and brushes strands of hair from her wet cheeks. She waits for Belle to speak and eventually she does. 'Everything is lost,' she says.

Lily takes up one of Belle's burning hands and holds it in hers, which is cool and soft.

'What d'you mean, Belle?' she asks.

'I mean that I know what's happened to me. I shall tell you, Lily, because you won't judge me, but I can't tell anyone else, or I will be ruined.'

Lily waits. She thinks in that instant that the picture her mind has always made of Belle Prettywood is of a woman in control of everything and everyone in her carousel of a life. From Monday to Monday, from one ambitious commission to the next, from the sequences of wild arithmetic assembled on her abacus, from lover to lover tangling and rejoicing in her apricot boudoir, she seems to surface with a striding step and a glittering smile. That such a person could now be talking about 'ruin' feels quite wrong.

'Belle . . .' she begins.

'I do not lie. I will be shunned. I will be nothing. Even the Wig Emporium will close. I will lose my house. I will become a pauper.'

'I don't know what you mean. You have a slight fever, that's all.'

'No, it is not a "slight fever", Lily. I am to be punished as soundly as God ever punishes anyone: I have the pox.'

Belle closes her eyes, as though the saying of this most terrible word has exhausted her. Lily looks down at her, remembering her recent agitation and recalling that she had been told in a lecture on 'moral turpitude' at the Foundling Hospital that this kind of restless behaviour could sometimes precede the arrival of other symptoms of the disease – symptoms which would, bit by bit, engulf you and bring your life to naught.

Lily is still holding Belle's hand. She strokes it gently as she says, 'There are cures. And are there not physicians who will administer them in secret, so that the world may not hear anything of it?'

'Yes. And I know one of them, who was my lover for a time. But he described the only known cure, which is mercury.'

'Well?'

'Mercury ravages before it cures. It peels away your skin. Your body feels as though insects were crawling on your flesh. Your teeth rot and your hair falls out and your heart is condemned to beat so fast, it will wear itself out and suddenly cease. Is this what I am to undergo?'

'They told us at Coram that all cures are painful. Acceptance of pain is part of what enables the cure to do its work.'

'Did you believe that?'

'Yes. I was shown it. Pain and shame, both. But we won't speak of that, Belle. We will speak of finding a cure for you. A cure that doesn't harm your heart.'

'It doesn't exist, Lily. I know I have been wanton. Look around this room and you will see how I made a little boudoir for pleasure. I have been no better than Violetta. Remember how she sings that nothing signifies in life but the joys of the body? It's been my way to indulge them all. And now I'm doomed to die a terrible death.'

Hetty returns at this moment, bringing water and rags, which she sets down beside the bed. She lingers until Belle turns her face towards her and says, 'Hetty, I know that you're very tired. You may take yourself to your bed now. Miss Mortimer is going to stay with me tonight and in the morning you must confect something nourishing for her: make pancakes and boil chocolate. Is that clear?'

Hetty gapes. Lily imagines that this look of astonishment has frequently afflicted this poor girl, showing, in her open mouth, teeth that appeared to vex each other by leaning this way and that and giving no ground in which they might have grown straight. Lily seldom sees Belle outside the workplace, but Hetty, all alone in the house (where – it has been rumoured – even the Prince of Wales himself could sometimes be found beached up in Miss Prettywood's bed), must have been witness to human behaviour she'd never thought to witness and consequently goes about her work in a state of almost perpetual disbelief. Now, Hetty manages to close her mouth, bob a tiny curtsey and retreat from the room as fast as she can.

As soon as she's gone, Belle says, 'I shall get rid of her before she can spread any rumours. You will move in with me, Lily, as I wanted you to do some time ago. Only now you will have to nurse me and keep everything a secret.'

Lily turns her attention to the bowl of water, wets a rag and begins to wipe some of the sweat from Belle's forehead. Then she says, 'I will stay, Belle, but I can't nurse you night and day. You know I must be in Long Acre doing my work. The Georgian wigs are yet to be finished.'

'Let Mrs Buchanan oversee it. What's the title of their foolish play? *The Murder of Lord Testicle* or some such nonsensical thing. And the down payment the Royal Victoria promised has never been received in total. I have a good mind to say to them, "Here, take your half-finished merchandise and make what you can of it. If you won't pay me, you are not entitled to my services."'

The night closes in on Seven Dials.

By candlelight, Lily is shown the rash at Belle's waist. She immediately remembers that Perkin Buck was once afflicted with something like this and took to his bed. 'I've seen this before,' she says to Belle. 'And it was not the pox, Belle. They called it "the shingles".'

'The shingles? I've never heard of that. I suppose one dies of it in due time?'

'No. Perkin Buck didn't die.'

'But did he have to suffer mercury poisoning?'

'I don't think so. He rested and we fed him apple sauce and he got well.'

'Apple sauce? Is that all? You mean I shouldn't despair?'

Lily takes up a hairbrush and begins to smooth Belle's hair and says, 'On no account should you despair, Belle,' and she sees Belle's face spread itself into a wide, relieved smile. She says nothing, but Lily watches her whole body begin to relax and then her eyes close and she lies her back on the pillows. Lily moves the candle further off so that Belle's face is in shadow. She waits until Belle's breathing becomes heavy and regular, then looks around the room for something soft to lie on. She's hungry, but she sets this aside. She crosses to a low chaise longue and covers herself with a silk peignoir she finds draped there and tries to rest.

She feels hot and exhausted. The air in the scented room is stale and close and Lily longs to open a window on the cool March night, but, afraid to wake Belle, Lily realises now what's happening to her: she's become entangled in the huge and complex web that is Belle Prettywood's life and she's afraid for where this is going to lead her. Then she remembers that nothing, really, is going to lead her anywhere. What waits for her is death, sudden and swift, and she has the feeling that it's coming closer.

A Cage of Larks

The night seems to deliver fresh terrors to Belle. Each time Lily manages to fall asleep, she's woken by loud shrieking and when the morning comes Belle is in a delirium, barely conscious, and the bed is soaked with sweat.

Near seven o'clock, with a dense mist greying the facades of Seven Dials, Lily goes to look for Hetty, to help her to wash Belle and change her sheets. She finds Hetty's room in the attic of the house. The narrow bed is stripped, Hetty's maid's uniform is folded on a wooden chair, the washstand is clean and empty and no possessions are visible on any surface. Lily says Hetty's name, as though she imagined she were hiding somewhere, playing a game of *cache-cache*, but she knows this is a vain hope; the girl has gone.

Lily sits down on the bed, resting her elbows on her knees. Outside, along the gutters, pigeons are peering through the fog, making their repetitive, companionable call, and Lily remembers asking Nellie Buck what the birds were saying and Nellie answered that they had only ever learned one lament through all the long cascade of years:

My toe bleeds, Nellie. My toe bleeds, Nellie.

'That's all they say, pet,' announced Nellie. 'You would have thought the toe might have healed itself by now, wouldn't you – unless they'd lost it altogether, like you did – but on they murmur, on and on,' and Lily said,

'I expect my toe did bleed when the wolf crunched it off,' and Nellie scooped Lily into her arms and kissed her cheek and said, 'No need to think of it any more. Look how you can run and leap on your nine toes!'

When the pigeons fall silent for a moment, Lily hears another sound and knows that it's Belle calling out for her, but she doesn't move. She feels so tired and confused that her body yearns only to be still. She's alone with Belle Prettywood and her illness, which might or might not become very grave, and she has no idea what she's going to have to do.

Again, with a numb sadness, she longs for Nellie to be by her side. She imagines Nellie rolling up her sleeves and saying, 'Very well, now steady yourself, Lily, one thing at a time. Let's just do one thing and then the next thing and the next.' And she knows that the first thing is to wash Belle and make her as comfortable as she can, but when she hears a clock sounding the half-hour, she remembers that she would normally be preparing herself to go to Long Acre, and it occurs to her that a message must somehow be taken to Julia Buchanan. Mrs Buchanan is one of those souls whose experience of life has been so meagre, it has left vacancies in her head which she has filled with a low murmuration of disapproval. But although her words can be tart, she's not unkind and seems to have been indifferent towards the favouritism shown to Lily by Belle.

Lily rises up from Hetty's hard bed, searches for paper and pen and ink and writes a hasty note to Julia Buchanan explaining where she is, alone in the house *with Miss Prettywood, who has taken a bad fever, which might signify the shingles,* and asking her, *in the absence of any other soul,* to come and help her.

She goes out into Seven Dials, where the sun is slowly creeping through the mist, and searches for one of those ragged children whose whole existence is lived out on the streets and whose knowledge of London is so wide and deep it enables them to survive by all the surprising means a child's mind can discover. She finds a girl trying to sell a little cage of larks for a sixpenny piece. Lily tells the girl she will pay a shilling for the larks if, in return, she will take her note to Mrs Buchanan at the Wig Emporium on Long Acre.

The child stares at the coin put into her palm, and quickly pockets it. Lily takes the caged birds and the girl takes Lily's letter and makes to run off. But Lily catches her by her torn sleeve and says, 'If my note does not arrive at the correct address, I will know, and I will kill the larks. And then, because I am a murderer, I will come for you.'

'Did you say *murderer*, miss?'

'Yes, I did. So you had better run as fast as you can to Long Acre.'

The girl rushes away. Lily goes back into Belle's house. She stands in the hall, listening for Belle's cries, but all is quiet.

One thing and then the next thing and the next.

Lily heats water in the kitchen. While she waits for it to warm, she searches for food in Belle's larder and finds a bowl of cream and a loaf of stale bread and she tears at this and dips the torn pieces into the cream and crams them into her mouth, and for some reason, she frames a picture in her mind of Joyce Trench cutting lamb chops on her china plate into smaller and smaller pieces before attempting to chew them. And these images at once guide her towards Sam. She looks at the larks, fluttering in their cage, and thinks, I would like to take one little bird and put it into Sam's hands, and he would be tender towards it and care for it, and whenever he saw it, he would think of me.

Then, she takes the cage to the window and opens it and holds it out into the air. For a moment, the larks don't move and then, suddenly, they are gone.

Washing Belle is a mighty task. Her body appears large and strong, but her illness has made her weak and her limbs seem to fall where they are not meant to fall and whenever Lily touches her waist, she screams in agony. All the time the washing is going on, Belle clings to Lily – to her arm, to her neck, to her waist, whatever is within reach – and Lily keeps talking to her gently, saying she is going to make everything dry and clean and then send out for laudanum to reduce her fever and her pain.

'Chloroform,' mumbles Belle. 'Find me that.'

Lily says she thinks a doctor would be needed to administer chloroform and when Belle hears the word 'doctor' she shakes her head violently. 'No, no, no,' she says. 'Because I cannot yet be sure this is not the pox, and if word gets out, I am ruined. Are there not … what might one call them … *booths* selling chloroform upon street corners?'

'No,' says Lily. 'I do not think so, Belle. I think you must have imagined that.'

'Ah,' says Belle, 'but I am certain they must be there. For who does not need oblivion from time to time? And this is what I must have now, for the agony is too much, Lily, too much …'

'I know,' says Lily, who has managed to turn Belle over and is now gently soaping her buttocks and the backs of her legs.

'You do not know,' says Belle. 'You have not suffered like this.'

'No,' says Lily. 'Not exactly like this. But at the Coram Hospital I suffered. I was tormented and violated by one of the nurses.'

'Violated? Is that the word you mean?'

'Yes. But I've put an end to it – to save the other girls who came after me.'

'Put an end to it, how?'

'I silenced her.'

Belle lies still. Lily begins drying her with a soft towel.

'Are you telling me that you killed her?' asks Belle.

'I killed her in my mind,' says Lily. 'She choked and suffocated.'

Belle is silent. She lies still and lets the drying of her legs go gently on. It's as if the mysteries of the conversation have distracted her from her own pain. After a while, she says, 'I don't believe you could kill, Lily. I've known men who have killed and they all have one thing in common: they believe they are exceptional, that no moral constraint touches them because they are in a category of their own. But you are not like them.'

It is now Lily's turn to be quiet. As she finishes her task and goes to find clean sheets for Belle's bed, she is surprised to realise that in the space of not more than an hour she has confessed to two people that she is a murderer. The idea that neither of them necessarily believes her is not significant. What counts is the realisation that a confession is rising and rising slowly within her, rising and rising of its own dark accord, and must soon enough come out. The admissions she's made today are brief rehearsals and neither, in the end, will matter one way or the other. She will betray herself to Sam and to no one else. And this is how she sees it, this inevitable confession, like the small bird she imagined putting into his hands and which he gently cradled.

As soon as Belle's bed is made up with fresh sheets and she can lie back on her pillows, she seems comforted a little and tells Lily to find Hetty and ask her to make some beef broth, 'for I have taken nothing for two days and I'm as hollow as a drain.'

'I will make it,' says Lily.

'No, no. You have done enough. When I've had the broth, I will sleep. You must go to Long Acre and report back to me on the progress of *Lord Testicle*'s wigs. And send a stern letter to the Royal Victoria saying we shall cease all our endeavours on their behalf if they do not pay the deposit owing. Just because I am dying, this does not mean I will surrender to bankruptcy.'

'You're not dying, Belle.'

'I warrant this "shingle" disease kills in the end, I'm sure it does. Now go and see what has become of Hetty.'

Lily smooths Belle's coverlet, then turns and looks towards the handsome window of the room and sees that the early mist has quite vanished and the sun is shining.

'Hetty has left,' she says.

'Left? Do you mean gone for good?'

'I think so. She left her uniform folded on a chair.'

'Well, good heavens,' says Belle, 'what are young girls made of these days? Spun sugar? The first sign of suffering and they run from the fairground. Now what am I to do?'

'I will care for you, just as you asked. I will make apple sauce.'

'No. I was quite wrong when I suggested you would do this. You are my best worker. You must take charge of everything at Long Acre.'

'Julia can do it. I won't leave you all alone, Belle. I cannot.'

'Well. We will think about what to do. Make the broth. There is always some beef in the larder. I keep it to feed my gentlemen. Making love to Belle Prettywood, I am told, augments the appetite for red meat.'

As she foretold, Belle falls asleep the moment she has taken a few sips of the broth. Lily closes the curtains and takes the bowl away and tiptoes out of the room.

She goes down to the kitchen and eats the rest of the bread and cream and some old apples she finds in a crate. She peels and cores the rest of the fruit and shaves a piece from a cone of sugar to put with them for the sauce. Once this is made, she sleeps for a while, with her head on the table, and wakes to see by the light outside that the afternoon has come on and she realises that there's no sign of Julia Buchanan and seems to know that her letter has never reached Long Acre. She imagines the ragged girl tearing up the paper and throwing the pieces into the air, then running on even as far as the river and sitting, watching the commerce that never ceases there, then taking her precious shilling out of her pocket and holding it in her open palm and being seized with a trembling excitement that the giver of the money called herself a murderer.

Seigneur

For three days and nights, Lily cares for Belle, spooning apple sauce into her mouth and only leaving the house to buy more beef for the broth, a loaf of new bread, a quart of milk, some hard cheese, a salve for the rash which has spread round Belle's waist and a jar of laudanum. She sleeps in Belle's room, on the chaise longue, and is woken by the conversations Belle has with the people in her dreams. One of these people is a man she addresses as 'Seigneur' and Belle seems to be made restless and excited by her reveries of him. With the Seigneur she appears to believe that she's dancing. She tells him that the quadrille is amusing, but why, she asks, does he not hold her more closely to him in a waltz?

'Who is the Seigneur?' Lily asks one morning, as she applies the salve and brushes Belle's hair.

'Oh,' says Belle, 'no one and everyone. All men believe they are lords, or even gods, isn't that so?'

'I don't know,' says Lily. 'I have no experience of them.'

'Well,' says Belle, 'that is just as well. They give you the pox in the end. But is there no boy that you have loved?'

Lily finishes the brushing and Belle lies back gratefully on the pillow. Lily looks down at the grey hairs trapped in the bristles of the hairbrush and says, 'Not a boy. There was a man I thought I loved.'

'You *thought*?'

'He held me once. Just held me to him. And I was at peace. But I've run away from him.'

'Why?'

'Because I think he will lead me to my death, one way or the other.'

'You mean you could die of love?'

'Perhaps I could. Or I will confess my wickedness to him and be punished.'

'What wickedness are you talking about?'

Lily realises that being told of troubles outside her own suffering seems to take away some of Belle's pain.

'Well,' she says, 'I have met this man's wife. She's a kind and tender person. Yet ... he and I ... we didn't speak of it, but I know that we could have betrayed her. I mean that we could have become lovers.'

'Oh, and that is all?' says Belle. 'You call that "wickedness"?'

'Yes. That is all. But it is very wicked in my mind.'

On the third evening, a gentleman arrives. He's portly and garbed in a coat with a fur collar and his hair is curled. Lily shows him into the turquoise parlour, where the white curtains have been drawn. He sheds his coat and tells her that he knows his way to Belle's boudoir and when Lily informs him that she has 'a high fever and can see no one', he swears under his breath, but then seems to collect himself and revert to some kind of aristocratic courtesy. He asks Lily what is being done to make Miss Prettywood well again.

Lily wants to say that a doctor should be found, but remembering how desperately Belle wishes to keep her illness a secret, explains only that she is all alone, after the departure of Hetty, and wonders whether a nurse might be hired somehow.

'A nurse? Well, naturally,' says the gentleman. 'It is only a question of money.'

Lily now remembers the drift of five-pound notes she discovered across Belle's desk at Long Acre and is about to speak of it when the gentleman says, 'Belle Prettywood, I think, is certainly not short of a shilling. Shall I ask her if she would like me to procure someone suitable for her?'

'I will ask her,' says Lily. 'What is your name, sir?'

'I do not give my name here. Belle addresses me as her Seigneur. I am quite in love with her, so I do believe I should be the one to go to her now.'

'No,' says Lily. 'She doesn't wish it.'

'Well, she may not wish it, but I do. Indeed, I have a very pressing need of her. Stay here, little child, and I will see to everything.'

Before Lily can protest further, the Seigneur sweeps by her and makes for the stairs. Lily wants to run ahead of him to warn Belle, but he blocks her way with his large body and out of his pocket takes a fistful of coins, which he drops at her feet.

'I've known Belle for seven years,' he says. 'I never harm her. Trust me, whoever you are. She and I have a very good understanding.'

Lily lets him go. He's too large and too insistent to fight with. She begins to pick up the money he's scattered around her and is surprised to find that the coins include a golden sovereign. She doubts that he meant to give her this, but she pockets it, then creeps back upstairs to listen outside Belle's room.

She hears nothing for several minutes, but after a while a loud bellowing noise begins, like the strange, agitated cry of the walrus, and she knows what this is and wonders that Belle, in all her sufferings, can endure it. Lily is at first repelled by the sound, but then, sitting mute on the stairs, struggling with her own exhaustion, she closes her eyes and allows herself to imagine at last how it would be to let Sam Trench make love to her.

She lets him come near and he enfolds her, as he did before. Then he kisses her mouth and his kiss is deep and abiding and can only lead them onwards towards the thing she has forsworn to do. Always, she has thought of this as an act of great wickedness – on her part and on Sam's – but listening to the animal rapture of a stranger now suddenly obscures all idea of sin and transgression and replaces it with longing. But then she reminds herself, as the noise from above becomes louder, diminishes and then stops, that it cannot be, it can never be. Sam Trench saved her life but cannot be her lover. Her gift to him will not be her virgin body, but her confession. She covers her ears with her hands, as if this gesture could stop her untamed thoughts, but still they linger.

Lily goes down to the kitchen and boils water to make coffee to calm the longing which seems to be felt deep in her womb and to keep herself awake through whatever the night will bring. Her neck hurts from sleeping on the chaise longue. She thinks with affection of her basement room and her cot and her scarlet dress hanging on the curtain rail and how the dress seemed to make her beautiful. She lays her head on the kitchen table and is soon asleep.

The Seigneur finds her there. His curled hair is wild.

'Just a fever,' he says. 'That is all she has.'

'Why do you say "all", sir?'

'Because these come and go when you live the life Belle Prettywood has. It is nothing serious. If she could accommodate me in her usual immoderate style, which she did, then she cannot be in the grip of anything profound, can she?'

'She is ill, sir. There is a rash on her body. I have cared for her the best I can for three days.'

'I saw no rash. Or only a very small one. And the fever will pass. It *must* pass, because I cannot live sanely without Belle Prettywood. But I will send a nurse to her tomorrow. She needs a maid, too, by the look of her room. I will pay and store up credit for my visits here. I like her so much, I expect she will bankrupt me in the end, as, perhaps, she is bankrupting half the noble lords in London, but I do not seem to be able to do anything about it.'

He passes a hand through the disarrangement that is now afflicting his hair.

'Do me a favour, Miss Lily,' he says. 'You see, I know your name now! Rearrange my curls, will you? I must go from here with all my dignity intact, to enjoy a peaceful late supper with my wife.'

'Your wife?'

'Yes. Now attend to my hair, little lamb. Be a peach and do that. Then I will be on my way.'

'I have no brush or comb, sir.'

'Use your hands. You have small, sweet fingers, I note. Just settle the style the way it should be.'

She hesitates, but then does as he asks, smoothing and primping his brown hair. The smell of his body is strong, slightly sour, and she remembers that the scent of Sam

Trench is not like this, but like the smell of sunlight on the harvest at Rookery Farm.

'So, Miss Lily,' he says as she works on his hair. 'Tell me, does Belle ever speak of me? I'm tormented to find myself yearning for her affection.'

'Yes. She does. She calls you her Seigneur.'

'Is that all? Does she never speak of me with longing?'

'I don't know about "longing". I think she dreamed, once, that she was dancing with you.'

'Dancing? I'm an infernally clumsy dancer. But on the other hand, that might be a sign of her affection, might it not?'

'Indeed it might, particularly if she knows you do not dance very well.'

'Hah! A little mockery. Good. I like mockery, especially in the very young. And it serves me right for parading my feelings. Now, are my curls in place?'

'Yes, sir, I think they are in place.'

The Seigneur gets up. 'Tell me one last thing, Miss Lily,' he says. 'Is it true that the Prince of Wales comes here?'

'I wouldn't know, sir. My lodgings are in Le Bone Street.'

'I see. I've heard it put about that he's in love with Belle Prettywood too, but who can say? Now, you take care of the dear lady and I will make sure a nurse is sent over tomorrow.'

The Seigneur hoists on his heavy coat, then looks hard at Lily and touches her face tenderly with his gloved hand.

'Beautiful,' he says. 'Almost.'

★

Belle is sleeping when Lily goes to her room. Her bedclothes are tangled, but when Lily lays a hand on her forehead, she finds it cool for the first time in three days.

After a while she crosses to the chaise longue and lies down and closes her eyes. Something like hunger gnaws at her, but she can't say whether it is for food or for sleep or for love, or even for death.

Kensal Green

The following day, two women arrive at Belle's house. They tell Lily they have been hired by 'Monsieur le Seigneur' for a period of fourteen days. They have agreed upon nursing duties and housekeeping, but wish to be addressed courteously by their surnames, which are Miss Smith and Miss Smythe. They are 'trained professional people', not servants.

When Lily tells Belle of their arrival, she laughs. 'How will I ever remember which is which?' she says. But then she draws Lily to her and says, 'Instruct them to treat me kindly – as you would treat me.'

'I will, Belle.'

'And now, listen to me. Go back to work. Make sure the Georgian wigs are correct. Send a letter to the Victoria Theatre reminding them what they owe me. Forge my signature. Threaten them with my wrath.'

'Should I not stay here with you?'

'No. Smith and Smythe will care for me. What else is there for them to do? And work at Long Acre must go on, or I shall be ruined. But in the case that I am dying, I want you to go, after work, to see the men at the General Cemetery Company and reserve me a place at the Kensal Green interment park.'

'What, Belle?'

'You heard me. Some people I know have joined what they call funeral clubs, but I know they are wretched

226

things, full of trickery. You pay them money every year you're living, then you die and they bury you, but in two years they dig you up again, to make room for someone else. But I've heard that at Kensal Green there are cata- combs. Is that the word? I think it is. You can reserve your place in a niche there and then nobody disturbs you for all eternity.'

Lily looks at Belle. She notices that there is a little more colour in her cheeks and she wants to protest that, surely, her illness is passing and there is no need, yet, to book a final resting place. But she knows Belle. Once an idea has taken possession of her mind, it will lodge there and not be moved.

'I will give you money,' says Belle. 'The word "deposit" is such a wretchedly favoured term with people these days, I have a good mind to make use of it myself. I will give you five pounds. I've heard that Kensal Green is costly because it houses lords and dukes and so forth. But in return, I want a paper showing me what niche I am to inhabit. And tell them I wish for a peaceful location. Make sure they show it to you, the exact spot. Insist upon it, Lily. I do not wish to be disturbed by noisy neighbours.'

There is more laughter then (a little fainter than Belle's usual boisterous laugh, but there nevertheless) and when Lily and Belle have recovered from this, Belle takes Lily's hand and says, 'Will you tell me, one day, about the man you think you love?'

Lily looks away from Belle, out at the untidy room, which still seems to reek a little of the Seigneur's body, and says, 'I *do* love him. It's not merely that I think it.'

'Well then, why do you not go to him?'

'He's married, Belle. I told you. We would betray his vows, only to give ourselves heartache.'

Belle looks towards the window. She lets go of Lily's hand to begin smoothing the folds of the nightgown over her breasts. 'Or,' she says, 'you might not necessarily fall prey to that. Happiness exists, you know.'

At Long Acre, Julia Buchanan has moved into Belle's office. The little stove burns with what feels like volcanic heat. The desk has been tidied and is now being used as a work table. The wig Mrs Buchanan has created, already magnificently huge, with tier upon tier of brown curls, is being further augmented with ribbons and feathers.

Lily stands and admires the creation and Mrs Buchanan says, 'The character who will wear this is called Lady Pumpernickel. Can any living soul believe that? At least in an opera, they do not seem to have foolish names. Perhaps it's because they're mostly Italian. What's wrong with English playwrights? Now tell me, dear, about our patronne? You have been gone a long time. I sincerely hope she is not dead?'

'No,' says Lily. 'But she is ill. She is in pain with the shingles.'

'Oh dear. That can be lethal, if one is not careful. And can be mistaken for the pox. I hope you have not caught it. There was a policeman here yesterday asking for you.'

'A policeman?'

'Yes. But he would not say why he wanted you, so I thought it best to tell him I had no idea where you were. Was I right? He said he had been to your lodgings and not found you ...'

Lily now finds the heat from the stove oppressive and backs away a little, nearer the door.

'Did the policeman say ... did he say what rank he was?'

'What rank? No. And I didn't ask. They all look the same, don't they, in that black uniform they wear?'

'And he left no message?'

'No. He just said he was seeking you. That was the word he used: "seeking". I thought it sounded a touch biblical.'

Lily is silent for a moment, then she says, 'Could you describe him to me a little, the policeman?'

'Describe him? Well, no, not really. He carried his hat under his arm. I thought at first he'd come to tell us Belle was dead, or some such affrighting news, but no, not that. It was you he wanted.'

'Was he tall or short?'

'Neither, as far as I can remember. A middling kind of man. Nothing much to look at. But his voice was kind.'

Rather than go alone to Kensal Green Cemetery, Lily asks Julia Buchanan to come with her. The days are getting longer and from the windows of their northwest-bound omnibus Lily notes the way the early-evening sun lays upon London a deceptively gentle and golden light. Then the grey buildings gradually give way to more and more green spaces and poplars shivering with silvered leaves and Lily sees the beauty in all of this and asks herself, What else will I know of beauty before the hangman puts the rope around my neck?

Arriving at the cemetery gates, noting a smart little chapel on a high knoll and commodious family vaults in polished granite and marble, laid out with their own miniature gardens surrounding them, Mrs Buchanan says, 'Look at this, now, Lily. It's not for the likes of us, is it? How much is it going to cost Miss Prettywood?'

Lily replies that she has a five-pound deposit in her skirt pocket and Julia Buchanan says, 'That won't be anywhere near enough, to judge from the look of these edifices, but I suppose she wants to keep good company after she's left Long Acre.'

'She isn't asking for a vault, just a niche in the catacombs.'

'Is that where we're headed, then, down into those? I wouldn't like that myself, would you? I'd rather have a little view.'

Lily smiles. She thinks, I have never thought about this – where murderers are put after they're dead. I have never thought about it because I will only be dust, so it doesn't matter. But in answer to Julia's mention of the 'little view', she says, 'There's a place I would like, in a field at Rookery Farm, where a big oak tree stands. We sometimes drank cider out of a stone jar in the shade of that tree, and then slept. But a pit of lime will do.'

'Why do you say that?'

'Because it is all one to me. Where would you like to rest?'

'Me? I suppose I should say Scotland. I grew up in the Highlands. But we were poor as sparrows. People say it's beautiful and so it is, but what I remember most is the snow, which stayed all winter and made walking a heavy thing. And when I think of my body being buried under that suffocating snow, I don't like it.'

At the mention of Scotland, Lily says, 'I had a benefactress once, who was going to take me to live with her in a Scottish castle.'

'Really?' says Julia Buchanan. 'Would you have known how to conduct yourself in a castle?'

'No. I don't suppose I would have done. I expect Lady Elizabeth realised this and that is why she changed her mind. Yet I was only a child. She might have been able to school me, mightn't she?'

'Yes.'

'The thing I think I never imagined falling on the castle was snow. But I suppose it was there all along.'

'It would have been, Lily. Snow has a love affair with the Scottish hills. A love affair that never ends.'

Lily and Julia Buchanan go through the gates and are stopped by a young man who announces himself as one of the 'curators' of Kensal Green Cemetery. He looks critically at these visitors, wearing cheap bonnets and working clothes, and is, perhaps, about to tell them they've come to the wrong place when Lily unfolds the five-pound note and explains that they're here on behalf of Miss Belle Prettywood of Prettywood's Wig Emporium to select and reserve a niche in the catacombs 'in good advance of her death'.

'Ah,' says the curator, 'well that is always essential. We are a bespoke cemetery. You cannot snatch at places here as you might snatch some trinket off a market stall.'

'You mean, you sometimes turn the dead away?' says Mrs Buchanan.

'We *always* turn the dead away, madam, unless they have paid a deposit and reserved their spot. Wig Emporium, did you say? I have never heard of such an endeavour. I thought wigs went out with the last century. But as long as Miss Prettywood can pay, we will accommodate her. Follow me and we will descend to the lower regions.'

They descend some narrow brick steps and as they go, the sun, which had burnished the world so kindly while they rode the omnibus, disappears behind the trees and they find themselves breathing in a sudden shaft of cold and musty air. The steps arrive at a dark, vaulted space and Mrs Buchanan says, 'Goodness me, what will Belle do down here without her stove?'

They follow the curator to where, on either side of the vault, coffins have been placed in narrow niches. Here and there, torches burn feebly, as though they are on the point of being extinguished, but this flickering light reveals to Lily and Julia that hundreds of dead have already been crammed in here. They have to walk some way to find a section of wall where the niches are empty and when they get to this, the curator stops and points to these and like a salesman in a haberdasher's shop showing off his shelves of ribbon, his bias bindings and his silvered lace, he declares, 'You may select from any niche at this location. Niches carved out at human height are more costly than the lower ones because people seem to think they will be visited after their interment and are afraid that people will not want to bend down to see them, but you would be surprised how few relatives come here. The cold puts them off, I think, and the scent of . . . what might one call it . . . mortality. The dead are a lonely race.'

Lily and Mrs Buchanan stand and stare at the empty niches. A scuttling shadow nearby reveals a large rat making for the further darkness and in a low voice Mrs Buchanan says to Lily, 'Did you see that rat, Lily? On mature thought, I believe I would prefer a high Scottish glen.' And Lily thinks about Belle, dressed in some ultimate scarlet taffeta dress, with rouge on her face and plumes in her hair, and decides that no, she cannot be put in here, to lie unvisited except by rats.

'What do you think?' asks the curator. 'If your Mrs Wig is a large lady, she of course would not fit. Further along, we have some wider spaces, if you would care to inspect those?'

'No, thank you,' says Lily. 'We have seen enough.'

'So, which level are you going to choose? The niches are numbered. We are at numbers four hundred to four hundred and five here. Four hundred and five is the superior accommodation. Do you wish to reserve that?'

Lily is about to announce that they will go away and think about it, and consult with Miss Prettywood, when Mrs Buchanan says, 'You know, sir, rats are a disgrace. The directors of the Cemetery Company should ensure that at least there are no vermin here. And until they have, I don't think we could possibly make a reservation, could we, Lily?'

'No,' says Lily quickly. 'No. We must leave now. We must go back into the air.'

They turn and walk as fast as they can towards the steps and the very last of the evening light. Lily replaces Belle's five-pound note in her pocket. When they come out into the fading green of the park, Lily looks once again at the marble mausoleums and says to Julia, 'I think one of those would be more to Belle's taste, wouldn't it?'

Mrs Buchanan takes them in with her careful wig-maker's gaze and shakes her head and says, 'Even for Belle, I think that would be too costly. In every life there is a limit to aspiration.'

Lily nods but privately wonders whether the Seigneur, in his adoration of Miss Prettywood, might foot a substantial bill for her last resting place and imagines him arriving here and looking at the tomb he's bought and standing still and remembering the grand flurry and frenzy of his ardour and the way Belle made him puff and pant like a walrus on his way to an ecstasy no one else could give him, then touching the cold marble and feeling an unaccustomed sorrow.

She turns to the curator and points to a monolithic structure in polished granite and asks, 'How much would Miss Prettywood have to pay to reserve one like that?'

'My dear young woman,' says the curator, 'those are not *reserved*. They are family vaults, architect-designed edifices, built to the most exacting standards by the nobility and the highest-standing personages of London, among whom your Mrs Wig does not entirely fit.'

'I do not see why,' says Lily, 'when she is a paramour of the Prince of Wales.' Then she tugs at Julia's arm and the two women walk briskly away, but Mrs Buchanan can't resist a backward glance at the curator and says to Lily, 'Well, his mouth is still hanging open! If the wind changes, so they say, it will hang that way forever.'

His Coat

Days pass and the spring turns cold once more.

Lily works hard at the Georgian wigs, which are nearly finished. Belle returns to Long Acre, looking pale and moving more slowly than is usual, but there again in her booth, soothing her pain with tots of gin, displacing Julia Buchanan, banking up her stove. Lily tells her about the terrible catacombs at Kensal Green and the marble mausoleums housing the corpses of the rich and all Belle does is sniff and say, 'Well, we shall have to *see* about that!' And, almost as if this news has cheered her, she begins to play amused hostess to the young actresses from the Royal Victoria Theatre, who come to the workshop, laughing and screeching, to try on their mountainous wigs and who prance about the place in a gaudy kind of rapture.

Lily looks at these girls, who seem so free of care, so satisfied by their own noise and commotion and self-love, and wishes she could be more like them. She wants to ask if any of them were abandoned at birth by the gates to a park where the wolves came out of the dark and gnawed at their feet. She wants to say, 'Were any of you walled up in a prison for five years, let down by your benefactress and abused by a cruel woman? Did one or more of you have a friend who pined for the coffee scent of a dry-goods store and hanged herself from a weaver's loom?' But she stays quiet and only watches as they parade their wigs to each other, parade their transformations from poor young women to aristocrats by the simple addition of banks of curls and ribbons and lace, and find themselves filled with excitement and hope.

Hope.

Lily knows that she's a fool to long for it. She has to comfort herself with the notion that, perhaps, others have it now, others who thought it was lost: the girls at the Foundling Hospital who will never again find themselves in Nurse Maud's room and who will, in time, feel their shame begin to depart. As they work at their sewing or their spinning, they will begin to allow themselves to imagine an honest future, a kind employer, a husband, a place to call home. And she decides that when her trial for murder arrives, this is what she will say, that she killed to set others free.

After her time caring for Belle, she's begun to copy one of Miss Prettywood's 'stratagems against pain' and dose herself with gin – just to give herself the right to an hour of beautiful dreaming. She keeps a bottle under her bed in Le Bone Street and when she gets back there in the evenings she lies down and drinks until the room trembles. Then she lights a fire with a shaking hand and kneels by it and takes herself to some distant wooded place, never named, but far from London, where she sits under a great and sheltering tree and sees sunlight touch a clearing and fall on the shy flowers she used to name with Nellie on the lane that led to the Swaithey Road. Sometimes, she lets a stranger enter the clearing. She tries to make the stranger young and handsome, but when he begins to walk towards her, she sees that he's neither of these things, he's the ordinary man she keeps trying and failing to eject from her heart.

Then, one evening, when the fire has burned low and the room still dances like the air danced above the hedge-rows when Lily drank cider with Perkin Buck, she sees him arrive. She knows it's him before he's knocked on her door. For a moment, she doesn't move from where she kneels by the fire. The sound of his footsteps on the stone of the basement steps makes her heart race. She hides the gin bottle under her bed, blinks to try to stop the room from trembling. He stops outside her window and looks in and when he sees her, he presses his palm on the pane of glass, as if he thought she might vanish unless he kept her there with his restraining hand.

When she opens the door to him, she sees that he looks woebegone. He's removed his tall hat and holds it over his heart like a shield. His shoulders are hunched inside his heavy coat.

'Lily,' he says, 'I'm glad to find you ...'

They stand face-to-face. A gust of cold wind sends a swirl of dust into the little space where he stands.

Sam Trench.

Lily knows that whatever happens on this night, his name will be in her mind forever. Its echo will keep repeating and repeating, like two notes of music striving to become a song.

'I came to Long Acre, to look for you.'

'Yes.'

'And you were not there. And you were not in church.'

'No.'

'I was afraid you'd gone away.'

'No. Belle Prettywood was ill and I had to care for her and sleep in her house.'

'I thought something had happened to you.'

She turns back into her room, still warmed by the grey coals, and Sam Trench follows her and she closes the door behind them. She wishes she hadn't drunk the gin, so that she could think clearly what she wants to say, but she can't think very coherently, except to wonder why he looks so downcast. She manages to ask him if he'd like to take off his coat. He begins to unbutton the thick cloth, then he does a strange thing. He removes the coat and comes to her and puts it round her shoulders and, still holding the lapels of the coat, pulls her towards him. So then she's enveloped in the scent of him, his heavy coat, warm from his body, and her face is now pressed against his shoulder and his arms gently wrap themselves around her.

She wants to lift her head and look at him. She yearns for him to kiss her but she's embarrassed to be so tainted by the taste and stink of gin, so she stays very still, leaning against him, her cheek on the dark serge of his uniform, and she thinks, This is how it has to be between me and Sam Trench – tainted by the frailty of the human world. And it can never be other.

After minutes of silence, he whispers to her, 'I have something to say, Lily.'

And suddenly she knows that it's going to arrive now, the reckoning. But this feels unbearable to her, that he should accuse her now, even while she's wrapped in his coat and can feel the beating of his heart against her breast. So, without moving from his embrace, she says, 'You don't need to say it. I know what it is and now I'll tell you how it was done.'

And so she lets it come out. In the shelter of Sam's embrace, she describes how on her very first day at the Foundling Hospital, she was tugged away from Nellie Buck by Nurse Maud and was afterwards called 'Miss Disobedience' and beaten and punished, and how, in time, Nurse Maud stole the letter from her benefactress and after this knew that Lily Mortimer was in her power and that she could do anything she liked with her. And what she 'liked' was to degrade her and shame her, so that she, Lily, went about her days in a condition of blank misery.

Sam says nothing. With the fire almost out, Lily begins to feel cold and is glad of the heavy coat wrapped around her. It's almost as if the coat, which both warms her and conceals her, is not an object any more, but a *place*, a safe and familiar room, and her confession will come out here and only here and when it's out she will feel that a colossal burden has been lifted and go calmly towards whatever awaits her. But she has to tell the story correctly. It's hers and will always be hers and what's important now is that Sam Trench understands this. There is only this: *her truth*.

She describes how she went to Coram to retrieve the sack and while she was there saw Nurse Maud with her hand pressing down on the neck of another girl, no older than nine or ten, and she thought of all the years passing and all the lives ruined by Maud's particular evil. 'I looked around,' she says, 'as if there might be someone else to take responsibility, to put an end to Nurse Maud, but I knew there was nobody else. It felt lonely. I was afraid. But I had to do it. I felt that Maud's wickedness was no less than the wickedness of my own mother, who left me to the wolves.'

Sam's arms unfold and he puts his strong hands on her shoulders and holds her apart from him, so that he can look down at her face. She sees his expression of helpless sadness and understands now why he looked woebegone when he arrived, knowing that when the morning came she would be locked in a prison cell and all his longing for her would remain unsatisfied for the rest of his life.

'What did you do, Lily?' he whispers.

'Maud was sleeping. I saw her white hair on the pillow. The old should be kindly, but she was not. Her hair matched the hair in the sack, so I took this out and put it in her mouth and stoppered it with my hand. Her eyes opened for a moment. I believe I wanted her to know that it was me who was going to end her life. Then she began to choke and the sound of this was the most terrible sound I've ever heard. I couldn't endure it. It made me sick with horror. I had to smother it. So I took up a pillow and put it over her face and held it down. My arms are strong from all the work I've done in my life, so I could hold it there and not flinch and I think only a few minutes passed before her body went limp and still.'

Even in the darkening room, Lily can see that Sam looks pale. His eyes are large and fearful. He walks a few paces from her and sits down in an old chair and clings to its arms, as if to keep himself from fainting. Holding the coat around her, Lily goes and kneels at his feet.

'I've always known,' she says, 'how a thing like that has to come out, in due time. But it was important to me that you hear the truth of it from my mouth. I realised you already knew it and were coming to take me away, but—

'No. No, Lily …'

'You said you had something to say to me, and from your sorrowful look—'

'I wasn't coming to take you away. I had no inkling that you could be guilty of such a crime. The thing I had to say to you was this: you are all I dream of. I lie beside my wife and I imagine I'm holding you, making love to you. I know it's shameful and wrong, but this is what I feel. I was coming to confess. No, that's not quite right. I was coming to ask for love.'

'You weren't coming to arrest me?'

'I never imagined that you might be responsible for the death of Nurse Maud. You told me you'd never gone back to Coram.'

She stares at him. Then she puts her head in his lap and after a moment, his hand relinquishes its grip on the chair and his fingers gently stroke her hair. But in leaning forward, she lets the coat slip from her shoulders and it's as if, now, she's crept beyond the possibility of shelter and is exposed to the cold terror of the world, with nothing and no one to comfort her.

In her distress, she pulls Sam's head towards hers and kisses his mouth and her kiss is returned and Sam begins to claw at her, to raise her up and set her astride his lap, and she has the thought that now, in what they're about to do, he's chosen to share her burden, to make himself her accomplice. But then he seems to wake out of his trance of desire, to master his need. His mouth leaves hers and gently, as if she were as light as a dancer, as light as an armful of flowers, he lifts her away from him and stands up. She thinks that this is only so that he can lead her to her bed, but quickly understands that no, he has faltered, the world has laid its chill hand on him, too, telling him that loving her is impossible, the price is too high.

He takes her hand, folding it into a fist and putting both his hands around it and holding on to it so tightly that he hurts her. She tries to take her hand away, but he won't let her escape.

'Listen to me, Lily,' he says. 'I can only say this once and then I must leave you, or everything will be lost. Early tomorrow, go to Belle Prettywood and tell her you can't work for her any more. Say nothing of what's happened here tonight, nothing of what you've told me. Are you listening to me? Beg a little money from her. Collect what you need and then leave this place and never come back.'

'Sam ...'

'I've told you, I can only say this once, or I will falter. I will become the man I am for most of my life's waking hours, the police superintendent. You see? And then I will have to take you away and bring you to trial for your crime. But there is this brief time ... this moment of dreaming ... when I am not that man; I'm just a raging soul, in love. But it will pass. I will soon enough be pulled back towards duty and the law of the land. So there is only one way out. You must leave London. You must relinquish your life here.'

'Leave London? Where will I go, Sam?'

'It doesn't matter where. But let it be far away. Go to where I can never find you.'

He lets go of her hand now. She looks down and sees it bruised from his grip and thinks, There will always be pain in it, from this moment on. He has left his mark on me and it will never heal.

She stands by silently as Sam reaches down for the fallen coat and puts it on. He picks up his hat and without looking back he walks to the door.

'Suppose you did find me?' she asks. 'What would happen then?'

But he doesn't answer. He opens the door and walks out into the night. He runs up the stone stairs and she counts his footsteps as he goes. Those eight familiar steps and then he's gone.

The Missing Key

She banks up the fire and sits by it until morning, staring into the little darting flames. Then, when the light comes, she falls asleep at last and dreams about the stone-picking at Rookery Farm and the thing which gladdens her in the dream is being lifted up by Jesse Buck so that she can tip the flints she's gathered into the hopper and she watches them fall and feels the weight of the sack slung round her neck disappear, and then Jesse sets her down on the plough and she can smell the earth and hear Jesse laughing.

When she wakes, she seems to know that there is no other destination for her now but Rookery Farm. She has no idea whether Nellie and Perkin are still alive or what has become of Jesse, James and Joseph, or whether, in the eleven years that have passed, the farm has fallen to ruin and sits abandoned and choked with thistles and ragwort and ground elder, with no one to hear the cries of the nameless boy from the bottom of the well. Perhaps she will arrive there, walking all the way from the tiny station at Swaithey, up the road, then along the narrow lane, past Miss Oldroyd's tea-kettle school, under the firs that shed little coverlets of snow onto Peggy's mane, and find everybody gone? Or perhaps, if they are there, she will not be welcome? Perhaps they will only think of her as a burden – even Nellie, who showed her such love and kindness – and perhaps Nellie will take her aside and say,

'If you were hoping to stay, pet, this is a false hope. Rookery Farm was never your real home.'

All of these fears run through her mind, but Lily also knows that she has to make the journey. She has to make it because there is no other place to go.

She does as Sam suggested and goes to Belle and when she tells Belle that she's leaving, she sees Belle's face fall into a trance of sadness. But Belle Prettywood is not stupid. She says, 'I know you must have a very potent reason for abandoning me, or you would not do it. You wouldn't hurt me like this. Would you?'

There is much that Lily would like to say to Belle, but she is choked and can't speak and what Belle understands is that this is someone in need of rescue. She remembers how patiently and tenderly Lily cared for her when she believed she was dying of the pox, without thought for her own safety, and how she never turned away, and it has often been on her mind that she owes Lily some reward for this, but has never worked out what that reward might be. Now, Belle sees what it can be. She reaches for the locked tin where she keeps her money, searches for the key in amongst the discarded hairpins, packets of blocking tacks, stubs of pencils and recipes for ink in her desk drawer, and holds it up with a flourish.

'What I hope,' she says, 'is that your trouble is not so great that you can't recover from it and return to me. But meanwhile ...'

Belle unlocks and opens the tin, counts out three five-pound notes and folds them into a tiny, crisp package, then reaches for Lily's hand and presses the package into it. 'This,' she says, 'will help you to stay alive.'

Lily takes the money. She feels a burning tear spill down her cheek.

'I'm sorry,' she says.

'No,' says Belle. 'No need.' And she pulls Lily to her and holds her for a moment in a scented embrace and Lily can sense, at her back, the other wig-makers, who are just arriving for work, watching the scene and wondering what is suddenly occurring. When she passes through the workshop, Julia Buchanan asks her, 'What is it, Lily? Is everything all right?'

'Yes,' says Lily. 'You are all so kind and good. But I have to go away for a little while,' and she strides on before more questions can come her way.

On her way back to Le Bone Street, she thinks of buying a tin trunk, so as to take with her the scarlet dress and the few other possessions which furnish her meagre life, but she realises that she has so few of them, they can be bundled into the sack she's taken from the workroom at Long Acre.

She packs her best boots, her sewing basket, her hair-brush and ribbons, her underwear and stockings, two nightgowns, two wool dresses, a candleholder, a tinderbox, a few tallow candles and the old rag doll she named Bridget. In a muslin bag, she puts a piece of cheese and some dried currants. The sack is still only half filled.

So then Lily lays the red dress on the bed and spreads out the skirt, as if offering it to another wearer. She imagines who this might be: the young girl who will pay half a crown a week for these lodgings, walking in and seeing it displayed there, this beautiful gown, and then taking it up and holding it against her body and uttering a cry of delight. Lily is about to walk away from it when it occurs to her that even if she never has a reason to wear it again, it's a thing of value and who knows what is going to happen to her if Rookery Farm has been abandoned and she's alone without shelter in Suffolk. She folds the dress carefully, making it as small as she can, and stuffs it into the sack and ties up the neck of the sack with string. She has the thought that the scarlet dress is the nearest thing to a companion she will have for a long time.

On the train to Ipswich, she sleeps through all its many stops, clutching the sack to her as tightly as one might clutch a baby.

She wakes and boards the slow locomotive to Swaithey and sees, going by in slow succession, the flint churches and the low thatched cottages, clustered about with apple blossom and plum blossom, and a few children running in the fields or along the towpaths, and birds in sudden, marvellous flocks, wheeling over the hedgerows. For a time, she feels her heart lift at these sights, remembered from so long ago, but as Swaithey comes closer she begins to feel afraid of arriving there and half wishes she could just go journeying on forever, live her life on the train, watching each day come and go, speaking to no one, living on dried currants, existing between one life and another, asking nothing and getting nothing except the feeling of the iron wheels turning.

But then the train stops and she hears the guard announce, 'Swaithey! Swaithey station! Anyone for Swaithey?'

Lily notices that the afternoon is already darkening to evening and that in the tiny stationmaster's cottage a lamp is burning. Her heart is knocking on her ribs as she gathers up the sack and opens the carriage door and steps down onto the platform, where dock and ragwort are beginning to push their way through the gaps in the stone slabs. And at once, she remembers it: the scent of Swaithey, which has a caramel sweetness to it, of roses and burning logs and the perfume of linen, dried in the sun. She stands and breathes. For a moment, she's shrouded in steam as the train leaves, then this evaporates and she looks beyond the stationmaster's house to the path leading to the market square and her fear lessens and she decides to hold her head up high. She thinks of Belle's money concealed in the bodice of her dress – riches by the standards of the people of Swaithey – and she remembers how strangers could sometimes be made welcome in the village and given a bed for the night in return for a precious shilling.

Darkness still falls early at this time of the year and although Lily is planning to walk from here to Rookery Farm, she doesn't want to arrive there, like a revenant, out of the shadows. She wants to see everything clearly, by early-morning light – every cluster of violets, every drift of straw, every shadow cast by the oaks, every thistle, every stone.

She knocks on the stationmaster's door and when his wife opens it, tugging a black shawl around her, Lily asks where she might enquire about a bed for the night. The woman looks at her in surprise, as at someone arrived from a distant land, and Lily knows what she can see and smell on her: the stink of the metropolis. The woman doesn't answer directly but calls to her husband who's returning from seeing the train onwards to Framlingham. He, too, stares at Lily and at the sack she's holding. Both are young and wouldn't have been there when Lily was a child and she supposes that most of the people who embark upon or disembark from the little train are known to them by some means and that the presence of a well-groomed stranger from London disconcerts them.

'I could pay a florin,' says Lily firmly.

The stationmaster's wife looks at her husband and he nods and Lily recalls Belle Prettywood once saying to her, 'Remember one thing as you go through life, Lily: money always speaks very loudly.'

'We have a back room here,' says the wife, pulling the shawl more tightly around her. 'It's the station office and a little choked with lost property, but there is a couch which can serve and we can find blankets for you, for the two shillings.'

'Call it three – three shillings,' says the stationmaster, 'and we can offer you some tripe and onions for supper.'

Tripe and onions.

And Lily thinks, Sam Trench will be in my heart forever and when Sunday comes I will think of him cooking the onions, then sitting down to his meal with Joyce, but with his mind far off, in some invented place where I am his and he is mine.

'Thank you,' she says. 'May I see the room?'

It's a cluttered place, with, on tilting wooden shelves, a collection of all the things left and found on the trains between Ipswich and Framlingham: gloves and books, empty bags and baskets, umbrellas, pairs of spectacles, men's hats and scarves, children's toys and, on the top shelf, an iron birdcage containing a stuffed bird on a tiny perch.

Lily remarks on the bird and the stationmaster's wife, whose name is Susan, says, 'Gathering dust, that is. Nobody's come to claim it. There's a place for a key and we think that when you turn the key, the bird will sing. But the key is missing.'

'Oh,' says Lily, 'but somebody could make a new key, couldn't they?'

Susan gives Lily a rigid stare. 'Happen they could,' she says, 'or else they think it's not worth the trouble.'

The couch has been placed under the tilting shelves and Lily can imagine all these lost things falling in the night and drifting down on her – a fugitive fleeing from death by fleeing from love – and this might be how her seventeen years reach their end: the iron cage would strike her head and the jolt of it turn the tiny cog that allows the bird to sing, and the unexpected singing of the bird would wake Susan and her husband and they would wonder what they should do with her body and try to find out to whom it belonged.

'Well?' says Susan. 'Will it suit? Not worth your while going from door to door, begging for shelter in the darkness, is it?'

At the Time of the Stone-picking

Lily wakes early. In the half-dark of dawn, she clambers up to reach the birdcage on the top shelf and sets it down on the couch where she's passed an anxious night and wipes the dust from it with the sleeve of her nightgown. She opens the door to the interior of the cage and touches the bird on its perch. Its feathers are sleek, its eyes the colour of amber, and Lily decides that she will try to buy it from the stationmaster's wife, to take to Nellie as a gift. She thinks that Perkin Buck could surely manufacture a key from all the bits and pieces of iron to be found among the detritus of his barn, and then Nellie could sit in her rocking chair and sew and listen to the bird with a little astonished smile on her face.

Susan makes Lily a breakfast of bread and dripping and hot milk. Susan watches her all the while, as though she's afraid this girl from London might mock this meagre meal. When Lily asks whether she can buy the birdcage, Susan asks, 'Why in the world would you want that?'

'Oh,' says Lily. 'I thought it would make a gift for someone ...'

'A gift for who?' says Susan.

Now Lily falters. She can't bear to ask the stationmaster's wife if she knows the Buck family in case the answer comes back that Nellie and Perkin are dead. If they are dead, Lily wants to go to Rookery Farm and at least inhale the air that they breathed and see the thistles growing in the fields. She doesn't want to be told of their death by a suspicious stranger.

'I lived here when I was a child,' says Lily. 'I would like to take something to the school, for the children there now.'

'Oh,' says Susan, 'well, I'm not sure they would want a birdcage. And I'm not certain I can sell it. Suppose the person who left it on the train comes a-calling?'

'You said it was just gathering dust.'

'Perhaps it is. It's been here a long few months. But you never know.'

'I could give you another florin for it.'

'It's worth more than that. There's craftsmanship in it.'

'A half-crown, then.'

'You could have it for three shillings.'

Lily doesn't argue. She pays six shillings for her board and for the bird. She tidies her hair and puts on her bonnet and says goodbye to Susan and her husband, the stationmaster, who stands by the door, puffing on a pipe and staring at the breaking day. Then she walks out into the early morning, carrying her sack of possessions and the heavy iron cage, and goes through Swaithey as its shops and businesses are opening their doors. All the buildings appear smaller than she remembers them being, not joined together like a London street, but each in its separate patch, as though inviting in the companionship of the big Suffolk sky. She sees nobody she recognises, but the blacksmith's boy touches his cap to her and at the bakehouse door a man unloading flour sacks from a dray asks her, 'Does the bird sing, then, miss?'

'No,' says Lily. 'But it might one day.'

The lane that leads to Rookery Farm comes off the road a half-mile beyond the village, beyond the stand of firs that once shook wedges of snow onto the cart. The turning was always almost concealed by a clustering of dog roses, pale pink in summer. And here they are now, just coming into leaf, but grown denser with time, as if they aspired to curtain off the lane and let nobody pass.

Lily sets down the birdcage. She looks and listens and her heart is full of terror. Birds flutter in and out of the hedgerows, a rabbit goes hopping along the dusty path and the sky is a calm and ordinary blue. But suppose, at the end of the lane, where the house once stood, there is only a ruin? Sam Trench commanded her to go where he couldn't find her. She understands that the world is vast. Some part of her imagined she might board a steamship and cross an ocean, putting herself way beyond his reach, but this thought didn't linger. She knows that he's capable of tracking her down to Rookery Farm, but she also knows that it's the only place where she might find peace.

In a few minutes, she will know what still stands in this place she once loved. She picks up the cage and walks between the encroaching bushes and sets her foot on the lane. She remembers how James Buck, who loved counting everything in the universe, counted his steps from the door of the house to the Swaithey Road, but she can't remember the number he arrived at. She begins counting all the same: thirty-five steps and then the lane veers left. Another thirty and it veers right again, and round the next bend, the third bend, there she will get her first sight of the house.

Once again, she sets down the heavy cage. She tries to see the state of the fields – the fields where the thistles always conquered the grass – to see if they are tended or abandoned, but the hedges have grown too high. She's hemmed in. All she can do is move forwards.

A few more steps. Twenty-seven steps and then the lane makes its final turn and there it is: Rookery Farm. In front of it an orchard has been planted. The trees are bright with blossom. The grass at their feet is uncut, the new growth just pushing through the old exhausted stems of last year, and among them stands a dilapidated wooden cart with its shafts pointing to the sky, but the brick path that leads to the front door is free of weeds and the morning sun falls on a house still luminous with recent whitewash. From the old, tilting chimney comes a skein of pale woodsmoke and Lily talks to some god of past times, saying, 'Please, oh please let the smoke mean that Nellie is standing at the range, frying bacon for Perkin ...'

She goes quietly up the path to the door, as if afraid to be heard. She knocks and hears a dog begin to bark, a dog who can't be Shadow with her yellow eyes, a dog who might belong to some new owner of the farm, who would shake his head and say, 'No, sorry, my lass, but the Buck family fell on hard times and are long gone.'

But then the door is opened. A young man with a wide, open face framed by brown curls stands before her. Round his neck is a coloured kerchief and his big hands fumble with this as he stares at Lily, as though, seeing this girl in her neat London attire, he wished to knot it differently.

He doesn't speak. Lily lifts her face and says in a choked whisper, 'Jesse Buck?'

He nods. The barking of the dog intensifies and then a black-and-white collie comes trotting to his side. Jesse reaches out to the dog, trying to quieten it, and Lily waits for the dog to calm itself before she says, 'Perhaps you won't remember me, but I lived here long ago, when I was a child. Your mother took me in. At the time of the stone-picking, you used to lift me up so that I could reach the hopper to pour in the stones I'd gathered.'

Jesse Buck still finds no words.

'I'm Lily Mortimer,' says Lily. 'I was six years old when I left the farm.'

'Lily?'

'Yes. I hope you'll forgive me, I have no real right to come here, but I . . . I had such a great longing to see the farm again and to put my arms around Nellie . . .'

She hadn't intended this, but she finds herself breaking down into tears. Perhaps it's the saying of Nellie's name? She hopes that her crying will be quickly over, but, after all that has led her here, to this door, she feels as though she might cry forever.

'Oh,' says Jesse Buck. 'Oh . . .'

As Lily tugs a handkerchief from her coat pocket, Jesse brings the dog close to him and strokes its head, as though he, too, needs consoling. Still keeping hold of the dog, he says, 'Will you come inside?'

Leaving her sack and the birdcage at the door, she follows him in and he leads her through into the kitchen. He pulls out a chair for her at the table, which is the same table where she used to sit with Nellie and do her needle-work, and she notes that it's clean and that the scrubbed wood has gone almost white with time. She watches Jesse pick up a blackened kettle and put it on the range. She blows her nose and tries to apologise to Jesse Buck for the weeping and she sees him turn towards her from the range and put his hands on his waist: a man perplexed, not knowing what to do or say.

Lily dries her eyes and looks around the kitchen, which, in eleven years, has hardly changed, and she manages to say, 'Do you remember Peggy sticking her great head in through the window and breathing her carrot-breath?'

'Yes,' says Jesse. 'Peggy was a good horse, but stubborn. The shire mare we have now is called Sally. She has a nice nature.'

'And does your father still drive the cart to Swaithey on market day?'

Jesse turns back to the range, to give his attention to the kettle. He reaches for a tin tea caddy and an old blue china pot. Then he says quietly, 'My father died of an apoplexy some few years back. They say that is a good way to go.'

'Oh. He died? He was always so kind to me. And he always seemed very content in that barn full of old things ...'

'Yes. He was content. And I believe he taught me that – to accept my lot. He never pretended that the farm wasn't hard work, back-breaking labour, but he wanted it passed on to one of us. My brothers had different ideas, but I was willing to take it on. I toil from dawn till dusk, just as my father did.'

'So you're alone here?'

'In one sense I am. Quite alone.'

Lily clutches her handkerchief. She looks round the kitchen for the things Nellie used to leave here: her white aprons on a peg, her rubber overshoes for wet weather days, her old umbrella, but doesn't see any of them.

Seeming to read her thoughts, Jesse says, 'Nellie is here. She can no longer help much with the farm work, but she's as happy as a goose.'

'Happy as a goose?'

'She is. Going here and there, just like an inquisitive bird, never still. But I should admit to you that something has been lost.'

'Something has been lost?'

'Just a little piece of her memory. But she doesn't know it's gone. It seems not to trouble her. And on certain days, it comes back and then she says, "Where have I been, Jesse? Have I been away?"'

Lily is silent. The collie comes to her and puts its paws on her knee and she strokes its head. Then she asks, 'Will Nellie remember who I am?'

But before Jesse can answer, they hear footsteps shuffling to the back door and it opens with the slight squeak that it always had and there is Nellie. Her head is wrapped in a shawl. Her face is lined, her gentle eyes a little pouched underneath, but she carries her heavy frame well, as she always did, and when she sees Lily she smiles and says, 'Good day to you, miss. Or I should say good morning, for what do we know of the day yet? Will the rain come? Will there be a letter from Africa?'

Lily stands up.

'Nellie,' she says, 'it's Lily.'

'Lily, did you say?'

'Lily Mortimer. I was here for a long time and then you took me back to London, to the Foundling Hospital.'

'Oh,' says Nellie. 'What is she saying, Jesse?'

'She's telling you that she's the foster-child we used to call "our girl" – the one you said you always missed when she went away.'

Now, Nellie gazes at Lily. Her blue eyes fill.

'Lily?' she says again. 'My little girl?'

'Yes.'

'Oh. Oh, I don't know what ...'

Jesse comes to Nellie and puts his hand on her shoulder. 'It's a bit of a shock for you, to see Lily, all grown up, is it?' he says.

'Yes. I think I'd better go outside and come in again, shall I? I was only feeding the chickens. I could feed them again, they wouldn't mind, and then I'll come back inside – to see if she's really there.'

'She's there, she's there. She's here. No need to go out. She's standing right in front of you. And a pretty face, at that. Eh? Why don't you give her a little kiss?'

'A little kiss? Oh, Jesse, this is breaking my heart. We sent her away. It was the law. The law said we had to give her back. Give her back to who? I never understood.'

'You did understand, Mother. We all understood. But it was a sad day.'

'Oh, and it was dark there. And the sky was full of dying birds ...'

Nellie seems at a loss. She starts to turn, as if to go outside again, but then stops and holds on to Jesse to steady herself. Lily goes to her and puts her arms around her and after a moment she feels Nellie hold tight to her and then she and Jesse hear a low, almost musical sound coming from Nellie's throat, a wailing they've never heard before, a lament for all the things in Nellie Buck's life which were never meant to happen.

Because it was the Law

They sit in the kitchen for a long time. Jesse makes the pot of tea. Nellie holds Lily's hands in hers and strokes them and her gaze barely leaves Lily's face. The dog whose name is Joey whines, scenting in the air something that it can't fathom, something which is no longer sorrow but is not yet joy.

Nellie's mind seems to be choked with questions, on which she tries to embark, but then has to stop each time, not knowing how to form them, and then she looks blankly at Jesse and he attempts to guess what they were and ask them for her.

'The Foundling Hospital,' he says. 'Nellie would like to know what happened to you there. I think she hopes they were kind to you.'

Lily is silent. Images return to her in a confused crowd, each one jostling for a place: lying in a soaking bed with Bridget, being beaten with a willow wand for trying to write a letter to Nellie, finding the sheep named Bert, knitting the scarf with which Bridget hanged herself, making dolls out of rags, being pushed by Nurse Maud's hand on her neck up the stairs to where the terrible room waited ...

'They thought ...' she begins, '... they meant to be kind, but it was not really so.'

'Oh,' says Nellie, 'but that sort of thing, it should be so, shouldn't it? I believe in kindness, don't I, Jesse?'

259

'Yes, you do.'

'It should be like a little housefly, to land on you gently.'

'A housefly?'

'Yes. Something which touches you with its wing.'

'But I found kindness later on,' says Lily quickly. 'I went to work in London, at Belle Prettywood's Wig Emporium, and we made wigs for operas and plays and all the sewing you taught me, Nellie, helped me in my job and Miss Prettywood was always kind to me.'

'And do you still work there, Lily?' asks Jesse.

'No. I've begun to find ... in London ... I've found that it's difficult for me to go on there. Miss Prettywood owed me a little money and it came into my mind to come here and ask you ... in return for my board and for all the work you could find for me to do ... if I could stay a while. Might you agree to that? I could help Nellie in the house and—'

'Nellie?' interrupts Jesse. 'Would you like Lily to stay with us, just for a short while?'

'Lily stay here?'

'Yes. Just for a time.'

Nellie reaches out and touches Lily's face. She is smiling. 'Why don't you take off your bonnet?' she asks. 'That way you will be more comfortable.'

'I will,' says Lily, 'but let me fetch something from the front step first. I brought you a little present.'

'A present?' says Nellie. 'I don't know what in the world it could be.'

Lily gently pulls her hand out of Nellie's grip and goes to the door. A thin rain is now falling and Lily remembers that just such a sudden rain came when Nellie took her hand and led her to the waiting cart and she was driven away from Rookery Farm forever. Lily stares at the lane, almost believing that she can still see it, the old cart drawn by Peggy, with a makeshift tarp sheltering her and Nellie from the sky, then she turns to pick up the broken cage and finds an inquisitive brown hen pecking at the iron bars, as though it thought the manufactured bird was a little beaker of grain.

She takes the cage back to the kitchen and sets it down among the teacups. Both Nellie and Jesse stare at it in perplexity. Lily says, 'I thought it might hang in here, or in the parlour. The bird will sing, if you can make these cogs turn, and you could listen to its song, Nellie, while you do your needlework.'

'Oh,' says Nellie, 'I can't hear any singing.'

'No. Because the winder key is lost. But I think Jesse might be able to make a new one, mightn't you, Jesse?'

'My father could have done it. I'm all thumbs when it comes to small things.'

'Still no singing,' says Nellie. 'But the time for night-ingales is past, that's what I heard.'

'I'm sure Jesse can make a key, can't you, Jesse? A little iron key? From your father's tools?'

Jesse examines the cage and the rusty cogs and the small spindle which leads to the silent bird. He rotates the spindle with his earth-blackened hands and the bird's beak opens and a tiny sound comes out, like the first squeak of the fire's flame as it finds the chimney and begins to burn.

'Oh!' says Nellie. 'Well now ...'

Nellie stares at the bird, but then turns away from it, as if it were no longer there. 'When Perkin went away,' she says, 'I said to Jesse, she should be here to say goodbye to him, that girl, that one I sang to, those silly old songs which made no sense, but which soothed her to sleep. I said there is something all wrong, didn't I, Jesse? At the time when Perkin left us. I said she used to work in the barn with Perkin and never tire. She used to pick up the baby rats with her naked hands. And then I asked James to go and fetch her ...'

'It was Joseph, Mother. James was gone into the army by that time.'

'Was he? Oh, yes. James went away, you know, Lily. To be a scarlet soldier. He went to what they call the Cape of Good Hope.'

'The Royal Engineers,' says Jesse. 'He's defending the British Empire in Africa. He always wanted to see the world. We get letters from him sometimes, full of words in a new language we don't really understand.'

'But there is good hope,' says Nellie. 'You see? Good Hope. That's what he told us and I trust in that. It will keep him safe. But I did say to him, at the time, I said he ought to go to London to bring the girl back, to say goodbye to Perkin, but he said, "She is gone, she is quite gone and couldn't be found anywhere ..."'

'It wasn't James. It was Joseph.'

'Perhaps it was. Anyway, what was I saying when Perkin died? I said, "She used to stroke my ear lobes when I kissed her goodnight. She always wanted to sit on my knee when we went to market day in the cart and Joseph was on my knee beside her and when the cart stopped, she'd fall down into that muddy old cart, into all that dust and straw, but she never cried, she only laughed." I told James – or Joseph – all of that and I said it never should have happened, that thing that happened, and it only happened, not because I wanted it, but because it was the law.'

There is silence in the kitchen while the three of them think about this: the law which said no child from the Foundling Hospital could remain with their foster family for more than six years. And Lily knows that if she'd been able to remain here, then she would have committed no crime. She would have worked hard with Nellie to run the house and wash and mend clothes and do whatever she could on the farm. She would have run in the sunshine with Shadow and helped with the spring lambing. She would have had her own little piece of ground and planted beans and nasturtiums and loved the red and orange of their flowers. She might even have learned to drive the cart.

She waits for Nellie or Jesse to speak, to tell her that she can stay a while. They are both looking at her, but it's as if now that they've remembered her, they can't think of anything more to say. She's a stranger to them and perhaps they are both trying to imagine how the intervening years have unfolded and what joys or sorrows are in her heart.

'Well,' Jesse says at last, 'Lily has come a long way to see us. I feel – if she would like this – she should stay with us, until London calls her back. Would you be happy to give her the room she once had, Mother? Would you like that?'

Nellie nods. Her pale eyes fill and she just lets the tears fall.

Nellie is lame. She says that someone – and it might be God, but it might also be the lamplighter who visits Swaithey to go round at dusk illuminating the new lamps in the marketplace and putting them out again when the dawn comes – has given her the gift of pain in her hip and she doesn't know quite what to do with it.

'It seems ungrateful to complain,' she says, as she and Lily go up the narrow stairs, which always curved round too steeply for comfort and were dark.

'Do you think pain is a gift?' Lily asks.

'Oh yes. For we each have our own. And pain is someone to talk to when I'm alone.'

'And you are alone, I suppose, when Jesse is out in the fields. But where is Joseph?'

'Oh,' says Nellie, 'he's a scarlet soldier. But I have good hope.'

'I thought the scarlet soldier was James.'

'James?'

'Yes.'

'Is that James in the faraway place?'

'I think so. But tell me about Joseph.'

They are nearly at the top of the stairs now and Nellie is out of breath. She stops and leans on the narrow bannister.

'I can't remember about Joseph,' she says. 'Sometimes he used to come in covered in white dust and I had to say, "You must find a brush and get that away or it will soon cover everything and then we wouldn't know where we were."'

'White dust?'

'Yes. I don't know what it was. Ask James.'

'Ask Jesse, you mean?'

'Do I? Did you know they were all named for the Perkin uncles, who went away to India and died in a ravine?'

'Yes. I knew that.'

'I've never seen a ravine, have you?'

'No. I don't think so.'

'Well, it doesn't matter. Now we have to remember which room you had. Every room in this house is small, but there was always space for me to come and sit on your bed, and we sang songs, didn't we?'

'Yes. We sang songs. Sometimes we saw the moon outside the window.'

'Oh, the moon. I never see it any more. It might be the fault of the lamplighter.'

Lily leads Nellie to the room where her cot used to be, and the crocheted coverlet of six or seven different colours, and they stand at the door, looking in.

'Terrible,' says Nellie, 'that you went away. But now look. We could pretend you never left.'

To be in that room. To look at the iron bed which is there now and to know that, when the night comes, she will climb into it and sleep and then wake in the morning sunlight and realise that she's at Rookery Farm: this makes Lily tremble with happiness.

She and Nellie sit down on the bed and Nellie holds her close and says, 'In Swaithey, they think I'm soft in the head. They think I sometimes fly up into the clouds. Once, I stole a little skein of silk thread from a market stall because I thought you would like it for your sewing. But they caught me red-handed. They said, "You could go to prison for that, Nellie Buck. You could spend the rest of your days fed with gruel and sleeping on straw." And besides this, they told me you were gone, which was the thing that I'd forgotten, so I said, "Oh excuse me then, pardon me, good sirs, good, honest gentlemen," and gave the silk back. But that's when they decided I was up in the ... whatever they call it ... up in the firmament … and James had to explain it was only the passing of time, that the world gets confusing at its end. But it was very awkward for him.'

'For Jesse, you mean?'

'Jesse. Do I? I expect I do. Something of an embarrassment.'

'I don't suppose he minded, Nellie.'

'Perhaps not. He's a beautiful, strong boy. But it all came in among his other trouble. Poor Jesse.'

'Why d'you say "poor Jesse"?'

'Well, he was disappointed, you know. Is that the word?'

'Disappointed?'

'He had his heart broken.'

'He did?'

'By the daughter of the schoolteacher. Esme. I think that was her name. Something like that. She went away with a bookbinder. Jesse said it was because of his hands. You see, Jesse's hands, they're all creased with dirt. So criss-crossed with grime after all the years he's spent toiling. A farm is nothing but toil and I think this Esme … or was it Esther, I can't remember … when she understood that, she decided she preferred nice clean white hands and so she chose the bookbinder and they went away to the North somewhere to bind books, because that is where books are bound, in the North. But when she told all this to Jesse, he didn't know what to do, and what could I do? I'm his mother, that's all.'

'When did that happen, Nellie?'

'Who knows, pet? A year ago, or more. It might have been three years. I can't remember. People's hearts are broken all the time. That's why I sometimes fly up into the sky, to escape from all the broken hearts. Maybe yours is broken and that's why you came back to me.'

Lily is silent. Then she strokes Nellie's cheek and says, 'There was somebody I thought I loved, but he had a wife, so there never could be anything honest between us. Yet he watched over me for a while.'

Nellie nods. 'Like the moon,' she says. 'They tell me it watches over the earth, but, you know, it's very neglectful. You go out into the dark and search for it, but all the sky is dark. I think that's why the lamplighter came to Swaithey.'

Later, there is a mid-morning dinner: bloaters bought from the travelling fishmonger who visits each Wednesday, stewed apples from the new orchard, stored across the long winter on slatted shelves in the larder.

Halfway through eating the apples, Nellie falls asleep in her chair and Jesse says, 'She doesn't like to be woken. She says the Land of Sleep is a beautiful place. I'll fetch her blanket and cover her and then I'll show you round the farm.'

While Jesse is gone for the blanket, Lily looks at her beloved Nellie and decides that this is her task now, to wait and watch for the moments when Nellie's mind goes wayfaring into a world known only to her, and then try – so gently that she doesn't take fright – to bring her back. And she finds herself hoping that she, who once looked to Nellie for her every need, is now the one to whom Nellie will often turn for comfort.

The Two Hands

The sky is blue again now, but the sweet, wet glitter of the rain clings to the hedgerows. The dog, Joey, sees a hare bound across the first of the meadows and, like Shadow in days gone by, flies off in pursuit.

Jesse is much taller than his father was and walks with a strong stride and Lily has to take little skipping steps now and then to keep up with him. She asks to see the old barn, and they go in there and Jesse shows her a pit dug deep into the ground where all the things of no value hoarded by Perkin are buried. Yet some heavy and broken parts for the plough and the harrow remain and Jesse says, 'If Joseph had stayed, I could have made better progress here, but sometimes loneliness makes me lazy. I go towards a task and then I feel frail at the thought of it.'

'I understand,' says Lily. 'Why did Joseph leave?'

'He tired of the place. He didn't love it in the way that I love it. He tried for a while to live a life here, but he told me he thought he would die if he spent his days trying to run the farm, and I understood that.'

'Nellie talked about white dust.'

'Oh, yes. He was clever with his hands, like my father. He was apprenticed to a stonemason and he became quite skilled at that and he liked the work.'

'Where is he now?'

'He went to Bath. He tells us Bath is a grand stone city, not a backwater of old lathe-and-plaster cottages, like Suffolk. I believe he thinks I envy him, but I don't, Lily. I've never been inclined to leave. A few good crops and hens laying and a goose at Christmas-time: that's what my life has always been.'

'Are those things all you still hope for, Jesse?'

'Mostly. But at other times, my head fills up with ideas. You see the size of this old barn? I've done some mathematics. I wasn't very good at it at school, like James was, but I can do simple sums. I've worked out that when I've finished all the clearing and repaired the roof, I could raise pigs in here. Room enough for ten sows, each with a farrowing pen. Feed them up with dandelions and sowthistle and snails and all the old peelings from the kitchen. You can get ten shillings for a weaned piglet. So then where might we be? All awash in piglets and plenty of money in the jar!'

'Oh,' says Lily, 'and there is something touching about them, with their little eyes like currants, and ... well ... couldn't I help you with them?'

'Help me with them?'

'Oh no, I don't mean ... I never presumed ... I only thought, if I could pay my way, do some housework, help Nellie with her sewing ...'

'You'd like to stay here through the summer?'

'Only if I would be no trouble. I'm used to rising early, working hard.'

He says her name then. 'Lily. Our Lily.' He stares at her, then he rubs his eyes, as if waking from some lingering dream, and says, 'After you left, Nellie brought back another baby, a boy. I can't remember his name, poor little mite. Perhaps he had no name? He used to scream in the night. And Nellie told me she couldn't love him, couldn't love any more foster-children, after you.

So she travelled back to London with him and asked the Governors of the Hospital to find a new home for the baby. She was ashamed to do it, but she said if she just couldn't love him, as she loved you, he would become "no better than a beggar". Those were the words she used: "no better than a beggar".'

'I understand what she meant. If a child isn't cared for, he or she becomes a beggar. The thing we beg for is love.'

'I don't think my father understood this. He couldn't see it quite like that. He just kept mentioning the money we got from the Hospital for the foster-children, and it rankled with him that Nellie wouldn't earn this any more. And it was the beginning of his decline. He grew very morose and his appetite went and he was all sinew and bone, but he never gave up on the farm. He kept working until the day he died and he taught me every-thing I needed to know about the land.'

'He was a kind man,' says Lily. 'A good man.'

'Yes. Until very near the end, when money was scarce and he became short-tempered with the world. But what do you think about the raising of piglets in here? Would my father have done this, if he'd thought about it? I don't know. There would be some laying out of money, to buy the sows, but after that, if there was no swine fever, if I could make the barn warm enough through the winter . . .'

'I think it's a fine idea, Jesse.'

'What I dread is becoming poor – so poor that I can't look after Nellie properly. But I think, with the pigs, we would all survive, wouldn't we?'

'Yes,' says Lily. 'We would survive.'

Jesse and Lily walk out of the barn. The dog Joey returns, panting, with the hare, broken-backed and bleeding but still alive in its mouth. He drops the wounded animal at Jesse's feet. Jesse reaches for one of the heavy bits of iron still lying by the barn entrance. Lily forces herself to watch as Jesse raises the weapon and brings it crashing down on the skull of the hare. Blood flows into the weeds.

Jesse finds a rope halter for the mare and lifts Lily onto her back. She holds on to the horse's mane while Jesse leads her with the halter and they walk slowly across the fields. The mare's foal trots along behind them and the dog bounds ahead, sniffing for rabbits. They go into the wood, where the first primroses are lit by a glancing sun, and Lily says, 'I used to dream about all this, about the thistledown and the smell of spring flowers, because there is nothing like that in London.'

It's very quiet in the wood. The mare picks a dainty path across fallen twigs and they hear the drilling of a woodpecker and stop to listen and Jesse says, 'I will do my best to make a key for your mechanical toy, but it was a strange gift to bring – a creature in a prison – when the birdsong here is so loud. What made you think of that?'

Lily is silent for a moment. She wants to admit, 'Since I left Swaithey, I drag some prison with me wherever I go, and I always will.' But all she says is, 'I don't think Nellie likes the cage, does she? It was a mistake. We could sell it in the village on market day.'

'Yes,' says Jesse. 'I think that's best. Get a few ounces of sherbet for that ole thing, eh, or a spool of thread?'

They come out of the wood and go by a tall straw stack, neatly made from last year's wheat stalks, but some of the land is still grey with stubble, waiting for the plough, and Lily is struck by how great an expanse of earth this is for the capabilities of one man. She looks down at Jesse, holding the halter. He now wears a frayed old cap on his curls and his boots are clogged with mud, and she finds that these things move her, but to what, exactly, she can't say. To sorrow or pity, but also to something else – to something like remembered affection?

They approach the Swaithey Road, going back onto the rough dirt of the lane, and when they pause by the wild-rose hedge, they stop once more because they have both heard an unmistakable sound.

'Coach and pair,' says Jesse. 'Not many of these come past here.'

Lily clutches at the horse's mane. Jesse loops his arm round the neck of the foal, to stop her straying onto the road, into the path of the coach, and they stand and wait. The dog shivers and begins barking. And then suddenly, Lily thinks, I must run and hide, I must run now and wait for the darkness, then make my way back to the station . . .

The sound of the coach and pair is very near. Lily scrambles off the horse and begins to run back into the stubble field. Jesse calls out to her, but she keeps running, for she knows why this coach is coming. She knows that Rookery Farm was never far away enough, never a place where Sam Trench would fail to find her, and now he's here, he's commandeered some heavy old coach and the coach will turn into the lane and keep going until it stops beyond the new orchard and Sam will step down into the spring grass, wearing his tall hat, wearing the heavy coat that he once wrapped around her, and then the rest of her life will vanish. By nightfall she will be in a prison cell.

She stands behind an oak, on a bit of rising ground, and she can just see the hedge on the opposite side of the

Swaithey Road. She puts her arms around the tree, lays her cheek against the rough bark. Then she see it come into view: grey horses, a coachman wearing black, the coach large and swaying and creaking on its axle. As she waits for the coachman to tug the reins to the left, to turn into the lane, she realises that running away is futile. Her sack of possessions is stowed in her old room. Nellie will wake from her sleep and greet the police superintendent and say, 'Oh yes, she came back. The girl I had to give away. She will be here soon. I've forgotten her name just for a moment, but I always loved her. And she will look after me now.' And Sam Trench will shake his head and say, 'That would have been a fine idea. But it cannot be.'

Then the coach goes on by. Lily keeps clinging to the oak, watching it pass. It rounds a bend in the road and is lost to sight and the sound of it begins to get faint and then to disappear altogether. Lily waits. All she can hear now is her own breathing. Jesse calls out again and she slowly walks towards him.

'I'm sorry,' she says. 'I take fright, sometimes. At the strangest things. It's difficult to conquer. It's how we were at the Foundling Hospital: always afraid.'

She asks to see the pond. Jesse helps her back onto the mare and she knows that she's still trembling, but Jesse makes no mention of it. When they reach the pond the horse bends her neck to drink and the foal drinks and the dog Joey bounces into the water and swims to where the geese are going in lazy circles and they start up their honking call and flex their wings and flurry to the further bank, to where, now, the willows are putting forth tiny yellow shoots.

Without waiting for the dog, who seems preoccupied by the water, they pass to the back of the house to where the well still stands, half covered with ivy. Lily feels calm now. She gets off the horse and walks to the well and puts her hands on the edge of the stone wall and remembers the feel of this and how, for her, the story of the boy with no name lying far down in the darkness, under the mud, was something she never stopped believing until much later in her childhood, when all her woes started to crowd in on her and she began to say to herself, It wasn't a boy trapped in a freezing shaft, where he could hardly breathe, it was a girl, it was me, for this is what my life became: a foul and suffocating half-life from which there was no escape.

She stands very still. The sun falls on her neck, from where her hair is gathered up into a simple knot. Jesse is still too, at her side, but after a while, he lays his wide hand next to hers and she is moved to see this, the two hands side by side, the two hands holding on. She looks down and the depth of the water seems greater than it once was, as if it might go into the very centre of the earth.

And she says to herself, If another coach arrives, if Sam Trench does come for me one day, to take me away to the scaffold, I will escape from him just long enough to climb up here and let myself fall into the well. Before I die, before I cast myself into the unknown, as my mother cast me away into the unknown at the park gates, I will take a gulp of sweet water. And then I will shout my name up into the air – this air which bathes Rookery Farm with a tender balm. I will shout my name, *Lily*.

Acknowledgement

I have one person to thank above all others: Mr Siong-Seng Liau, Consultant Surgeon at Addenbrookes Hospital, Cambridge, for saving my life in the autumn of 2019.

the reforms it has advocated. Inevitably, this has been reported in terms of fraud, even where the Court's actual words may not have justified this.[62] Opportunities for fraud are best minimized by careful design of the programmes in question and by appropriate processes of financial control, accounting and internal audit. The primary responsibility for preventing and detecting fraud rests with management. External audit may aid management by advising on weaknesses in processes and identifying risks which might lead to problems and, as such, external audit is a deterrent to fraud. So, although external audit is an effective way of evaluating the capacity of such processes to prevent and detect fraud, it is doubtful whether it is useful in combating fraud directly.

VFM Audit

VFM audit can be unpopular.[63] Assessing 'effectiveness' means asking whether policy objectives are being achieved. Economy and efficiency also depend on the existence of clearly defined and coherent objectives. The less success the auditee has in defining and achieving his objectives, the more difficult it is for the auditor to draw a clear line between questioning the merits of policy objectives and assessing whether *vfm* has been achieved in the pursuit of those objectives.[64] The legitimacy of the public sector auditor is thus likely to be most precarious precisely when his function is most important.

The Court's 'Stuttgart report', produced in 1983 at the request of the Council, identified significant failings in Community policies and legislation.[65] The report was not well received by the Commission, which regarded the Court as trespassing into areas that are not properly its concern. More generally, the Commission has tended to resist the Court's increasing focus on *vfm* issues, claiming that these raise policy questions which are for the Commission and Council. Its view has been that the Court should be concerned primarily with regularity and legality.

The Court's difficulties in pursuing *vfm* audit have two main origins. First, *vfm* audit is not accepted in all states as a legitimate part of the work of an external audit body. The idea that the proper role of the auditor

[62] Contrast for example the title and the content of Kok, C., 'The fight against Euro-fraud', December 1994, *European Brief*, 30–1. The Court's Report to the 'Reflection Group' on the operation of the Treaty on European Union in May 1995 also draws attention to the Court's role in the fight against fraud.

[63] See, for example, the ECA's Special Report of the EU Administration in Mostar, OJ C287/1, 1996.

[64] Cf. National Audit Act 1983, s.6; see, further, Ch. 5.

[65] *Report in response to the conclusions of the European Council of 18 June 1983*, OJ C287/1 1983. See also Kok, *supra*, n. 2 and House of Lords, Select Committee on the European Community, *The Court of Auditors*, HL 102, 1986–87.

The Significance of the DAS

The DAS is supposed to be about regularity and legality,
but otherwise the Treaty is silent about its form and purpo
put into effect, it is hard to see the DAS as a major step forw
ing the management of Community finances, or the effec
Court. The requirement to provide an assurance can, of co
ing directly to improve the quality of financial control, or
of the Community's accounts (the possible indirect effect i
below). The proponents of DAS appear to have had a numb
ives in mind, including:

(1) providing a basis for the Parliament to make a global judg
    the work of the Commission in the discharge process;
(2) providing a lever for the Court to use in getting better acces
    mation; and
(3) putting pressure on the Court to adopt a more coherent ap
    its work.

The role of the DAS in the discharge procedure (see below) is un
has probably been an important factor in the Court obtaining a
the results of the Commission's internal audit and in a revision
Commission's rules about access more generally (see below). Th
process has also put pressure on the Court to reassess its own me
and to devise a corporate approach, but it has not yet led to a more
nal allocation of its resources. Unlike the position in the UK or Swe
for example, there is no formal division of staff at the ECA as fina
or *vfm* auditors. The staff who perform the DAS work are assigned to
different divisions of the ECA and do not operate from a central unit.
will the DAS help the Court to define the scope and purpose of its o
role in relation to the other institutions (see, further, below).

   The indirect impact of DAS will depend on how it is received b
the various audiences for the Court's work. Here, there is a considerabl
risk of a gap between what the Court thinks the DAS means and wha
others may understand it to mean.[61] This is especially so in relation to
fraud. The DAS is not intended to detect or measure the extent of fraud.
However, there is a danger that it will be misinterpreted. Euro-fraud is
big news and politically sensitive. In recent years, the Court has pursued
a high-profile strategy, seeking to mobilize public opinion in favour of

private firm of auditors, or part of a ministry of finance, or an NAI, or part thereof. Where
an NAI does this work, it is in its capacity as agent for the Commission and not as an NAI
per se. In the UK, the NAO won a three-year contract to perform this certifying task. See
Council Regulation 1663/95, as amended, and the NAO Annual Reports for 1995 and 1996.

   [61] The 'expectations gap' has been extensively analysed in relation to private sector
audit, see Power, M., *The Audit Explosion*, (London: Demos, 1994).

is confined to issues of regularity and propriety has found supporters amongst the members of the Court, as well as in the Commission. Second, effective financial management depends in practice on a hard budget constraint. Without such a constraint, there is little incentive for those responsible for spending to engage in a serious attempt to achieve *vfm*. Expenditure restraint requires priorities to be established between competing policy objectives, which in turn requires that those objectives be clearly identified and defined. This encourages—and is encouraged by— a focus on *vfm*.

In the Community, both Parliament and Commission have tended to regard expansion of the Community budget as per se a good thing, because it represents a growth of European competences. The result has been a tendency towards a 'spending culture', where it is more important to spend money than to set priorities or obtain *vfm*. By pointing out the results, the Court has made itself vulnerable to the accusation of being anti-*communautaire*; not a 'house-trained animal', as one Commission official put it to us. In the Community context, it is difficult to combine the role of 'house-trained animal' with that of effective watchdog.

Access

The Treaty and FR give the Court rights of access to information and to documents necessary to perform its duties.[66] It may perform on the spot audits in the states and in other Community institutions. However, the Court does not possess effective means of enforcement that it can use against states.[67] Even in respect of information held by the Commission, the latter's co-operation in providing or securing access is of considerable practical importance. An internal Commission document, consisting mainly of an exchange of letters, forms the basis of the rules on access. These rules were originally quite simple, but additions and revisions left them complicated and less effective. They were redrafted, following a problem concerning access to DG VI.[68] If the Court experiences difficulties with access to Commission records it may seek help from DG XIX. Parliament currently has no formal role in disputes about access, but conflicts may be brought to its attention.

The Court's new-found institutional status opens up the possibility of legal action against the Commission under Article 232 EC if it fails to

[66] Article 248(3) EC *(Article 188c(3))*; Articles 85–87 FR.

[67] Giving the Court the right to bring member states before the Court of Justice was proposed in the Court's report to the 1996 IGC 'reflection group'.

[68] Referred to in a 1993 Special Report, 8/93. The revised rules are contained in the *Vademecum des dispositions relatives à la Cour des comptes*, DG XIX 12 June 1995, which is an unpublished internal Commission document.

provide access to documents.[69] A litigious approach would clearly not be conducive to a good working relationship and the Court is likely to use its new powers with caution.[70] Likewise, the Commission is unlikely to want to see the scope of the Court's legal powers tested.

The 'Contradictory Procedure'

The Commission has the right to have its replies to criticism by the Court published together with the Court's report.[71] If the Court disagrees strongly with the Commission's eventual replies it may include a further 'réplique'. The final shape of the Court's report and the Commission's replies is determined in a dialogue between them known as the 'contradictory procedure'.[72] This process is not expressly provided for by the Treaty, or the FR, though it flows naturally from the right to reply. In the case of the annual report, the Court sends drafts of chapters to DG XIX, which forwards copies to the relevant directorates general. Copies are also sent by the Court to the Chair of the Budgetary Control Committee of the Parliament and the Committee's *rapporteur* for the discharge (see below), although Parliament has no *locus standi* in the negotiations between the Commission and the Court. The directorates general responsible for each policy area draft replies and send them to the unit in DG XIX which is responsible for liaison with the Commission, the ECA and the financial committees of Parliament. At an inter-service meeting, DG XIX offers advice on the revision of draft replies. Representatives of DG XX, the Secretariat General and the Commission's anti-fraud unit (UCLAF)[73] are also present at these meetings. Meetings then take place between the Court and the Commission (*réunions contradictoires*) before the final wording of the report and the replies is determined. The aim is, at a minimum, to agree on the facts. The process has sometimes been confrontational.

Previous practice has been to hold the réunions contradictoires concerning the annual report in September. There has been a change in the level at which the contradictory procedure occurs. It used to be conducted between Directors in the Commission and audit staff from the Court. Since 1995 the procedure has also involved Commissioners and Members of the Court and meetings between Commissioners in the preparation of

---

[69] Article 232 EC (*Article 175*) permits 'other institutions of the Community' to bring proceedings against the Parliament, Council or Commission for failure to act. The Amsterdam Treaty further recognizes the standing of the ECA under Article 230 EC (*Article 173*) to challenge the legality of Community acts for the purpose of protecting its prerogatives. However, it cannot bring proceedings in the Court of Justice against a Member State.

[70] HL 75, 1993–94, evidence of A. J. Wiggins, current member of the Court.

[71] Article 248(4) EC (*Article 188c(4)*).

[72] '*Procédure contradictoire*'—more accurately translated as 'adversarial procedure'.

[73] Unité contre la fraude.

replies to the Court.[74] These changes are part of an attempt to achieve a more effective working relationship between the Commission and the Court (see further below).

Reporting

The Court's main output has traditionally been its annual report, which now includes the DAS. The annual report is a mixture of regularity and *vfm* findings and is published in November of the year following the year to which it relates. The Council and Parliament take it into account in the discharge procedure (see below).

The Court also produces special reports, most of which are concerned with issues of *vfm*. Not all of them are published.[75] As a result of amendments to the Treaty by the TEU, special reports are also to be taken into account in the discharge procedure.[76] The special reports have the advantage of focusing on one issue, rather than being part of a long, varied and variable annual report. However, a major weakness of the Court's special reports is that it may take up to two and a half years to complete them. This means that some of the findings and recommendations may be out of date by the time the report is published.

The Court also communicates some of its findings privately to those whom it audits. It does this through 'sector letters', some of which later form the basis for special reports. Where the relevant audit has taken place in the Commission, the sector letters are sent to DG XIX. If the audit has taken place in a member state, the Court sends them to the NAI, and the relevant government department, with a copy to DG XIX. Both types of letter are forwarded to the appropriate Commission departments for information or action.

THE COURT'S AUDIENCE(S)

The Court's audit findings are potentially a source of information which can be used both to call those responsible for administering the Community budget to account, and by those same persons, to improve their own performance. The impact and effectiveness of the Court depend on its relationship with its audience(s) and what action is taken as a result of its reports. It is therefore important that the Court should be able to identify its audience(s) and gear its reports to them.

[74] SEC(95)772 'L'amélioration de la procédure contradictoire avec la Cour des Comptes', Communication de M. Liikanen en accord avec M. le President, adopted 18/5/95.
[75] Unpublished special reports are copied to the Council and the Budgetary Control Committee.
[76] Article 276(1) EC *(Article 206(1))*.

The Commission

The Court has repeatedly criticized the Commission's internal control systems. As noted above, it has argued that the system of *ex ante* control by the contrôleur financier discourages those making spending decisions from taking responsibility for ensuring *vfm*. The Court has also argued that the contrôleur's role effectively involves the incompatible functions of authorizing expenditure and then subsequently evaluating the *vfm* of the same decisions.[77]

The possibility of a good relationship between the Court and the Commission is limited by the nature of the Community's financial system. We have already noted that, despite its responsibility for implementation of the budget, the Commission exercises little managerial control over the end use of the majority of Community spending. The extent of the delegation of functions to states makes it difficult for the Commission to establish a robust financial control system and for the Court to monitor it. The Commission is under pressure from the Parliament to do more and spend more. It also has to cope with the results of deals and compromises between the states, reached in the Council, which may have obscure or conflicting objectives and which may make little sense in terms of the practicalities of implementation.

In the past, the Commission's responses to the Court's reports have often suggested that the Court is interfering in matters that are not its business, that it is bringing stale news, or that it is plain wrong. It is no secret that relations between former Commission President, M. Delors, and the then President of the Court, M. Middlehoek, were less than harmonious. Following the appointment of the Santer Commission in 1995, there has been an attempt to re-establish good relations between the Court and the Commission.

The DAS process may put the improved relationship under renewed strain. The sampling technique being used raises complex statistical issues and judgment is required in assessing the significance of errors detected in the sample. This means that there is room for disagreement about what the results of the DAS audit really mean, especially when the Court takes the view that it cannot give an unqualified assurance.[78] Even if the meaning of the DAS is clear to professional auditors, there is further scope for conflict about how it can best be communicated to the Parliament, the Council and the public. It may prove hard, in practice, to

---

[77] See 'Study of the financial systems of the European Communities', OJ C 342 1981.

[78] In response to the ECAs' 1995 DAS report, the Commission commissioned a private management report on the ECAs' work. This report has led to further dialogue between the Commission and the ECA about the DAS methodology: *Report to the European Commission on the Approach of the Court of Auditors in arriving at their 'Statement of Assurance' on the reliability of the income and payments of the Commission in 1995*, December 1996, unpublished.

separate disputes about what the DAS means from those about how it is to be communicated.

The European Parliament[79]

The Discharge Procedure

The Council and the Parliament jointly constitute the budgetary authority. Since 1977, however, it has been the Parliament alone, acting on a recommendation from the Council, which grants discharge to the Commission for implementation of the budget. Discharge is given to the Commission as an institution, not to individual Commissioners, and in respect of the budget taken as a whole.

The discharge procedure is one of the key parliamentary levers over the Commission, but its precise constitutional nature is somewhat obscure. It is both a formal act, marking the final closure of the accounts and a political verdict on the performance of the Commission.[80] Neither the Treaties nor the FR provides for any specific sanction against the Commission in the discharge procedure. The consequences of a refusal of discharge are disputed as, indeed, is the question of whether Parliament even has power to refuse discharge, rather than merely postpone it.[81] The then budget Commissioner Christopher Tugendhat told the Parliament in 1977 that the political consequences of a refusal of discharge would be extremely serious; a Commission thus censured would have to be replaced. However, the only occasion when Parliament refused discharge was in 1984, for the 1982 budget. At that point, the Commission was only a few weeks away from the end of its normal term. The Commission did not resign, nor did the Parliament take steps to dismiss it under the then Article 144 EC.[82] Discharge was later granted to the new Commission, though the Parliament regarded this as relating only to the formal closure of the accounts.

As amended by the TEU, the EC Treaty requires the Commission to 'take all appropriate steps to act on the observations in the decisions giving discharge and on other observations by the European Parliament relating to the execution of expenditure'.[83] The first part of this provision reproduces wording that was already contained in the FR.[84] The second part was new. Its effect is to extend the obligation to act on observations

---

[79] See, generally, Theato, D., and Graf, R., *Das Europäische Parlament und das Haushalt der Europäischen Gemeinschaft*, (Nomos Verlag, 1994).

[80] *Community Public Finance: The European budget after the 1988 reform*, (Luxembourg: Office for Official Publications of the EC, 1989).

[81] See Strasser, *supra*, n. 18, p. 291.

[82] Dismissal under Article 201 EC (*Article 144*) requires a two-thirds majority, whereas the Parliament's rules provide for a refusal of discharge to be by simple majority.

[83] Article 276 EC (*Article 206*).   [84] Article 89(4) and (5).

to include those attached to a *postponement* of discharge. This is significant because, if Parliament decides to postpone the discharge, it must give reasons and state the conditions on which the granting of discharge depends.[85] Hence this provision encourages Parliament to use a form of political censure that, in principle, is directed towards ensuring improved performance in the future rather than punishment for past failures. The Parliament's rules mention the possibility of Article 232 EC proceedings in the event of the Commission failing to comply with the observations in resolutions accompanying discharge.[86]

As already noted, approximately 80 per cent of the general budget is actually disbursed by the administrations of member states, but it is the Commission which is held to account through the discharge procedure. This would cause no problems if the Commission were able to demonstrate that it effectively monitors and evaluates the relevant activities of the states' administrations. There are few who would argue that the Commission does this, but there is less agreement about who is responsible for the fact that it does not. Is it the Commission itself, member states, one or both of the component parts of the budgetary authority, or some combination of all of them?

Making the Commission responsible through the discharge procedure would be effective if all states had the administrative capacity for sound financial control and management and if the Commission had sufficient levers to make them use it. There is a strong similarity between the problems faced by the Court in relying on the work of NAIs to support the DAS and those faced by the Commission in relying on national administrations to spend Community money properly. The difference is that the Court has no executive responsibility, whereas the Commission does. The Court takes the view that the Commission can delegate functions, but not responsibility. The Commission could refuse to implement budget lines where there is functional delegation to the states, but no satisfactory mechanism exists to monitor and evaluate the spending. However, this would immediately bring it into conflict with the states and with the budgetary authority. It is therefore unsurprising that the Commission should appeal to 'subsidiarity' to argue that responsibility for money spent by the national administrations rests with the states themselves.

Whilst DAS will do nothing to solve this fundamental problem of accountability, it may re-open the question of the meaning of the discharge process. Financial audit directed by the C&AG in Britain leads to certification and reporting on individual accounts. DAS, however, relates to the budget as a whole. If the DAS is unqualified (or positive), does this

---

[85] See, for example, the Parliamentary resolution explaining why discharge for the 1992 accounts was postponed, OJ C128/322 1994.

[86] (*Article 175*): European Parliament Rules of Procedure, 8th edn., 1993, Annex V Article 7.

not pre-empt the discharge decision? On the other hand, if the Court detects so many irregularities in the underlying transactions as to cast doubt on the reliability of the accounts and/or the legality and regularity of the underlying transactions, how can discharge properly be given at all? In relation to the 1994 general budget, for instance, the ECA found that it could not give a positive global assurance as to the legality and regularity of the transactions underlying payments.[87] It appears that the ECA was saying that, on the basis of its work, it cannot give either a positive, or a negative, assurance on the legality and regularity of payment transactions. Nevertheless, in April 1996, Parliament gave discharge to the Commission regarding the general budget.[88] Accordingly, it would seem that the ECA's opinion on the 1994 budget is not clear enough to be linked to the discharge process. The relationship between the DAS and discharge remains obscure.

The Budgetary Control Committee

When the ECA was being planned in the early 1970s, the European Parliament approved in principle the creation of a 'Public Accounts Committee', based on the analogy of the British PAC.[89] Eventually, responsibility for control of budget implementation was given to the Budgets Committee, which was requested to delegate the task permanently to a subcommittee on the Budget of the Communities (Control of Implementation). The subcommittee was described as appearing to be 'completely dormant' in the mid-1970s. Only in 1979 was it elevated into a separate Budgetary Control Committee (BCC). Parliament's rules of procedure provide that in carrying out its functions, the BCC is to 'cooperate closely' with the Budgets Committee.[90] There is a substantial overlap of membership between the two committees, although they are served by separate secretariats.

The BCC is the Committee responsible for the discharge process. The Committee is the Court's main Parliamentary audience and often bases its own work on reports made by the Court. However, it also responds to legislative proposals from the Commission, and produces 'own initiative' reports. As a result, the Court's and the BCC's reports sometimes compete with each other.[91] BCC meetings are attended by representatives from the Commission, the Court and, less regularly, the Council. Like the

---

[87] This was also the case regarding the 1995 and 1996 budgets.

[88] The Parliament did refuse discharge regarding the implementation of the European Development Funds for 1994 following the ECA's negative DAS: see OJ L148/56 1996.

[89] The Commission proposed the establishment of a Court of Auditors in 1973 (COM (73)1000). For Parliament's response see OJ C 87 1973.

[90] European Parliament Rules of Procedure, Annex VI, October 1993.

[91] Compare, for example, Chapter 17, 'The European Parliament's building', in the Court of Auditors' 1993 Annual Report (OJ C 327 1994) with the Budgetary Control Committee's report (PE 208.238/fin, rapporteur: John Tomlinson).

PAC at Westminster, the BCC tries to function in a non-partisan way and has had some success in achieving this. Its reports are usually adopted by the Parliament. However, this is not because the Committee has a high status. On the contrary, it is low down the pecking order of committees and attendance is relatively low; of the 27 members, only a handful are fundamentally interested in what happens and active in following up the Court's reports. Attendance is low at the plenary session of the Parliament when the Court's report and the BCC's draft discharge resolution are considered.

The Committee's profile has begun to rise as a result of the prominence accorded to the 'fight against fraud'. Attendance has improved as a result, but at the same time the Committee is having more difficulty in maintaining a bipartisan approach. It is also having to protect its own turf against other committees which have wanted to set up inquiries in areas that the BCC would normally cover, making use of the power which the TEU gave to the Parliament to conduct ad hoc investigations.[92]

Spending and VFM

The procedure for establishing the Community budget was briefly outlined above, where it was noted that Parliament has the last word on 'non-compulsory' expenditure. Within the Parliament, the Budgets Committee plays the role of 'gatekeeper' in relation to amendments to the draft budget. Amendments proposed by subject committees are forwarded to the Budgets Committee, which decides whether or not to endorse them. It may also propose amendments of its own. The draft budget then goes to a plenary session of Parliament, which votes on all the proposed amendments. In practice, amendments which have not been endorsed or proposed by the Budgets Committee have a much lower chance of success.

Most Parliaments—and the European Parliament is no exception—find it easier to establish new spending programmes than to cut old ones. The reason is simple; the benefits of any particular item of spending are concentrated on a smaller group than the savings that result from not spending. Hence, there are greater incentives for groups to 'log-roll' (that is, form spending coalitions) than to form coalitions to resist, or cut, spending. Furthermore, the European Parliament has ambitions actually to make, not merely to scrutinize, the policies which spending represents. The activities of the BCC should therefore be seen in the context of a larger

---

[92] Article 193 EC (*Article 138c*). See also the Decision of the European Parliament, the Council and the Commission of 6 March 1995 on the detailed provisions governing the exercise of the European Parliament's right of inquiry: OJ L 78 1995. See, for example, the Report of the Committee of Inquiry into the Community Transit System, (PE 220.895/fin, rapporteur: Edward Kellett-Bowman).

enterprise of seeking to consolidate and expand the budgetary power of the Community *vis-à-vis* the states and of the Parliament *vis-à-vis* the Commission and Council. Most members of the BCC are also members of other Parliamentary committees and, as already noted, there is a high degree of overlap in the membership of the BCC and the Budgets Committee. These factors mean that many BCC members are more concerned with the policy issues behind spending than with the spending issues behind policy. Although the BCC has criticized the Commission's financial management on *vfm* grounds, it has also focused on the Commission's failure—or refusal—to undertake spending, particularly on items which Parliament has put into the budget.[93]

Whatever may have been the intentions of those who established the BCC, its resemblance to the PAC is no more than superficial. Historically, the search for waste and inefficiency has had a high profile at Westminster because Parliament granted taxes reluctantly and jealously scrutinized the use which the executive made of the money that Parliament provided. In more modern times, the PAC has prestige because the MPs who sit on it are just about the only backbenchers who have any real power over the executive. The UK Parliament has no power to increase spending, or to reorder priorities in the budget. The BCC and the PAC are different creatures, operating in different environments.

There is now considerable tension evident between the BCC and the Court.[94] In the view of the Committee, the Court should be no more than a technical adjunct to its own work rather than a free-standing body with its own role in the institutional balance of the Union. This general perception (which may be based in part upon misconceptions about the constitutional role of the NAO in the UK) feeds into more specific complaints. A long-standing source of grievance is that the Court has provided information to the Commission which it refuses to give to the

---

[93] The Commission would probably never explicitly refuse to spend money appropriated by the Parliament because of the political implications. It may however not spend the full amount appropriated by Parliament when it considers it impracticable or undesirable to do so. There is also a difference of opinion between the Commission and Parliament over what constitutes an adequate legal basis for expenditure. Parliament has argued that the budget itself is all that is needed. The Commission position is that, in addition to budgetary authorization, there must be a specific legal basis, such as a Regulation, for the programme in question. A related dispute concerns pre-emption of the budget process by the use of legislation to prescribe particular amounts of spending. See, further: Edsberg, J., 'The European Community's budget: budget discipline and budget accounting', 10 (1994) *Financial Accountability and Management*, 1–16; the *Interinstitutional Agreement* of 29 October 1993; the Commission Communication to the budgetary authority concerning legal bases and maximum amounts SEC (94) 1106 (final); and the Committee on Budgets Working Document No. 2, 21 December 1994, PE 211.073.

[94] See, for example, the memorandum to HL 75, 1993–94 by John Tomlinson (a member of the BCC) and the BCC report on relations between bodies responsible for the control of the Community budget, PE 206.004/fin A3-0320/93 (rapporteur: John Tomlinson).

BCC.[95] The BCC would also like to have power to direct the Court to conduct audits in particular areas. There is also resentment at the Court's attempts to raise its own public profile and to mobilize public opinion in support of its criticisms of financial control and management.

The Council

The main interface between the Court and the Council is also the discharge process: in giving discharge to the Commission, the Parliament acts on a recommendation from the Council.[96] The Council's recommendation is prepared by its budgets committee, which is part of the Committee of Permanent Representatives (COREPER). At ministerial level, the Council has not accorded the annual or special reports of the Court much political priority.[97] Until recently there has been no mechanism by which to ensure, for example, that the Agriculture Ministers consider the Court's findings in relation to agricultural spending. However, ECOFIN[98] has decided that in future every special report from the Court will be thoroughly examined by a relevant Committee or working party designated by COREPER.[99]

As a Community institution, the Council's role is essentially to forge agreements on policy through compromise. Efficiency therefore may be sacrificed in order to achieve consensus. Public opinion tends to lay the blame for waste and fraud on the Commission and, less often, the Parliament, rather than the Council. These factors militate against the Council acting effectively on the basis of the Court's findings and limit its value as an audience. The Council's role in representing the interests of the member states is considered in the next section.

Member States

The states, in particular the net contributors to the Community budget, might seem to constitute an obvious audience for the Court. The BCC is making efforts to encourage national Parliaments to get involved in the fight against fraud. The problem is that, even for net contributors, there is little incentive to examine the use of the funds they themselves receive to see if better *vfm* can be obtained, or more effective measures to prevent

---

[95] In one case, the Court conducted a study at the request of the Commission. It considered that the resulting information belonged to the Commission, hence it was for the Commission, not the Court, to release it.

[96] Article 276 EC (*Article 206*).

[97] HL 75, 1993–94, evidence of A. J. Wiggins, current member of the Court. See also Kok, *supra*, n. 2.

[98] The Council meeting in the composition of economic and finance ministers.

[99] *European Community Finances*, Cm. 2824, 1995.

fraud be put in place. The aim of the national agencies who actually spend Community funds is to make sure that they get as large a share as possible.[100] National finance ministers might be expected to have a different perspective. They typically have responsibility for taxation and government borrowing as well as spending. This gives them an incentive to limit total Community spending, because their national contribution to the Community budget is thereby reduced. Finance ministers are also under pressure to limit spending in order to help meet the EMU convergence criteria. For any individual state, however, the likely advantage from taking effective national measures against fraud and poor financial management would be tiny. Any savings made would be shared by all 15 states, whether or not they themselves had taken such measures.

Since lack of positive incentives means that norms of sound financial management and fraud-prevention are not self-enforcing, Community institutions have turned to sanctions as an alternative. The Commission successfully brought a case against Greece in the European Court of Justice for failure to apply the same standards of control to Community as to national money.[101] This principle was reinforced by provisions in the TEU.[102] At present, however, the Court has no powers to invoke legal sanctions against national officials who obstruct its audit work.[103]

THE FUTURE ROLE OF THE COURT OF AUDITORS

The Union needs an effective external audit body. External audit is essential to ensure both the effective management of public money and the accountability of those who make decisions about it. Its scope should not be confined to the regularity and legality of expenditure, but also include *vfm* examinations. The potential value of the ECAs' *vfm* work is shown by the best of its reports, which have drawn attention to lack of clear objectives and to poor and confused systems of accountability and financial management in the Community.

However, the conclusion we draw from the analysis in previous sections is that the effectiveness of the ECA could be substantially improved. So far, it has:

(a) achieved an uneasy relationship with the Commission;
(b) found itself in conflict with the Parliament's BCC;

---

[100] Levy, R., 'Audit and Accountability in a Multi-Agency Environment: The Case of the Common Agricultural Policy in the UK', 10(1) (1994) *Financial Accountability and Management* 65.

[101] Case 68/88, *Commission* v. *Hellenic Republic* [1989] ECR 2965.

[102] Article 209a EC (*Article 280*).

[103] See HL 75, 1993–94, evidence of Jo Carey (a former Member of the Court); Court of Auditors Annual Reports, OJ C321/32 1986; OJ C336/39 1987; OJ C312 1989.

(c) been largely ignored by the Council; and

(d) remained virtually unknown to most of the national Parliaments.

This situation is the result of factors which are, for the most part, beyond the control of the Court itself. The structure and organization of the Court are part of the explanation, but even they are not wholly under its own control. The other part of the explanation relates to the broader framework in which the Court operates and which its power to influence is even more limited. We shall examine these matters in turn.

Structure and Organization

To perform effectively, the Court needs internal agreement on its purposes and methods. Trying to forge a common understanding and a clear identity out of 15 different national traditions of public sector audit is destined to fail within a collegiate structure which gives individual members a high degree of autonomy. It remains the case that the delegation of tasks to officers of the Court must be specifically notified to the authorities with which the officer is to work.[104] This system—combining fragmentation with obstacles to delegation—seems almost designed to limit the Court's effectiveness. We have also noted that staff resources are divided relatively evenly between members rather than being allocated on the basis of the amount and importance of the work to be performed in different areas.

The enlargement of the Community in 1995 resulted in a corresponding increase in the number of members of the Court. It is doubtful whether there is enough high-level work to occupy 15 members fulltime. With further enlargement of the Community almost certain to happen in the medium term, there is a strong case for reassessing the convention of having a member for every state and/or the current role which members play in the Court. Possible reforms (not necessarily alternatives) include:

(a) strengthening the role of the President, perhaps abandoning the collegiate structure in favour of an institution headed by a single individual. However, it would be a mistake to base a reform of this kind on an analogy with the British NAO, headed by the C&AG. In the Community context, an audit body headed by a single individual would probably have to become subordinate to another institution (unlike the NAO). If it were not, what method of appointment for a 'Community Auditor General' could be devised?

---

[104] Article 83 FR.

(b) reducing the number of members of the Court. The problem here is the same as in the case of the Commission: states are unlikely to agree to losing 'their' member;

(c) appointing a small number of members as an 'audit board' with direct management responsibility for the audit staff—the role of the plenary Court could be confined to approval of strategic management and policy decisions; and

(d) dividing the Court into a small number of chambers, thus retaining the collegiate structure, but limiting the fragmentation and irrational allocation of resources involved in giving each member a personal fiefdom. The creation of 'audit groups' (see above) could be regarded as an initial step in this direction. This route to reform would provoke least opposition in the Court itself and involve least risk of unexpected consequences.

Streamlining the Court in one or more of these ways would make the process of appointment of members and of the President even more important, adding weight to the argument that the role of the European Parliament in the appointments process should be strengthened. This could help remove doubts about the independence of members from the governments of member states. An additional or alternative safeguard would be the introduction of a longer, non-renewable, term of office.[105]

There may be legal scope for some changes to be made by agreement in the Court itself, particularly as regards (d) above. In practice, however, amendment of the Treaty would be necessary for most of them. Any such amendment needs also to address the framework of financial control and budgeting in which the Court operates.

The Framework of Financial Control and Budgeting

It has been argued that the conceptual conflicts implied by the absence of a 'European audit fraternity' can be understood in terms of a north/south divide.[106] 'Southern' states, it is argued, tend to see the job of the public sector auditor as being to sit in judgment on public accounts. The judicial approach is associated with an approach to financial control based on detailed legal requirements and personal liability of officials. The 'northern' states tend to see the public auditor's role much more in terms of evaluating the adequacy and appropriateness of systems of financial management and *vfm*. Although this analysis reflects debates within the

---

[105] Cf. membership of the Executive Board of the future European Central Bank, Article 109a(2) EC (*Article 112(2)*).

[106] See HL 75, 1993–4, evidence of Jo Carey, former UK Member of the Court.

Court and elsewhere, it does not completely explain the Court's failure to establish an identity for itself. Germany, for example, does not fit neatly into the north/south divide.[107] The German system is governed by detailed legal provisions, but is also directed towards *vfm*. The French system—on which those of the 'southern' states and the Community are based—also manages to combine a strong legal culture with a concern for good financial management.[108] There is no necessary conflict, therefore, between a strongly legal approach and concern with *vfm* issues. Rather, the key difference is that between a legal culture in which rules and procedures are understood, interpreted and applied as part of a purposive enterprise and a legalistic culture, in which the prevailing ethos is—as one Commission official told us—'just follow the rules and you sleep easily at night'.

However, perhaps the most fundamental problem in finding a role for the ECA is that the Community does not have any equivalent of a ministry of finance.[109] French contrôleurs financiers are appointed by, and responsible to, a powerful Ministry of Finance. As well as being responsible for *ex ante* control of legality and regularity they are, in effect, the eyes and ears of the Ministry of Finance in the spending ministries. The French Ministry of Finance is the institutional guardian of overall spending restraint; hence the necessary precondition for taking value for money issues seriously is in place. The Cour des Comptes and the Ministry of Finance are basically pushing in the same direction. The same is true (though in very different constitutional settings) of the British NAO and the German *Bundesrechnungshof*.

In the Community, responsibility for budgets and for financial control is divided between DG XIX (budgets) and DG XX (financial control).[110] The Commission's contrôleur financier is not part of a powerful ministry of finance. Even if the two Directorates General were put together, DG XIX does not have a powerful, strategically dominant, role in the budget process.[111] In these circumstances, it is unsurprising that the relationship

---

[107] As noted in Ch. 5, the *Bundesrechnungshof* is also a collegiate body and operates within a highly structured public sector where financial controls are governed by detailed statutory provisions. It does not however act as a judicial body and devotes the greater part of its resources to value for money investigations.

[108] Although the French system has been criticized for paying relatively too much attention to legality and too little to good management: see the contribution of Loïc Philip to Cassese ed., *supra*, n. 13.

[109] A point made by the ECA in the 'Stuttgart report', *supra*, n. 65, para. 1.2.1.

[110] In the last Commission, one Commissioner headed both DG XIX and DG XX, however there are currently two separate commissioners.

[111] For the importance of such a role in large states, see von Hagen, J., and Harden, I. J., 'National budgetary processes and fiscal performance' in *European Economy: Towards Greater Fiscal Discipline*, Reports and Studies 1994, No. 3, pp. 311–418 (Luxembourg: Office for Official Publications of the EC, 1994).

between the Commission (in the sense of the *spending* DGs) and the Court is clouded by mutual prejudices.

Where does this leave the Court? Its problem is not simply to define a Community model of audit, though it certainly needs to develop a more co-ordinated approach to its work and to seek to expand the possibilities of co-operation with the NAIs of the states. The more fundamental problem is constitutional. NAIs differ not only in their understanding of audit, but in their constitutional relationships with other organs of government. At present, the Community constitutional framework provides no obvious niche for the Court to occupy.

For the reasons already given above, it seems unlikely that the Court can find a sustainable long-term role by putting itself in the front line of the fight against fraud. An alternative possibility would be to seek to become more like the Parliamentary auditors of Sweden and Finland.[112] Finally, and most likely, the Court could essentially play a waiting game, relying on a gradual strengthening of its natural allies: those within the Commission and Parliament seeking to push an agenda of good management and *vfm*.

There are a few encouraging signs. In the Parliament, there may be the beginnings of a recognition that the budget constraint imposed by the financial perspective makes attention to *vfm* a sensible political strategy.[113] In the Commission, the budget Commissioner now has a stronger role in the process of developing new proposals with expenditure implications.[114] However, for the Commission to develop an effective ministry of finance role would require mechanisms to review and change existing expenditure priorities. Aspects of the Union's constitutional structure make this especially necessary, because they create a strong bias against cutting existing spending programmes. Factors of particular importance are: the intergovernmental nature of decision-making in the Council; the status of the *acquis communautaire* (the body of European law); and the relatively powerful role of the Parliament in the budget process.[115] These same features, however, militate against a role for the Commission in questioning the value and purpose of existing Community programmes. Part of its institutional role is to be the guardian of the acquis. Furthermore, it lacks

---

[112] As was noted in Chapter 6, in these countries, there are two separate bodies: Parliamentary auditors, appointed by Parliament and with an overtly political role; and a national audit office which reports to the Ministry of Finance and government.

[113] See Committee on Budgets, draft report and explanatory statement on the guidelines for the 1996 budgetary procedure, PE 211.743.

[114] SEC (95) 82, 23 January 1995, approved by the Commission 25 January 1995.

[115] Intergovernmentalism has a status quo bias because of the size of the majorities needed to achieve change. The *acquis* tends to be defended in terms of specific policies (e.g., agricultural price support) as well as areas of Community competence. On the Parliament see above.

the democratic legitimacy to challenge the two parts of the budgetary authority.

This does not necessarily exclude better financial management of existing programmes. The Santer Commission adopted a three-stage initiative for this purpose.[116] Stage 1 aimed to produce improvements within the present administrative and legislative framework; the Commission adopted its conclusions in June 1995.[117] Stage 2 concerned the internal organization of the Commission's services and possible changes to the FR. There has been a rationalization of the prior control exercised by the contrôleur financier over payments using sampling methods, and this is to be extended from 'payments' to 'commitments' on a test basis.[118] This rationalization appears compatible with the current FR and no major modifications to the FR have been proposed to date. Also, greater emphasis is being placed on *ex post* internal audit with particular reference to developing a common approach to methodology with the ECA.[119] This could facilitate the work of the Court by opening up the possibility of reliance on the Commission's internal audit work.

Stage 3 has the more ambitious aim of 'reinforcing partnership with the member states', through Commission initiatives 'to improve co-ordination with the responsible national authorities in order better to manage, control and audit the use of resources of the Community and to evaluate the results'. The scope for doing this through sanctions—forcing officials and states to comply with Community rules—is limited. In the longer term, there is no satisfactory alternative to a degree of harmonization of national systems of financial control and management and of external audit. The Commission appear to be adopting the latter approach and to date, eight 'protocols' have been signed with member states in the area of Structural Funds, and negotiations are continuing regarding the remaining states.[120] The objective, it would appear, is to align audit methodologies between member states and the Commission, taking into account the methodology used by the ECA. This may herald the beginnings of a 'Community' model of financial control and audit.

[116] Sound Financial Management, SEC(95)477.
[117] Improvement of Financial Management, Phase 1. Communication from M. Liikanen and M. Gradin in agreement with the President, 20 June 1995.
[118] Unpublished Memorandum to the Commission from M. Gradin, in agreement with the President, 6 November 1996.
[119] Ibid.
[120] Ibid. Pre-SEM2000, progress had already been made in the area of agriculture where 'accredited agencies' are used to provide internal control checks: see further DG XX, *Financial Control and Audit in the European Union*, (unpublished, July 1997).

9

Conclusions

The previous chapters have sought to describe and analyse the constitutional role of public sector audit in Britain. We have focused mainly on the audit arrangements for central government, but have also considered audit at the local and European levels of governance. In this final chapter, we first bring together various threads of our analysis to identify the fundamental principles—institutional and substantive—of public sector audit, then consider some new tasks that audit could fulfil at central government level and conclude with an examination of the challenges presented by devolution.

A theme which has run through several chapters of the book is the series of changes in the public sector for which we have borrowed the label 'new public management'. For our purposes, the main importance of NPM is that the public sector has become much more like the private sector in terms of organizational structures, methods of operation and management style. This change has knock-on implications for audit. In particular, there has been a convergence of audit skills and techniques between the two sectors. The increase in the number of audits contracted-out by the NAO illustrates that private firms are capable of, and willing to, conduct public audit. The whole framework of public sector audit in local government and the NHS is evidence of this fact. More recently, the focus of training within the NAO has shifted from the standard public sector qualification (with the Chartered Institute of Public Finance and Accounting) to the standard private sector qualification (with the Institute of Chartered Accountants of England and Wales).

A fundamental difference remains, however, between the role of private and public sector audit. External audit in the private sector is an essential part of arrangements for corporate governance which are premised on private ownership and private profit as the mainsprings of action. External audit in the public sector is an essential part of a constitution which is premised on the accountability of government to Parliament and to citizens. This does not prevent a considerable degree of overlap between concepts, practices and standards of audit in the two sectors. In our view, however, it does mean that there should be recognition of a distinctive set of principles of public sector audit that reflect its constitutional importance.

To avoid misunderstanding, it should be made clear that we do not propose that a uniform set of institutional arrangements should be applied at all territorial levels of government. On the contrary, the constitutional role of audit implies that its institutional arrangements should reflect constitutional differences between layers of government, as well as the relationship between the layers. Nor do we propose that there should be a uniform method of audit that applies to all types of public sector body. One of the effects of NPM is greater organizational separation and specialization of function in the public sector. The activity of the auditor needs to be appropriate to the characteristics of the audited body.

However, despite the necessary differentiation in concrete arrangements, all public sector audit should embody a common set of fundamental principles. These principles concern both the institutional framework of audit and the substantive audit activity.

Institutional Requirements

The analysis in earlier chapters leads us to identify three fundamental institutional requirements for public sector audit: independence; an appropriate audience; and the right to follow public money to the final recipient.

Of these three requirements the most central, and the one which should be constitutionally secured, is independence. The independence of an audit institution must be understood to include the three elements of organizational, personal, and operational independence discussed in Chapter 5. In Chapter 7, we saw that a number of ministerial powers in relation to the Audit Commission are incompatible with this standard.

The second institutional requirement of public sector audit is the need for an identifiable and appropriate audience which can act on an auditor's reports and findings. In central government in Britain, the PAC is the long established primary audience for the findings of the NAO though, as was considered in Chapter 6, other audiences, potential and real, exist. The identification of an appropriate and effective audience for the European Court of Auditors is highlighted in Chapter 8 as one of the challenges which faces the Court.

The final institutional requirement is that audit institutions must have the ability to follow public monies to the final recipient, if necessary, to ensure that public monies have been spent in accordance with the proper authorities and in a way that achieves value for money. This right is afforded to the Audit Commission and to the European Court of Auditors, but not to the NAO. Contracting-out in particular means that large amounts of public money are provided to private bodies to provide public services. And yet, as described in Chapter 4, the NAO has no automatic right of access to the records of private contractors in order to check that the money has been spent for the purposes and in accordance with the conditions for which it was provided.

Substantive Requirements

The substantive practices and standards of audit that should apply in the public sector are largely a matter for professional auditors to determine, rather than lawyers. However, the procedure through which the substantive content of public sector audit is determined is a matter of constitutional significance. The process should be an open and accountable one. This point was made in Chapter 2 in relation to the setting of accounting standards under Resource Accounting and Budgeting (RAB). Similar arguments can be made here, when it comes to setting auditing standards for the public sector. Public sector auditing standards should not be determined through a closed bargaining process between the profession and the Treasury. One way in which this could be avoided would be to develop a standard setting role for the Public Audit Forum. As noted in Chapter 2 above, the Forum was established following a recommendation from the Nolan Committee on Standards in Public Life, in order to oversee the different audit frameworks and to bring together the key issues in public sector audit. Little information was available about the Forum at the time of writing and there was no material published as to its constitution, its functions, or its procedures for doing business. However, we would suggest that its remit should include the making explicit of fundamental principles of public audit. In doing so, it should seek to do its business in a transparent manner, and, in keeping with the desire for openness, should consult as widely as possible. Clearly, it would be important for the Forum to be representative of interested parties, including the audit institutions themselves, the Treasury, and the profession.

From a legal perspective, we have two main suggestions concerning the rules and principles of public audit. The first concerns their level of abstraction. Our view is that the more concrete the expression of these standards, the better. *Practice Note 10: Audit of Central Government Financial Statements in the United Kingdom* (February 1996) and the consultation draft Practice Note: *The Audit of Regularity in the Central Government Sector* (December 1997) are examples of more definite statements and, as such, are to be welcomed.[1] However, it should be noted that these standards apply only to central government. We have already noted that

---

[1] See Ch. 2 for auditing standards.

as more layers of governance develop in Britain, developing and maintaining a central core of substantive standards becomes more difficult, but also more important.

Our second substantive suggestion concerns a central core of issues with which audit should deal throughout the public sector: public audit should include an assessment of the *legality*, *regularity* and *propriety* of public spending and the auditor should also be competent to report on issues of *value for money*. At central government in the United Kingdom, regularity, propriety and value for money are central concerns. However, in contrast to the position as regards local government, issues of legality at central government are usually subsumed into the more innocuous sounding 'regularity'. In our view, it would be better to clearly distinguish between issues of legality and issues of regularity and propriety. The purpose is not to involve the courts *ex post*, but to use the system of audit further to buttress the system of financial control *ex ante*. Of particular importance in this context is what we described in Chapter 4 as 'the Pergau principle': *proposed expenditure by the Executive of money voted by Parliament is unlawful if, in relation to the object for which the money has been provided, no reasonable minister could think that it represented value for money.*

NEW TASKS IN CENTRAL GOVERNMENT

The system of external audit in British central government contributes to the democratic accountability of government by providing expert information to Parliament, which can be used to hold government to account. Audit also reinforces the internal system of managerial accountability which operates within government. Of crucial constitutional importance is that audit links democratic and managerial accountability, allowing Parliament to a certain extent to participate in the real business of government.

As the real business of government changes and develops, audit needs to keep pace, whilst maintaining the link between democratic and managerial accountability. A significant challenge is to enable audit information to be provided in a way which is meaningful for both purposes. For this to be possible, the information must be understandable to and useable by an audience which, though it must be prepared to make an effort of understanding, does not consist of accounting or audit professionals. RAB, examined in Chapter 6 above, presents both challenges and opportunities in this respect.

As seen from Chapter 6, there are examples of new types of information, in the form of resource accounts, and there are potential new audiences, including departmental select committees and the citizen. If the PAC is to continue as the primary audience for financial audit reports, the Committee needs to be willing to learn the skills needed to understand resource accounting. However, consideration should also be given to whether the PAC is the most appropriate audience for all the new information that could be provided. If not, is there a suitable alternative? This question is closely linked to two developments outlined below—the possibility of a 'whole of government account' and the C&AG's role in auditing macro-economic information.

Whole of Government Account

One potential area of development, which follows from RAB, is the production and audit of a whole of government account. The basic concept is not difficult. The term 'whole of government account' is used to mean a consolidation of all departmental resource accounts. In New Zealand, combined statements for the whole of government are required under the Public Finance Act 1989.[2] These statements are intended to provide an overview of the financial position and operating results of the federal government in a co-ordinated annual presentation. They can assist users in demanding accountability for actual results by comparison with earlier projections or budgets and provide a common database for analysing, developing, and debating, policy.

The 1994 Green Paper on RAB[3] dismissed the concept because it saw little practical value in aggregating departmental resource accounts given the differences between the various departments and other parts of government. The NAO generally agreed, but it identified a public and Parliamentary interest in whole of government accounts bringing together the income and expenditure and the assets and liabilities of central government. Accordingly, it recommended further research.[4]

A case could be made for consolidating the whole of the United Kingdom public sector on the ground that there is unified control. However, democratic arguments concerning separately elected local authorities, notwithstanding intensified central government control, suggest that they should be excluded. Other cases for exclusion can be made: for example, public corporations such as NHS trusts.[5] Another option which would resolve these difficulties is having a system of sectoral consolidation.

---

[2] To avoid ambiguity entities included in the whole of government account are listed in the legislation: see the Schedules to the Public Finance Act 1989.

[3] *Better Accounting for the Taxpayer's Money: Resource Accounting and Budgeting in Government*, Cm. 2626 (1994).

[4] NAO, *Resource Accounting and Budgeting in Government*, HC 123, 1994–95.

[5] Consolidated accounts are already produced in the NHS under legislation dating from the 1970s.

The Code for Fiscal Stability published by the Government in 1998 states that: *The Government shall ensure that accounts are to be produced for the whole public sector. Where reasonably practicable, these accounts shall also be produced on a consolidated basis.*[6] One of the advantages of such an account, which of course would have to be audited, is that it could offer an comprehensive view of the financial state of the nation to the citizens, and as such, could be an instrument of democratic accountability. Its use in assisting managerial control might be more limited. Nevertheless, if the account included a balance sheet showing assets and liabilities, it could have been useful at the time of the major privatization programmes in the 1980s and 1990s in order to evaluate fairly the impact on the public finances. Similarly, bringing into account future pensions liabilities could inform both Parliament and decision-makers. Again the key issue from a constitutional perspective is that the form and contents of the account should not be decided or altered merely at the discretion of government. The NAO should be involved and report to Parliament concerning the degree of transparency achieved by the account.

Given that a whole of government account would help to ensure democratic accountability, the most suitable audience for this information might appear to be the PAC. However, it is arguable that the Treasury Committee would be a more appropriate audience for such information, because not only could it achieve democratic accountability but it would also be best placed to create a link with managerial accountability.

The C&AG's Widening Jurisdiction

As was illustrated in Chapter 4, the scope of audit in central government is expanding in a number of different ways. For instance, a new material jurisdiction for the C&AG, an example of which was the C&AG's reports on the budget assumptions, was described there. These reports give Parliament and citizens an independent view of how realistic the economic projections underlying the government's public finance depend on developments in the economy. For example, if assumptions about growth are too optimistic, total revenue at given rates of taxation is likely to be less than expected.

The development of this new role for the NAO should not come as a surprise. An analogy can be drawn between the development of this macroeconomic role and the previous development of the C&AG's *vfm* jurisdiction. As noted in preceding chapters, the C&AG was conducting a type of *vfm* audit long before the National Audit Act 1983. But who is the best

[6] See paras. 13 and 14, see more recently, the joint study by the Treasury and the NAO into the development of Whole of Government Accounts for the UK: see Treasury News Release 128/98.

audience for this type of macro-economic information? Arguably, given its remit, the Treasury Committee would be more appropriate than the PAC, since it is the Treasury Committee which in general deals with issues of public finance from a macro-economic perspective. Given the distinctive nature of this information, there would be no danger of undermining the present role of the PAC.

AUDIT AND DEVOLUTION

At the time of writing, the constitutional framework for devolution to Scotland and Wales was being debated in Parliament, on the basis of the government's proposals set out in the two White Papers, *Scotland's Parliament* and *A Voice for Wales*.[7] The proposals for Scotland are very different from those for Wales. In Scotland, there will be a Scottish Executive and a Scottish Parliament.[8] The Scottish White Paper states that the Scottish Parliament will make laws in relation to devolved matters in Scotland and exercise democratic control over the areas where powers are currently exercised by the Scottish Office and other Scottish departments. Its competence is to be extensive: all matters not specifically reserved to Westminster will be devolved.[9] Ministers of the Scottish Executive will take over the statutory powers and duties in relation to devolved matters that are currently exercised by ministers of the Crown in Scotland.[10] The White Paper states that the Westminster Parliament will remain sovereign. Procedures to resolve cases where the Scottish Parliament and Westminster take different views of their respective legislative powers will be established. There will continue to be a Secretary of State for Scotland who will represent Scottish interests in reserved matters and promote communication between the Scottish Parliament and Executive and the Westminster Parliament and Executive. The Scottish Parliament's budget will comprise a block grant, determined using the existing formula, voted by the Westminster Parliament, the remainder being covered by the European Union and by borrowing. The Inland Revenue will collect any additional tax due to the Scottish Parliament should it use its revenue raising powers. The Scottish Executive shall have complete freedom to allocate resources across programmes.

[7] *Scotland's Parliament*, 1997–98, Cm. 3658, and *A Voice for Wales*, 1997–98, Cm. 3718.

[8] Elections to the Scottish Parliament are expected to take place in the first half of 1999, with the Parliament fully operational in 2000.

[9] The areas proposed to be reserved include: the UK constitution; foreign policy; macro-economic policy; monetary and fiscal affairs; policy on common markets; employment legislation; social security; regulation of certain professions; transport safety and regulation; and certain other matters subject to UK regulation.

[10] In relation to the Scottish executive, see, further, Brazier, R., 'The Scottish Government', *Public Law* [1998] 212.

4204A

udit

The Secretary of State for Scotland announced, in November 1997, the establishment of an all party Consultative Steering Group to consider the operational needs and working methods of the Scottish Parliament. A number of technical working groups have also been established, including a Financial Issues Advisory Group. Its remit is to develop proposals for consideration by the Consultative Steering Group for the rules, procedures, standing orders, and legislation which the Scottish Parliament might be invited to adopt for the handling of financial issues. The Consultative Steering Group is to submit a draft report to the Secretary of State by the end of 1998 to inform the preparation of draft standing orders.

In Wales, there will be an elected Welsh Assembly,[11] which will be a Crown body. The Assembly will take over certain functions of the Secretary of State to issue guidance and directions, in the areas of economic development, agriculture, industry and training, education, local government, health, and housing, for example. Other functions, such as foreign affairs, defence, and taxation, will not be transferred to the Assembly. The Assembly will make appointments to, issue directions to, and measure the performance of public bodies in Wales. Some bodies will be jointly sponsored with Westminster. Westminster will continue to be the principal legislator for Wales, though. The Secretary of State for Wales will represent Welsh interests in the British Cabinet, but, although he will be informed by the views of the Assembly, he will not be obliged to support them. The Assembly will also be funded by a block grant from Westminster, using an existing formula, and it will have discretion as to the allocation of funds between different programmes.

In relation to the provisions for audit, the two original Bills vary considerably as to their content and detail—in large, a reflection of the constitution differences between the Assembly and the Parliament. The Scottish devolution White Paper was minimalist in its approach to audit. It stated that the grant to the Scottish Parliament will be audited by the C&AG, though there was no definition of the scope of that audit. The White Paper made no mention of a C&AG for Scotland. Rather it stated that the detailed arrangements which the Scottish Parliament makes to control and scrutinize the spending of the Scottish Executive will be a matter for the Scottish Parliament. In keeping with this minimalist approach, Clause 66 of the Scotland Bill, as introduced, deals with financial control, accounts and audit. It places a general obligation on the Scottish Parliament to establish effective scrutiny and audit arrangements for the spending by the Scottish Executive. In particular, it states in subsection (1) that rules made by or under the Scottish Parliament shall provide, *inter alia*, for the appointment

---

[11] Elections to the Assembly are scheduled for May 1999, with functions being transferred to the Assembly in July 1999.

of an independent person to exercise the functions mentioned in subsection (2). The functions mentioned in subsection (2) are: issuing of credits for the payment of sums out of the Scottish Consolidated Fund; examining the accounts prepared by Scottish ministers, and others, and certifying and reporting on them; and carrying out examinations into the economy, efficiency and effectiveness with which the Scottish administration have used their resources in discharging their functions.

The Government of Wales Bill is more explicit about issues of financial control and the nature of audit and its audience, than the proposed Scottish legislation. For instance, it is proposed that the Treasury will direct the form of the Assembly's accounts and shall designate the accounting officer(s) for the Assembly. Clause 90 of the Government of Wales Bill provides that there shall be an office of Auditor General for Wales, appointed by Her Majesty.[12] The Welsh Auditor General will have jurisdiction to conduct a financial audit of the Assembly's accounts and to carry out *vfm* examinations, subject to a prohibition on the questioning of the merits of policy objectives, into how the Assembly has used its resources in discharging its function. As a longstop, the C&AG is given jurisdiction to carry out examinations into, and report to Parliament on, the finances of the Assembly, in consultation with the Auditor General for Wales.

We do not yet know all the details concerning the nature of the devolved governments for Scotland and Wales. As such, it is not possible to make specific comments about the audit arrangements. However, given that any audit arrangements should comply with the fundamental principles identified in the first part of this chapter, we can make some general comments. In particular, attention should be paid to securing the institutional requirements of constitutionally protected independence and an identifiable audience.

Looking first at institutional independence. As stated above, the Scotland Bill provides for the appointment of an independent person to exercise a number of functions set out in Clause 66, subsection (2). Subsection (4) of that Clause states that, for the purposes of this section, a person is independent in relation to a function if he is not subject to the direction or control of any member of the Scottish Executive or of the Parliament in exercising that function. While the Scottish Bill provides for the appointment of an independent Comptroller and Auditor, the definition of independence offered in the legislation is inadequate. As can be seen from Chapter 5, securing constitutional independence is not a simple exercise. The Scottish Parliament will need to be aware of the multidimensional nature of independence (that is, it requires organizational, personal and operational independence) and the various means through which such

[12] A schedule to the Bill provides that the C&AG can act as the Auditor General for Wales.

independence can be secured in order to fill in the gaps left by the legislation.

The same principles apply to Wales. However, unlike the position in Scotland, the procedures for appointment, dismissal, terms of service, staffing, budget, reporting, and so on, are provided for in the Bill. If the Bill is enacted in this form, then at least the arrangements for audit are constitutionally secured in the Act, and the position of Auditor General for Wales (AGW) will be protected. More complicated issues arise however, when one sees that, for example, the AGW will be appointed and dismissed by the Crown, after consultation with the Assembly. Protecting the AGW's independence when it comes to appointment and dismissal is tricky—it would not be good to have the Assembly responsible for appointment and dismissal given that one of the auditees of the AGW will be the Assembly itself. But, having central government responsible for these powers also raises problems, given that the relationship between central government and the Assembly may not always be rosy. Other potential problems for the independence of the AGW lie in the budget arrangements, whereby the AGW's budget will come out of the Assembly budget and will be overseen and approved by the Audit Committee—a committee made up of members of the Assembly. However, there are some positive aspects of the Bill in relation to independence—for example, the AGW will draw his staff from the NAO in addition to being able to appoint his own staff. The main difficulty when securing the audit arrangements for Wales, is reconciling the AGW's independence with accountability. At committee stage, concerns were voiced that the Bill was not clear about who the AGW's 'master' would be—the Assembly or the central executive.[13] The question is mistaken. The AGW should be independent, he should not have a 'master'. What it does need, however, is a clearly identifiable and effective audience for its reports.

The Welsh devolution White Paper states that the Westminster Parliament will remain sovereign over the Welsh Assembly. The Government of Wales Bill reflects this sovereignty in relation to the audit audience. It is proposed that the PAC will continue to be able to question accounting officers in Wales about the way in which they exercise their functions, though the PAC can delegate the task of taking evidence to an Assembly Audit Committee. Clause 61 of the Government of Wales Bill provides that the Assembly shall establish an Audit Committee, to be elected from the members of the Assembly and to reflect, as far as possible, the balance of the parties in the Assembly. There is provision for a chairperson but a member who represents the largest party in the Assembly cannot chair the Committee. The Audit Committee, as well as acting on behalf

---

[13] See *Hansard*, 3 February 1998, col. 904.

of the PAC in taking evidence and reporting to it, may consider and report on, any accounts and reports of the Welsh Auditor General.

The proposals for the Welsh Assembly appear to be reproducing a PAC model audience for the reports of the Welsh Auditor General, while at the same time maintaining a direct link to the PAC. As was shown in Chapter 6, the PAC model can work to produce democratic accountability and, where there is an identifiable manager, such as the Treasury in relation to central government, managerial accountability. It is not clear, however, whether there will be an equivalent to the Treasury in the Welsh Assembly to perform this managerial function. Reporting to a Welsh Audit Committee may deliver a form of devolved democratic accountability but, without an equivalent of the Treasury, any link with a form of devolved managerial accountability cannot be developed.

The issue of an audience for the findings of audit in Scotland is left open by the proposed legislation. Clause 66(3) of the Scotland Bill, states that standing orders shall provide for the consideration by Parliament of accounts and audit reports laid before it. The details of this provision will have to be addressed by the Financial Issues Advisory Group and in turn the Scottish Parliament. As well as the NAO/PAC model of audit, other models exist, including the AC model of an independent quango, or the Swedish model with two sets of auditors, one acting on behalf of the Government and another acting on behalf of the Parliament. Whatever model is chosen, it is vital that the framework of financial control and audit holds together. The relationship between a public audit institution and its audience should not be based on false analogies, as is the case with the European Court of Auditors and the Budgetary Control Committee of the European Parliament.

The development of new audit arrangements in the public sector, or altering existing ones, is no easy task. Audit is fast becoming a major player in the accountability of government, at whatever level. As such, that accountability can be either democratic or managerial, and can exist at any level of government—central, local, European or devolved government. However, in order to meet the expectations of those relying on it, mechanisms must be in place to secure what we have identified as fundamental principles of audit. Additionally, any substantive standards which may in the future be set by, for example, the Public Audit Forum, need to be applicable to all levels of the public sector, taking into account that a Parliament in Scotland and an Assembly in Wales may not be the only changes to the structure of the United Kingdom that take place.

Select Bibliography

ACCOUNTING STANDARDS BOARD, *Foreword to Accounting Standards*, (1993).

AUDIT COMMISSION AND DEPARTMENT OF ENVIRONMENT, *Accounting For Independent Audit–A Joint Statement of Responsibility and Accountability*, (London, 1994).

AUDIT COMMISSION, *Who Audits the Auditors*, (London: HMSO, 1994).

AUDITING PRACTICES BOARD, *Central Government Practice Note, Practice Note 10*, (1996).

BAINES, P., 'Financial Accountability: agencies and audit', in Giddings, P., ed., *Parliamentary Accountability: A Study of Parliament and Executive Agencies*, (London: Macmillan, 1995).

BOSTON, J., MARTIN, J., PALLOT, J., AND WALSH, P., eds., *Reshaping the State*, (Auckland: Oxford University Press, 1991).

BOWERMAN, M., 'The National Audit Office and the Audit Commission: co-operation in areas where their value for money responsibilities interface', 10 (1994) *Financial Accountability and Management* 47.

—— GRAY, I., AND REEDMAN, M., *Audit Management Letters in Local Government. Aspects of Accountability* Research Papers in Accounting, No. 2, (Sheffield: Sheffield Hallam University, 1996).

BRAZIER, R., 'The Non-Legal Constitution: Thoughts on Convention, Practice and Principle', 43 (1992) *Northern Ireland Legal Quarterly* 262.

BUTLER REVIEW OF THE AUDIT COMMISSION, (February–July 1995).

CARTER, N., AND GREER, P., 'Evaluating Agencies: Next Steps and Performance Indicators', 71 (1993) *Public Administration* 407.

CIPFA, *Statements on Internal Audit Practice–Public Sector*, (1979).

COMMITTEE FOR STANDARDS IN PUBLIC LIFE, *The First Report of the Committee on Standards in Public Life*, Cm. 2850, 1995.

—— *The Second Report of the Committee on Standards in Public Life: Local Public Spending Bodies*, Cm. 3270, 1996.

—— *The Third Report of the Committee on Standards in Public Life: Standards of Conduct in Local Government in England*, Cm. 3702, 1997.

COMPTROLLER AND AUDITOR GENERAL AND THE CONTROLLERS OF AUDIT AT THE AUDIT AND ACCOUNTS COMMISSIONS, *Spending Public Money: Governance and Audit Issues–A Joint Response*, (June 1996).

COUCHMAN, V., 'The Audit Commission', in Sherer, M., and Turley, S., *Current Issues in Auditing*, (London: Chapman, 1997).

DAINTITH, T., 'The Techniques of Government', in Jowell, J., and Oliver, D., eds., *The Changing Constitution*, (Oxford: Clarendon Press, 3rd edn., 1994).

DAVIS, K. C., *Discretionary Justice: a preliminary inquiry*, (Urbana: University of Chicago Press, 1971).

DEPARTMENT FOR THE ENVIRONMENT, DEPARTMENT FOR HEALTH, WELSH OFFICE AND THE AUDIT COMMISSION, *Accounting for Independent Audit–A Joint Statement of Responsibility and Accountability*, (1994).

DEPARTMENT OF THE ENVIRONMENT, TRANSPORT AND THE REGION'S CONSULTATION PAPER, *Modernising Local Government. A New Ethical Framework*, (1998).

DEWAR, D., 'Value for Money Audit: the first 800 years', August (1985), *Public Finance and Accountancy*, 10.

DICEY, A. V., *Introduction to the Study of the Law of the Constitution*, (London: Macmillan, 10th edn., 1959).

DISTRICT AUDIT, *Framework Document*, (undated).

DUNN, J., *Auditing–Theory and Practice*, (London: Prentice Hall, 1996).

DWORKIN, R., *Taking Rights Seriously*, (London: Duckworth, 1978).

Erskine May's Treatise on the Law, Privileges, Proceedings and Usages of Parliament, edited by Limon, D. W., and McKay, W. R., (London: Butterworths, 22nd edn., 1997).

EUROPEAN COURT OF AUDITORS, *Stuttgart Report*, OJ C 287, (24 October 1983).

EXPENDITURE COMMITTEE Eleventh Report, HC 535, 1976–77.

EXPENDITURE COMMITTEE Twelfth Report, HC 576, 1977–78.

EXPENDITURE COMMITTEE (GENERAL SUB COMMITTEE), Fourteenth Report, HC 661, 1977–78.

FLEGMAN, V., 'The Public Accounts Committee: A Successful Select Committee?', (1980) *Parliamentary Affairs* 166.

FULTON COMMITTEE, *Report of the Committee on the Civil Service 1966–68*, Cm. 3638, 1968.

GARRETT, J., 'Developing State Audit in Britain', 64 (1986) *Public Administration* 421.

—— *Westminster, Does Parliament Work?*, (London: Gollancz, 1992).

——, AND SHELDON, R., *Administrative Reform, the Next Steps*. Fabian Tract 426 (London: 1973).

GENERAL ACCOUNTING OFFICE, *Government Auditing Standards*, (1988).

GLAUTIER, M. W. E., AND UNDERDOWN, B., *Accounting Theory and Practice*, (London: Pitman, 6th edn., 1997).

GRAHAM, C., AND PROSSER, T., *Privatizing Public Enterprise*, (Oxford: Clarendon Press, 1991).

GREEN PAPER, *The Role of the Comptroller and Auditor General*, Cm. 7845, (1979–80).

—— *Better Accounting for the Taxpayer's Money: Resource Accounting and Budgeting in Government*, Cm. 2626, (1994).

—— *Spending Public Money: Governance and Audit Issues*, Cm. 3179, (1996).

GRIFFITH, J., AND RYLE, M., *Parliament, Functions, Practice and Procedures*, (London: Sweet & Maxwell, 1989).

HARDEN, I., 'Money and the Constitution: Financial Control, Reporting and Audit', 13 (1993) *Legal Studies* 16.

—— 'Regulating Government', 66 (1995) *Political Quarterly* 299.

——, HOLLINGSWORTH, K., AND WHITE, F., 'The Control and Audit of European Community Spending', 23 (1996) *Auditorium* 8.

——, ——, AND ——, 'Value for Money and Administrative Law', [1996] *Public Law* 661.

HEALD, D., AND GEORGIOU, G., 'Resource Accounting: Consolidation and Accounting Regulation', 73 (1995) *Public Administration* 571.

HENDERSON, R., *European Finance*, (London: McGraw-Hill, 1993).

HENLEY, D., HOLTHAM, C., LIKIERMAN, A., AND PERRIN, J., *Public Sector Accounting and Financial Control*, (London: Chapman & Hall, 4th edn., 1992).

Hood, C., 'A Public Management for all Seasons?', 69 (1991) *Public Administration* 3.

House of Lords, Select Committee on the European Communities, *The Court of Auditors*, HL 102, 1986–87.

—— *Financial Control and Fraud in the Community*, HL 75, 1993–94.

Institute of Internal Auditors, *Statement of Responsibilities of the Internal Auditor*, (New York, 1947).

INTOSAI, *Auditing Standards*, (June 1989).

Jones, R., *Local Government Audit Law*, (London: HMSO, 1985).

——, and Pendlebury, M., *Public Sector Accounting*, (London: Pitman, 4th edn., 1996).

Jowett, J., and Rothwell, M., *Performance Indicators in the Public Sector*, (London: Macmillan, 1988).

Klein, R., and Day, P., *Accountabilities: five public services*, (London: Tavistock, 1987).

Kok, C., 'The European Court of Auditors: The Other European Court in Luxembourg', 26 (1989) *Common Market Law Review* 345.

Laffan, B., *Finances of the European Union*, (London: MacMillan, 1997).

Layfield Committee, *Local Government Finance: Report of the Committee of Inquiry*, Cm. 6453, (1976).

Likierman, A., 'Resource Accounting and Budgeting: Rationale and Background', 73 (1995) *Public Administration* 562.

—— 'Applying Accruals-Based Accounting and Budgeting to UK Central Government', 4 (1997) *Irish Accounting Review* 55.

McEldowney, J. F., 'The National Audit Office and Privatisation', 54 (1991) *Modern Law Review* 933.

—— 'The Control of Public Expenditure', in Jowell, J., and Oliver, D., eds., *The Changing Constitution*, (Oxford: Clarendon Press, 3rd edn., 1994).

—— *Public Law*, (London: Sweet & Maxwell, 2nd edn., 1998).

National Audit Office, *A Framework for Value for Money Audits*, (London: undated).

—— *Helping the Nation Spend Wisely*, (London: undated).

—— *Pergau Hydro-Electric Project*, HC 908, 1992–93.

—— *Resource Accounting and Budgeting in Government*, HC 123, 1994–95.

—— *State Audit in the European Union*, (London: 1996).

—— *Audit of Assumptions for the Pre-Budget Report*, HC 361, 1997–98.

Normanton, E. L., *Accountability and Audit in Governments*, (Manchester: Manchester University Press, 1966).

O'Keeffe, D., 'The Court of Auditors', in Curtin, D., and Heukels, T., eds., *Institutional Dynamics of European Integration*, (Dordrecht: M. Nijhoff, 1994).

Pallot, J., and Ball, I., 'Resource Accounting and Budgeting: the New Zealand Experience', 74 (1996) *Public Administration* 527.

Pollitt, C., and Summa, H., 'Reflexive Watchdogs: How Supreme Audit Institutions Account for themselves', 75 (1997) *Public Administration* 313.

Power, M., *The Audit Explosion*, (London: Demos, 1995).

Price Waterhouse (in association with Sir Brian Cubbon GCB), *Examination of the Impact of the NAO and PAC Process on Value for Money in Government Departments*, (unpublished, 1992).

PROSSER, T., *Nationalised Industries and Public Control*, (Oxford: Blackwell, 1986).

PUBLIC ACCOUNTS COMMITTEE FIRST SPECIAL REPORT, *The Role of the Comptroller and Auditor General*, HC 115, 1980–81.

PUBLIC ACCOUNTS COMMITTEE EIGHTH REPORT, *The Proper Conduct of Public Business*, HC 154, 1993–94.

PUBLIC ACCOUNTS COMMITTEE SEVENTEENTH REPORT, *Pergau Hydro-Electric Project*, HC 155, 1993–94.

PUBLIC ACCOUNTS COMMITTEE FIFTEENTH REPORT, *Resource Accounting and Budgeting*, HC 407, 1994–95.

RADFORD, M., 'Auditing For Change: Local Government and the Audit Commission', 54 (1991) *Modern Law Review* 912.

ROBINSON, A., 'The Financial Work of Select Committees', Ch. 17 in Drewry, G., *The New Select Committees*, (Oxford: Clarendon Press, 1985).

SCOTT, G., BUSHNELL, P., AND SALLEE, N., 'Reform of the core Public Sector: New Zealand experience', 3 (1990) *Governance* 138.

SELECT COMMITTEE ON PROCEDURE, First Special Report, HC 588, 1977–78.

—— *The Workings of the Select Committee System*, HC 19, 1989–90.

SHERER, M., AND KENT, D., *Auditing and Accountability*, (London: Chapman Publishing, 1983).

STRASSER, D., *The Finances of Europe*, (Luxembourg: Office for Official Publications of the EC, 3rd English edn., 1992).

THAIN, C., AND WRIGHT, M., *The Treasury and Whitehall: The Planning and Control of Public Expenditure, 1976–1993*, (Oxford: Oxford University Press, 1995).

TREASURY, *Government Internal Audit Manual*, (London: 3rd edn., 1996).

—— *Government Accounting: a guide on accounting and financial procedures for the use of government departments*, (2 vols., loose leaf) (London: HMSO, 1989 and seven amendments 1989–97).

—— *Regularity and Propriety–A Handbook*, (July 1997).

—— *Audit of Assumptions for the July 1997 Budget Projections*, Cm. 3693, (1997).

—— *Output and Performance Analysis Guidance*, (December 1997).

TREASURY AND CIVIL SERVICE COMMITTEE FOURTH REPORT, *Simplified Estimates and Resource Accounting*, HC 212, 1994–95.

WHITE PAPER, *The Role of the Comptroller and Auditor General*, Cm. 8323, (1980–81).

—— *Better Accounting for the Taxpayer's Money: the Government's Proposals: Resource Accounting and Budgeting in Government*, Cm. 2929, (1995).

—— *A Voice for Wales*, Cm. 3718, (1997–98).

—— *Scotland's Parliament*, Cm. 3658, (1997–98).

—— *The Governance of Public Bodies: A Progress Report*, Cm. 3557, (1997).

WHITE, F., AND HOLLINGSWORTH, K., 'Resource Accounting and Budgeting: Constitutional Implications', [1997] *Public Law* 437.

Index